More praise for
KISS OF THE VAMPIRE

"Terrific . . . The unrelenting tension between the monstrous and the human propels this unique tale of gripping suspense."
—KATHERINE RAMSLAND
Author of *The Witches' Companion*
and *The Vampire Companion*

"Nancy Baker's KISS OF THE VAMPIRE is a bullet train of a suspense novel. It's almost impossible not to finish it in one frenzied, chocolate-donut-munching sitting. It's also impossible not to root for its feisty, feminist vampiress heroine."
—CHARLES BUSCH
Author of *Vampire Lesbians of Sodom*

"Nancy Baker writes horror with an originality and imagination that dares you to put it down. You won't!"
—ANDREW NEIDERMAN
Author of *The Solomon Organization*

"Intriguing . . . Baker's novel is guaranteed to cause a stir."
—*The Toronto Star*

KISS OF
THE VAMPIRE

Nancy Baker

Formerly titled *The Night Inside*

FAWCETT GOLD MEDAL • NEW YORK

A Fawcett Gold Medal Book
Published by Ballantine Books
Copyright © 1993 by Nancy Baker

A portion of Chapter 9 appeared previously in the story "Cold Sleep," published in *Northern Frights*, Mosaic Press, 1992.

Page ix: "This Big Hush," words and music by Dave Allen, Barry Andrews, Martyn Barker, Carl Marsh. Copyright © 1985 Point Music Ltd. Used by permission. All rights reserved.

Page 9: "Midnight Maps," words and music by Dave Allen, Barry Andrews, Carl Marsh. Copyright © 1984. Used by permission. All rights reserved.

Page 37: "The Only Thing That Shines," words and music by Dave Allen, Barry Andrews, Martyn Barker, Carl Marsh. Copyright © 1985 Point Music Ltd. Used by permission. All rights reserved.

Page 131: "Shark Walk," words and music by Barry Andrews, Martyn Barker, Mike Cozzi, Wendy and Sarah Partridge. Copyright © 1988 Point Music Ltd. Used by permission. All rights reserved.

Page 193: "Everything That Rises Must Converge," words and music by Dave Allen, Barry Andrews, Martyn Barker, Carl Marsh. Copyright © 1985 Point Music Ltd. Used by permission. All rights reserved.

Library of Congress Catalog Card Number: 93-25553

ISBN 0-449-14957-9

Manufactured in the United States of America

First Ballantine Hardcover Edition: January 1994
First Ballantine Mass Market Edition: November 1995

10 9 8 7 6 5 4 3 2 1

For Richard and Kim

Thanks to: Gillian Holmes, friend, bat fan and test reader extraordinaire; Neil Bissoondath and Ann Montagnes, for encouragement when it counted; Bill and Aileen Jamieson and Jim and Margo Scott for the use of the cottage and farm; Cynthia Good and Mary Adachi for making this the best book it could be; Shriekback for the soundtrack; Kim Kofmel, for lunches, dinners, writing weekends and unending inspiration; and Richard Shallhorn, who watched me turn his big ideas into little ones and who married me anyway.

Aching with a passion inside
Deep as the river of desire,
The ashes and the fire
Turning this night inside . . .

Prologue

It took him two days to wake.

His heart, which had beat only once every day, gradually began to expand and contract more rapidly. The blood that had crawled along the interior miles of his body as sluggishly as a glacier now began to melt and flow. Nerves sparked into life and set muscles twitching in reaction as contact was reestablished with the long-forgotten territories of hands and feet.

As his body woke, so did his mind, drifting up from midnight oblivion to a twilight plain where dreams bloomed like Rousseau flowers, bright crimson, with teeth.

Finally, after two nights of the moon's rise and fall had dragged his blood like tides through his body, he opened his eyes and stared into utter darkness.

His hands jerked then flopped back, twitching like pale fronded sea creatures. As his control over them returned, they moved again, lifting up to touch the wood that surrounded him. Nails now long and sharp as razors clawed desperately at his prison walls before he overcame the suffocating panic. He was not trapped, he told himself, the thoughts coming sluggish and heavy. This was his hiding place, his sanctuary.

The hands sank to his sides, as reason subdued his rebellious body. He took a deep breath (there was next to no oxygen, true, but that hardly mattered). Wait, the slow pulse in his body told him, wait.

Several timeless hours later, when the moon had reached its zenith over the silent city, he moved again. This time, his hands raised to brace themselves against the wood above him. He pushed, and waited for the creak of the lid rising, the tearing sound of nails dragged from their beds. There was only silence and darkness.

Irrational panic suddenly raced through his mind, snapping at his barely reestablished reason with teeth of terror. Be calm, be calm, he told himself, fighting the fear. He had never experienced this before, this failure of his body to obey his commands. But then, he had never waited so long before. Could he have misjudged his strength so? Had it been too many years, and now he was too sapped of strength to escape from his hiding place? If he were trapped here, then what? Could he starve here, hunger accomplishing what bullets, swords and more than four hundred years could not? If so, how long would it take? Would his mind crack before his body could rot away? For a horrifying moment, he contemplated an eternity of gibbering, ravenous madness, trapped in the twin tombs of wood and bone.

A sound escaped his lips, a hoarse guttural groan of denial, and he thrust upwards again. He held the pressure until he heard, over the roar in his temples, the crack of the wood as it split above his hands.

He opened his eyes again. There was no light, but he needed none, not to see the three-foot crack in the wood above him. He thought he could scent the wild sweetness of the night air and the illusion gave him strength.

Ten minutes of thrust and claw and there was a rent in the wood large enough for both his arms. The fraying cloth of his jacket ripped on the wooden splinters as he snaked one arm out through the hole to grip the edge of the lid. Hard, ragged talons slid beneath the edge and tugged until, with a faint shriek of protest, the metal nails yielded their grip on the wood. One more thrust and he was free.

He rested for an hour that for the first time seemed that long, and then clambered slowly to his feet, leaning on the wood box for support. The space was not much wider than the box. He looked about slowly, feeling the weight of the building over him. He reached for the wall at one end, felt a sudden dizziness sweep over him and clung to the box again.

He bent there for a long moment, letting his muscles re-adapt themselves, and then became aware of the ache deep inside him. The exertion of the last hours had awakened his slumbering hunger. His belly cramped and nausea shook him again. He would have to feed, and soon, to maintain even the shadow of strength he still possessed.

He shook himself slightly and reached for the hidden mechanism that had sealed him into the wall years ago. For a moment he thought it too would not open, but then the internal machinery crawled into creaking life and the hidden door opened out into the darkened warehouse.

He stepped out onto the deserted upper floor and felt a rush of strength as the clean air touched his face. This part of the warehouse had been empty when he had locked himself away and was empty still, except for the heavy iron pulleys and winches hanging like skeletal ribs over the barren floor. The great windows that lined one wall were dirt-caked and blackened, but the faint moonlight crept through the narrow cracks to lie like a shining web on the dirty floor. He stepped into one shaft of pale glow and breathed in the quicksilver light.

Closing his eyes, he lifted his face to the faint gleam of sky above him, then stretched out his mind slowly, feeling for some scrap of life, some tiny heartbeat in the upper emptiness of the warehouse. There, oh there . . . he felt a faint pulse, and the dim awareness of a rodent brain. "Come," he breathed, a dry, dusty sound. "Come."

The rat chittered nervously, its squeak echoing in his ears, but it crept from the wall and began to scurry through the sea of dust towards him. He watched it come, then bent down to let it crawl onto his hand. For one moment, the tiny black eyes stared up into his and he had a dizzying vision of himself through the rat's eyes—a grey, grimacing monster whose glowing eyes were almost obscured by the tangled, ashen hair.

He felt fastidious disgust then, but the hunger was so much stronger and the warm life pulsing in his hands too tempting. He drowned his ancient revulsion in an act even more ancient.

After a moment he dropped the lifeless body and crouched there, panting. The creature's blood ran like fire down his throat and through his veins. It was sweet, oh so sweet . . . but not nearly enough to assuage the maddening hunger he felt. If anything, the brief satiation had only heightened his need.

He wiped his face, licked his stained fingers absently and stared back up at the moonlight, its mercury-silver glow brighter now. How long had it been, he wondered. More than fifty years, he guessed, but perhaps less than one hundred. Rising, he went slowly to the stairs that led down to the main floor of the warehouse. The cracking leather of his boots creaked with each step, the floor echoing the sound to a reverberation that throbbed in his head. He started down the stairs, clutching the railing whenever his head spun again.

Halfway down, he realized he was not alone.

Heartbeats sounding like thunder in his head, breathing like a hurricane in his ears . . . the sensations flooded through his mind with a power that shook him. More than one, more than two . . . that was all his confused senses could make of the input for a moment. Then he lifted his head and saw them, flaring bright and hot in his nightsight. They were clustered at the other end of the empty warehouse, three of them standing over a machine that hummed a maddening frequency in his hypersensitive ears.

Stay away, his reason cautioned, they are many, you are weakened . . . stay away. But the smell of their blood was intoxicating, the hunger a red-blooming flower in his mind. Only one. Only one and he would be strong again, strong enough to take the others too, if need be. Only one—and then he would be free.

He moved down the rest of the stairs carefully, clinging to the scraps of cunning that kept him in check while the blood-hunger raged. They mustn't see him, mustn't know he was there until he was ready. The machine's whine filled his ears, battering his tightly strung nerves.

At the bottom of the stairway, he moved into its shadow and waited. There was no cover in the empty warehouse, concealment existed only in the darkness of the shadows and in his own impossibility. He stood very still, and though his body ached with hunger, he waited while the voices of the men filtered slowly into his consciousness, past the annoying thrum of the machine.

"One more pass and we'll have finished this floor," one announced.

" 'Bout time too. You know Roias said we weren't supposed to do night work," the second said.

"Shit, Tucker, he'll never know. We get the five grand whether the job takes a week or a month. Me, I could use a vacation."

"Me too. But this place gives me the creeps," Tucker replied.

"If you can't hold your water, you can leave. Simpson and I will split your share," the first man suggested.

"Not a chance, Theo," Tucker snapped back, then glanced around the warehouse nervously. "Do you ever wonder what the hell he's looking for?"

"Al Capone's hidden vault?" the third man drawled, fumbling in his pocket. Their laughter scraped along the watcher's nerves like dull razors.

"It'd serve Roias right if all he found was a dirty bottle . . . oh Jesus, Simpson, put that shit away. You know I can't stand that stuff."

"That's why you're pussy, Theo, my man," Simpson said, as he struck a match that burned and beckoned.

"Oh, go smoke that shit over there," Tucker intervened, and Simpson shrugged and started to stroll across the barren floor.

Under the stairway, the vampire felt his muscles tense in preparation for attack. Predatory instincts honed in a thousand ice-sharp nights moved him out to the edge of the shadows as Simpson moved closer, pacing casually beneath the halo of aromatic smoke. The tip of the hand-rolled cigarette glowed faintly, the only spot of light in the dark figure silhouetted against the circle of lights at the far side of the warehouse.

Three steps more, two ... the count sounded like bells in the vampire's mind. The man paused suddenly, stared into the darkness, and the vampire froze. Then Simpson took another slow drag, tilted his head back and exhaled. The movement exposed the dark curve of his throat, outlined its arching strength against the lights. The vampire could feel the beat of the blood, and the scent of the life in the man's veins filled his nostrils. It was more than he could bear, and he came out of the shadows in a feral leap that brought him almost to Simpson's side.

The man's eyes opened suddenly, the glaze over the dark depths fading as uncomprehending shock took the place of drugged pleasure. "Holy shit ..." He had time for only those words, then the vampire's hands had closed on his shoulders as his second lunge tumbled them both to the floor.

Distantly, the vampire was aware of the other men turning, crying out, but then there was only the hot flesh and hotter blood filling his mouth. Simpson thrashed beneath him, head whipping from side to side, until taloned hands closed on the man's forehead, drawing blood from the temples as they held his head still. Even then his strength was barely enough to hold the man down until he could tear open the throat wide enough to turn the frenzied struggles into death spasms.

Then he was deep in the blood-thrall, the hot liquid burning down his throat, splattering on his face from the pumping artery. The world narrowed to the taste, the scent and the dizzying pleasure that coursed along his veins with each gulp of the sweet blood.

When someone seized his shoulders, tried to pull him away from that rich fountain, he struck out, dimly aware that it was Theo he sent sprawling across the floor. He could hear Tucker shouting, a thousand miles away, then suddenly the dull mosquito hum in his ears shrieked up into a knife of sound that sent him staggering to his feet, clutching his head.

He forced his eyes open to find this new threat. It was the man called Tucker holding something in his hand, a small device strung on cables to the strange machine that must be the source of the agonizing sound. He was halfway to the man, holding his ears, snarling and gritting his bloody teeth against the pain, when the sound jumped again, arcing off into a stratosphere beyond his imagination.

He screamed then, howling in sudden, mindless anguish, and fell to the floor, writhing beneath the lash of the white-hot pain in his head. He barely heard Theo's obscene shouts. But he felt the man's heavy boots as they thudded into his ribs, Theo's fury driven by the blind determination to obliterate the creature that had dared to terrify him and, most importantly, shame him with that terror.

The blows that hammered his sides could not kill him, or even shatter his bones, but that did not stop them from hurting, an agony he felt even above the roar in his mind.

When the sound at last eased, the blows went on, sapping away the strength he had found in the blood. Arms wrapped around his head, he retreated back into the darkest corner of his mind. Distantly, he heard the men talking, sharp, panicky voices no more than ragged peaks of sound over the steady wail of the machine.

"Jesus fucking Christ, what is it?"

"I don't know! How the hell would I know!"

"Is it dead?"

"I don't know! But it fuckin' killed Simpson."

"What are we going to do?"

"I'm gonna call that bastard Roias, and tell him to get the fuck down here, that's what I'm gonna do. Hold the machine on it and if it moves again, crank it up."

Dimly, he knew he had to get away, before these men called others and he was trapped. It should not have been like this, it had never been like this before ... he was stronger than they, smarter ... he was the predator and they the prey. He started to lift his head, to see where the men were, if Tucker had lowered that infernal device. The sound stabbed through him again, full volume this time, and the vampire screamed wordlessly, arching backwards until the pale moonlight filled his eyes, and then he passed back into darkness.

Midnight Maps

I'm putting markers on the
midnight maps . . .

From the Diary of Ambrose Delaney Dale

13 March 1898

Some news at last! I had almost begun to doubt my original conclusions, so quiet has the city been. But just before dinner tonight, a message came that Mr. Collins was waiting to see me and I dared to hope. When he was shown into the library, his expression lifted my hopes even higher. And when he told his tale . . .

He has, as I've recounted before, been keeping company in the bars and streets of the Ward, where the workers and the poor live, where the mysterious bloodless body was found, listening for any unusual stories. The few leads he had been able to pass along so far had proven to be no more than drunken ramblings, but tonight's tale promises to be different.

It seems that one of his cronies has as an acquaintance a woman who makes her living as a whore (sad to say, even this most respectable of cities is plagued by her kind). According to Collins's friend, a group of whores meet from time to time to discuss the revolting details of their profession and warn each other of police efforts to stop their trade. One of the subjects of their latest gossip was a client who had visited several of them. A man of middling years and foreign extraction, he was reputed to be generous with his money and considerate in his treatment of them. Yet they were all, according to Collins's informant, surprised to discover that none of them could remember the precise details of the transaction.

I suggested that this was hardly surprising, considering the drunken state in which many of these women must exist, but Collins insists that his friend was adamant that several of these harlots restricted their imbibing only to their leisure hours. There were other oddities about their encounters with this customer that mystified them. Several recounted falling prey to an unusual lassitude after his visits, and one or two specifically stated that, though they believed that they had performed the usual acts of intercourse, they found no physical evidence of it, though such was usually to be discovered in their dirty sheets.

Upon the completion of this story, I paid Mr. Collins as usual and sent him out with instructions that I would be willing to pay to interview one of these whores. Collins, of course, has no idea what my true suspicions are (he seems to believe that I seek some damaging information about a business rival) and my name is never to be mentioned in connection with his inquiries.

After he left, I sat down to write this. Reviewing these words—and the previous evidence that led me to pursue this line of inquiry—I am more convinced than ever that I am right.

I hear Henry at the door, with no doubt yet another of his business schemes. As much as it relieves me to leave my wealth in such good hands, I sometimes wish he held my research into the occult secrets of the world in as much respect as my fortune. For what is another bank, or company, or rail line, when compared to the reward I now seek?

Chapter 1

The party was going to end with people passed out on the floor. Ardeth Alexander could tell that the moment she stepped in the door to be enfolded in Peter's beerily effusive embrace.

"Welcome to the end-of-the-world bash," he said as he released her.

"I thought this was your birthday party."

"So did I. But it's the end of term, and that means we have to face life outside the ivory tower. That might as well be the end of the world for most of us. Everyone is much too depressed about that to celebrate only the most momentous event in the twentieth century."

"Was it?"

"Of course!"

"Well, if you say so. My specialty's the nineteenth century, remember? We never notice anything after 1899," Ardeth said and handed him the silver-wrapped bottle of Rémy Martin. More booze, she thought wryly, just what this party needs. "Happy Birthday anyway."

"Thank you," Peter replied with an exaggerated gentility that was at complete odds with his appearance. "Early mountain man," his girlfriend, Lise, termed it. He stepped aside to let the noise of the party drift out to envelop her as surely as his earlier embrace. "Now bring out that other bottle I see in your purse and come in and get stinking drunk with the rest of us," he instructed.

I may do just that, Ardeth thought, moving into the long corridor down to the kitchen. The party was in full swing, music thumping from the stereo, each of the old house's small rooms crammed with people.

The kitchen, as usual, was a focal point of social action. She squeezed her way through a knot of women she didn't recognize to reach the counter. She had just managed to pour herself a generous glass of wine (the plastic glasses helped, she thought), when she heard a voice call her name.

Ardeth turned to see Carla waving to her from the far corner of the kitchen. She slipped between two men in deep conversation about economic theory and reached the small space Carla and her friends had claimed.

She recognized Danny and Roger, both from the history department and both due to submit their theses at the same time as Ardeth; Richard, who'd quit after his Masters and found a job with some obscure government agency; and Conrad, who'd forsaken the University of Toronto for the wilds of a suburban university for his Ph.D.

"Ardy, you made it!" Carla exclaimed and reached out to hug her. Ardeth returned the embrace briefly and then drew back to smile into the other woman's dark face.

"Of course I did. Did you think I'd miss this?"

"Well, the way Roger tells it, you've had your nose so close to the grindstone you'll end up needing plastic surgery." She didn't mention the other reason for expecting Ardeth's absence; no one did.

"Roger exaggerates," she said with a quick glance at the fair-haired man lounging against the wall. And he usually exaggerates much more graphically, Ardeth thought. It's not the grindstone he says my nose is up against. "I wouldn't have missed this, and I imagine we're all pretty busy now."

"How is the world of 'Public Transportation and Private Ownership in Toronto: 1865 to 1900'?" Conrad asked. "Or maybe we shouldn't ask each other these things."

" 'Public Transportation and Private Ownership' is fine, and I trust 'Political Doctrine in Nineteenth Century Russia' is equally well. And I agree, let's *try* to make theses a forbidden topic for this evening."

"That leaves us with politics and religion then," Richard observed. "Has anyone changed parties or gods lately?"

"If those are the only topics left, I'm planning to change locale right now. Con, pass me another beer and we ladies will leave you gentlemen to debate who's right—or left," Carla said firmly. Con flipped her the beer can, which she caught two-handed. She took Ardeth's arm and steered her out of the kitchen.

"How are you doing?" she asked carefully.

"I'm fine, Carla."

"Peter almost didn't have this party . . . after what happened to Tony. Lise talked him into it."

"I'm glad she did. We can't pretend our lives are all going to stop because Tony's dead. It was over between us anyway, you know that."

"Yeah, I know. So, now that that's out of the way, down that wine, girl, and we'll try to find someone here who isn't talking shop." Ardeth laughed, swallowed down enough wine to make her scalp tingle a little, and let Carla lead her through the crowd.

The party progressed as parties do, with Ardeth shifting among the knots of people, joining and abandoning conversations to the backdrop of music, smoke and the never-voiced fear of being left standing alone in the centre of the crowd.

Later, momentarily unoccupied, she glanced around the room and thought that Peter was right. It did feel like the end of the world. It was almost April, and time for exams or theses or dissertations; the end for some of them of the long scholastic grind. Conversations seemed to turn inevitably to the future—jobs, yet more degrees (some in an attempt to avoid option one), marriage, going home to replenish drained finances before facing the world.

And no matter what she or Carla said, none of them could really forget Tony's death. Two weeks ago most of them had been together at another party. On the way home that night, something had happened to Tony. Death by misadventure, the police ruled: too much cocaine and a long fall from the bridge on St. Clair Avenue. Ardeth remembered hearing the news on the radio the next morning, seeing the television reports with the bland, blonde reporter speaking in measured tones in front of the body-bag being carried up the edge of the ravine. Then the funeral, which they all attended, shocked for the moment from their invulnerability, from the comfortable belief that it couldn't happen to them. And though it was true that she and Tony had broken up six months earlier, their one-year relationship having died in slow, frozen inches, it was not true that there was no grief inside her.

All of which was why, she supposed, she was drinking far too much wine tonight. She dreaded the future as much as any of them. She'd tried to avoid thinking about what she would do when her thesis was done and the letters Ph.D. firmly affixed after her name. Teaching positions were scarce and the competition fierce. She had no illusions of finding any great need for her particular field of study in the world outside academia.

At times like this, I wish I *could* pass out on the floor, she thought, taking another sip of wine, knowing that she wouldn't. And that she wouldn't share the joints already being passed around the room. Too practical, too conventional or just too scared—whatever the reason, she'd never been able to take any of the oblivions the world so considerately offered. Your problem, my girl, she said to her distant reflection, is that you think too much. Somewhere in the shadows of her mind, in the place she carefully locked away everything that did not fit into her well-ordered world, she felt the dark shiftings of dreams, of unarticulated longing for something that could *make* her stop, just once, thinking so much. Ardeth shivered and lifted her wine to her lips. It was only pretend-oblivion, but it was better than the promise of darkness she had felt beckoning in her mind. Then someone bumped into her, and the noisy reality of the party closed in again, dragging her back into a too-long conversation about the byzantine powerplays currently being enacted in the Department of Medieval Studies.

Much later in the evening, in retreat from the smoke and heat of the house, she ended up sitting on the battered couch set out on the narrow balcony of the upper floor. The party had spilled out onto the back lawn and she listened idly to the conversations drifting up from beneath the oak trees.

At the sound of the door opening behind her, she twisted around to see Conrad stepping through the narrow doorway. "Care for some company?"

"Yes. Have a seat. No one else seems to have remembered how to get out here yet." He settled onto the couch, offered her his beer bottle, which she declined in favour of another sip from the wineglass resting on the railing in front of her.

"How's it been going?" Conrad asked casually, and Ardeth laughed.

"If one more person asks me that in that careful tone of voice . . ." She sighed, shook her head slightly. "I'm fine, Con, honestly. But everyone seems to think I should be wearing black and a suitably tragic air. I hear my students whispering about it all the time. I'm sorry Tony's dead but I'm not exactly planning to play Queen Victoria to his Albert over this."

"Well, I sure wouldn't expect you to. I never could figure out what you saw in him anyway, pompous ass that he was some days. Though I shouldn't speak ill of the dead, should I?" The repentance in his tone was so false that she laughed. You should tell him, a voice in her mind whispered. It's dark and quiet and if he thinks you're crazy, you can always claim to be drunk. If you ask, at least then you'll know.

"Con," she began casually, "did Armitage Historical Research ever call you again? I mean, after that party where you and I and Tony talked about our work for them?"

"Yeah, now that you mention it, they did. They asked for my original research notes."

"They asked me too. Did you give them to them?"

"Of course."

"Didn't that strike you as odd? I've never done a job where someone wanted my notes."

"So it's a bit odd. For the bucks they paid me to do that work, they could have every note I've ever written. Even the naughty ones."

Ardeth shifted a little to face him. When she spoke, her voice had unconsciously shifted down, pitched below the laughter from the yard. "Con, if I tell you something, will you promise to hear me out and not laugh till I finish?"

"I'll try."

"Two nights before that party, there was a fire in an abandoned warehouse downtown. I saw it on the news the same time I heard about Tony. That warehouse was one of the ones I did my study for Armitage on—you know, tracing the history of ownership from the mid-1800s until now. There were three men killed in that fire but no one knew what they were doing there. Then Armitage called and asked for all my original notes. I gave them, but I made a copy first."

"Why?"

"I don't know. It was just something that nagged at me. I couldn't give all that information without something to show for it." She shifted again, to stare out at the dark bulk of the trees. It was easier to tell if she couldn't see his eyes, she decided. "Maybe it was to keep from thinking about Tony, maybe it was to keep from thinking about my thesis, but I went and looked at my notes again. The warehouse had been abandoned for a long time and before that it was owned by numbered companies and bank trustees and a vanished Russian wool merchant and a Scottish shipping company. Nothing unusual about it at all. I forgot about the whole thing until a couple of days later, when a guy from the Land Transfer Office called me. I'd given him my number when I was doing my research there. He told me that the River Street warehouse had been sold again. Two weeks after I filed my research, a numbered company bought the warehouse. I thought I'd call Armitage and tell them that."

"Scoring brownie points again, Ardy?" Con inquired with a touch of malice.

"If you like, yeah. And I wanted to know what they were doing with the work I'd done for them. When I tried to call them, I just got a message saying that number was no longer in service. They weren't in the phone book either."

"So?"

"So that means that Armitage hired you and me and Tony—and maybe some other people we don't know about—to do research. Then two weeks after I submit my report, someone buys one of the buildings on my list. Two weeks after that, the building burns down with what the police call 'suspected drug dealers' inside. And Armitage disappears."

"I repeat the question. So? Do you think Armitage, if it exists, is up to 'no good'? That they're involved in some deep, dark plot to buy worthless old warehouses in Toronto and burn them down?"

"Maybe. That warehouse wasn't worthless, Con, and it was worth a hell of a lot more burned down. None of the historical building regulations could apply to it then. Maybe they *did* burn it down, maybe those men were hired to commit arson."

"I sense a 'but' coming here."

"But if that's all it was, why my research? Why yours and Tony's?"

"Exactly. I can't see what Russian dynasties and sixteenth-century magicians have to do with burning warehouses for insurance money in Toronto. Ardeth," Conrad paused, suddenly serious, "how's your thesis going? Really?"

"It's not. It's going nowhere. I keep trying to work on it but I can't seem to concentrate."

"And Tony's dead and you'd rather not think about that either."

"You think I'm just being paranoid."

"Ardy, if it was anybody but you I'd be tempted to say you should join the line-up for alien encounter stories and JFK assassination conspiracy theories. But it *is* you."

"And I don't have an imaginative bone in my body, is that what you're saying?" She managed to make it sound like a joke. Almost.

"You don't have a *crazy* bone in your body. What you're doing makes perfect sense. You have a thesis that's stalled and your ex-boyfriend just died. Rather than think about that, you're thinking about this admittedly mysterious string of coincidences. There, Dr. Freud has spoken. You're cured. I'll send you my bill in the morning."

Ardeth laughed, the sound a little unsteady with relief that was stronger than she had expected. "I'm relieved to hear you say that, Doctor. I suppose rampant paranoid is better than having people really out to get you." Conrad gave an evil chuckle and put a companionable arm around her shoulder.

"Who says no one's out to get you, my dear?"

"Con, I'm not your type."

"True enough. But that blond over there by the barbecue, do you think I stand any chance with him?" Ardeth leaned over to look down at the group assembled on the patio below them. The blond in question had a sharp, pretty face framed by spiky hair and a dangling skull-and-crossbones earring.

"I think he's strictly a U of T type. Downsview's too far away."

"I didn't say I wanted to marry him, Ardy. Just . . ." he trailed off suggestively and she laughed.

"You're wicked, Con."

"And you're naïve. You ought to try recreational sex sometime."

"I thought that was dangerous these days."

"Not if you do it right. Oh well, I suppose someone around here has to play the goody two-shoes type."

"And it'll never be *you*, that's for sure. So it might as well be me. After all, I'm good at it." Ardeth heard the undercurrent of discontent in her voice and wished she could have hidden it.

"You're sweet, Ardy, you know that? If I were straight, I'd marry you." Ardeth laughed and rolled her eyes in mock horror.

"Now I do need a beer." As they retired from the balcony to descend back into the noise and heat of the party, the sense of relief that Con's sensible explanation had caused faded a little. There was one thing you didn't tell him, the voice in her mind whispered. I couldn't, she thought back, it sounded truly paranoid. I just couldn't tell him that I think someone has been following me.

As she had predicted, there were at least two people sprawled on the floor, oblivious, by the time she left the party at two o'clock.

The night air was refreshingly bracing after the hot, smoky haze in the house. The back streets of the Annex were almost deserted, only the constant hum of activity on Bloor Street two blocks south breaking the silence. She walked more quickly than usual, not looking up at the huge old houses, now subdivided into rooming houses, or renovated and converted into trendy duplexes. She loved this part of town, loved the air of age and the heavy, overhanging trees, and the infinite variety and convenience of the city at her doorstep. Even if all she ever did was go to the Korona for cheap Hungarian food or succumb to temptation at Book City once in a while. But tonight, out of the warm safety of the party, the warm certainty of Con's rational psychoanalysis, she didn't want to linger even in this familiar territory.

At the corner of her street, she automatically paused for a moment to check the sign outside the Doric-columned First Church of Christ, Scientist. The sign announced that week's sermon, and the letters were cut from a black plastic sheet, which was placed into a lighted box. She had been impressed by the expense they went to, until she realized that they recycled the signs every three months or so, covering the same topics over and over again. This week's subject was "Necromancy, ancient and modern (including hypnotism and mesmerism) explained."

Ardeth smiled a little as she passed. She'd always intended to catch that one someday. Behind her, a car door slammed, echoed by a second one. Ardeth automatically began to walk a little faster, but she didn't look back. You're almost home, she thought, don't get paranoid.

When she reached the circular drive of her building and cut across it to the stairs, she glanced back instinctively. The two men walking up the street had been closer than she thought. They were moving quickly, hands in pockets, not speaking. There was no one else on the street.

She ran up the wide brick stairway to the landing of the porch that ran the width of the building. It was an old mansion, built in 1912, and since renovated with a five-storey addition on the back. Even though she lived in the new section, it was the broad, red-brick porch with its balustrades and pillars that represented "home" to her, that never failed to evoke a rush of wonder, bordering on satisfied smugness, that *she* lived in such a place. She had just opened the battered oak front door when a voice said her name.

She jumped, heart going still for a moment, and turned to face the figure emerging from the shadows at the far end of the porch. At first, all she saw was a pale face, crowned by a shock of copper-coloured hair. A guitar case and duffel bag banged against the black-clad figure's knees as it stepped into the light. "Sara. Jesus, you scared me," Ardeth said, after she could breathe again.

"Sorry. Where have you been? I've been waiting for hours."

"I went to a party. I didn't realize you'd be coming over to visit." The sarcasm went unacknowledged.

"I didn't either."

"Did you and Tyler have another fight?"

"Yes. But can we talk about it inside?"

"All right," Ardeth sighed and fumbled for her keys. She didn't offer to take Sara's bags, but just led her younger sister to the apartment.

"Do you have anything to eat here? I haven't had dinner."

"Whatever's in the fridge or cupboard," Ardeth replied resignedly. It would be a while before she got to sleep now, she might as well get some work done. She dug out her pocket calendar and sat down to review her schedule for the next week.

After a few moments, Sara emerged, munching on a ham and cheese sandwich. She peered over Ardeth's shoulder. "Jesus, Ardeth, do you schedule everything? Do you schedule sex in too? I can see it now. Foreplay 11:15 to 11:30."

Ardeth unclenched her jaw and tried to make her voice even. "I'm very busy, Sara. It's end of term. And no, I don't schedule sex. But then, I generally know who I'll be having it with."

"That was a low blow." Sara's voice aimed for flippancy but skidded perilously close to pain.

"You're right. I'm sorry. What happened tonight?"

"I walked in on Tyler fucking one of those peroxide clotheshangers he claims are 'modeling' for his paintings," Sara admitted, voice back under control.

"You've left him for good this time, I hope."

"Yeah." She dragged out the word reluctantly. "He was holding me back anyway. And the guys hated him." Sara looked up at her. "So can I crash on your floor for a few days?"

Ardeth turned in her chair to look at her younger sister. Sara had changed her hair again in the month since she'd last seen her. Then it had been purplish mahogany, left long and shaggy; now it was coppery, caught up in a crude, spiky topknot. She was wearing black pants, pointy-toed ankle boots and a white T-shirt. Her leather jacket was on the floor beside her. The T-shirt bore the red logo "Black Sun" over the stylized image of the band's name, the usual sun image rendered in ominous black. It had once been good quality—now it had been run through the laundromat a few too many times and the sun had faded to grey. Sara had a large collection of the T-shirts—they advertised the band she fronted. "The guys" were, with her, the core of the group's shifting membership. Beyond them, Ardeth never managed to keep names and faces straight.

She realized that Sara was still watching her expectantly, waiting for the inevitable affirmative response to her question. For a moment, Ardeth wanted to say no. For once, she wanted to refuse to be Sara's hotel, the place she went when money ran out or relationships ran cold. For one moment, she wanted to say "You messed up your life, you fix it." But she couldn't. Sara was all the family she had left.

"Sure. My couch is your couch."

"Thanks, Ardy. You're a life-saver, as usual. I'll be no trouble."

"So you say. But I still get up at 6:00 in the morning. I have work to do."

"6:00 ... AUGH. How do you stand it?"

"I don't go to bed at 4:00 in the morning," Ardeth replied, but her smile took the disapproving edge off her voice.

"The price of rock and roll," Sara said with a shrug. Even as children, Ardeth had been up and noisy at the first sign of sun, while Sara would slumber until noon if left undisturbed. Ardeth sometimes wondered if Sara had adopted her profession to suit her lifestyle, not the other way around.

"Is that everything you've got?" she asked, gesturing to the duffel bag and guitar case.

"All I'm carrying. The band gear is with Pete; I've got some stuff in a locker at the Gold Rush. Gotta learn to travel light, Ardy," Sara said, gesturing at the bookshelves lining the walls, the television and VCR, the stereo, the couch and chairs. Those represented the first decent furniture Ardeth had ever owned, bought when she purchased the condo with the money left after their parents' car accident. It had taken her six months to even think about spending her inheritance without a nagging guilt. And then, the fact that Sara was already a quarter of the way through her money financing her band had had some influence on her decision. As if this were another competition—who can spend Mommy and Daddy's money better.

"If I travelled light, you'd be sleeping on the floor in my dorm room," Ardeth pointed out tartly. She hated herself when she got this way, the lecturing older sister, but almost every conversation she had with Sara ended up like this. She found herself forced even harder into the role of the stable, dependable and slightly dull scholar—if only in contrast to Sara, who changed boyfriends and living accommodations almost as often as she changed hairstyles. Ardeth stood up, yawning. Best to get out of this while she still could. "I've got to get some sleep. I'll see you in the morning."

"6:00, right," Sara moaned.

"Well, maybe 8:00. It's the weekend." She smiled and her sister laughed.

"Oh well, I guess I'll get to see what the world looks like before noon. Will you take me out to brunch?"

"*Take* you?"

"Well, we don't get paid for the gigs this week until tomorrow night, so I'm a little short of cash." She had the grace, or the good sense, to sound apologetic.

"OK. Brunch it is. But you'd better be up by 10:30," Ardeth warned. Sara opened her duffel bag and a flurry of crumpled black clothing tumbled out.

"For free food? You bet." Sara contemplated the scattered clothing as if they were tea leaves and there was some message in their pattern on the grey carpet, then glanced up. "Thanks, Ardeth. I appreciate it."

"Any time," Ardeth replied and was relieved to discover that, deep inside, she meant it.

Sara left Sunday afternoon, departing in the band's battered van with Pete and Steve, the two other constant members of Black Sun. She promised to call when she had a new phone number. Ardeth sighed and added another black stroke to the column of deleted phone numbers in her address book.

Chapter 2

Talking to Conrad had helped after all, Ardeth discovered. She resumed work on her thesis with renewed energy, as the ideas that had seemed so formless a week ago began to take shape. She no longer felt that someone was following her around the campus. She confined any thoughts about the Armitage mystery to idle speculation during dull moments in the library.

Then Conrad was murdered.

She heard it on the news Sunday afternoon a week after the party at Peter's. For the next two days the rumours were passed through the Grad Students pub, the library, the classrooms. Con had been stabbed, bludgeoned, shot. The villain was an old boyfriend, a new boyfriend, a complete stranger. There wasn't much in the papers, beyond the coroner's confirmation that death had come from a blow to the head with a blunt object, and that police were canvassing the areas frequented by gays for information on Con's movements that night.

Somewhat to Ardeth's surprise, she cried more for Con than she had for Tony. Cried and tried to ignore the cold weight in the pit of her stomach, the irrational, terrible suspicion that *she* was somehow responsible—that her peace of mind had come at the expense of Conrad's life. Behind the illogical guilt was the frightening compulsion to see the patterns that Conrad had so neatly dismissed. Armitage's disappearance, the fired wirehouse, Tony's "accident," Conrad's murder, the echo of footsteps behind her in the night. She wondered if it was better to be crazy or really in danger.

Routine offered some refuge from grief and speculation, so she kept to the established rhythm of her days as best she could. One ritual she clung to was her early morning walk. At 6:30, the neighbourhood was quiet, the sun just beginning to touch the empty streets. She had a usual route, so she trusted her feet to keep to the path and let her mind wander, drifting from one of her thesis arguments that was still giving her problems, to Conrad's funeral, to Carla's upcoming dinner party, and back to her thesis.

She paused briefly at the foot of the hill leading up to Casa Loma. She could turn left here and follow the street to climb the hill or take the steep stairway cut into the hillside. She could see the turrets of the castle rising over the trees, the elaborate folly of a wealthy merchant as tribute to the wife who never lived to see it finished. Now, it was a tourist attraction and a site for extravagant weddings or tasteful corporate Christmas parties.

You need the exercise, she told herself. And climbing the stairs was hard work, or at least hard enough to keep her mind from things she'd rather *not* think about this morning.

She was halfway up, pausing on one of the landings to catch her breath, when she heard footsteps behind her. She glanced back and saw a fair-haired man climbing the second flight of stairs. He was moving quickly, not looking at her. Ardeth started up again, feeling vulnerable and exposed on the long stairway. She didn't stop again, despite the burning in her thigh muscles and the beginning of a painful stitch in her side, but the footfalls behind her grew steadily louder.

She started up the last stretch of stairs two at a time, using the railing to help haul herself up. Halfway to the top, she dared a glance back and saw that the man was almost at the landing below her. Something shifted sickeningly in her stomach and she turned around to run up the last steps.

There was someone standing at the top.

She had a brief impression of dark hair, dark clothing. Run, the terrible chill in her spine urged her. Don't be a fool, her reason answered. It's just a jogger, or someone out for a walk. He's not waiting for you. Ardeth looked up again and saw the smile he tried to hide.

She knew that her widening eyes betrayed her. He was already moving towards the first step when she ducked under the railing and fought to get her balance on the almost vertical slope of the hill. Slipping on the dew-damp grass, she started to scramble up and to her left, hoping to reach the top before he could head her off. If he came out onto the hillside, he'd have the same trouble moving as she did and she might be able to beat him to the top. If only he didn't go back up the stairs . . .

A quick glance to her right revealed that he'd done just that and was running across the top of the hill to cut her off. This isn't happening, a part of her mind whispered in dull panic, this can't be happening. She was slipping again, gasping as her body hit the ground and she started to slide down backwards. The ache in her side had turned into a knife-sharp pain.

Twisting around, she saw that the fair-haired man had left the stairway and was scrambling across the grass directly below her, to intercept her if she tried to tumble down the slope to safety. There was nowhere to go but across the face of the hill.

She wanted to scream for help but couldn't get her voice past the band of terror that seemed to have tightened around her throat. She could only listen to her gasping breaths as she struggled over the slanted ground, grabbing saplings for support to halt her slow, steady drift downward towards the man moving below her. A glance upward revealed that the dark man had sprinted ahead of her along the hilltop and was working his way down through the scrubby trees towards her. There was no escape, no way they wouldn't catch her. Don't let them get me, Ardeth prayed and lunged forward, hands clawing at the grass, feet slipping in the dirt.

The dark one caught her as she reached the edge of the denser growth, one hand closing over her shoulder and pulling her around to deliver the backhanded blow that tumbled her to the ground. She skidded down the hill a little, struggling to free her shirt from his grip, then he sat down hard on her stomach and drove the air from her body.

For a moment, darkness swamped her as she fought only to breathe. When the sudden rush of oxygen back into her lungs cleared her vision, the man was crouched over her. There was a long knife with a wickedly serrated blade moving in hypnotic rhythm in front of her eyes. "Another sound, another move out of you and I'll leave your guts here for the birds to eat, understand me?" he whispered.

Ardeth's head spun again but she found herself nodding without thinking about it. She felt a distant sense of relief that some part of her had managed to maintain an instinct for self-preservation. She felt the sudden cold kiss of metal against her skin as he laid the knife beneath her jaw.

"That's good. Now sit up, nice and slow." She managed to get her hands under her and ease herself into a sitting position, aware of the knife poised just below her chin.

The blond man emerged from behind the dark one, breathing hard, eyes angry. "You could leave her in the bushes here. Nobody'd find her for weeks. It'd be even better than the ravine where we left the other guy," he suggested helpfully.

"No. We'll take her with us. Get her up," the dark man ordered and, with a shrug, the blond moved around to grip Ardeth's shoulders and pull her to her feet. They held her firmly as they struggled back up to the top of the hill. "We're going to that van over there. You walk nice and steady, Alexander, and I won't cut your throat."

My name, he knows my name, Ardeth thought dazedly as she let them guide her towards the van waiting by the curb. The blond one went ahead to open the back doors.

This is it, last call, Ardeth thought as she was pushed around the back of the van and sent stumbling inside. I ought to scream, I ought to do something. Someone might hear, someone might save me. But it was too late, the hands were closing over her again, jerking her hands behind her back to bind them tightly, forcing a greasy rag between her lips.

The back doors of the van slammed shut, then she heard the front door echo them. The engine sputtered into life, then the van into motion.

"Where do you want to dump her?" a distant voice asked.

"Go back to the base."

"You want to do it *there*?"

Ardeth didn't see the blindfold coming, then all light was gone. Pain sparked briefly behind her eyes as her hair was tangled in the knot as it was jerked tight. Finished with her, the dark man answered, "We're not going to do her, Wilkens. Our guest needs her."

There was a sudden outburst of laughter, echoing wildly through the darkness in her mind. "I get it . . . kill two birds with one stone."

"So to speak." Another harsh burst of laughter was drowned by the roaring in Ardeth's skull. I'm going to faint, she thought distantly, before the last coil of fear inside her tightened and stopped her heart.

Chapter 3

Don't panic, Ardeth told herself, when she found herself awake again, don't panic.

Of course, suggested a tiny voice in the back of her mind, *if* you did decide to panic, only *if* mind you, you would be excused as having every reason. You are, after all, bound, gagged and blindfolded in the back of a van driven by two maniacs who've already killed someone else. Someone they left in a ravine. Someone who might have been Tony. And they know your name. They knew where you'd be. They were waiting for you.

But they hadn't killed her yet. They had even said they weren't going to "off" her. Ardeth tried to console herself with that thought, but the tiny voice only cackled and remarked that if they hadn't killed her yet, it was because they had some other use for her. And what might that be, it mused. Maybe they want you to teach a Sunday School class. Maybe do some research for them. Maybe they just want to have a little gang-bang and then kill you.

The vision of that fate was so overwhelming that Ardeth's mind screamed in protest. It wasn't until she heard the choking whimpers that she realized she'd screamed out loud as well.

"Shut the fuck up back there," a distant voice shouted and Ardeth buried her head against the rough carpet of the van's floor and willed herself to be quiet.

Right. Don't panic. Don't faint again. She bit down on the gag to keep from crying. She had to think. OK, Ardeth, think, she told herself. How long before someone missed her? A couple of days, maybe even a week before anyone got concerned enough about her absence at class and her endlessly ringing telephone to call the police. Maybe less if someone was worried (maybe Carla, oh please Carla be worried, be worried soon!) enough about her mental state after Conrad's death.

Then . . . if they tried to find her, what would they find? Nothing. She couldn't remember seeing anyone on her walk. How long would it take the police to reconstruct her movements? Days? Weeks? Months?

All right then, all right. She caught herself on the verge of hyperventilating and slowed her breathing. No help from outside for days, if ever. She'd just have to make it through this on her own.

Why me . . . oh God . . . why me? I've been good . . . I don't deserve this . . . I can't face it, I can't, I can't, I can't!

You don't have a choice.

That thought steadied her a little. She was a coward, true enough, and physically weak. But she was smart, surely smarter than these thugs. And no matter what they did to her, all that mattered was that she stay alive until help came. Just stay alive.

All right, Ardeth thought again, clinging to the clear, final sound of the words in her mind. So she had to make it on her own. Think then. Where were they taking her? She'd started up the hill at 6:45. How long had she been unconscious in the back of the van? She had to remember to check her watch when they arrived . . . wherever. Yeah, that'd be simple. She was only blindfolded with her hands bound behind her back. Still, it was something to try for.

Now, the van. She'd had only a glimpse of it, but even if she'd seen it clearly, she wouldn't know more than the colour. Too bad you didn't pay more attention to Tony's car lectures, Ardeth told herself, then clamped down on the hysteria-edged laughter she could feel bubbling in her throat. The carpet in the van smelt like spilt beer and gasoline. A unique smell, surely. She could see it now, the headline screaming "Kidnap victim identifies culprits by smell."

The men. That's right, she told herself, try to remember the men. What do they always say on cop shows? Male, Caucasian, early thirties, one dark, the other blond, eyes ... she shuddered when she thought of their eyes. No. Don't think about the men.

Just think about the van, the motion. How far are we going? How far? The steady hum of the van's engine and the rough vibration of the floor beneath her seemed to dull her senses. She let her thoughts dissolve into the sound and motion. Even if she couldn't faint again, it was easier, so much easier to be in shock. She just wondered how long the state would last.

She made it last until the van jolted suddenly, sending her body rolling against the side, and bruising her hip on the wheel cover. She'd been drifting, her mind filled with peaceful, grey fog. Distantly, she'd heard the men talking, a foreign language of business deals and baseball scores that she could not stir herself to try to understand. The only thing that made sense to her was the dark man's name— Roias.

The van jerked again. One of the men swore and Ardeth bit back her whimper as her back slammed into the side of the van. They must be in the country now, off the paved roads.

At last the van coasted to a halt. "Well, bitch, we're here," one of the men, Wilkens she guessed, said cheerfully.

"Open the door and get her downstairs," Roias ordered. Ardeth heard the front doors slamming. The side door slid open.

"All right, I'm gonna take you out now. And you're going to march nice and pretty where we tell you, or I'll start cutting you up into little pieces right here."

"Be sure you have a bucket handy if you do. I don't want any of this to go to waste," Roias remarked, which set the other man off into gales of nasty laughter that turned Ardeth's spine to ice. Any *what* to go to waste? she wondered and then shied away from the horrific possibilities her mind insisted on presenting. They want you alive and unharmed, she told herself. That's something to hang on to.

When Wilkens hauled her to her feet, she struggled obediently along beside him, straining to hear every sound around her. It was oddly quiet, no street noise. They were definitely in the country.

She stumbled on the stairs and Wilkens cursed, hauling her up by her bound arms. She counted the stairs to keep her mind busy. There were fifteen of them. Inside, she felt the change in the air and in the sound of her feet on the floor. She was being marched down a long, echoing hallway, with wooden floors.

There was a pause and Ardeth heard the snap of bolts and the heavy grinding of a metal door being pulled aside. "Move it," Wilkens snapped, pushing her forward. She staggered into a rush of dank, chilly air. A basement, she thought, as Wilkens began to manoeuvre her down a long set of curving stairs. The steps were narrow and she could feel the vast emptiness tugging at her. One misstep or an overzealous thrust from Wilkens and she could end up with her brains splattered all over the floor. It might be better that way. This could be your last chance, the nasty little voice whispered. It might, she acknowledged, but knew she wasn't brave or desperate enough to take that way out. Not yet.

They reached the bottom of the stairs and kept moving. "Wake up, Your Highness. Din-din's here," Roias called out, from somewhere ahead of her. "I know it's early, or is that late for you? But if you don't take it now you won't get any more." Wilkens laughed and quickened his pace, dragging Ardeth along beside him.

She heard the clink of metal on metal, then the long protesting squeal of a rusty door opening. "Bring her in here," Roias instructed, and Wilkens pushed her suddenly forward. She stumbled and fell to her knees, then crouched there, afraid to move. Wilkens's hands closed on her arm, then she felt the cool blade of a knife between her wrists. She cried out once, the sound mercifully muffled by the gag, before she realized that he was cutting the rope that bound her. Freed, her hands tumbled limply to her sides. She could barely feel her fingers.

"The wrists are no good, no circulation left. It'll have to be the arm," Wilkens said and then shoved her forward again. Ardeth sprawled onto the stone, unable to catch herself with her lifeless hands. Hands seized her hair and hauled her up again, thrust her forward until her aching body met cold metal bars. A cell, she thought distantly. I'm in a cell. Or a cage.

"Put your arm through the bars," Roias ordered and she tried to lift her arm. Disoriented, she couldn't find the opening in the bars. Someone took her arm and thrust it through. Wilkens's hand was still in her hair. "Now hold your arm out straight. And don't move it, no matter what."

Ardeth nodded against Wilkens's grip, against the bars that pressed into her cheek. "All right, Your Highness. It's all yours," Roias said mockingly. In the sudden silence, Ardeth heard the faint clatter of chains moving, the fainter rustle of material on stone. The sound drew near and instinctively she tried to shrink away. Wilkens's hand rammed her head harder against the bars and he hissed a warning.

She straightened her trembling arm and waited, realizing suddenly that she was crying.

Something brushed her wrist and she started to jerk away. Wilkens's warning held her still as the cool, smooth touch settled on her hand, then moved up, as if searching. Finally, the coolness settled on the vulnerable inner curve of her elbow. Warmth replaced the chill and Ardeth realized what was touching her. It was a mouth. It sucked at her skin for a moment, the warm tongue tracing the throb of her veins.

She tried desperately to understand what was happening, what this strange ritual had to do with any of the fates she'd envisioned after her kidnapping. Wilkens's grip on her hair and shoulder suddenly tightened and she had only time to wonder why before two pinpoints of pain shot through her inner arm. The pain faded almost instantly, but she could feel at its source, beneath the warm mouth, a strange pressure.

In the echoing black silence, she heard the soft, almost sensuous sound of sucking.

She almost screamed then, as she realized what was happening. Someone—or something—on the other side of the bars was sucking her blood.

Wilkens's hand moved to loosen her gag and she spat it out. "Go on, scream if you'd like. His Highness probably expects it by now." Roias's voice was a croon of pleasure and Ardeth bit her lip to keep from obeying him. It doesn't hurt, she told herself. No matter what else, it doesn't hurt. I won't scream. I won't give them the pleasure.

She felt the tears tracking down her face and pressed her cheeks harder against the bars. How long could it last? Her arm already felt like lead and her panic had begun to dissolve into an almost welcome lassitude. After another moment, she heard Roias say "That's enough for now." The mouth did not move; the steady pressure did not abate. "I said, that's enough. We've got work for you tomorrow night, and we all know you work better hungry."

He's not stopping, Ardeth thought dizzily, he's just going to keep going until there's no blood left in me. Then she heard Wilkens's curse and a sudden groan from beyond the bars. The mouth left her arm. Someone was pulling her arm back, undoing her blindfold.

Ardeth opened her eyes carefully, squinting against the dim dazzle of the lights. Roias crouched beside her, smiling. Wilkens stood beyond him, a long pole in his hand, the end pointed through the bars. A cattle prod, Ardeth thought, with distant satisfaction at her own knowledge. That's what they use to control ... "Go on," Roias said, as if reading her mind. "It's time you met His Highness, the Count." He took her chin in his hand and forced her head around to face the cell beside hers.

She bit off her scream, choked it down into a strangled gasp. She was staring into hell-bright eyes, burning in a skeletal face shadowed by tangled grey hair. Beneath the torn clothing, the form looked like a man's, but there seemed nothing human in that hot gaze.

"This is our guest, the Count. Count, this is your dinner for the next little while. I'm sure the two of you will get along just fine." Roias released her chin, but she found herself unable to look away from the creature crouched across from her. She was drowning in the molten gaze, caught by the mad hunger burning there.

Far away, Ardeth heard hard laughter, the creak of the cell door closing, footsteps on the stairs. The metal door at the top of the stairway slammed, the sound suddenly so loud it hurt, the echoes rippling in to batter her mind.

The creature's head turned, lifting to swing towards the doorway. Lips curled back and she saw the glitter of eye-teeth, like bone knives dipped in ice. She closed her eyes.

It's not real, this isn't happening. Please God, let me wake up and have it gone.

Trembling, she opened her eyes to discover that, as always, her prayers had gone unanswered.

The Only Thing That Shines

Only say that word and I will
pour myself like wine

. . .

And you are
The only thing that shines.

From the Diary of Ambrose Delaney Dale

4 April 1898

Success! If not complete yet, then so close I can taste its nectar . . .

Collins brought the woman to the house tonight, taking care to bring her in the back entrance, suitably blindfolded so that she cannot recognize the house again. She was an Irish wench, with dark hair and brilliant blue eyes, though past her first prime and with many of her teeth missing. The scent of smoke and alcohol clung to her shabby clothes. Collins settled her into the chair and took off her blindfold. She blinked a few times and seemed to squint about her. I had kept the fire deliberately low and lit no candles, but if she were afflicted with poor eyesight it would be so much the better.

"Here's the gentleman I was mentioning to you, Maud," Collins said, then turned to me. "This is Maud." He was careful not to use my name.

"It is good of you to come, Maud," I said, to put her at her ease, for this would go better if she were relaxed and unresisting.

" 'Tis my pleasure, sir, and your coin," she replied. "Your man here said you wanted some information and no more."

"Very true. You have been visited by a certain client whose identity interests me."

"They don't hardly give me their names, sir. Not their true ones."

39

"Nonetheless, there may be details about him that are of use to me. So tell your tale and I will ask you questions after."

Her story was nothing I had not heard from Collins before; a middle-aged man with a European accent who came to her rooms, paid her the agreed fee and then seemed to require the usual service from her. "But I don't rightly remember it, if you catch my meaning, sir. I remember him undoing my dress then things got a bit muzzy and I must have gone to sleep. When I woke up he was gone. I thought at first he must be some kind of thief, one of those low scum that prey on hard-working women such as I, but there weren't nothing missing from my room. And he left me a little extra, a coin or two, on the table."

She could recall no details about him beyond his accent and his grey hair. A "middling man" she called him— middling height, middling weight, middling appearance. His clothes she described as "gentleman's things, but not flash."

When I brought out the subject of mesmerizing her, she protested, citing her fear of being made to act like a chicken, as she had seen some stage magician do at a town fair. But money is the great persuader and at the prospect of leaving the house with no coin to show for her time, she submitted. Despite her initial resistance, she was an easy subject and soon her eyes drooped and will submerged. I sent Collins out to wait for me in the drawing room beside the study.

"Now Maud," I said quietly, moving into the light for the first time. "It is the night the stranger came to your room. You have just closed the door. Tell me what happens."

"He takes off his hat and puts it on the chair. I see his face clear for the first time." Her voice was slow and clear but I confess I crouched closer in anticipation.

"Describe it to me."

"Oh, but he's a fine-looking one, finer than I had thought. His hair is grey but he's younger than I had thought as well. His face is all sharp and fine and clean. His eyes . . ." she frowns, concentrating, "his eyes are grey too."

"What happens next?"

"He takes the money from his pocket. 'In advance is the usual arrangement, I understand,' he says and I nod and he puts the money on the table. I go and sit on the bed to take off my hat and my gloves. He watches me with them grey eyes." Her voice falters for a moment and I urge her on. "When I starts to unhook my dress he comes to sit beside me. 'Let me,' he says and I laugh and shake out my hair so it falls over his hands when he touches me. When my dress is undone, he pulls it down to my waist. Then he looks at me. I . . . I . . . I start to say something but . . ."

"But what? What happens, girl?" My voice is sharper than I intend and she winces, shrinks in her chair.

"His eyes . . . My head is spinning around, like I've had too much to drink. There is a voice in my head, telling me . . . telling me to go to sleep. So I do . . . but I'm still sitting there with my eyes open. But I can't see anything or hear anything so I must be asleep. He takes my hair in his hand, gathers it all up, and pulls my head to one side, not hard, not so that it hurts. Then he leans over and kisses me on my neck." In the firelight, her eyes are wide and staring, her mouth works as she talks. She takes a sharp, in-drawn breath. "Aah, that hurts. It hurts. But then . . . then it doesn't any more."

"What is he doing to you?" She shakes her head.

"Don't know, can't tell. Then the voice is back in my head, only it's like a dream now, like I can feel something happening to me but it ain't."

"What are you dreaming?"

"That he is taking off my dress and having me, just like all of them do. Then the voice is telling me to go to sleep, shut my eyes, go to sleep. . . ." Her voice trailed off as her body slumped, as if hypnotized by the memory of mesmerism, for I am sure that is what was done to her. It took a sharp slap to bring her back to even the level of consciousness I had left her.

"Then what happened?"

"I went to sleep. He went away." I can get no more from her so I lay my own instructions in her mind, to prevent her loose tongue from wagging *my* business, wake her, pay her off, and send her back to town with Collins. I cannot have them gone quickly enough, so that I can sit here in the quiet and record this.

There is no doubt in me now. There is a vampire here. The whore has given me some clues to his appearance and bearing and I will find more, if I must mesmerize every trollop in the stews. *I will find him.*

Chapter 4

A vampire, dear God, it's a vampire. Ardeth put her head down against the dirty blanket and tried to think clearly. Abandoned in the cell, dizzy from blood loss and shock, she had crawled onto the cot against the wall and kept her eyes resolutely from the presence in the next cell. She had not as much luck keeping her mind from it as well. It's *not* a vampire, her rationality said. It's a lunatic who *thinks* he's a vampire.

Vampires do not exist, except as metaphors. The voice of the professor in her undergraduate Victorian fiction course echoed in her ears. She remembered regurgitating the phrases for a subsequent exam: "Vampires represented the repressed libido breaking out to wreak havoc, causing both death and unfettered sexuality." *She* had no dreams of darkly handsome midnight lovers (are you sure? very sure? the little voice asked) though she remembered passing a movie poster and Sara's laughing voice saying that the spiky-haired lead "lost boy" could bite her neck any time he wanted.

We all say things like that, she thought suddenly, because we know it can't come true. Because it's just a projection of our own subconscious minds. Because there are no such things as vampires.

But metaphors did not cast shadows or leave darkening bruises on the veins of your inner arm.

And human lunatics did not have teeth that could pierce skin without tearing it or eyes that refracted red.

So she was back where she started, trapped between the impossible and the inconceivable.

Her mind gave up then, unable to organize chaos or to categorize all the levels of her fear. She closed her eyes and let the dark shadows hovering all around take her in.

She drifted back into wakefulness much later, blinking into the dim light that glowed in the centre of the room. She had just begun to wonder where she was when a movement to her left caught her eye.

The vampire was standing in the centre of his cell, staring up at the door to the cellar. As Ardeth's drowsy, disoriented mind tried to explain him to itself, he flung back his head and closed his eyes, mouth opening in a long, soundless howl.

This is a dream, Ardeth thought vaguely. I'm sure that in the dream this all makes perfect sense. Then she went back to sleep.

When she woke up again, there was no denying reality. Her stomach was cramped in hunger, her bladder aching, and the arm that had twisted under her while she slept was numb.

She sat up slowly, shifting her shoulders to ease the stiffness from her neck. What time was it? she wondered, peering at her watch. Sometime during the abuse of the previous night, the hour hand had snapped off. It was twenty past something. It must be after noon or else she wouldn't be so hungry.

The thought of hunger reminded her of the silent presence in the cell next to hers. Carefully, she glanced to her left. That's funny, she thought absurdly, I always thought they were supposed to sleep in their coffins, flat on their backs, with their hands crossed. The vampire (may as well call him that, she told herself, it doesn't mean you believe it) was sleeping on the cot, face to the wall, half-curled into a fetal crouch.

She stood up carefully, keeping a wary eye on the sleeping figure. The leg-iron she could see circling one ankle did not reassure her at all. She knew that the chain was long enough to allow him to reach the edge of her cell. Her legs felt heavy and stiff and she stood still for a few moments before braving a step forward. Her knees did not give out and the vampire did not stir. Ardeth walked to the edge of her cell and looked around her prison.

The walls and floors were of unevenly cut stone and it looked, in the light of the one bare bulb that hung from the ceiling, as if both had once been whitewashed. Now there were only cracks of white tracing their way through the greyness and the dirt. On the wall behind the cot where the vampire lay, she thought she saw the suggestions of dark stains. They looked old; she hoped they were.

The stairs were not quite as treacherous as they had felt last night but there was no railing. In the alcove beneath them, she could see the vague bulk of machinery and furniture, some covered in cloth as well as shadows.

There were eight cells, five in her row, three on the other wall, starting just past the alcove. All but hers and the one beside it were empty. There were no mattresses on the bare metal cots bolted to the walls.

What was this place? Ardeth wondered. An abandoned prison perhaps, someplace outside the city. She inspected the lock on the door. It was new, the metal shining mockingly against the rusted bars.

She turned to lean against the door and stare back into her cell. There was a covered plastic pail and a roll of toilet paper under the cot. Curiously, she crossed the cell and crouched to pull them out. She lifted the lid of the pail carefully. It was empty but the unmistakable odour of urine emanated from inside.

Wonderful, Ardeth thought. I haven't used a chamberpot since I was three, at Grandpa's farm. She stared at the roll of paper for a moment. The last sheet had been pulled off unevenly and the remaining edge was ragged.

She didn't think Wilkens or Roias had brought the pail and paper with them, so it must have been under the cot already. It had obviously been used more than once as a chamberpot. Which meant that she was not the first person to be kept in this cell. Someone else had been imprisoned here, someone else who had probably had her (she knew, somehow, that it was a woman) arm thrust through the bars to let the vampire feed. Someone who wasn't here any longer.

Shaking suddenly, Ardeth thrust the pail and paper back to their resting place and scrambled onto the cot. She pulled her knees in tight to her chest, wrapped her arms around her legs and wished desperately that she could just faint again. She settled for the momentary release of tears.

She was still sitting there, though dry-eyed, when the door at the top of the stairs opened. Wilkins appeared at the top, and as he descended the stairway, Ardeth realized that he was carrying a tray. "If you want to eat, get over here," he snapped, stopping outside her cell. Ardeth got to her feet and walked carefully to the door, watching him uneasily.

Wilkens thrust the tray through the horizontal slot in the bars and she barely had time to grab it before he let go, backing away. As he turned, Ardeth opened her mouth. But she had no idea what to say, so she let him go.

The door upstairs slammed behind him, and she thought she could hear the snap of locks closing.

Retreating to her bed, she examined the tray. At least, for now, I won't starve, she thought ruefully, surveying the ham sandwich and jug of water on the tray. Her stomach cramped and complained, but she ate as slowly as she could, not trusting that her captors' largesse would continue.

When she finished, she knew she could no longer ignore the ache in her bladder. Ardeth glanced towards the next cell. The vampire had not moved. At least it . . . he . . . is a sound sleeper, she tried to console herself. Of course, he'll probably wake up at the most inopportune moment.

Still, there was no way around it. It was an awkward process, but she managed. The vampire stayed asleep.

In fact, he stayed asleep the whole of the longest day of Ardeth's life. It became evident quickly, once she had eaten, and explored her surroundings, that there was nothing to do in the cell. For a while she found herself glancing compulsively at her watch every few minutes. But, with no hour hand to mark the passage from one hour to the next, she seemed to be trapped in an endless cycle of repeating minutes. She also found herself subject to crying fits or attacks of panic that sent her stumbling to the cell door to clutch and tug at the bars, as if the lock might have somehow answered her silent pleas and unlocked itself in the time since her last futile attempt. She paced the short diagonal length of the cell, tried to sleep, desperately attempting to hold off the soul-curdling fear she could feel prowling around the edges of her mind. She thought more than once that she might willingly put her arm into the next cell, if only someone would bring her a book to read.

When her watch read ten-to-something, Wilkens reappeared with another tray. He retrieved the old one in silence and again, she did not dare to try to talk to him.

He paused at the vampire's cell. "The sun's down, monster, so I know you're awake. Time to get up. We've got work for you to do soon."

The vampire turned and sat up slowly. He focused on Wilkens for a moment, then his eyes shifted to Ardeth. She froze, clenching the tray between trembling fingers. Then the dead gaze dropped to stare, unblinking, at the floor.

"Jesus," Wilkens muttered and stamped up the stairs. Ardeth withdrew to the farthest corner of the cot and ate her dinner, barely tasting the tinned spaghetti and packaged cake dessert. When she finished, she set the tray down slowly, and huddled back against the wall.

If you keep still, stay quiet, maybe he won't notice you, she thought desperately. She dreaded the weight of his gaze, the memory of the avid hunger she'd seen there the night before. Still, she couldn't help the careful glances she stole at him. He held a dreadful fascination for her, like the perverse human desire to stare at death that manifested itself at traffic accidents.

He was not as inhuman as he had appeared the night before. The face that had seemed like a skull was, in profile, rather fine, with pale, translucent skin stretched over arched, Slavic cheekbones, a straight nose, and a narrow jaw unshadowed by beard. His hair was long over his neck, ears and brow and was an odd shade of grey that was not the colour of age, or perhaps of age so great it was beyond reckoning. He was wearing a white shirt and dark pants, but the fabric of both was fraying and decayed. His feet were bare but he did not seem to be bothered by the cold stone beneath them.

The vampire shifted a little, head coming up, and Ardeth hastily looked away, fearful of being caught by the hot gaze, transfixed like a rabbit before a snake. She closed her eyes and willed herself not to look at him again.

For a moment, she was almost relieved when the door opened and Roias bounded down the stairs. His entrance at least broke the empty stillness and interrupted her aching awareness of the thing she was trying to ignore. Then she saw the anticipation in his sudden grin and her stomach churned, as the fear edged hungrily closer.

"Come on, Alexander," he called. "Time for the show."

Chapter 5

"What show?" she asked, taking a step back and shooting one nervous glance at the silent vampire. Roias opened the door to her cell and stepped inside.

"You'll see. Now turn around." When she obeyed, he jerked her arms behind her and she felt the chill of metal handcuffs snap about her wrists.

"Let's go." He seized her arm and pushed her out of the

cell ahead of him. The stairs were easier this time, without the blindfold. On the other side of the metal door, he went through the ritual of relocking it. Two locks, two keys. Ardeth noticed that he put them back in the front pocket of his pants. That's three locks so far, the cynical little voice noted. Do you think that Wilkens or Roias will just drop the keys by accident in your cell someday?

Roias escorted her down the long corridor, towards the centre of the building. Small rooms with barred doors lined the hallway. "What was this place? A prison?" Ardeth dared to ask.

"An asylum. Not that it's any concern of yours," he answered with a warning glance. Ardeth lowered her eyes and hoped she looked sufficiently cowed. She felt it. After a moment, Roias took her arm again and drew her to a halt in front of a solid doorway. He unlocked this door as well and pushed her through into darkness.

She blinked, her eyes adjusting to the dim light. They were in a long, narrow room, dominated by a huge window. The back wall was lined with shelves of electronic equipment: televisions, videocassette recorders, cameras and items whose purposes were more obscure. Some were on, red lights blinking in time to some hidden rhythm. The window did not open onto the outside, but looked out over a huge room. The asylum common room perhaps, Ardeth thought, for the room was almost two storeys high and at least as long. Now it housed a strange assemblage of draperies, floodlights and people. A dais was set up in the middle of the room. Men were moving hooded lights into position in front of it, focusing on the white-draped table there.

A film set, Ardeth realized suddenly. And the glass in front of her was not a window, but a one-way mirror. From this room, Roias could watch the proceedings without anyone seeing him. He caught her look of sudden comprehension and smiled slightly. "Have a seat." He gestured to one of the chairs set up in front of the mirror. She sat, awkwardly aware of her hands still cuffed behind her back.

"It's not exactly Hollywood, but it serves the purpose. Ever want to be in show business?"

"No," Ardeth said automatically, mistrusting the gloating pleasure in his voice. Whatever he had brought her up here to watch was not going to be pleasant, she knew. Roias liked to watch people suffer, she guessed, remembering his reaction to her fear of the vampire.

"There's our director, Leseur. He's a genius, or so he says." Roias pointed to a small, rabbit-faced man surveying the set. "Thinks he's Steven fucking Spielberg or something." Roias seemed to find this comment intensely amusing and chuckled to himself. Ardeth decided it was safer not to say anything.

She looked at the set again. Despite the bright lights, there was an air of decay about it. The drapery on the table was fraying into mouldy strands of silk at the bottom. There were crystal glasses filled with pale liquid at the eight places set along one side of the table and she could see the pale drift of cobwebs running from cloth to glass. They must be fake, she thought, though the grime and dust on the walls behind the table were undoubtedly real. Whoever had designed the asylum had not been interested in pure function. The mouldings on the walls were heavily carved and a crooked, dusty chandelier dangled twenty feet down from the ceiling. The religious edification of the mad patients had not been left to chance either. A dust-coated mural covered the upper wall behind the dais. It was a poor copy of *The Last Supper*. The proportions were slightly off, giving the impression that the heads of Christ and the apostles were too large for their bodies.

One of the men scurrying about the set emerged with a large, two-tier wedding cake and set it on the table. The scene suddenly reminded Ardeth of Dickens's *Great Expectations*. She waited for the mad old woman, Miss Havisham, to appear in her rotting wedding dress.

The dress was old, that was obvious, the silk yellowing, the train now moth-eaten, but the girl in it was no old, raddled crone. She was young, far younger than herself, Ardeth suspected, and pretty. Her blonde hair had been left loose about her shoulders, one bared by the too-large neck-line of the dress. She was nervous and trying not to let it show, though there was something ominously feverish about the way her hands darted about, tugging up her dress, toying with her hair.

More actors had entered, representing the rest of the wedding party. As with the bride, their clothing was a strange, twisted version of tradition. The single bridesmaid wore a blood-red dress, red elbow-length gloves and a veiled hat of black lace. High black leather boots disap-peared beneath the swirl of the dress over her knees. The male attendants wore tuxedo coats or tails but one wore no shirt, another leather pants. All of them wore half-masks of black or red, edged in jewels, studs and feathers.

A man approached the bride, spoke reassuringly to her. He was young, with blond, slicked-back hair and a grey suit that Ardeth guessed must have cost thousands at one of the exclusive Yorkville stores. The girl smiled nervously and he kissed her slowly, one hand sliding into the folds of silk between her thighs. When he stepped away, she was flushed but laughing.

"That's Greg. He's our talent scout," Roias said conver-sationally, then leaned over to flick a switch on the panel in front of his chair. A speaker above them crackled into life. A hum of conversation filled the room. "There's not much dialogue in this film but there'll be some good sound ef-fects," Roias told her with a wide grin that seemed to hang, Cheshire catlike, in her vision after he had turned away.

"Positions everybody, we're going to start. You know the rules. Ignore the cameras, and we won't interrupt you," Leseur said from below them and waved the two camera-men into position. They carried portable cameras, to sup-plement the main stationary camera aimed at the table. There were some last-minute adjustments to the lights, as the cast assumed their positions.

"Wait a minute. Where's the groom? Get him out here!" Leseur yelled and a man came dashing out of one of the side doors. Like the others, he was masked with black leather. He wore antiquated evening dress and a long cloak was slung over his shoulders. Unlike the others, there was no visible twist to his clothing. He waved an apology to Leseur and assumed his seat beside the bride.

"All right then, let's go. Action!" the director cried and red lights blossomed on the tops of the cameras. For a moment, the group at the table remained still, a tableau of odd elegance, then the groom inclined his head. Whether it was in acknowledgement of an unheard command or the giving of one, Ardeth could not tell.

The man to his right, the one with the red feathered mask, rose and stepped behind the groom to stand beside the bride. He held out his hand to her and she took it slowly. He drew her to her feet and escorted her to stand in front of the table. He bowed briefly to the groom, then took the neckline of the bride's dress in both hands and tore it down the front. The rending of the fabric jerked Ardeth up in her chair, her eyes widening.

"Well, what kind of movies did you think we were making?" Roias asked with a malicious chuckle. Ardeth shook her head dazedly, lowering her eyes from the window. "Keep watching. It gets better."

The bride had clutched the torn dress to her but when Red Mask took her chin in his hand, she let it go, to tumble in a froth of rotting lace and silk at her feet. Beneath it, she wore a tiny white lace bra, white panties, garter and stockings. Red Mask's hand slid over her throat, lingered for a moment in the hollow between her breasts as if he would tear her bra from her as well, then withdrew. He stepped back and Ardeth realized that beneath his evening coat he wore leather pants with a special leather codpiece. When he began to remove the codpiece, the bride sank to her knees.

"They're all amateurs, you know," Roias commented. "A group of people with certain ... tastes ... that don't normally find such an interesting outlet."

"What about the girl?" Ardeth asked, her voice a faint whisper as she watched the blonde head moving against the leather.

"One of Greg's ... stable." Red Mask was done, and he left the bride crouched on the floor. The shirtless man was next and he removed the girl's bra with a knife before sprawling her across the floor on her back to turn his attention to her bared breasts. He kept the knife at her throat the whole time and when he rose Ardeth thought for a terrible moment that she could see the marks of his teeth on the girl's skin.

It went on for an hour. Each attendant took a turn and in the end the bride was naked, her body gleaming with sweat and semen. Roias watched Ardeth as much as he watched the show and every time she dropped her gaze, his hiss of warning would jerk her head back up. She did not know which was worse—watching the endless use of the girl and listening to the sounds, the cries, the crack of the whips, the slap of flesh on flesh—or wondering what Roias was planning to do to *her* next. Or perhaps it was the guilty memory of her own half-conscious erotic dreams of being taken, overwhelmed by some force strong enough to blot out fear, and doubt, and even rational thought itself. But in the dark, secret depths of her fantasies, she was a god, even in chains. She had complete control of her own domination, and the power to make her own ecstasy the ultimate goal of her dominator. Here, she'd be nothing but the next victim, the receptacle of others' dreams, and there was nothing erotic about it at all. Not me, please God, I know I don't believe in you, but please God, don't let them do that to me, she prayed helplessly as four of the chosen gathered around the bride for one final assault.

When they were done, they lifted her body, shaking with sobs, and laid her across the table before the groom. "Cut!" yelled Leseur, and Ardeth let her breath out in one long shudder. They were through, it was over, she thought in relief.

"One more scene. The best one of all," Roias said, as if reading her mind. On the set, Leseur was shooing off the attendants and the groom. Greg had brought the bride a robe and wrapped her in it, helping her to sit down on one of the abandoned chairs.

"You were great, baby, just wonderful," he told her, wiping away her tears. Ardeth could hear their voices faintly, over the activity on the set.

"Can I have some now, Greg?" she asked, her voice shaking.

"Now, honey, we had a deal. You do this job for me, and I'll give you all the stuff you want. You just have one more scene."

"Please, Greg. I ... I need it. I did all that for you, please ... just one," the girl pleaded.

"Suzy," the name was a warning. "When it's over, like I promised." He kissed her forehead briefly. "Just one more scene. For me." Suzy stared at him for a moment, mouth working as if she wanted to beg him again. Then she bit her lip and nodded slowly. "That's my girl. You just finish this scene, then I'll let you have as much as you want." She bent her head against his shoulder and Ardeth looked away, torn between anger and pity.

The set had been emptied of everyone except Leseur, one of the cameramen, Suzy and Greg. Leseur was moving the main camera closer to the dais and instructing the remaining cameraman on the best angles. When the actor-groom reappeared, Wilkens at his heels, Greg abandoned Suzy, with one more quick kiss on her bruised mouth, and disappeared out the main door. Ardeth watched the groom return to his seat. There was something about the stance beneath the black cloak, the tilt of the pale head behind the leather mask that made her uneasy. She felt her palms turn clammy. She shrank as far back into her chair as she dared.

"Finally," snorted Leseur with a glance at Wilkens. "All right, my dear, please take your place." Suzy shed her robe and walked shakily around to the front of the table. She was shivering and Ardeth waited for Leseur's order to control herself. But the director said nothing as the girl draped herself across the table. The marks of the earlier scene were still etched in red across her skin.

Wilkens hovered behind the groom, then bent to whisper something behind the mask. The man nodded slowly. With a last warning glance, Wilkens retreated from the dais.

"Ready?" Leseur called and the cameraman moved slightly.
"Go!"

The actor's hand came up and curled into Suzy's dishevelled blonde hair. She whimpered slightly as he dragged her
off the table and to her feet beside him. Ardeth knew the
sound of pain and fear was not feigned.

The other narrow, long-fingered hand slid slowly up the
girl's side from hip to breast, lingering there a moment.
Suzy's eyes closed beneath the caress and Leseur shouted,
"Open your eyes!"

She did, and Ardeth did not have to see her face to know
there were tears in the blue depths. The groom's hand con-
solidated its position in her hair, pulling back her head to
reveal the line of her throat.

They posed there a moment in tableau. Then, with elegant theatricality, the actor took off his mask.

"Oh my God," Ardeth whispered when the black mask
fell away and she saw the pale, chiselled features and
ragged fall of grey-smoke hair. The cameraman was close
now, shooting up into the revealed face. Unable to look
away, Ardeth watched as the vampire smiled.

Suzy's scream came a second after Roias's laughter.

Ardeth saw the vampire's head dart down like a grey
snake striking, and she closed her eyes as tightly as she
could. Roias was on her in a second, forcing her up against
the mirror. "Open your eyes!" he ordered, twisting her
cuffed hands up behind her. "Open your eyes and watch,
bitch, or it'll be you up there next!" Helplessly, Ardeth
opened her eyes.

The vampire was hungry and not particularly neat. When
he was done, he dropped Suzy's body over the table. Blood
was smeared across her breasts and shoulders, painted
across her face in a parody of cosmetics. Her blonde hair
was dark with it, but not as dark as the gaping hole in her
throat. When he let her fall, one limp arm knocked over the
wedding cake and left its remains decorated with red icing.

The vampire straightened slowly and looked down at the
body for a moment. Then he lifted his hand and wiped the
blood from his mouth. Ardeth watched his shoulders rise

and fall in one long breath and then he turned away from the table. Roias's grip on her head had loosened and she shrank back from the cold glass. But she was unable to look away from the cloaked back, the grey head bent slightly over the dark rise of the cloak's collar.

When Wilkens appeared, cattle prod tilted like a lance, the vampire stepped off the dais and walked out the far door.

Roias let her go and her knees buckled. She slid down the glass wall to huddle at his feet. "You see what will happen if you give us any trouble. You may not be as pretty as that strung-out junkie, but they'll have fun with you anyway. And we'll make sure His Highness is particularly hungry that night. So you're going to be a good girl, aren't you?"

Ardeth nodded, wishing her breath wasn't coming in faint whimpers, wishing tears weren't tracing the dust on her face. "You're going to be good, aren't you?" Roias repeated.

"Yes," she managed to gasp out. "Yes."

"All right then. Stand up and we'll go back to the basement."

She stood up.

Chapter 6

Wilkens had herded the vampire back into his cell by the time they arrived. He stood in the centre of the cell and did not glance their way as Roias returned Ardeth to her own prison. "Get the suit off, Your Highness. You're not going to any parties for a while," Wilkens ordered mockingly. The vampire did not move for a moment, then one hand lifted woodenly to unfasten the cloak.

Ardeth willed herself not to look, not with Wilkens and Roias there, but her curiosity was too much for her and she risked one surreptitious glance from beneath lowered lashes. The vampire's skin had a smooth, matte gleam beneath the lamps. She saw the pale tracings of scars across his chest and stomach. He looked like a man; arms, chest, legs all finely proportioned, muscles shifting in silver planes of light as he moved. Even his genitals looked human. What did you expect, girl? she asked herself, returning her eyes to a fixed gaze at the floor. That they shrivelled up and fell off when he became a vampire? But she hadn't expected him to look so human, and so vulnerable, though he himself gave no indication that his nakedness made him uncomfortable.

She kept her eyes on the floor until the rustle of material indicated that he had dressed again in the pants and torn shirt he had worn earlier. Wilkens held the cattle prod in front of the vampire's chest and Roias fastened the leg-iron about his ankle. "You were very good tonight, Your Highness. For that, we won't even give you a dose of the old ultrasound," Roias said casually, leaning brazenly on the vampire's cell door. The vampire gave no sign he had heard him. He retreated to the cot and sat there, staring at a point past Roias's head.

"You see," Roias said, to Ardeth, "we can make him do anything we want. And we can make *you* do anything we want too. Remember that." Ardeth wished she could mimic the vampire's complete disassociation from her captors, but she didn't dare. Instead, she nodded as quickly as she could. Wilkens laughed and Roias clapped him lightly on the shoulder. She could hear their laughter echo back as they climbed the stairs.

They sat in the semi-darkness, Ardeth on her cot, the vampire on his. When she let her trembling breath return to normal, Ardeth thought she could hear the faint rasp of the vampire's own breathing. She inhaled deeply to blot out the sound. It didn't blot out her images of the movie. She thought that it would run forever through her mind, an end-less tape loop of horror. She saw the final image projected on her eyelids, Suzy laid out across the table, clad only in her skin and her blood, the red-streaked tablecloth, the roses of blood on the cake. And the vampire wearily wiping his crimson mouth.

Ardeth glanced at the vampire carefully. He was sitting absolutely still, head bent slightly. It wasn't until she saw his hands, clenched together so tightly the knuckles had bleached to the colour of bone, that she realized he was even truly conscious. There was no pretending he was an escaped lunatic, not any more. The solid, undeniable reality of him terrified her. Her universe had been very ordered, the line between reality and fantasy clear and unmistakable. Now that line had been moved, no, shattered forever and she was left in a world without foundations.

This would be endurable, she thought suddenly, if I only could *understand* it. All her life she had believed that if she could comprehend something, from a historical fact to her own emotions, she had some sort of mastery of it. In des-peration, she had spent the last day refusing to think about her situation, as if that would somehow change it. But now, perhaps if she could make some sense of the madness she was trapped in, she could restore her bearings in the world.

But here, in the darkness of her prison, there were only questions. Did Conrad's murder have anything to do with her situation? Who was the "other man" they had referred to—and could it have been Tony? Who were Roias and Wilkens and did they have anything to do with Armitage? If so, what? Who was the vampire and what did he have to do with the answers to the other questions?

Ardeth wrapped her arms around her knees and stared out into the darkness. Thinking seemed, momentarily, to blot out her painful, almost physical awareness of the crea-ture in the cell beside her. Maybe it would be her defense, her refuge after all. Maybe it would shield her now, protect her from the embodied death so close to her.

She started with Roias. Surely not all the films produced here were snuff films. Most must be legitimate pornographic films, available by mail, in video stores and by the secret chain of VCR owners that served as the conduit for such things.

She couldn't believe that there was any direct link between Roias and Armitage. But why would men who made porno movies want to kidnap her? It was clear that they had been pursuing her, otherwise how had they known her name? In fact, kidnapping her had been an afterthought. They had obviously intended to kill her, just as they had killed "the other guy." She shuddered suddenly, remembering her flight across the hillside, the jagged knife's cold kiss against her skin. But if Roias and Wilkens didn't have any reason to kill her, perhaps someone else did. Someone who had hired them to do it because that was what they were good at, that was what they *did*.

Assuming her suspicions about their deaths were correct, why had Tony and Conrad been killed? The obvious answer was that they knew something they weren't supposed to. But what on earth would either of them know about porno films? Unless it didn't have anything to do with pornography at all—but with something else, some other secret they knew. Or that they *could* know. And there had to be some connection between the deaths and her own predicament—or else how had Roias and Wilkens known her name? That thought led straight back to the only thing that linked her, Tony and Conrad beyond their status as graduate students—their work for Armitage.

Still, it seemed dangerous to her, to hire three people and then kill or kidnap them. Surely the police would be made suspicious by the sudden propensity of history grad students for misadventure, murder and disappearance. If Armitage had something to hide, surely it would have made more sense to hire only one person to do all the research and then risk only one murder.

Unless, she thought suddenly, the killings had not been anticipated. Perhaps the original plan had been to simply let them collect their fees and gradually forget about the essentially tedious research work they had done. Then *something* had happened—something that could make the knowledge they had dangerous to the company.

Ardeth shifted on the cot, her eyes still focused, unseeing, on the bars. She was close, the scent of her quarry making her heart pound.

If she was right, then the research she, Conrad and Tony had done was connected somehow, despite appearances. If she could find that link, then the puzzle would finally take shape in her mind. But what possible link could there be between sixteenth-century magician-scientists, a Russian dynasty and the ownership of buildings in nineteenth-century Toronto?

One subject was medieval, one continuous and one relatively modern. Two were European, one about North America. Ardeth ran the comparisons through her mind carefully. Two were about people, or families, one was about buildings. No, she corrected herself slowly, not about buildings but about the people who owned them. Still, there had been more than forty-five names on the list she had drawn up, forty-five owners of more than twenty-five buildings. Most of those people were long dead, and many of the buildings long demolished.

But only one of those buildings had recently been bought by a nameless company. Only one of those buildings had been burned down, with three men inside. Only one building had long ago been owned by a man whose name tied him to Conrad's research.

When the answer hit her, she sat up straight and held her breath. She rolled the solution around in her mind for a moment, prodding it for defects, weaknesses. It held, solid and undeniable. The reason for the research, the burning and the signing of death warrants for them all. The name Armitage had wanted—that of a long-forgotten Russian wool merchant who had vanished from the city one hundred years earlier, leaving behind an empty, unclaimed warehouse on River Street.

Carefully, she looked over at the vampire. "You're Rozokov. Dimitri Rozokov."

His head came up slowly, like a creature wakened from

sleep. In the faint light, she could not see his eyes, only the narrow line of his profile beneath the cindered silk of his hair. "You are, aren't you?" She turned on her cot to face him, elation suddenly wiping away fear.

"Yes." His voice was faint, a rusty scrape that hurt her own throat with its dryness. "I am Rozokov."

"They found you, in the warehouse. Then they burnt it to hide where you'd been." There was no reply, only the slow susurration of his breathing. "What happened there . . . in the warehouse?"

"I killed one," Rozokov said slowly, as if remembering something that had happened centuries before. "I woke up . . . so hungry . . . there were men there and I killed one. The others had a machine . . . the pain." His head bent suddenly, shoulders shuddering beneath an unseen lash.

"Who found you? Was it Roias?" she asked, but he was gone again, eyes blank, features closed as carved marble. She said his name once more, but he did not stir. Before she turned away, she said, softly, "My name is Ardeth," because it suddenly mattered that he should know.

Chapter 7

The second day was, if anything, longer than the first. Ardeth paced restlessly across her cell. Movement helped to keep her calm, if only in the illusion of activity. It also kept her warm; the cellar's chill dampness seemed to have seeped into her bones.

Two days. It seemed like an eternity to her, an endless age of darkness and cold, punctuated only by the bright heat of fear. But outside the cell, two days was nothing. It was only Monday. She had no classes on Monday, no place she could be missed from, and no one to know she was gone from the safety of her routine. How many more days until someone missed her . . . and how long after that till they did anything about it?

How long until they make you put your arm through the bars again? the cruel voice in the back of her mind asked. She turned to push away that thought and failed. She stopped, closed her eyes against the waves of panic surging up through her mind, and took a deep, shuddering breath. The moment of terror passed, as they all did, unsustainable in the face of the endless hours, and she resumed her pacing.

The vampire (Rozokov, she reminded herself) was sleeping, face to the wall. Unconsciously, she paused in her restless movement to look at him. The intellectual elation she had felt at the discovery of his identity had worn off somewhat, blunted by his steadfast withdrawal from the world for the remainder of the previous night. So you know his name, so what? the cynical voice in her mind mocked. The two of you can now exchange pleasantries after he drinks your blood. It matters, she told herself resolutely. It makes a difference. For one thing, it was something Roias did not appear to know—or want *her* to know.

She settled back on her cot and retrieved an apple from the breakfast tray Wilkens had brought. She had finally worked up the nerve to talk to him. Now that, she reflected, had been an exercise in futility. She had asked the time, to which he had growled, "Don't see what difference it makes to you." There had been no response she could give to that, so she had watched in silence as he climbed the stairs back up into the light.

Later in the afternoon, another man had come down the stairs. He was younger than Roias and Wilkens, barely out of his teens, and had an awkward nervousness about him. His long brown hair and faded heavy metal band T-shirt made him look like one of the suburban high-school kids who hung out on Yonge Street in search of big-city excitement. The band's leering skeletal mascot grinned across his chest at Ardeth.

He had ducked under the staircase and begun to hunt through the equipment stored there. He had been careful not to look at the vampire, but, watching him, Ardeth caught his curiously guilty glances at her. When he had at last emerged with a tangled handful of cables and started up the stairs towards the door, she thought that she could hear barely restrained relief in his steps. She had felt absurdly comforted to discover that someone else was afraid of the vampire.

There was a rustling sound from the next cell, as the vampire stirred, began to wake. The sun must have gone down, Ardeth thought. At least that's what all the books and movies said; vampires can only rise after sundown. Of course, the same books and movies also said that vampires slept in coffins, feared crosses and garlic, and could turn themselves into bats or mist. The first and last were obviously myths; Rozokov had no coffin and if he were capable of transforming, he would undoubtedly already have done so and escaped. She doubted somehow that crosses and garlic would have much effect.

She watched surreptitiously as he rose and walked to the length of the chain. He stared up at the door for a moment, then turned to pace towards her cell. Ardeth fought the impulse to shrink back against the wall. Instead, she sat very still and watched him.

He stared at her for a moment with pale, puzzled eyes. His gaze was devoid of the red hunger she feared. Talk to him, she thought. If you can make him talk to you, at the very least, it'll pass the time down here a lot faster. "Rozokov," she said quietly, unable to think of anything else. Something moved under the gaze, flickering like a fish beneath the ice of a frozen river. She groped desperately for something to say, any line she could cast to draw that shadow of awareness to the surface. Something about him . . . something that would make him remember . . . Then she heard Tony's voice, telling her more than she had wanted to know about Renaissance magician-scientists. She had been more interested in the coincidence of their sponsorship than the details of his subject, but had been momentarily intrigued by the fact that magic and science were so intermingled in the past he studied and so separate in the one she did. "Were you an astronomer?"

The lines around his eyes deepened as he frowned. "I . . ." The word was no more than a whisper, the faintest of tugs on the line she had thrown.

"Is that what you were, long ago? A scientist? A magician?" Ardeth persisted, keeping her voice low. She was suddenly aware of the strength of the hands hanging loose at his sides, remembering the mad, feral hunger that had burned in him two nights earlier. She felt her leg cramping beneath her and shifted a little to ease it.

The movement seemed to distract the vampire, whose gaze slipped from her face to her throat. She fought the urge to put her hands up to protect herself from his eyes. The hunger was returning, like a distant fire in the grey depths of his gaze.

Ardeth froze, torn between the desire to maintain the fragile link between them and her fear of his terrible, alien need. "Did you discover the secrets of the stars? Did you ever change lead into gold?" she asked. The questions drew his eyes back from the pulse in her throat and she struggled to identify the emotion lying beneath the icy gaze.

"No." As he turned away, she heard the echoes of his eyes' emotion in his voice and knew that it was sorrow.

The clank of his chain as he began to pace signalled the end of the conversation.

The young one, whose name she didn't know, brought dinner. He was nervous, glancing edgily at the vampire, who continued his restless pacing. Ardeth was surprised when, rather than handing her the tray through the door, he sidled into her cell, keeping as far from the adjoining cage as his pride would allow. He locked the door behind him.

"Dinner," he announced brusquely and set the tray down on the floor by her cot.

"Where's Wilkens?" she asked casually, emboldened by his entry into the cell.

"Busy."

"What's your name?"

"Peterson."

"Thanks for dinner, Peterson." He shrugged uncertainly, backing away from her. He was at the door, sliding back the bolt, when Ardeth stood up. She still had no real idea of what was going on, and Peterson was the only one of her captors who had shown any inclination to talk to her. "Wait . . ." He paused, watching her. "Could you just talk to me for a minute? It's lonely down here with just *him*." Jesus, girl, you are so transparent, Ardeth thought, but Peterson's nervousness was melting into uneasy interest. His eyes flickered over her as if gauging possible threat and reward.

"All right, but don't try anything," he warned.

"What would I try?" Ardeth asked. "I just get lonely down here. It's pretty creepy."

"Yeah," Peterson breathed, his eyes drifting almost unwillingly to the oblivious vampire.

"I guess *he*" she gestured with her head to the vampire, "must be pretty valuable."

Peterson drew a breath to answer, then the sound of the upper door opening sent him scrambling back through the cell door. He was busy locking the padlock and Ardeth had retreated to the cot when Roias started down the stairs.

"Well, good evening, Ms. Alexander. Good evening, Your Highness." He looked at the pacing vampire, who made another savage, tigerish circuit of the cage without glancing up. "I think he's hungry. What do you think?"

Ardeth shook her head uneasily, dreading the feverish glitter in his eyes. Even Peterson had shrunk away from him, retreating into the shadows pooling at the base of the stairs.

"Well, I think he's hungry. And I think he's gonna stay that way a while yet. I think he's getting a bit too energetic in there. Maybe a dose of the old ultrasound would do him some good." The pacing stopped, the clank of the chain dying to a rattle. "Oh, you understand that well enough, don't you?"

Roias's bright, hectic smile matched his glittering eyes. He's on something, Ardeth realized, some drug that crystalized all his sadistic impulses into diamond resolve. "Come here, bitch!" he snapped suddenly and she stumbled to her feet. "Come here." Ardeth forced herself to walk across the cell to stand by the door. "Give me your hand." Seizing her wrist, he jerked her savagely forward, slamming her into the bars.

When Roias took the knife from his pocket, she started to struggle involuntarily. He won't cut me, she told herself desperately. My blood's too valuable, he won't, he won't . . .

When he did, she barely felt it, the quick, light cut that drew a line of rubies across her fingers. "Oh, Your Highness," Roias crooned as he held up her bleeding hand.

Ardeth watched Rozokov's head turn slowly. His eyes sparked, reflecting the blood, and he swallowed convulsively. "Want some? Of course you do. But in this case, the pleasure's mine." Ardeth gasped in surprise as Roias took her fingers into his mouth and sucked away the blood. The touch made her skin crawl, made her soul shrink in a way even the vampire's feeding had not.

Rozokov watched helplessly and Ardeth saw the long fingers clench. Roias lifted his head and laughed, squeezing Ardeth's hand to make the blood blossom forth again. Then he dropped her hand and gestured to the silent Peterson. "Bring the ultrasound." Peterson started nervously and, when Roias's head half-turned, scrambled under the stairs to drag out the machinery. The drug-bright eyes focused back on Ardeth. "Put your hand into the cell."

She remembered the vampire's almost incoherent murmur about "a machine" and pain and suddenly realized Roias's intention. He was going to torture Rozokov and use her blood as the lure. "Go on!" Roias snapped and she moved slowly forward, aware of Rozokov's eyes on her. She put her shaking hand through the bars. The chain on the vampire's ankle would not prevent him from reaching her outstretched hand and Roias knew it.

"There it is, Your Highness. All the sweet blood you want. Who knows, I might let you drain her dry. Or, I might turn on the ultrasound." He gestured with the narrow, wandlike device in his hand.

Ardeth watched Rozokov's eyes fasten on her hand. His tongue slid out across his lips. "Don't," she breathed helplessly, though she was not sure whether the plea was aimed at Roias or the vampire. She could see the yearning in every line of Rozokov's gaunt body, in the fearful light in his eyes.

Finally he moved. It was only a step, a shuffle really, but it was enough. Roias laughed and turned on the machine.

Rozokov screamed almost immediately, a wrenching, anguished howl that sent Ardeth staggering back from the bars to collapse on the floor. The vampire had fallen too, arms wrapped about his head, his face to the floor as if he sought to muffle his cries against the stone.

Ardeth willed herself not to scream in accompaniment but in the end, she was crying, her own hands over her ears to shut out the vampire's agony.

Roias turned off the machine and Rozokov's screams ended as suddenly as they had begun. In the silence, the only sound was Ardeth's broken sobbing. "You feel sorry for him?" Roias inquired. "How touching. He'll still kill you. Remember that."

The cold words helped. She wiped her face and sat up, looking at Roias. I shouldn't have cried, Ardeth thought. He mustn't suspect I've talked to Rozokov, that I know who he is. She stumbled to her feet then to the edge of the cell.

"Don't leave me down here, please. Don't leave me here . . ." She was suddenly grateful for the tears she didn't have to feign. Roias laughed and turned away, gesturing for Peterson to follow him up the stairs. "No, please, don't leave me! Don't leave me here with him!" Ardeth cried after the retreating backs until the final echoes of mocking laughter were cut off by the heavy slam of the upper door.

She felt her muscles fail her, relief crumpling her knees and leaving her to slide to the floor in the corner of the cell. She crouched there, shaking, while the echoes of screaming died in her ears. Roias was gone, gone without seeming to suspect that . . . That what? That he frightens you more than the monster in the next cell? That Rozokov may not be the mindless creature they've assumed? That she'd been trying, however clumsily, to get information from Peterson? Don't let him come back, she prayed to the darkness. Let him find somewhere else to play out his sadistic urges.

There was a faint sound from the next cell and she turned to see the vampire still huddled on the floor. After a moment, she crawled unsteadily along the side of the bars to crouch across from him. "Rozokov," she whispered his name like a talisman, the only tie she had to the brief moments when she had seen sanity in his eyes. "Rozokov. They're gone. It's all right, they're gone."

Slowly he moved, arms shifting to bare the grey head. She saw his shoulders shudder, heard the aching rasp of his breath. "Kill him . . . I will kill him," he muttered at last, his voice as molten as the hunger-light in his eyes.

The ferocity of his voice frightened her, but Ardeth stayed where she was, waiting out the horrifying litany of the vampire's sworn vengeance. At last, Rozokov lifted his head. There was a raw scrape from the stone floor on the arch of one cheekbone. His face looked old and gaunt, skin stretched taut over the skull. Ardeth shivered, the icy touch of fear feathering down her backbone.

"What," he began, then coughed as if the words were caught in his throat. "What is your name?"

"Ardeth."

"Ardeth . . . I thought so." The red-reflecting eyes met hers. The fire in them had faded, leaving only dead, grey marble. He tried to pull himself to his knees but failed, balance shattered by the ultrasound. Ardeth watched him, torn between her memory of Suzy's savaged throat and the echo of his pain in her ears. They keep him mad with torture and hunger, she thought slowly. Mad, he would certainly kill her. But sane . . . could he be persuaded not to? There was nothing she could do about the torture, but the hunger . . .

Ardeth realized that she was holding her wounded hand protectively against her stomach. The cut throbbed, but the blood had dried to a thin line. She should wash it now, in case it became infected. But . . . she looked at Rozokov again. His eyes were on her, watching her with dull curiosity. He's weak, she thought suddenly. I could make him stop.

Hesitantly, she reached out her hand. It stopped, almost of its own accord, at the line of the bars, then she forced it through. The vampire's gaze settled on her stained fingers and she heard his breath catch. "It's all right. They'd make me do it eventually," she said slowly, the reassurance more for herself than for him.

He crawled across the floor to the edge of the cell, the chain clanking behind him. Ardeth forced herself to keep still, but her hand was shaking and she had to bite her lip to keep herself from crying out when he began to lick her fingers.

There was not much blood left and after a moment he lifted his head. The pale face was strained and tight, the hunger shining like a light in his eyes. But he did not move to take more than she had offered, simply watched her face with desperate eyes.

When she turned her arm to bare her wrist to him, he let out a long, shuddering breath and bent back over her arm. He was restraining himself, she knew, pausing to draw her veins to the surface. The pain was a swift stab that stiffened her, then there was only the steady pressure of his feeding.

It feels so strange, Ardeth thought. I'm giving him life. Is this what mothers feel when their babies feed, this odd combination of maternal compassion and sexual desire? The realization that his hunger aroused her was suddenly terrifying and she started to pull back. Long fingers closed on her arm and held her still.

Shaking, already feeling the dizzy lassitude of blood loss, Ardeth leaned against the bars and watched him. It was easier this way, giving him her blood freely. She was not even frightened any more, drowning in the swells of pleasure and emotion that seemed to flow through her to the rhythm of his sucking. Even Roias couldn't touch them now.

The thought of Roias jerked her from her hazy stupor, her heart racing with the enormity of what she had nearly allowed to happen. "Rozokov, stop," she hissed, starting to pull her arm out of his grasp, thrusting against the bars to brace herself against the iron grip of his fingers. "Stop!" He lifted his head with a snarl, his fingers clenching cruelly around her wrist. The grey eyes glowed with blood-hunger, the upper lip curled back from eyeteeth as sharp as needles. There was blood on his mouth. "Rozokov," Ardeth whispered in sudden terror.

After a moment, the madness began to drain away and she saw that the sharp angles of his face had softened a little. He looked closer to thirty now than sixty. "Ardeth." Her name was the barest breath of sound. His grip on her arm loosened, though he did not let her go. His eyes searched her face for another moment, as if memorizing it, then he bent his head again. She caught her breath in fear but it was only his tongue that touched her, gently stroking the wounds on her wrist. His tongue slid across her cut fingers and she felt a distant throb of reluctant desire deep inside her.

Rozokov raised his head and curled her fingers within his for a moment. "It will heal more quickly," he said slowly and then pushed her limp arm back through the bars to her.

"Thank you," she said automatically. "Are you ... are you all right now?" She blinked as the world whirled before her eyes.

"You must eat. I was," he paused, suddenly awkward, "careless." His withdrawal was abrupt, just the ghost of a shadow across his face, then he was moving back towards the cot.

Ardeth watched him for a moment, then tried to stand. She barely managed to get up on her knees. Rozokov was right, she had to eat. She crawled leadenly to the tray and devoured the cold steak, washing it down with the orange juice. She ate the chocolate bar slowly, with the thin blanket around her shoulders, waiting to stop shivering.

Chapter 8

She must have gone to sleep. When she woke up, she was still sitting up, her neck stiff from the odd angle at which she had tilted it against the wall. The empty tray was beside her on the cot; she leaned over to put it on the floor and instantly regretted it when it made her head spin. "Damn," she muttered and stretched out on the cot, trying to will away the throb behind her temples.

But sleep refused to come and join her in the relative comfort of her prone position. Fuelled by the steak and juice, her body had recovered the strength it had lost with her blood. That realization led inevitably to the memory of what she had done earlier. In the dim light, Ardeth peered at her hand with uneasy curiosity. The lines on her fingers had already begun to heal and the marks on her wrist were no more than pinpricks.

It had been sheer madness to put her hand into that cell. Even injured, the vampire had been quite capable of holding her there until he had drained every drop of her blood. But he hadn't. Rozokov had waited until she offered, then been careful not to hurt her. She remembered Suzy's savaged throat and fingered the marks on her wrist again. No, it didn't hurt, she thought unwillingly. There were a few moments when she had even enjoyed it. Maybe she was suffering from a variation of the Stockholm Syndrome, with her loyalty being transferred to her . . . your what? your killer? rather than her captors.

Whatever the reasons, there was no denying that she had moved beyond her initial blind fear of the vampire. Knowing his name, knowing that he must once have passed as a successful businessman meant that his savage, withdrawn state could *not* be normal, that his madness could be only temporary. Of course, sane, he could turn out to live up to the evil reputation of his fictional counterparts. But perhaps if she could further penetrate his shell, she could persuade him that they were *both* captives and that she could help him.

Help him what? Escape? Why not? Ardeth thought, staring at the ceiling. She'd come up with a hundred desperate and totally impossible plans during the endless hours of the previous days. All of them were so improbable that she had unconsciously abandoned them to the fruitless, but much easier, longing for rescue, for the *deus ex machina* that would somehow get her out of this tragedy. But with the vampire's help, were her plans still so impossible? She added Rozokov to the scenarios and ran a couple through her mind. It did not help much. None of her captors were careless around her, let alone around Rozokov. They did not venture within range of the vampire without being well armed with the cattle prod or ultrasound. But he'd been passive and withdrawn for so long, perhaps that was all they expected of him. Perhaps if he were sane, and Wilkens dropped his guard for just a moment . . .

Ardeth sighed and closed her eyes, daunted by the sheer impossibility of it. Even *if* Rozokov were sane, even *if* he could be persuaded to attack them and not her, even *if* one of the guards were careless, would *she* know the opportunity when it presented itself and would *she* be able to take advantage of it? Would she have the nerve to risk what little safety she had left? The paralysis that seemed to grip her returned. She felt herself teetering on the edge of despair, felt the hot tears behind her eyes. She dragged herself back to her original line of thought. Escape or no, she had to try to convince the vampire that she had value beyond nourishment.

Ardeth rolled onto her stomach and looked at Rozokov. He had resumed his customary position, sitting on the cot, arms on knees, staring at the floor. His face was so still it looked like the carven image of some alien deity, unknowing, merciless. Her fear of him came nosing back into her mind, to feather a chill down her spine.

What the hell, she thought at last. What *else* did she have to lose? At least talking to him would give her something to do.

She pulled the blanket over her shoulders and stood up, teetering there uncertainly for a moment, doubts flaring, then she moved over to the bars before she lost her nerve. She sat on the floor a foot or two from the edge of the cell, within Rozokov's line of sight if he lifted his head.

"Rozokov." There was no reaction. "I know you can hear me. You can hide from them. . . . I know that's what you're doing. But you don't have to hide from me." She paused, waiting, but he didn't move. "All right, you don't have to talk. I suppose it's been a while since you have. All you have to do is listen. My name, in case you've forgotten again, is Ardeth Alexander. . . ." So she talked. She told him about herself, her thesis, Sara, Tony's death, her suspicions about Armitage, Con's murder, her kidnapping. "So, here we are. How many were there before me, I wonder?" The question was rhetorical only; she no longer expected a reaction from him.

"I do not know." His voice was quiet and calm. He did not look up.

"How many movies did they make you do?"

After a moment, "Two."

"They made me watch." He nodded slowly.

"It was quick this time."

"They made you do it. I know that."

"No choice. Her heartbeat . . . the blood . . ." His head went back, eyes closed, and she saw his fingers clench into fists. Ardeth tensed, ready to scramble back from the bars. He drew a deep shuddering breath and opened his eyes. "I had to." She knew that he was not thinking of the cattle prods and the ultrasound. He'll "have to" do it to you too, she thought in despair, but dared not lose the tentative hold she had on his awareness.

"Why do they want you? What are they planning to do?" she asked. Surely no one who had a vampire would simply

make snuff movies with him. The grey hair stirred and settled as he shook his head. "Have they ever said who pays
them? Who wanted you?" The line of inquiry held no interest for him, and she sensed his waning attention. "Are you
better now, after what Roias did?"

For the first time in the conversation, he looked at her.
"Yes."

"Does he do that often?"

"Enough." She thought she heard an edge of bitter
humour in his voice.

"Rozokov, what's my name?" His head turned and the
cool, grey eyes met her squarely.

"Your name is Ardeth Alexander." She felt like laughing.
He had heard, really heard, the long monologue of her life.

"Why did you do it?" he asked suddenly.

"Do what?"

"Give me your blood."

"Oh," she paused, debating what to say. "You're as much
a captive here as I am. And, they'd have made me do it
sooner or later. At least this way, I had some control over
it." She shrugged and met his gaze. "I felt sorry for you."

He regarded her for a moment with a faint air of bewilderment. "Felt sorry for me," he murmured at last and
closed his eyes. A sudden weight dragged lines of pain and
weariness into his face.

"Rozokov," she began.

"Let me be!" he snarled suddenly, rising to turn on her
with eyes bright with anguish and anger. The ferocity in his
voice was like a blow, tumbling her back to sprawl in awkward fear well away from the bars. Rozokov stepped forward to grip the bars, knuckles whiter than the ashen
strands of hair shadowing the feverish gaze. He can't be
that strong, she thought in sudden terror. Not enough to
bend the bars, to tear down the walls of iron that suddenly
seemed more like protection than prison. "Let me be," he
repeated, the words ground out between clenched teeth,
then he spun away from the edge of the cell and began to
pace.

You see, you can't trust him, you can't ever stop being

afraid of him, the voice inside her warned and her pounding heart and shaking limbs offered no argument. Ardeth slid carefully back to her cot, to curl up in a fetal ball beneath the blanket. At last, she fell asleep to the harsh lullaby of the clattering chain.

It was getting easier to sleep most of the day, Ardeth discovered. She spent the third day of her captivity in a restless doze, waking only to eat and, dreading that she would have to do it while Rozokov was awake, relieve herself.

She tried to tell time by her meals, though she suspected they were brought whenever it was convenient, and not because the hour bore any resemblance to conventional mealtime. Sometimes the vampire was awake when it arrived; tonight, he was still stretched in a thin, tense line along his cot.

After eating, Ardeth rinsed her mouth out with water and spat into the unoccupied cell beside her. Her mouth tasted sour and when she ran her hands over her hair, it felt lank and dirty. What I wouldn't give for a nice long hot shower, she thought and eyed the jug of water. If she was willing to spend a thirsty night, there might be enough water to wash the worst of the dirt away.

It was worth it, she decided, and tipped some water into her hands, scrubbing at her face and throat. Then she crouched and bent her head, pouring as much water as she dared over her hair. Without soap, she could do no more than squeeze the cold water through the tangled strands, but her spirit rose just from the illusion of cleanliness.

That done, she contemplated the water's lowered level, then shot one quick glance over her shoulder at the sleeping vampire. What the hell, Ardeth thought, and unbuttoned her shirt. With the rest of the water, she washed her arms, torso and shoulders, wishing she had the nerve to shed her bra as well.

Shivering in the chill air, but reluctant to cover her freshly clean skin with the dirty fabric of her shirt, she sat combing out her hair with her fingers. She was engrossed in untangling one stubborn knot when she heard a faint sound behind her. She turned and found Rozokov propped on one elbow on his cot, watching her.

Ardeth froze, hands still fanning her hair over her shoulders. His eyes were shadowed by the ragged fall of his hair, but she thought she saw a spark of red there. For a moment, she sat still, hands in her damp hair, the column from her chest to groin suddenly tight and aching. Then she dragged her gaze from his and reached for her shirt. Her fingers were shaking as she fastened the buttons and she took a deep breath to ease the acid residue of fear from her limbs.

Some of her equilibrium restored, she smoothed back her hair once more and stood up. "So you're awake," she said and turned to face him. "Are you talking to me again?" He swung his legs over the edge of the cot and sat up, eyes drifting away from her. "You may as well, you know. We're stuck with each other down here and I, for one, would rather talk, even to an unresponsive lump, than sit here and watch the walls sweat." She settled onto the floor in the place she had sat the previous night. "If you don't talk to me, I might be forced to give you my dissertation." You're babbling, she thought, but still the sound of her own voice gave her some comfort.

"What year is it?" Rozokov asked suddenly, without looking at her.

"Year? Oh, it's 1991. What year was it . . . the last time that you remember?"

"1898. It was 1898 . . . in the summer."

"It's April now, the 8th, I guess. Then you were in that building for more than ninety years."

"Ninety years," he repeated softly. "Longer than I thought."

"What were you doing in there?"

"Someone suspected me. They were too close . . . there was no time to escape." He paused, disbelief still lingering in his expression. "Ninety years. That does explain some things." His voice seemed stronger now, she noticed, and his sentences more complete.

"What things?"

"The machines, the men, those 'movies.' You."

"Me?" Ardeth echoed in surprise, then laughed, envisioning the refined ladylike women he must remember, well-bred denizens of Toronto the Good. "There have been a lot of changes in the world."

"Tell me," he urged suddenly, shifting to look at her.

"Tell you what?"

"Everything that has happened. Everything I have missed." Ardeth thought of the long hours ahead, of the darkness waiting beyond the circle of light above her, waiting beyond the few days she could see into the future.

"All right. It'll probably be more interesting for you than my dissertation anyway."

She was attempting to explain the sixties counter-culture movement when there was a sound from behind the door at the top of the stairs. Before she realized it, she had scrambled back to her cot. A glance at Rozokov revealed that he had dropped into his customary position.

Ardeth tucked her legs up under her on the cot and leaned back against the wall, watching the door from beneath half-lowered lids. A sudden shaft of brightness heralded the descent of Roias and Peterson.

"Rise and shine, Your Highness," Roias called his customary mocking greeting. "It's dinner time." He crossed the room to unlock the door to Ardeth's cell. "What do you say, Peterson? I think the Count must be pretty hungry by now. Shall we just take the bitch and toss her in?" Peterson didn't answer; he wasn't expected to. Roias's attack was as leisurely as the vampire's had been swift—he knew his prey wasn't going anywhere. He sauntered casually over to Ardeth's cot, giving her plenty of time to wonder what he had in mind. "Should we do that, eh, Alexander?" His hand closed on her arm, hauled her easily to her feet. "Just toss you in and let His Highness have a little party? I wonder how long he'd make you last." He squeezed her upper arm experimentally and she gritted her teeth against her wince of pain. "You've still got a little flesh on your bones. I bet he could make you last all night."

He's just bluffing, Ardeth thought. He just wants to make

me suffer first. Surely he couldn't afford to let Rozokov have her so soon. *That's what you thought last night,* the voice in her head mocked. She tried not to think about what would happen if Roias really *did* put her in with the vampire.

He swung her around to face the other cell and held her tight against his chest. "Oh, come on, Your Highness. I know you want it. You wanted it last night," Roias taunted, drawling out the words to make the most of the mocking *double entendre.* "Just have a look at what I've got over here for you." His hand, tangled in Ardeth's hair, jerked her head back so hard she couldn't stop her gasp. She couldn't see Rozokov any more, could only stare helplessly at the ceiling as Roias kept her head tilted back.

The chain clattered suddenly and Roias began to laugh. Pain spiked through Ardeth's scalp and neck as he gave one final savage tug on her hair, then she found herself released from his grasp and hurled forward to stumble helplessly into the bars. She caught them to steady herself, sparks scattering behind her eyes as her forehead hit the metal.

Then her head cleared and the vampire filled her vision. He was very close, the feral smile bright with icy fangs, eyes seeming to swim with blood. There was nothing there of the sad, weary creature who had asked her to tell him of the world. She'd cried out before she realized it, trying to back away from the bars. Hard hands on her shoulders pressed her inexorably forward.

Rozokov's fingers closed over hers and slowly pried loose her grip on the bars. He drew her arm towards him. Ardeth bit her lip against the pain in her hand, in the body forced against the cold metal, and most of all, against the desire to beg him to stop, to betray everything to spare herself this sudden, shocking assault.

If you do, then Roias wins, she told herself and felt a rush of hatred so potent it dizzied her, even as it closed her throat against her cry of pain.

She heard Roias's low laughter in her ears as Rozokov turned her arm, baring her wrist. But though his grip on her arm was cruelly tight, the mouth that settled on her vein was gentle, almost caressing.

The seal on her lips broke only once. Ardeth prayed that Roias thought it was a sound of pain.

When Roias ordered him to stop, Rozokov held Ardeth's wrist for a moment longer, then dropped it so quickly her arm fell lifelessly to her side, banging painfully on the crossbar. He turned his back on both of them.

Roias's grip shifted to her shoulders and he spun her around, jamming her back against the bars. His face was very close, cold dead eyes holding hers. "Wasn't that fun, Alexander? Didn't you like it?"

Ardeth closed her eyes against his and shook her head. It was more than a denial to him—it was a denial to herself of the moment of white-hot pleasure that had pierced her, sharper than vampire's teeth, at the feel of Rozokov's mouth on her skin.

"Well, *I* liked it. I'm going to miss the Count here when he moves on to bigger and better things," Roias said with a laugh, stepping away from her.

Ardeth's knees buckled and she almost fell, but caught herself on the bars. "Yeah," continued Roias conversationally, "His Highness here's been a bundle of laughs—a lucrative bundle of laughs at that. Works cheap too." He grinned at her. "Just feed him the leading lady." He was still laughing as he locked the door and led Peterson back up the stairs. " 'Night, children."

Ardeth closed her eyes and held on to the bars until she heard the last echoes of the slamming door fade. She felt as though she might shatter if she moved, or that the floor might open and swallow her into a blackness that was fearfully inviting.

"I regret if I hurt you. I tried not to . . ." a quiet voice said, too close behind her, and she found the strength to turn around, still clinging to the bars. Rozokov stood a foot away, hands spread a little at his eyes, palms upturned. There was no madness in his eyes now, only a cold and ancient sorrow.

"I thought you were . . ." she stopped, groping for the words.

"Mad for your blood? Not wholly mad, not this time. But I needed it, and they needed your fear."

"You didn't hurt me. Not nearly as much as Roias did." She acknowledged the ache on her scalp, the bruises from her impact with the bars.

"I knew your name. I did not know the others." There was a terrible distance in his voice, a momentary movement back towards the bright, sheltering heat of madness. "It was easier that way." She realized then the reason for his anger the night before. He knew her name and her sympathy for him—and he knew he would have to take her blood anyway. Even in her sudden surge of hope she felt an edge of sadness; the price of his sanity was the pain of that knowledge. But the very fact that he cared at all, that ruthless slaughter was not his normal means of survival, meant that perhaps her half-conscious, desperate plan could work.

He was drifting away, she realized, hovering between the sorrow of awareness and the tempting balm of mental and moral oblivion. "Let me see, where were we? Oh yeah, the sixties. They landed the first manned spacecraft on the moon in 1969, did I tell you that?" she said quickly, forcing herself to yield up her grip on the bars.

Rozokov looked at her in surprise, bewilderment then memory passing like shadows beneath the ice in his eyes. "No," he said at last, "you had not told me that."

Ardeth eased herself to the floor, crossed her legs to hide her shaking knees, and began to talk. After a moment, Rozokov settled onto his cot and leaned back against the wall to listen.

Chapter 9

The next night, Roias was too preoccupied to play out his tormenting games. He and Wilkens arrived later than usual and did not bother to unlock her cell.

"Get over there, bitch. You know the routine," Roias snapped. Ardeth stood up slowly, glancing from the men by the door to the silent vampire. When Roias put his hand on the door of her cell, she moved to crouch by the cell bars. Rozokov stalked over and stood waiting, until she put her arm through. He drank from her inner elbow. Ardeth turned her face away from Roias, pressing it against the cold bars, and closed her eyes. The act had a terrible impersonality about it, as if she were no more than a vessel containing blood, a glass to be drained dry. She would have preferred even the unsettling pleasure of the previous night to this silent, dreadful feeding.

Roias stopped it far sooner than usual, without a word. The cattle prod caught Rozokov on the side of the head, sent him snarling back from the bars. Roias laughed and jabbed at him again, driving him back to the far side of the cell, where he stood beyond the prod's range, watching Roias with burning eyes.

Ardeth sat back from the bars, cradling her arm against her. She kept her head down. "Jesus!" Roias swore, in anger or disgust, and she heard the rattle as he tossed the cattle prod to the far side of the room. She waited for the door upstairs to close before she lifted her head.

Rozokov had risen and was staring up at the door, body tight and terribly still. Ardeth reached out to the bars to pull herself up again and he looked at her. She almost jerked her hand away when she saw the hatred in his eyes. "Are you all right?" she ventured carefully.

"Do not ask me that!" Rozokov snapped. "I am not 'all right.' I cannot be 'all right' here." His voice was icy with contempt.

"Who can?" she asked, her own voice rising as anger overwhelmed her fear of him and threatened to swamp the calm rationality with which she maintained the fragile bridge she had built between them. "Do you suppose I am all right? You should know the answer to that best of all."

"I cannot help what I am, what I need to survive. I have not lived four hundred years to let them starve me to death down here." There was no apology in his tone.

"I don't suppose it's occurred to you that *I* want to survive too. They're not going to starve you to death. If you get too hungry, they'll just give you another junkie to kill for the camera," she said bitterly. "What do you suppose they mean to do with me, eh? What are they going to do with *me*?"

She was crying before she knew it, shattered by the sudden onslaught of all the pain and fear she had kept so carefully controlled over the last days, distracting it with her hopeless flirtation with the thing that would destroy her. Ardeth bent her head against the bars and let the sobs shudder through her. It seemed so much easier to surrender than to go on fighting against the darkness that was all around her.

When his hand brushed her hair, she was too tired to move away, though she knew she should. He could kill you, the voice inside warned. Let him, she thought and for the moment, that seemed the best way out.

The hand settled on her head, and gently smoothed her hair. "Child." The word was a whisper. "I am sorry. I am selfish—it is my nature—but I am sorry. You have been kind, far kinder than I deserve."

"I'm not kind," Ardeth muttered, though she didn't raise her head. He did not stop stroking her hair.

"I know. You think that you are clever, that you are making an ally of me against them." Her head moved beneath his hand, the only sign of her surprise. "I would have done the same, had I been sane enough. Now I am . . . almost returned to myself. But I am afraid I am a poor ally. They have kept me too weak to do anything against them."

For a moment, she wondered if it was all a lie, his remorse, his gentleness, all to persuade her to yield up what he truly wanted. But she didn't care; hollow or not, his sorrow moved her, and his touch was the only thing of warmth in the coldness of her prison. "You need more." It was not a question, but she lifted her head to catch his nod. "You could take it. I couldn't stop you."

"I could. There might be a time when I would. But now . . ." He paused, watching her, his hand still on her hair, inches from her cheek.

"All right." She let go of the bars and put her right arm through. Rozokov took her hand, uncurled her fingers gently. He bent his head and kissed her palm. The sudden, unexpected sensuality of it took her breath away. She felt her fingers curl again, to brush one high cheekbone and touch the loose strands of grey silky hair that obscured his face.

"What is it like?" Ardeth asked breathlessly, struggling to be detached, analytical. To be safe.

"It is like food," he said, pausing to glance up at her, "or love. Some meals are sustenance, some feasts of delight." He leaned over to put his lips against her wrist, to run his tongue along her vein. "Some acts of love are mere biology, some a sacrament." She felt his breath against her skin as he spoke.

"What is this?"

"Whatever you want it to be," he replied before his mouth fastened on the soft inner curve of her arm. Ardeth closed her eyes at the irony in his answer. I don't *want* it to be so good, she thought in despair. But it is, oh God, it is.

Ardeth woke up on her cot, with no memory of how she got there. She turned over groggily and opened her eyes. The dim light above her seemed to be glowing through a dense fog and she struggled to blink the haziness from her mind.

What had happened? she wondered. There had been those moments of terrible pleasure while Rozokov drank her blood (even now, the memory left her with a queasy sense of excitement deep inside), then his voice urging her to sleep. She must have crawled back to her cot, though her memory of it was uncertain.

She closed her eyes again, drifting in the lassitude that cocooned her. Everything seemed very far away; the harsh chill of her prison, her life outside, her friends, her thesis. They all seemed light years in the past, fading quickly down the tunnel through which she moved towards the future. There was no light there, at the end.

After a while, she sat up, brushing her hair out of her eyes, and looked into the next cell. Rozokov was on his cot, leaning back against the wall, one leg up, elbow propped on knee. For the first time, the remote stiffness was gone; he looked lazily graceful. When he glanced over at her, she saw that the lines in his face had smoothed out.

"How long have I been asleep?" Ardeth asked, then wondered why she supposed that he would be able to tell time down here any better than she.

"A few hours. How do you feel?"

"I've felt better," she admitted with a shaky laugh. She shifted into a more comfortable position, trying not to notice how the simple movement made her head spin. When she looked up, he was still watching her. She could sense the words of gratitude waiting on his lips. Don't say it, she thought suddenly. I don't want to hear it. I don't want to remember what it was like.

"So," she began awkwardly, to deflect him, then shivered in the silence as her train of thought failed and left her with nothing to fill the gap. She caught a question and flung it out, to distract him. "How did you become a vampire? I assume you weren't born that way."

"That would have been a grave shock to my mother," Rozokov agreed seriously, rising to wander over to the bars. He leaned against them and looked past her into the darkness. "No. I was, as I recall, a perfectly ordinary child. I was born in 1459, in what you now call Russia. I went to Germany to study and stayed there, in the hills where I could pursue my work. In truth, I was more dabbler than scholar. Astronomy, philosophy, medicine. I tried out each of them." He laughed softly, but it was not a sound of joy. "We were so innocent then, so eager to believe that all the world lay before our hungry minds. I also dabbled, sometimes, in necromancy, but with no great success. Then one night I called and something came. She knocked on my door and stood on the snow like a shadow, and when she came in it was as if a sliver of night had entered, the same way the sun would come through the high windows in the Great Hall." His eyes were far away, mist over the ice. "I did not know what she was until she smiled, but then it was too late. I woke with the next dusk and for two nights we ran the hills like wolves. Then I told the parish priest where her coffin lay. He drove a stake through her heart and cut off her head, then filled her mouth with garlic."

"Why did you do that?" His shrug was eloquently, elegantly cynical.

"I tired of her. And . . ." he paused, "there was still enough human in me to hate what she had done. Or perhaps it was the first inhuman act I was to commit." Bitterness edged the calm voice, the shadows of a darker and, she guessed, more recent sorrow.

"What did you do then?"

"I fled. There was a whole world waiting for me, at least at night, and I fled into it. That was the first law of my new state—keep moving or die. I dared not stay in one place long enough for them to realize I did not age. Of course, I gradually learned the lies to tell, the shells within shells of reality to create, so that I could be myself, then my cousin, then my nephew and on down the years. There are places, I suppose, that are still empty and waiting for a Rozokov to return. Though, from what you have told me of the world, I may not recognize them any more."

"They might not recognize you. Things are much more—organized—these days. You need a Social Insurance

Number and three kinds of identification to open a bank account. You need a passport to travel. Almost everything you do nowadays leaves a paper trail—or a computer trail. Which will be very convenient for historians two hundred years from now, but I imagine it would make things rather difficult for vampires."

He hesitated for a moment, and she wondered if she had lost him in the flurry of unfamiliar words and concepts. But if he had questions, he didn't ask them. He just said, "It does seem so. I suspect that now, more than ever, existence would be much easier if all the myths about my state were true."

"Yes. I noticed you hadn't turned into a bat and flown away yet."

"I cannot transform myself into mist either, more's the pity. Still, I suppose I should be grateful I do not require a coffin to sleep in. They had one here, put it in here with me. When I ignored it, they took it away again."

Ardeth laughed. "It's probably a prop. For the movies." That thought started the terrifying flicker of the snuff movie rolling in her head again, and she forced it from her mind. "Is any of it true? The stories about sunlight, and garlic and crosses?"

"As with most myths, there is a small nugget of truth in the dross of invention. The sunlight will not melt me with a single ray, but I prefer not to move about in it. Garlic is unpleasant, but hardly a deterrent. As for crosses, I am no demon, else one so far below God's notice that he does not bother with me. I have prayed in the Cathedral of Notre Dame and walked through the Vatican without harm. A stake through the heart would probably kill me, as would fire, or beheading, but under normal circumstances, I am much stronger and more agile than a mortal man."

"Under normal circumstances," Ardeth began hesitantly, weighing how much she wanted an answer to her next question. But curiosity won out and she continued. "How often do you have to . . ."

"How often must I feed? After my long sleep, I needed nourishment desperately. That is why they have been able to use that need against me. Normally, I need sustenance once or twice a week. It can be less, but then," he paused for a moment as if searching for a word, "I must do lasting harm. And that would leave a trail of corpses like breadcrumbs behind me." Ardeth tried not to laugh at the image, but failed.

"I *did* wonder about that," she confessed.

"When I first changed, the hunger was as it is now. If I had not been very lucky, I would probably have been caught and destroyed. That is no doubt the root of the stories that are so prevalent in my old lands. A newly made vampire abandons all caution in the search for blood, often returning to his own family in blind need. Most were caught and given a true death soon after they awoke."

"Are there many vampires?"

"Not to my knowledge. I have only known two—she who created me and . . . one other. But there may be more."

"Can you make someone a vampire? Or does it happen automatically?"

"It is a conscious thing. A choice, at least on my part. I have never done it."

"Why not?"

"It is not something to do lightly. Every new vampire would increase my own danger of exposure and I would prefer not to perish for another's carelessness. And those I met who did long for my state were hardly the type of person with whom I cared to share eternity. The truth is, we are a solitary lot. It does not do for us to forget that." She heard irony in his tone and the bitter pain gliding, sharklike, beneath it. Ardeth felt the sudden pang of sympathetic sorrow, wondering for the first time what it was like to have almost a century pass in a moment's rest, to face a life that could go on forever, if only under the pale light of the moon. But to live it always alone. She had always thought of herself as a solitary person, who enjoyed the quiet of the library, the peace of her own apartment. But there had been friends, and Sara, and the expectation of love someday.

"How did you end up in Toronto? Was it just next on the map?" she asked, to keep away both their sorrows.

"I suppose so. I had never been to North America . . . a month-long sea voyage was not something to be contemplated lightly. But Europe had grown . . . hard for me to bear . . . and I needed to put it far behind me."

"I imagine Toronto must have seemed very provincial to you."

"Oh yes. But I needed its routine, its simplicity. It was very easy to survive here. It was a good place for careful men—it bred them, rewarded them. So it and I suited well."

"Toronto the Good. We still call it that, with a kind of embarrassed pride, I think. All our politicians wish we were New York, but without the crime and garbage," Ardeth said and caught the edge of his half-smile.

"New York. I have never been there. I remember when the Dutch bought it from the Indians however." The reality of his age hit her then, the fact that all the things she had read of and studied he had touched and felt, that the worlds she had so carefully reconstructed for essays and exams had been the ones in which he lived and breathed.

"Tell me," she said suddenly, as eagerly, as desperately, as he had once commanded her. Rozokov glanced at her curiously. "Tell me what the world was like, what you've seen. God, do you realize that half the historians in the world would kill for a chance to talk to you." She stopped suddenly, her stomach dropping sickeningly as she realized what she had said. Would they die for it? Would you? a voice asked mockingly in her mind. Will you?

"Ardeth . . ." Rozokov's voice caught her, dragged her back to look at him. "Eyewitness accounts from vampires do not hold much academic weight, I am afraid. I have received more than one lecture from a learned professor for presuming to question his version of the truth."

"It doesn't matter. I just want to know," she said, the sudden terror over. I do want to know, she told herself fiercely, to escape the suspicion that she clung to the irrational belief that their recited histories could somehow hold back the future, like Scheherazade holding back the executioner's axe.

Deliberately, she drowned herself in his stories of the places he'd been—Europe, the East, Africa. He was an eloquent storyteller, patiently accommodating her interruptions of "but that isn't what . . ." and "are you sure?" There were things he would not discuss, times and places dismissed in a manner that told her nothing except that those memories must hurt him. He had had his share of narrow escapes, such as the time he had been inadvertently stranded in the Spain of the Inquisition, and his share of pleasures, like hearing Bach's Mass in B Minor for the first time ever.

"Was it easier being a vampire in the sixteenth century or the Victorian age?" Ardeth asked curiously.

"All ages have their own dangers. The world was larger, more unknown, in my youth, but it believed in my kind. In the 1800s, the world was far more organized, but the belief in rational science was so strong that I would surely have had to turn myself into a bat in order to convince anyone that I was not merely some lunatic who believed he was a vampire. Of course," he mused, with a faint smile, "there was a brief, difficult period when vampires seemed all the rage in penny dreadfuls and the like. That infernal book by that Irish author was the worst of them all."

"You mean *Dracula*?"

"Exactly. Suddenly to be Eastern European and of noble birth was enough to make you the object of considerable suspicion or, at least, considerable interest."

"It's still very popular. I read it for Victorian fiction class. The professor explained that vampirism was a metaphor," Ardeth said, with a sudden, giddy smile.

"A metaphor," Rozokov echoed with quiet amusement.

"For . . . oh yeah, 'dangerous, unfettered sexuality,' " she explained, then regretted it, for it called up the image of his head bent over her outstretched arm, the memory of his mouth on her palm.

"Ah." There was a long pause. "Then it seems I should be right at home in this new age. From your description, it seems to be rather more liberal than the last time in which I lived."

"Well, it was, I suppose. AIDS has changed a lot of that." At his curious glance, she continued. "It's a disease that's transmitted by bodily fluids, usually through sex, or by sharing needles for drugs. It's fatal."

"I am immune to most diseases now, however I shall keep that in mind," Rozokov said seriously and Ardeth eyed him for a moment, certain that he was teasing her in some manner, though his face remained solemn. She started to yawn, then tried to catch and cover it. "You should sleep," he said.

She thought of protesting that she was not tired, then yawned again and abandoned that idea. It was easier to just lie back down and close her eyes, to surrender to the bone-deep weariness that claimed her. The darkness was warm and gentle, enfolding her so softly she barely noticed when it wiped all thought from her mind.

Chapter 10

Ardeth crouched beside her cot, washing her face and hair with water from the jug she had kept after her breakfast. She shrugged off her shirt and looked down at herself. The nightly loss of blood had begun to show; her arms were thinner and her ribs were etched in high relief below her breasts. What a way to lose weight, she thought with the absurd, detached humour that was becoming easier each day.

She splashed the water up onto her arms. Had he woken up and now watched her, she wondered, but refused to look, not even before she reached back to unhook her bra and let it fall. It didn't matter any more, all her former modesty and self-consciousness about her body. She felt as if all the layers of conventions of the outside world, the rules she had obediently, even slavishly, followed were being peeled away. Where had all her careful conformities got her, after all. To this state, crouched half-naked in a dungeon, her world reduced to twice daily meals and the ritual offering of her blood to the vampire.

Ardeth scrubbed at her shoulders and breasts, trying to ignore the itch between her shoulder blades that gave her the feeling she was being watched. She had not heard the vampire move; she thought that he was still asleep. He had been dragged from his stupor an hour earlier by Wilkens, who supervised another brief, perfunctory feeding. When it was done, Rozokov had returned to his cot and vanished back into sleep.

There was a sound from the door and she froze, hands poised to scoop more water from the jug. As the door began to open, she seized her shirt and pulled it on, turning her back as her fingers fumbled with the buttons. Her bra she tucked under the mattress, unwilling to let whoever was descending the stairs see it.

When she turned around, Peterson was at the door of the cell, carrying her dinner tray. Tonight he was wearing a T-shirt bearing the logo of the heavy-metal band Megadeth.

Ardeth stepped forward to receive the tray through the slot but stopped as Peterson opened the door and slipped into the cell with her. "Here's your dinner," he said, then set the tray down on the floor. His eyes never left her.

He wants you. The thought flared through her and she knew with blinding clarity that it was *now*, that moment she had not believed would come, that chance she had feared she would not recognize.

"Thanks." The smile felt like a grotesque mask but she held it in place. She glanced down at the tray. Steak this time, supplemented with pills. "What are those?"

"Vitamins." When she looked doubtful, he said cruelly, "Look, it's vitamins. Roias says you have to last another couple of days."

Ardeth felt the blood drain from her face at the words. She knew, had known from the first night, that she was not to live. But this was the first time any of them had said so straight out.

She was aware that Peterson was still in the cell, that the moment had not passed yet, that the chance was still there. She let her knees bend as if in weakness, settling herself down by the tray. The utensils were all plastic but the tray itself was metal, hard enough to hurt. She looked up at him. "How many others have there been?"

"Four, including the last one—the other night."

"What . . ." she began, then took a deep breath to steady herself, "happened to them . . . . after?"

"We took them out to the woods and put stakes through their hearts and buried them."

"Stakes?"

"Yeah. Roias told us to," he said, watching her with eyes almost as bright as Rozokov's. "I took the last two. It was funny you know, how they got more beautiful at the end. Like you." Ardeth felt her heart contract but she could not look away from his face. "I've watched you, getting more and more beautiful," Peterson whispered, crouching down beside her. "Your skin is cool." It was all a mask, that youthful friendliness that had made him seem less frightening than the others. It was a shell of normality that only seemed normal in comparison to Roias's dark and subtle sadism and Wilkens's gleeful brutality. But Peterson was the darkest, the most subtle of them all.

"You're almost gone now, just another night or two. Then I'll take *your* body out and put it on the ground. Then take off your shirt," his fingers fumbled with the buttons, "and put the stake right here . . ."

"No," Ardeth whispered and the tray came up in her hands, aimed at his head. The narrow metal edge struck his cheek and rocked him back. She swung again before he could find his balance and the panic-driven blow seemed to stun him. The keys, just get his keys, the cold voice of reason whispered behind her fear. She scrabbled in his pocket, found the cool, jangling metal and lurched to her feet, staggering towards the door.

Hands caught her before she reached it, spinning her

around to take a blow that sent her sprawling back across the cot. Her head struck the wall and the world spun into sparks and darkness. When her senses cleared, she felt Peterson's weight across her. He was tearing at her clothing, kissing her still mouth desperately.

Ardeth twisted her head away in revulsion and started to struggle. The sound of their breathing echoed through the dungeon, pounding in her ears. Even if she'd been healthy, it would have taken all her strength, and considerable luck, to hold him off. But she was weakened by blood loss, and in a moment he had torn open her shirt and tugged her jeans and briefs down to her ankles.

For a few moments Peterson contented himself with exploring her naked body to murmured declarations of pleasure at her coolness, at the stark bars of her ribs beneath her breasts. When at last he reached down to unzip his own jeans, Ardeth made one last attempt to push him away. He swore, her sudden action destroying the illusion her passivity had created, and his open-handed blow rocked her senses again.

Distantly she felt him forcing her thighs apart, heard his panting breaths and her own faint whimpers. Then she heard the slow, echoing rumble of the vampire's snarl.

Peterson froze, poised over her, and with her clearing vision, she saw him struggling not to glance up into the next cell. Ardeth started to twist her head to look, but Peterson's hand tightened in her hair and held her still. "No," he whispered harshly and thrust down on her. Ardeth screamed as his hard flesh rammed against her, missing her closed entrance.

The vampire said something sharply, in a guttural, snarling tongue, and Peterson's gaze lifted to the next cell before he could help himself.

Ardeth lay still, her head immobilized by Peterson's grip, and watched the blood leave his face. His erection wilted against her thigh. Then, cursing in sobbing breaths, he flung himself from her and scrambled from the cell, hastily locking it behind him. He didn't bother to do up his jeans until he was on the stairs.

Shaking, Ardeth turned her head to look at Rozokov. He was staring after Peterson, eyes glowing fierce and crimson with contempt. His lips curled back from the bright fangs. Was that what Peterson had seen, the primordial savagery that looked on his own perversion with cynical contempt? Had that ancient, knowing glance withered his erection and driven him in terror from the cell?

With a faint cry, she turned away, curling into a tight ball on the cot, clutching her arms across her breasts. "Ardeth." Her name was a whisper, the vampire's voice tentative and almost fearful. "Child, I am sorry. I did not know what to do to stop him." What was he talking about, Ardeth wondered. He *had* stopped him. The voice was an intrusion on the safe, numb world of her withdrawal and it annoyed her. She pushed her face against the cot as if to block it out. She shivered, the chill seeping into her naked skin, but took perverse pleasure in the discomfort, letting the shudders of cold replace the luxury of sobs.

"Ardeth?" the voice came again. "Are you hurt?" She supposed she must be. Her cheek stung from where Peterson had hit her, and her scalp from the steady drag on her hair. There might be other places too, but perhaps if she didn't move they would let her be.

There was a long silence, then she felt something brush the top of her head. The contact brought memories of the last hands on her body and she jerked up, away from whatever had touched her. Rozokov was crouched in the corner of his cell, body pressed to the bars, arm extended as far as it would reach. His hand rested on the end of her cot. When she met his gaze, he drew his hand back and sat away from the bars.

"Ardeth."

She shook her head to keep his voice out of her consciousness. "Leave me alone."

"No."

"Why not?" She kept her face turned away, staring down into the deserted cells beside her, knowing she should ignore him, that questions would only lead to answers, and eventually she would have to acknowledge the reality of it all again.

"Because I know what you are feeling. Withdrawal is easy; so is despair. But there is no point in it. *You* showed me that."

"Maybe I was wrong. What else *is* there?"

"It will change nothing."

"Will hope? I tried that already." She looked at him then, a brief, bitter glance.

"Surely hope is easier to bear than misery."

"What is this? 'Zen and the art of dying gracefully'? I was just assaulted by a necrophiliac. Am I supposed to find hope in that?"

"No. But you could find other things. Anger. Hatred."

"Is that what kept you so sane?" She despised the bitter cruelty in her voice, but could not help herself. Rozokov shook his head, unwounded.

"No. But it kept me alive. Until you came to make me sane again."

"Do you thank me for that? Maybe this would be easier to take if we were both crazy."

"Perhaps it would. But it is not over yet. Madness may have kept me alive for a purpose my sanity will find." His voice was so solemn that Ardeth could not help her laughter.

"I don't believe this. I'm sitting here, half-naked, nearly raped, discussing Philosophy 101 with a vampire."

"At least it made you laugh." She glanced over at him. Rozokov was smiling faintly, with an air of patient amusement.

"So it did. Of course, I've never seen you laugh."

"I have had nothing to laugh about in the last month. But we do laugh, believe me. In the end, we are no less human than we ever were. Whatever we had in us as mortals, we have as vampires. It is only the proportion, and the expression, of those things that sometimes differ."

"I suppose being a vampire isn't so bad then," Ardeth said slowly, reaching down to tug her underwear back up over her hips.

"It is not an easy life." There was no irony in his tone, only a faint edge of warning.

"But it is life."

"It is life," Rozokov conceded.

Ardeth tried to do up her blouse. Most of the buttons had popped off and the ones that remained barely held it closed. She was too tired to care. She leaned her head back against the wall. They were going to kill her, just like all the others. Just like Tony and Conrad. They would put her arm through the bars one last time and Rozokov, no matter how gently he did it, or how much pleasure he gave her, would drain her dry.

It was impossible to believe in escape now. Peterson might keep the secret of her attempt along with the secret of his own perversion but the moment when the future might have changed was gone. She had tried and failed and now the chance would never come again.

She had no choice but to sit here and wait for death, just as she'd been doing all along, despite the illusions she'd maintained. Sit here until too much blood had been drained from her, and Peterson came to carry her body away like a prize. He'd dump her with the others. . . . A vision of a pile of naked, violated bodies, each bearing a stake like a grave marker through the heart filled her mind.

And another victim would take her place, arm outstretched beneath the vampire's teeth.

The hatred was white-hot, blazing so suddenly along her cold, numbed nerves that it almost took her breath away. It was more than anger at the train of circumstances that had brought her here, more than fury at the men who ended lives with such casual ruthlessness. She wanted them to *pay*. She wanted it more, it seemed, than she had ever wanted anything in her life. Oh, to be able to terrorize Roias the way he had so casually tormented her. She pictured him on his knees, begging her for mercy (as *she* had never done), cringing in fear from her savage triumphant smile, the cruel heat in her eyes . . .

And then she knew.

Ardeth straightened up and sat very still for a moment. It

was madness—and the fact that she had accepted it so easily was madder still. Had it happened and she hadn't even noticed, that moment when she slid over the line into insanity? But mad or not, it was the only way out now.

She opened her eyes and looked at Rozokov. He was watching her from his cot, curiosity slowly replacing concern in his eyes. "Would the other girls . . ." she began carefully, "have come back?"

"No. Merely dying from a vampire's . . . attentions . . . does not make one a vampire. If that were so, there would be far too many of us. It requires a sharing of blood and," he paused for a moment, "death soon after. Why do you wish to know?"

"Because I'm not going to get out of here alive." Said, in the stillness, the words were a relief. She felt as if a great burden had been lifted away, the weight of decision gone.

"Ardeth," Rozokov began, then stopped, because there was no lie he could offer.

"If I don't die from loss of blood, they'll shoot me."

"Yes."

"They wouldn't expect me to come back."

"They stake the bodies," Rozokov pointed out slowly.

"I know. If there were only some way to make sure they didn't . . ."

"And if there were a way?" There was reluctance in his voice, a distance she could not quite understand.

"Then you could . . ." She paused, the words not coming as easily as she had thought. It was much simpler to talk around the meaning, much harder to say it plainly. "You could make me a vampire. I could come back."

"Ardeth . . ."

"It's the only way," she said stubbornly and looked at him. There was despair in the hunched shoulders, the bent head.

"I know. I've known for some time now."

"Then why didn't you tell me?"

"Tell you what? That the only way for me to escape from here was to kill you, transform you into a creature like myself, then make you rise from a pile of corpses to come back to me? Ardeth, I would not force that upon you. They have made me commit atrocities here, but I will not do it of my own free will."

"It's my will now. I don't care about dying any more. But I want them to pay for it," Ardeth said, her voice suddenly hot and venomous. "I want to tear this place down around their ears for what they've done to me, to you, to all those girls. I don't think I'll rest any easier, knowing I was just another helpless victim."

"Ardeth, this is not a simple decision," Rozokov began.

"Yes, it is. It's the simplest decision I've ever had to make. I die or I survive . . . we *both* survive."

"There is a price for that survival. It is not a price that comes without regret."

"Will either of us regret it less if I die for good?" she challenged him, and he stared at the floor for a moment.

"No." He lifted his head and smiled at her. "Very well. Leave the stakes to me. I will solve that problem somehow. When do you wish it done?"

"Now, tonight."

"So soon?"

"How much longer will I last?" She had to do it now, while she was well past the fear that held her passive or the hope that could make her cling to life too long.

"Now, then," Rozokov agreed quickly and he rose from his seat to step towards the bars. Ardeth crossed to meet him on shaking legs, stumbling on the jeans around her ankles before kicking them aside, then sank to the floor. He lifted his wrist to his mouth for a moment. When he held out his arm to her, a line of blood had blossomed across the pale skin. Ardeth stared at it in dizzy fascination, her hands tightening on the bars.

Two steps brought him to the edge of his cell. Slowly, he extended his arm until wrist and forearm had passed the boundary between his prison and hers. Crouched on the cold floor, she stared at the marble hand, the long fingers loosely curled, and the pallid arm, scored with the bright, heavy blood.

If you do it, there's no going back, she thought. Back to

what? Every other choice she might have made seemed very remote now. The only real thing in the world was that line of red before her. Ardeth licked her lips, not daring to look anywhere else, especially not up into the vampire's eyes.

She knelt forward slowly, put one hand out to curl around his. When she laid her trembling lips over the wound, she heard his distant sigh. It took her a moment to master the rhythm, but when she did, the blood flowed easily, warm and strangely sweet. It filled her mouth and its heat ran like fire along her veins. Somewhere deep inside, she felt the last barriers crumbling in.

When he tried to draw his arm back, she clung to his wrist as he had once clutched at hers. His hand touched her hair, seemed for a moment to hold her mouth against his open vein, then he pulled her gently away, whispering her name.

Ardeth kept her head down, shocked by the abandon with which she had clung to him. When Rozokov spoke, she realized that he had crouched down on the other side of the bars. "Give me your wrist."

"No," she whispered, before she could stop herself.

"It is too late to change your mind."

"I haven't. But . . ." She dared to look up then, at the narrow, shadowed face. She remembered the touch of his mouth on her skin, fever and ice, and her breath caught in desire. "I want it the real way."

"The real way?" Rozokov echoed in bemusement. His eyes flickered to the bars between them, then back to her face. He smiled suddenly, a slightly surprised smile that softened the angular lines of his face. He put one hand through the bars and brushed back her hair. The long fingers drifted along the curve of her jaw.

They tightened on her chin, drew her gently to lean against the bars. He, in turn, moved to press against them from his cell. One arm moved about her waist. It was maddening to feel his body so close, and know she could get no closer.

Ardeth closed her eyes when Rozokov kissed the corner

of her mouth. His kiss, like his blood, was warm and sweet. But he did not press her, and it was she who finally opened her mouth beneath his. When her tongue touched the edges of his sharp eyeteeth, he drew back and smiled.

Rozokov's hand moved to unbutton her shirt, push it back over her shoulders. It was awkward at first, with the bars between them, but in the end she clung to them gratefully as even her bones seemed to melt beneath the caress of the cool fingers, the burning mouth.

When he lifted his head to kiss her mouth again, she reached with shaking fingers to unfasten his torn shirt. His flesh was smooth and cool but she could feel his heart, warm and strong, against her palm. He watched with curious eyes as she pulled off his shirt and traced the silver scars that crisscrossed the pale skin, a map of the dangers he had endured in his long life. She bent her head and followed the same lines with her lips until they led her to the hollow of his throat. When she bit him, his soft laughter dissolved into a croon of pleasure.

Rozokov tangled one hand in her hair and tilted her head back to bare the curve of her throat angled against the opening in the bars. Ardeth's breath caught as he ran one finger down her neck and across her collarbone. A thread of fear slid along her backbone, woven among the tapestry of desire. But he saw the involuntary doubt in her eyes, and his hand drifted down to brush her breasts, her hips, her thighs. By the time he pulled her forward and settled his mouth against her throat, she was trembling in pleasure, not fear.

I'm not afraid, Ardeth thought with sudden clarity. For the first time in my whole life, I'm not afraid. The vampire was kissing her, lips drifting from the curve of her shoulder to the soft, secret spot behind her ear. Suddenly, she wanted the final kiss, the sweet, perverse penetration, more than she had ever desired a mortal lover. "Now. Do it now."

He groaned and his teeth slid into her flesh. Ardeth cried out, in pleasure and pain so intermingled she could not have told where one ended and the other began. She was shattering in his arms, over and over, her senses breaking and reassembling to be dissolved again in ecstasy. But each climax was weaker than the last, until she was drifting in a dizzy netherworld of pleasure.

Rozokov was holding her so tightly that the bars were pressed hard against her flesh, but she barely felt them. I should be cold, she thought distantly, but felt nothing but the heavy weight of her limbs. She had a remote awareness of Rozokov stroking her hair, whispering something against her ear. She thought that she should try to listen to him, but something was beckoning to her from the darkness, calling her out beyond the borders of reason and consciousness. For the first time in her life, she went.

Chapter 11

Peterson stood at the doorway, the tray balanced on one hand. He didn't want to go down there again—not with that monster there.

It hadn't been his fault. He couldn't help it. She had been so beautiful, with her hair slicked back from her pale face, the shirt clinging to her damp body. She was the first one he had touched while she was still alive. It had been incredible, the combination of her cool skin and still soft, supple body so much more exciting than the chilling rigidness of the others. And she had it coming, for trying to hurt him like that.

The thought of her swayed him, warred with his memory of the monster's terrible, knowing gaze. You think she's yours, don't you? Well, she'll be mine in the end. Buoyed by that realization, he opened the door.

Halfway down the stairs, he realized that something was very wrong. He took the next steps as quickly as he dared, spilling orange juice all over the tray. At the door to her cell he stopped.

She lay on the floor, by the bars to the monster's cell. She was on her back, wearing only white briefs, her shirt now spread open to bare the curves of her breasts and the sharp edges of her ribs. One hand, fingers curled up slightly, rested in the vampire's cell. Her eyes were closed, but he knew she wasn't asleep. Her skin was too pale, too glowingly white for that, and the bare breasts did not move.

Peterson put down the tray and unlocked the door. The dungeon faded around him, awareness of anything but her blotted out by the sprawl of her white body on the stone floor. He walked to where she lay and crouched beside her. He touched her face, caressing the still eyelids and flaccid lips. His hand slipped behind her head and he bent, aching to touch her chill lips.

"Peterson." For a moment, he thought it was her voice, crooning his name in welcome. Then he realized it came from beyond the bars. Don't look up, he thought, but it was too late. He fell into the grey emptiness and was swallowed by whispers.

He carried her body through the woods. She seemed lighter than the others, her body still soft and malleable. The arm he rested over his shoulder did not move as he walked.

Roias had not been nearly as angry as Peterson had expected he would be. "We'll just buy one of Rick's girls for tonight. We only have to keep His Highness happy for another couple of nights, then he's out of our hair forever." He stood in the control booth, staring out over the empty makeshift studio. "Well, what are you waiting for? You know what to do. And don't forget the stake."

The stake and shovel were in a bag slung over his shoulder. Don't worry, asshole, Peterson thought angrily. I won't forget your precious stake. I'll just do it last, that's all.

He shifted her in his arms and her head rolled against his shoulder, almost as if she were snuggling up against him. She would be the last one, he realized. It would have to end now, just when it was getting easy, getting perfect. As much as he hated the monster in the dungeon, if the vampire went away, so did the women. Without the vampire, Roias would just go back to making his porno movies, and those women didn't interest Peterson at all. Unless Roias decided to keep on making snuff movies ... but Peterson couldn't see him doing that, not without the vampire to make it special.

The monster had power—and both Peterson and Roias hated him for it. Roias's bosses needed the vampire a lot more than they did Roias, and that gave the monster power. That made Roias angry, made him play his stupid games with the ultrasound and the girls.

But that was what Peterson envied. The vampire wasn't at all like the smooth seducer he remembered from late-night movies, but it still had power. Power over the anonymous hookers that Roias snatched off "the track" in Toronto and put into the cell next door, until they grew pale and luminous and beautiful. Power over the desperate junkies that "starred" in Leseur's movies, then surrendered to the vampire's embrace.

He had seen it in all their eyes in the final moments; the longing for that gaunt, grey monster, the dizzying desire for death itself. The neon-scrawled deathshead logos he wore on his chest didn't seem to either scare or draw them. But they all went into that grey death with their arms open.

If it was death they all loved, couldn't he be it to them? he wondered. He was better, he loved them more than that monster, who only wanted their blood to hang on to his own awful life. He wanted them, wanted to worship their cool limbs and still lips.

He remembered the hot, contemptuous eyes and held the body in his arms tighter. *You'll* be gone, he thought at the memory. Roias will take you away and his bosses will do whatever they want to you. *I'll* still be here. *I'll* still be free. I know what to do now. I know how to do it.

He was almost disappointed when he reached the make-shift graveyard and had to lay her on the ground in order to dig the shallow grave. They were deep in the woods surrounding the asylum. The sky was overcast and the light shifting through the leaves of the overhanging trees seemed cold and grey. Peterson shivered, then started as leaves rustled beneath a squirrel's passage. He hated the woods, feared them with a city-born mistrust of the seemingly deceptive quiet in their depths.

He dug the grave, once or twice shifting its angle as the shovel struck one of the other bodies buried there. When he was done, he stood back to survey his work. It was a weirdly shaped hole, but he could bend her to fit in.

Peterson went back to take her in his arms, carried her to her new bed. He laid her gently into the shallow indentation and brushed the leaves from her hair. Spreading the sides of her shirt wide, he gazed at her for a moment. There were bruises on the sheen of her skin, spreading along one side of her breast, discolouring the point of one hipbone. The largest, darkest one was on her throat and he turned her head to hide it.

"Ardeth," he whispered, the first time he had said her name aloud. She was the most beautiful of them all, even the ones Roias bought for the movies. There was a glow about her, a silver radiance that none of the others had possessed. So beautiful that he could forgive her anything, even hitting him with that tray.

He put one hand on the soft curve of her stomach, then ran it up along her side, pausing over the ridges of her rib cage. A breeze touched her hair, sent it fluttering about her in a way that made it seem as if her head had moved. Peterson's hand froze for a moment, then shifted on to cover her breast.

Suddenly, he could not bear the thought of piercing the soft flesh that filled his hand with the stake waiting in the bag at his side. Roias said you had to, he reminded himself. Roias doesn't have to know, a cool, grey voice murmured, deep in his mind.

"Maybe," he whispered to the face tilted away from him. "Maybe if you're real nice to me . . ." He leaned forward to watch her, to wait for the welcome he could sense in the yielding of her limbs.

The chill came suddenly, like a wind he couldn't feel,

and the shadows from the trees seemed to thicken, lengthen out to caress her hair, tumbled among the leaves. Peterson shivered and reached out for her shoulders, to draw her up into his arms, to get warmth from her cool flesh.

What about us? a voice hissed in his mind, to be echoed by another. *Traitor . . . cheater . . . You said you loved us . . . we loved you . . . lie down and we will love you again . . .*

He froze, as the dead leaves heaped over the graves began to move, to ripple as if something shifted and stretched beneath them.

Come and love us . . . lie down and touch our cold skin again . . .

He looked at Ardeth, desperately searching for the sign of the welcome he had almost seen. He thought her eyelid flickered, then another, stronger voice joined the others.

Come and love me . . . come and love us forever . . . forever and ever and ever . . .

A vision opened up before him, of rotting bodies stirring beneath the leaves, of skeletal hands dragging him down and embracing him in a horrifying parody of all his secret dreams.

"NO!" he cried out, frantically scooping at the dirt by the grave and tossing it in to cover her beckoning arms and still, waiting face. "No. I don't want you . . . not like this. Leave me alone!"

When she was covered, he snatched up the bag and shovel and ran, pursued by feminine laughter that whispered through the leaves.

Halfway to the asylum, he remembered that he was still carrying the stake. He slowed down long enough to throw it into a shallow gully.

Chapter 12

Ardeth woke to the faint whisper of her name.

She was still for a few moments, letting the sound echo through her mind. She did not think about where she was, or how she had gotten there, only listened to the cadence of her name; the sensuous growl of the first syllable, the abrupt termination of the second.

Gradually, as the call died, she regained awareness of her body. She was lying down, a light blanket of . . . something . . . covering her. For some reason she could not define, she did not want to open her eyes. She tried, hesitantly, to remember falling asleep, but could not.

After a moment, she moved her hand a little and felt the cool blanket covering her crumple and slide across her skin. Fascinated by the sensation, she moved her hand again. She pierced the covering suddenly and her hand tingled as the warmth of the air surrounded it.

I'm underground, Ardeth thought with dim surprise. She flexed her fingers experimentally and felt the faint caress of the breeze. I suppose I should sit up. When she did, the earth and mouldering detritus of the previous autumn slid away from her with a sound like the patter of rain.

The air was warm on her skin, and unconsciously she tilted her head back, as if lifting her face to the sun. She heard the rustling of leaves, the distant chirp of crickets. Somewhere, an owl cried mournfully.

Ardeth opened her eyes and stared upward, into the overhanging trees and the silver glow of the moon. It did not seem at all strange that she had been lying under a blanket of earth, in the depths of a forest. The dappled light was cool and comforting. I could stay here, she thought. I could curl back into my little hollow and sleep forever.

But she didn't feel like sleeping. Something nagged at her, the vague memory of something she should be doing. There was also a hollowness in her gut, like hunger. She was not entirely sure what she was hungering for.

Ardeth lifted her hand and absently brushed away the dirt clinging to her cheeks and eyelashes. She shifted and felt something hard and uncomfortable beneath her. When she moved unsteadily to her knees and turned to look, she saw it was a hand.

The hand had lain beneath her in the hollow, the arm disappearing beneath the earth. It was a woman's, for the nails were red and had once been long. Now they were ragged and short, as if someone had bitten them, or worried them away on a wall. The flesh was swollen and glowed a ghastly, ghostly green in the moonlight.

Ardeth stared at the hand for a moment. She was not afraid. The hand was dead, and what had death to do with her? Whose was it? she wondered, with the shallow, conscious part of her mind. One of the others, came the answer, from deep inside her. What others? she wondered uneasily. Why had they put her here, with a dead hand?

She frowned, watching the hand uneasily, as if it would signal an answer. The others, the "they" her unconscious mind had thought of had something to do with the whispered call that was once more sighing through her mind. She lifted her head slowly, listening to the far-off voice.

He wanted her, he was calling her. She wasn't sure who *he* was yet, but there was a tantalizing familiarity about the whisper. She could almost see eyes upon her and her skin shivered with the memory of a caress. Wait for me, she thought back to the darkness around her, I'm coming.

The woods were bright with the moon and with her growing excitement. Only the crackle of dry twigs reminded her that her feet touched the ground as she moved. Ardeth looked down, watched her feet, her legs moving. She was wearing only a shirt and her briefs. The shirt was stained with dirt and seemed dull against the almost phosphorescent glow of her skin. Suddenly curious, she stopped and reached up to touch her face. It felt the same—lips, nose, eyes, brows. Her hair was tangled and she felt the brittle crunch of leaves as she ran her hand over it. She had started to tug at the worst of the knots when the call came in her mind, more insistent this time. At the sound of her name, her hands dropped and she began to move again, her body automatically adopting a steady, loping run.

The building came upon her suddenly, sending her to a staggering stop at the edge of the forest. In the moonlight it seemed huge, the two long wings on either side like arms reaching for her. Rows of blind windows watched her. She had been there, Ardeth knew, but she could not recall seeing it like this. If I was there, why don't I remember this, she wondered. Because you were blindfolded when they brought you in.

She remembered suddenly, remembered struggling up the line of stairs, remembered cruel hands on her bound arms. At the memory, rage swept her, washing the scene with red. *They* were in there, the ones with the hard hands, the taunting words. The ones who had hurt her. And him.

Ardeth stood there a moment, her breath coming hard and shallow, lips curled back in a snarl. *He* was still in there, trapped, calling to her. It was coming back to her, slowly. She remembered a face, angularly elegant, and hungry eyes, and a warm, sweet mouth. Remembered the sharp kisses and the enveloping darkness. "I'm coming," she whispered, her voice a harsh croak.

She was running across the yard towards the building when she saw the nose of the van jutting out of the shed to one side of the lawn. Memory thrust in again, memory of the smell of beer and gasoline and a long, dark, terrifying journey. Ardeth changed direction suddenly, dashing across the driveway. Her feet were bare but the sharp gravel left no mark on them. She felt no pain.

In the dark shed, she stared at the van. It was important that none of *them* get away. Not Roias, or Wilkens, or Peterson. The names rang in her mind, tangled suddenly in a rush of memories. She saw Wilkens coming up the long stairway, saw Roias bent over her bleeding hand. No, especially not Roias, Ardeth thought, then put her hands under the edge of the van's hood and forced it up to reveal the engine. She tore at it, tugging out wires and parts with dizzying abandon. When she was done, she wiped her greasy hands on her shirt and stood back to look at the mutilated engine. It had been so simple that it was hard to imagine that she had not always been able to bend and twist metal with such ease.

Heady with the feeling of strength, she walked to the stairs that led up into the building. The asylum, she remembered. With the memory came caution and she moved quietly up the steps to the door. The door was not locked but it creaked as she opened it. Ardeth ducked inside and ran, barefoot and silent, to crouch beneath the shadow of the stairs. In the empty silence, she could feel distant heartbeats, combining into a steady drone. The sound settled beneath her own ribs and reawakened the hollow hunger there.

No one seemed to have heard her entrance, so she moved from her hiding place to stand in the darkened foyer. Down the long corridor she could see a rusty metal doorway, heavily locked. They had taken her down there, she remembered now. Taken her down into the darkness where he was waiting. He was waiting still, and she ran, catfooted, down the hall. She tugged at the metal bolts, fumbled with the heavy locks, but even her newfound strength could not open the door.

Roias had the keys, Ardeth remembered. And Wilkens, and Peterson. One of them would come by soon, to laugh, or torment, or use their captive in their obscene games. She bit her lip against the surge of rage she felt. She must stay calm, must plan carefully and rationally. They had weapons they could use on her—guns, knives. They even had weapons with which to hurt *him*. They must have no chance to reach those weapons.

Far away, beyond the range of the hallway lights, Ardeth heard a footstep. She froze, her head lifting to scent the darkness as the steady, double-thump of a heartbeat asserted itself in the silence. It was one of *them* come to check on their captive. She darted into one of the doorways that lined the corridor, flattening herself into the shadows cast by the dim and uneven light.

He was humming to himself, the nervous uneasy sound of man's ancient denial of the darkness and its terrors. When he passed Ardeth's hiding place, she saw that it was Peterson. He was digging in his pocket for the keys to the basement.

For a moment, Ardeth was frozen in confusion. What am I doing? she wondered dazedly. What has happened to me? She put her hands over her mouth to keep from crying out and closed her eyes in despair. What happened to me? her mind wailed again.

There was a sudden musical jingle and she opened her eyes again. Peterson had dropped the keys and was crouching, his back to her, to pick them up. Now, a voice, hers or the other's, she was not sure, cried in her mind and she moved without thinking. Her body had an instinct of its own and it did what was necessary. One arm went around Peterson's shoulders and hauled him back, the other lifted to clamp her hand over his mouth.

He struggled, hands coming up to seize her forearm and try to free himself, but she was stronger than either of them knew. Fighting him, Ardeth felt the red rage surging inside her again. This man had held her captive, had tried to rape her, deriving his sick erotic pleasure from the scent of death on her. She hated him as she had never hated anything in her life and she wanted to hurt him, to make him know one fraction of the pain she had felt.

She had no weapons, and both her hands were occupied in holding his thrashing body. So, in her bitter fury, it seemed the most natural thing in the world to sink her teeth into the throat curved next to her face.

The blood caught her by surprise, welling in a sudden gush into her mouth. She almost gagged, then its intoxicating sweetness hit her, jolting along her nerves. Dizzily, she swallowed and the warmth filled her. She barely heard Peterson's muffled scream or felt his frantic struggles. She was drowning in the blood as it washed over her rage, feeding it even as it satiated the emptiness she felt.

Slowly Peterson's spasms stopped, his feet twitching to a stop. Ardeth lifted her head and drew in long, shuddering breaths. The taste of blood lingered sweetly in her mouth. What have I done? she asked herself, but knew the answer. She ought to be horrified. The person she had been would be. But she felt no horror, no regret. She felt only satisfaction and the warmth of the banked fires of rage within her.

She had to move the body. She found the keys beneath his body and unlocked the metal door to the basement. With her newfound strength, it was easy to lift his body through the doorway. She tossed it over the edge of the stairway and waited for the heavy, satisfying thump as it hit the floor. She paused to pull the door shut behind her, then looked down into the basement.

He was there, standing in his cell, waiting for her. He had a name in her mind now, and she remembered what he was. What she was. Ardeth walked down the stairs slowly, aware of Rozokov's wary gaze. She crossed to the cell where he waited, then bent her head to fumble with the lock. When the door swung open, she looked up at him.

"Ardeth." Her name was no more than a whisper, but it felt like a shout of affirmation.

"I came back," she said slowly. He nodded and stepped towards her. She could still feel him in her mind, like the memory of a fragrance that hung in the air.

When he kissed her, she felt none of the soul-shattering desire that had rocked her the night before but a deeper, sweeter satisfaction. She clung to the kiss. When he drew back, she saw a smear of Peterson's blood on his lips. The memory of it filling her mouth pulled her lips into a cold, tigerish smile. Rozokov's grin followed hers, but slowly, as if the savage expression were the symptom of a disease passed by Peterson's blood, and he was only beginning to feel the effect of the fever burning in her veins.

"The others," he said.

"The others . . ." she echoed, and smiled again, revelling in the sensations of her lips sliding up from her sharp teeth.

Chapter 13

Roias was in the booth, his private sanctuary. Outside, in the studio, two women writhed on the red-sheeted bed, while cameramen circled like greedy sharks. Roias barely noticed the scene. The regular fare of the company had lost its allure for him since he had discovered his "specialties."

But that was coming to an end. Rooke's call that night had been definite. They were coming to "collect the merchandise" in two days. That meant he'd better feed the Count. He glanced out at the women. He'd have to put out another couple of grand to buy one of the girls from Greg, but it would be a small price to pay to prevent Rooke's anger. Hell, it was Rooke's money.

At least the Alexander bitch was dead. If Rooke had arrived while she was still alive . . . Roias pushed aside that thought. His instructions had been explicit; kill the girl immediately. But it had seemed a shame to waste the opportunity. It had been easier to use her than shell out to Greg or grab some whore off the streets. Rooke was a mean bastard—and the old bitch he worked for was rumoured to be even worse—but what he didn't know wasn't going to hurt him. She was safely dead and he'd been spared the trouble of putting a bullet in her head.

Still, there had been something disturbing about her death. The image of the pale, nearly nude body sprawled across the dark floor seemed to flicker across his reflection in the window. The vampire had killed her, there was no doubt of that. There had been a massive bruise on her neck, others across her breasts and hip. The monster himself had been sitting on his bed, the icy eyes as blank and unconcerned as ever. But Roias had sensed something behind the glacial surface of that gaze, some edge of anticipation that disturbed him.

Why had Alexander let the vampire take her? he wondered. Had she finally realized that they were going to kill her no matter what and taken the quickest way out? Had she just wandered too close to the bars when His Highness was in a particularly savage mood? Whatever the reason, the Count hadn't made death easy for her. He thought of the marks on the white skin and felt a throb of desire. Too bad he hadn't installed those cameras down there. He might have had one final "specialty" film to sell. Not that he hadn't cleaned up on the three he'd made. Of course, the market for that stuff was limited, but at what he could get for a single tape, that wasn't a problem. And it was pure profit; he paid the cameraman and Leseur out of the company's money and pocketed all the carefully collected revenue from the films himself.

He lit another cigarette and let the smoke curl sweetly down his throat. Rooke would terminate this project soon, he could tell. None of these jobs ever lasted long. In a few weeks, he'd be scouting out new locations, new channels for obtaining the raw material (he glanced again at the flesh intertwining on the bed) he needed. This place had served its purpose, but he was damned tired of it. The long drive in from the city, then the days as a virtual prisoner in the empty corridors, all had taken their toll on him. The next site would be in the city, where he could hear the world again. He missed the smoky nights in the bars, missed the freedom to come and go as he pleased, missed the chance to see faces other than the increasingly annoying ones of Peterson, Leseur and the rest.

Roias leaned back in his chair and tried to watch Leseur's latest masterpiece. It still failed to stir him and after a moment he rose restlessly and went to the door, wondering if there was any beer left in the kitchen. He was already tasting the smooth coolness of the alcohol when he realized that, though the door knob had turned beneath his hand, the door had not opened. He pulled on it again but it didn't move. There was no exterior lock, so what was holding the door closed? And more importantly, who had done this? Not Wilkens. Maybe Peterson. The kid had been acting odd all day, come to think of it. Trying to cover up the bruises on his face, coming back from the burial detail all pale and shaky. Maybe this was that little nutcase's idea of the joke. Some fucking funny joke. The little shit wouldn't think it was so funny when he got out.

After a few moments of rattling the door, he decided he would have to call down to Leseur and have him send someone up. He returned to the console and switched on the intercom. "Leseur," he called, then switched the set to receive. And heard the screaming.

For a moment, he thought it was the movie they were making, that Leseur had decided to add a little S & M at the last minute. Then Roias realized that there was more than one voice crying out, and some of them were male.

He was at the window in one long step, in time to see Leseur's body, spraying blood, tumbling down the steps that led to the raised bed. On the top step stood the vampire. "Holy fucking Christ," Roias whispered as the gaunt figure spun to catch the blonde as she tried to scramble off the bed. She was dragged back onto the red silk sheets, screaming until the vampire's blow turned off the sound.

A movement in the other corner of the room caught Roias's eye. Fernandez was running for the door. He was almost there when a figure emerged from the corner and tackled him. Roias had a brief impression of a patterned shirt and a banner of fair hair before attacker and attacked tumbled into a heap on the floor. For a moment, Roias thought Fernandez might make it, as he rolled on top of the other man. Then the cameraman threw back his head and howled, a wail that ended in a bubbling groan. His body was tossed aside and the attacker rose from beneath it.

The shirt wasn't patterned, it was white. The red blotches were blood. The figure inside this gruesome covering was undeniably female; he could see the curve of her breast where the shirt had torn, and her legs were long and lovely. He dragged his gaze up to the face. Beneath the heavy make-up of blood and dirt, there was no doubt about her identity.

"Oh God," he groaned and ran back for the door. Alexander. It was that damned Alexander bitch. Peterson hadn't staked her. "Wilkens!" He hit the metal door with both hands. "Peterson! Somebody let me the fuck outta here!" He was still banging on the door when the screams from the intercom died. Helpless, Roias went back to the window.

They were all dead—Leseur, the two actresses, the two cameramen. Their bodies were flung carelessly about the studio like cast-off mannequins. Blood pooled around Fernandez, Leseur and the brunette. The blonde's head lolled across the silk at an impossible angle. The two vampires were nowhere in sight.

Maybe they don't know I'm here, Roias thought desperately, but the jammed door made a lie of that hope. Had they killed Wilkens and Peterson already? He had to assume so. He had to assume he was alone here with those two monsters. He went back to the door and snapped shut the bolt on the interior lock; he could keep them out as surely as they could keep him in.

Now, what did you use to kill vampires? Stakes, crosses, garlic? Yeah, where was his crucifix when he needed it? Abandoned long ago, with any semblance of the faith of his childhood. Too bad he didn't have the ultrasound. That'd stop the buggers fast enough. Roias froze, looking at the monitors and the console. Maybe he could do something . . .

He was crouched over the console, trying frantically to remember anything he had learned in high-school tech class, when the door rattled. He caught his breath . . . but it stayed shut. He had a few moments then, a few moments to make this plan work.

He had almost figured it out, just about remembered the buttons to push to make the machinery emit an ear-piercing wail, when the window in front of him shattered. Glass showered like glittering rain and he stumbled back, arms flung up. He lowered them in time to see her climbing in through the window. He heard glass crunching beneath her feet as she landed on the booth floor but she didn't even wince. How had she gotten there? he wondered, then remembered the lighting scaffolding rising up beneath the booth window.

"Hello, Roias," she said, smiling with crimson lips. He saw the sharp daggers of her teeth and felt his guts churning in terror. "Didn't think I'd come back, did you? And after you were such a charming host."

"Listen, I . . ." His voice trailed off. What could he say to her? That it wasn't his fault? Tell her anything, he thought desperately, tell her anything you have to.

"That's right, Roias. I'm going to listen. You're going to tell me everything."

"I don't know anything."

"Who hired you?"

"I don't know," Roias insisted, wishing he could keep himself from shrinking back as she stepped towards him, driving him farther away from the console, and his fading hope of finding a weapon against her. Her eyes were bright and avid, her lips parting to let her tongue flicker out over the blood-stained mouth.

"What did he want Rozokov for?"

"Rozokov? Who's . . . oh. I don't know. I swear that I don't know."

"You like blood, don't you, Roias?" she asked casually, stepping towards him again. He felt his knees give way and he collapsed. The shards of glass on the floor cut him, even through his jeans, but he barely felt it. "As long as it's someone else's. You enjoy your work. You liked those movies. You liked torturing him, didn't you?"

"I was feeding him," he said desperately. She was standing over him but he couldn't force himself to look up at her. He stared at her blood-stained thigh instead.

"How kind of you. Of course, now I like blood too. Especially when it's someone else's. Will you feed *me*, Roias?" Her voice was a seductive purr, half-threat, half-promise. He heard his last chance there. One boss was pretty much the same as the next, he thought. He could

serve either one equally well. He closed his eyes and made
his choice.

"Yes," he whispered. "I'll feed you. I'll do whatever you
want." He leaned forward, kissed the bloody curve of her
inner thigh. He forced himself not to think about whose
blood he was licking from her cool skin. She let him continue his worship of her until he reached up to tug aside the
thin stretch of silky cloth that barred his way.

Then her hands gripped his hair, dragging him to his
feet. "You'd like it, wouldn't you?" she said savagely, eyes
glittering red. "You could be my Renfield, find me blood,
when I got tired of yours. I might even let you watch. Well,
not a chance, you goddamn bastard, not a chance."

She swung him around by his hair, and he was still crying out from that pain when she thrust him forward onto
the jagged spikes of the shattered window. The new pain
was deeper, sharper than he imagined possible, and he
couldn't find the breath to scream as darkness sliced up
through his eyes.

Chapter 14

Ardeth came down the scaffold effortlessly, not looking
back up at Roias's body impaled on the glass. She hadn't
bothered to taste his blood; the thought of it nauseated her.

She felt a brief flicker of regret that her anger at him had
kept her from questioning him further—but killing him
had been so much more satisfying than suffering his revolting attentions.

Rozokov was waiting for her, standing by the bed. She
paused, looked at the bodies tumbled around the room.
"Are there more?" she asked, trusting his more experienced

senses. He shook his head. He was very still but she could feel him trembling on the edge of madness, the killing fury only partially sated by the deaths of their tormentors.

There was a wildness in her too, filling her up with a strength and certainty that was dizzily intoxicating. She stripped off her blood-soaked shirt and tossed it on the floor. There was still blood on her skin, in her hair, but she did not care.

Rozokov's eyes were bright, brighter than her memories of the sun, as she stepped up onto the dais with him. He reached out to run his hands from her shoulder to her throat, then up to cup her face. She turned to kiss his fingers, dark with blood.

On the bed, beside the blonde's body, they shared what love they could, the ecstatic mating of wolves after the kill.

Ardeth opened her eyes and saw herself reflected in a dead woman's gaze. For one terrifying moment she was hypnotized by the glazed, black marble eyes, the dull white skin. That's me, she thought, that's what *I* am. She had a sudden vision of herself through the dead whore's eyes, two lifeless sets of corneas reflecting death back and forth.

Then there was a faint movement behind her and she became aware of the warm pressure against her back, the weight of the arm draped loosely about her waist. She turned to meet another gaze, this one grey and undeniably alive. Wonderingly, she put her hand on the pale, scarred chest and felt the double-beat of his heart. He echoed the motion, pressing until she felt the beat of her own heart against his hand as strongly as she felt his.

"Ardeth . . ." he said softly, voice calm and reassuring though his eyes were wary. Ardeth remembered again, recalled all that had happened, all that she now was. She smiled and stretched in his arms, shifting on the red silk of the bed. His hand moved, slid into a caress, then fell away reluctantly. "We must leave, before others come."

Ardeth glanced over at the dead body on the end of the bed, then around the room. Her eyes rested on Roias's corpse hanging over the jagged parapet of the window. "Let them."

Rozokov took her face in his hands and forced her to meet his serious gaze. "Young one, we are not invulnerable. Especially not now. We must be very clever and careful. Did you discover anything of value from Roias?"

"No. I just killed him." It had been a mistake and she knew it, but the knowledge was not enough to keep the petulant defiance from her voice.

"Who do you think will find this?" Rozokov asked after a long moment whose silence was more eloquently disapproving than any words could have been.

Ardeth frowned, trying to think beyond the triumphant carnage in the room. "Their bosses, or accomplices."

"Will they report this to the authorities?"

"Not likely. They'd have to explain it then."

"Good. What about the movies?"

"They've probably sold them by now. But no one will believe them anyway . . ." She pulled from his restraining grasp and bounded off the bed, revelling in the strength and confidence she felt. "What are you worrying about? They're all dead." She spun a little to encompass the tumbled bodies about the room in the gesture of her outflung arms.

"Ardeth," Rozokov began patiently. "There are many lessons you must learn of this life. But the most important one is caution. The consequences of even one mistake can be fatal."

She sighed. He was right, of course, but caution seemed alien to her now, an unwanted remnant of a life she'd left buried in a shallow grave in the woods. "There are probably master tapes around here somewhere," she admitted. "We should erase them."

"Then we must find them. But first," Rozokov smiled with sudden amusement, "find yourself some clothes. You are far too distracting as you are."

She laughed and turned to look at him. He was sitting in the tangled sheets, pulling on his pants. The gesture was so commonplace, so human, it made her heart ache with sudden, undefined longing. "I didn't think vampires were attracted to other vampires," she said flippantly, to counter the intensity of the emotion.

"We disproved that theory a while ago. I must confess, I had not expected *that*." She could hear the thread of uneasiness under the humour in his tone. Until a moment ago, Ardeth had not thought to wonder at her hunger for him; she had desired him when she was alive, it seemed only natural to want him after . . . Though the pleasure had been different, lacking either the penetration of human or vampire lovers, it had been oddly satisfying. "Now, go find some clean clothes. Come back here after and we will find these master tapes."

She hovered at the edge of the dais for a moment, unwilling to leave him, then stepped down over the actress's sprawled body and headed for the door.

In the dressing cubicle provided for the actresses, she found a pair of black pants, only slightly loose on her thin form, and a pair of reasonably comfortable short black boots. She surveyed the two tops draped over the chair for a moment, then abandoned them in amusement. There was no way either the black bustier or leopard-patterned bra top would fit her much smaller figure. She settled for a white shirt she found in one of the other rooms. The room had been Peterson's, she decided, staring down at the jumble of heavy-metal tapes on the floor. A skeletal face surrounded by tangled green hair leered up at her from the pile. He had a T-shirt like that, she remembered, and the blinding, white-hot fury surged through her again. She kicked the pile of tapes savagely, sending boxes skittering across the floor. The action stilled the rage somewhat and she stood in the centre of the room, breathing deeply, until it subsided.

It was time to get back to Rozokov, to find and destroy the obscene record of his existence. Not that anyone would really believe it, she thought, they'd think it was all just another special effect. But he was right . . . it was too dangerous to leave for either the rest of the gang or the police to find. They would have to destroy the film in the cameras in the studio as well, in case any of the slaughter there had been recorded.

Rozokov was in the studio. He too had found new clothes, the expensive white shirt contrasting with a battered pair of black jeans. He had also thought of the cameras—they lay shattered on the cement floor, nested in a tangle of exposed film. "Will this suffice to destroy these movies—or should we burn them?" he inquired and Ardeth smiled.

"I think that'll do it. Now we have to find the masters, and any copies. I'd rather just burn the whole place down." The vision of the asylum flaming against the night sky made her smile again, though not as pleasantly.

"As much as that would please me as well, it would attract too much attention, I'm afraid. So—what do these masters look like?"

She found them in the room next to Roias's eyrie. Four shelves of videotapes lined one wall, over banks of dubbing and copying equipment. "Sorority Sluts," "Confessions of a Schoolgirl," "Robowhore." There were three identified only as "V1," "V2," and "V3." Ardeth pulled down "V1" and slid it into one of the machines, turning on the television monitor.

On fast forward, the torture of the dark-haired victim looked almost comical, but the Keystone Kops movement did not completely disguise the horror, and Ardeth felt the rage pressing, black and satisfying, against the back of her eyes.

As in the film she had been forced to watch, Rozokov came out only at the end. She let the machine switch back to normal play and stared at the skeletal features and hot, burning eyes. Her first vision of him came back to her and she felt the distant frisson of remembered fear. Rozokov leaned over and hit the stop button. "Enough," he said, in a low, unsteady voice. "Destroy them."

Ardeth set the machine to rewind and stared at the blurry images on the screen. They could erase each one, but that would take time. There must be an easier way. Her eyes moved around the room and settled on another machine, which was marked "Videotape Eraser." She went over to examine it and noted a warning to keep it away from the videotape stock to be preserved.

She returned to the VCR, removed the rewound cassette and tried running the tape across the top of the machine. She inserted it back into the VCR, and the tape offered up blank static, broken by the occasional fuzzy image and garbled sound. She smiled narrowly at her reflection in the screen. "That should do it," she announced and ran each of the "V" tapes over the machine. After a moment, she began to pull down the rest of the tapes as well.

"Are you planning to destroy them all?" Rozokov asked, watching her curiously.

"We might as well. Otherwise the bastards will just make more money from them." When she finished, some memory of caution made her test each of the vampire tapes. They were all blank. "We should check the control room, just in case."

With their combined strength, the lock on the door to Roias's last, ineffectual refuge shattered and Ardeth entered the booth. Glass crunching beneath her feet, she prowled around, checking machines and cabinets for more videotapes. Satisfied that there was no record of Rozokov's existence there, she turned to leave, then noticed a black leather jacket hanging over the back of a chair. She spared one glance at the body draped as lifelessly over the window frame then, smiling, shrugged on the jacket.

Ardeth was preparing to ease back out into the hall when she heard voices. She moved into the doorway until she could see Rozokov, standing in her line of vision, staring down the hallway. "I asked," a voice sounded from beyond her range of sight, "who the hell are you? Where's Roias?"

"Roias was called away unexpectedly. I am in charge now."

"Yeah? All right then, I've come to collect my fee." Ardeth recognized the voice, remembering it lying smoothly to a desperate, strung-out young woman.

"Your fee?"

"Yeah. For the girls. You keeping both of them, or what?"

"I see. What fee did you and Roias agree upon?"

"Ten thousand dollars for the two of them. That's if you keep them. Otherwise it's one thousand dollars each for the movie—and I want them back."

"Ah, then you are their procurer. I understand." Rozokov's voice was soft and dangerous. "Tell me, do you know what Roias does with the ones he keeps?"

"Uses them in those snuff movies of his, I guess. Look, I don't give a flying fuck what he does with them. I got places to be. So give me the money or give me the girls," Greg snapped angrily, but beneath the threatening tone Ardeth could hear a whisper of uneasiness.

"I regret to say there's been an accident. The women are dead."

"Then I want my money." Rozokov took a step forward, disappearing from Ardeth's view. She tensed, shifting closer to the hallway.

"They didn't deserve to die. However, *you* do." There was a scuffling noise, then Greg's incoherent shout. The blast of a gunshot launched Ardeth into the hallway, the roaring fury in her mind blotting out the dying echoes of the shot.

Rozokov stood over Greg, staring down at the body, with its head twisted at an impossible angle. The revolver was still clutched in one dead hand. Ardeth slid to a stop and Rozokov looked up. "I am fine," he assured her, before the question left her lips. There was a hole in the shoulder of his shirt, surrounded by a faint stain of red. "It will heal in a few moments." The red tide in her mind receding, Ardeth considered Greg's twisted form for a moment.

"Well," she said at last, "this does solve one problem."

"Oh?"

"He must have a car. I'm afraid I ruined all the ones that were already here." His glance was curious. "I didn't want them to get away," she explained awkwardly, preferring the rational explanation to the reality of the fury that had blinded her to any kind of logical thought.

"A car . . . you know how to drive one then?"

"It's been a while, but I'm sure I can get us back to the

city. Once I figure out where we are, that is." She crouched down to search Greg's pockets, retrieving his car keys and wallet. A quick thumb through the eelskin case revealed almost one thousand dollars in cash. Ardeth paused for a moment, the ghost of a long-dead morality tugging at her, until the absurdity of her reservations struck her. With a faint smile, she tucked the money into the front pocket of her jeans. She also took his watch, replacing the broken Hong Kong knock-off on her wrist with his heavy Rolex. She glanced around at the dim hallway, and felt a pressure behind her eyes, as if they were glowing. "Let's get out of this damned place."

Chapter 15

Greg's car was parked in the main driveway, one last gesture of defiance to Roias. "It looks rather like something from a tale by Wells or Verne," Rozokov commented and Ardeth remembered that the only cars he could have seen would have been the earliest prototypes.

"Well, they aren't all quite like this," she said, surveying the silver-grey BMW. She had thought that Greg would have gone for something small, European and expensive; a Porsche or Ferrari. Then she remembered the two women lying dead in the studio and realized that a pimp needed passenger room even more than image.

Settled into the plush grey upholstery, she ran her fingers hesitantly over the wheel. It had been at least five years since she'd driven a car, back at her parents' home in Ottawa. Thank God the BMW was automatic; she wouldn't have had the first idea what to do in a standard. But the old reflexes were still there, she discovered, and felt a surge of pleasure as she swung the car out onto the circular drive.

She turned on the headlights to negotiate the long, tree-roofed laneway. This could not have been the road Roias and Wilkens had driven on the endless trip to the asylum; it was too smooth. Her suspicion was confirmed when she reached the end of the drive. Looming before her were iron gates, patched with rust, held closed by a chain and padlock. They were flanked with high stone walls.

Ardeth cursed, and slammed the BMW into reverse, twisting to check the road in the tail-lights as she backed up. "You are going back?" Rozokov asked, as he turned in the seat to follow her gaze.

"Actually, I was thinking of going through," she replied, turning to him and catching the edge of her own manic grin in the rear-view mirror. She didn't give him time to protest, but hit the accelerator and aimed the car at the centre of the gates, adrenaline surging up through her. It washed away the voice that whispered warnings in her head, trying to remind her that this kind of thing only worked in the movies.

The car hit the gates at close to sixty miles per hour and, while the force wasn't enough to snap the gleaming chain, it was more than sufficient to break the rusted hinges. For a moment, Ardeth's head was full of the sound of grinding metal, and the sight of black bars as they tumbled over the car. Then the BMW was free and she spun the wheel frantically to avoid the ditch.

In a spray of gravel and dirt, she brought the car to a shuddering halt, stretched diagonally across the road. She took a deep breath and looked at her hands on the wheel. They were steady. Her heart was pounding, a quick tattoo that echoed up through her, but she realized with quickly fading surprise that it was with excitement, not fear. She had not been afraid. She let herself savour that realization for a moment, then looked over at Rozokov.

He was sitting very still in the seat, one hand resting on the door handle. White was fading from his knuckles. "Well," he said, after a moment. "That *was* quicker than going back." He glanced at the gate hanging like a broken wing over the driveway. "We should put that back as best we can."

"All right." Outside the car, Ardeth glanced at the front bumper and decided the dents were not too noticeable.

"I gather this was not something for which these vehicles were precisely designed," Rozokov observed carefully.

"Probably not," she conceded and felt a trace of amusement at his casual manner of confirming that his white knuckles had been justified.

After a few moments of manoeuvring, they managed to re-align the gate with the stone walls and prop it into a position that approximated its unwounded state. Ardeth stepped back and squinted at it critically for a moment. She guessed that traffic on this road was minimal, and limited mostly to locals. They probably no longer even looked at the gate; it was merely part of the scenery. Roias's confederates had been trained to use only the back laneway. It might be weeks before anyone noticed the damage.

Ardeth glanced back at the car. She supposed that they could get in and just start driving, trusting that she'd recognize some town or sign that would orient them back to the city. She looked up at the sky, regretting she'd never bothered to take any courses in astronomy. She wasn't even sure where the Big Dipper was any more.

Rozokov followed her gaze and traced the discontent on her face back to its source. "That way is north," he said, pointing back towards the asylum. "Is that of any use in solving your dilemma?"

"Well, I still don't know where we are, but if we go south, sooner or later we'll hit something I recognize. Even if it's just the lake."

"You still wish to go back to the city, then."

"You don't?" she questioned in return. "Don't you want to find out who knows about you, and how much?" She paused, stepping closer to him. "Don't you want to make them pay?" He shook his head slightly, then took one last look at the sky.

"Drive us south then, child," he said, smiling, but even

in the darkness she could see that it was fraying at the edges, "but try to avoid any more locked gates."

Ardeth willed herself to see the smile and not the sadness, then led the way back to the car.

They drove in silence through the dark back roads. She started left, for no more reason than that the car was pointed that way, then turned south on the first paved road she found. The BMW's headlights marked the only movement on the landscape, and nearly the only light. The occasional porch light glowed faintly across the fields, and once they passed a house with all the windows bright, looking like an illuminated dollhouse set in the dark playground of the night.

Gradually the signs of road names, distances and populations yielded one she could use: Toronto, 100 kilometres. She turned right onto a four-lane road, then caught an exit-ramp and gunned the BMW out onto a near-deserted highway. In the west, the sky glowed like a false dawn. "What is that?" Rozokov asked.

"The city." When the silence fell again, she could sense the great gap of years he faced, from a city lit with gaslight to a nuclear-powered sprawl whose lights were visible from space, banishing the purity of night.

Shaken, she reached for the radio dial, filling the emptiness with a burst of static, then the clamour of a heavy-metal song. "I hope that is not what this era calls music," Rozokov said, in only partially feigned horror, and she laughed.

"Some people do. Usually long-haired, pimply-faced adolescent boys." The description brought back memories of Peterson and his gloating deathshead T-shirts. Ardeth spun the dial quickly, sliding through chatter, bass riffs and commercial jingles until she reached the relative comfort of Mozart. "Is that better?"

He nodded, but turned his head to stare out the window, and the silence, dispelled, now seemed twice as heavy. The music ended somewhere in the suburbs and the announcer's voice came on with the perfunctory 2 A.M. newscast. Ardeth let the latest from Eastern Europe, the Middle East and the House of Commons wash over her. A lifetime had passed for her it seemed, but only a few days in the world. Very little had changed.

"Police continue to ask the public for help in locating Ardeth Alexander, reported missing Tuesday night. Anyone who may have seen the twenty-eight-year-old graduate student since last Thursday should contact police at 555-3636."

Not much of a eulogy. "A twenty-eight-year-old graduate student." She wondered who had reported her missing. Carla? Sara? It hardly mattered. They must have no idea what had happened to her; they weren't even sure when she had disappeared. She felt a distant twinge of bitterness at the memory of her grand and hopeless schemes of rescue. To think she had clung to those hopes of salvation, when her saviours did not even know she needed saving.

Rozokov had returned his attention from the dark passage of trucks outside the window. "Ardeth," he began and she shrugged, as if twitching off an unwanted hand on her shoulder.

"It doesn't matter. I'm not missing."

"You can't go home. You know that. Wherever you take us tonight, it cannot be home."

"I don't *want* to go home," she said, hands tight on the wheel. "Let them keep looking for Ardeth Alexander. Ardeth Alexander is dead."

"Long live Ardeth Alexander," Rozokov said with a smile, but under the humour she could sense the edges of mockery. Or warning.

"Long live Ardeth Alexander," she echoed and then saw the turnoff to the Don Valley Parkway. The BMW slid across three empty lanes of highway and down the throat of the off-ramp.

She found a place to stop just north of Bloor Street; the burnt shell of an abandoned brick factory shaded by trees and shielded from the road by a decade's worth of unchecked undergrowth. She pulled up behind the rusting remains of some ancient machinery and shut off the engine. Over the tick of its cooling, she thought she could hear the faint hiss of the sparse traffic on the highway, and the fainter whisper of the river as it swirled its slow, muddy way to the lake.

The car would be found sooner or later and traced to Greg. Could he ever be connected to them? She looked at her hands, pale fingers resting on the leather steering wheel. "Fingerprints ... we have to get rid of my fingerprints."

Rozokov nodded and hunted in his pockets, looking, she realized suddenly, for the cloth handkerchief that men always carried in his past. She was not surprised when he discovered only a tattered tissue secreted in the depths of his stolen clothing. Ardeth shrugged off her jacket, took one sleeve of her shirt and used teeth and nails to rip it off at the elbow. Carefully she rubbed the cloth across the steering wheel, turn signals, light switches and the clasp of her seat belt. When she left the car, she treated the door handles, locks and the edges of the window the same way.

She pulled the jacket back on and looked at Rozokov standing on the other side of the car. "Now what do we do?"

"We must find some place to spend the day; it will be dawn in a few hours."

"What kind of place?"

"An abandoned building, a tunnel. At the very least, some place deep in the trees, where no one goes."

"I don't know what's in this ravine." She frowned, trying to remember what she had seen from the subway as it ran beneath the bridge to the south. "There are abandoned houses and stores farther down. If we start walking now, it won't take long."

"Go then." She looked at him sharply. "We cannot stay together."

"Why not?"

"It would not be safe for you. You are right. This was not Roias's scheme. Someone else has planned all this. They know of my existence but you ... no doubt they believe you died a true death in the asylum. They will not be looking for you."

"If they're still after you, then that's all the more reason we should stay together. You don't know this city any more. You don't even know this century." The words came out more cruelly than she had intended, sharpened by fear.

"I shall manage," he replied drily. "I have some years' experience with these things, if you recall."

"What about me?"

"You shall manage as well. Only be careful. Do not go home; do not go any place where people might recognize you. No one must know that you still live."

"What if I won't go? You can't stop me from following you," she pointed out.

"But I can. You are very young, and you are my blood. I can force you—and I will, if I must." His voice was hard and the grey eyes cold and remote. "We are solitary creatures. It does not do for us to forget that."

"So now that you've got what you wanted, you remember that again," Ardeth said bitterly.

"It was your choice. And I made you no promises."

"No." There was a moment of silence, as if he waited for her to say more. She clenched her teeth to keep the words inside her. At last, he turned away and began to walk towards the trees.

"Damn him," she whispered. "Damn, damn, damn." He had known all along he would leave her. You'll see, you'll see it's not as easy as you think. You'll wish I was there. She wondered if he could hear the venomous thoughts but the retreating figure did not stop. You'll be sorry you left me.

She suddenly remembered the stolen money in her pocket. For a moment, she contemplated keeping it all, taking a bitter pleasure in imagining Rozokov fumbling through the labyrinth of the modern world with no resources at all. Then she remembered the cold, unforgiving dungeon, the colder, unforgiving future she'd seen there, and the pleasure melted into pain.

"Wait," she called softly and ran towards him. He paused and turned, waiting as she caught up to him. "Roias's money—take it." She pushed the bills into his hands and he smoothed them out, staring curiously at the coloured bills with the face of a queen that he did not recognize.

"What about you?" For a moment, she thought she heard regret in his voice.

"I'll get more." Rozokov shook his head and carefully counted out five hundred dollars. It was the final severing and she protested, but at last took the bills and stuffed them back into her jacket pocket. He stepped away, passing into the dark edges of the wood. "Dimitri . . ." Her voice slid up from the whisper to a cry and caught in her throat.

Nothing is forever, something whispered in her mind, so softly she was not sure whether it was her thought or his. Not even for vampires.

"This will not be forever," she said to the darkness. "You'll see."

Shark Walk

She's hungry all the time
—she do the Shark Walk.

From the Diary of Ambrose Delaney Dale

15 May 1898

Some progress has been made but it is slow work. One would not suppose there were so many Europeans in the city. Still, I have narrowed the field down somewhat—some several hundred men have been excluded. Collins's men have found nothing, despite all the nights they have spied in the taverns and the streets. No one has seen the man I seek, or else they do not remember it.

My own researchers have yielded only tantalizingly obscure clues. There is little reliable literature on the subject and, of course, no scientific studies. What occult works there are have nothing of substance to add to my search. But in more ancient texts I have found some threads worth pursuing. There are tales of undying alchemists, such as the notorious St. Germain, and so I have begun a search of the shipping manifests of our train and ship lines to seek those ingredients that would have to be imported for such work. Certain events in Paris twenty years ago implicate a Russian nobleman and my agents on the Continent are seeking the truth with the authorities there.

Henry, of course, scorns all this as a foolish waste of our resources. He continues to press me about the expansion of our mills and shipping lines, as well as urging me to buy out one of the faltering financial institutions in the city. He supposes, of course, that I do not know about the other schemes he has—and the "machinery" he ships to both the Americans and the Spanish for use in their war. We pretend we do not know each other's business—and it is better that way.

Carstairs has just come with a letter from my Berlin agent. It contained a list of names of those linked to magic and murder there, as well as what historical attributions of vampirism he has been able to uncover. Forty names—but that is better than four hundred. I will send for Collins and have his men begin the search for any in Toronto who bear these names.

Carstairs is back—the doctor waits in the drawing room. When he comments on my erratic heartbeat, as he always does, I will have to try not to laugh. Whose heart, after all, would not beat faster when its desire is in sight?

Chapter 16

She went home. She didn't know what else to do.

The apartment was dark and quiet, just as she had left it a week earlier. Ardeth turned on the hall light and looked around. Everything looked familiar, her books, her furniture, the shoes scattering the hallway. But nothing felt like hers any more. It was as if she stood in one of the showpiece homes used to display furniture and an interior decorator's idea of personal style. All the pieces were in place but no one lived there.

She drifted into the bedroom, and looked down for a moment at her unmade bed. Should she try to sleep here, when the dawn came? Don't go home, Rozokov had said. She felt a rush of anger filling her mouth with a sudden bitter taste. You left me, she thought accusingly at the darkness around her. *You left me.* He had reasons, she knew, and all of them were correct. But the anger felt better than the lost emptiness and she clung to it, letting it curl comfortably around her heart.

She could not stay here. Rozokov had been right about one thing—whoever was behind all this must never know she had not died at the asylum. She had to leave every trace of her former self behind. That would not be hard. "We are who we were," Rozokov had said. *But I don't have to be,* she thought defiantly. *I can be anything I want—and I don't want to be* her *any more.*

She looked around the dimly lit room and caught the edge of her reflection in the mirror. That story was a myth as well, it seemed. She stepped forward to stare at her reflected image. Her hair was tangled and dirty, and there was a dark blood stain on the collar of her stolen shirt. Her face looked thinner, cheekbones in high relief where they had once been merely the underpinning of her soft profile. Her eyes were still hazel but the russet in the mix had darkened. They would refract red, as Rozokov's had.

But she still looked like Ardeth. She would have to cut her hair, dye it too. She touched the lank tangles. She needed a shower badly. Her new vampiric body did not seem to sweat but her old human one had gone days without a proper bath. She glanced at the bedside clock radio. It was 4:30 in the morning— would anyone in the building be awake, or notice the sound coming from her supposedly deserted apartment? She weighed that thought for a moment then decided the risk was slight.

She went to the bathroom, quietly closing the door. She stripped beneath the bright overhead light and then stared for a moment at her body. The bruises had all faded, healing along with her rejuvenation, but she still looked pale and worn. Even the blood she had taken during the slaughter at the asylum had not been enough to counteract the days of hardship.

She turned away from the stark image in the mirror and bent over the tub. She turned on the taps and hesitantly put one finger underneath the flow. Another myth gone; the water was no more than a little too hot.

She slid into the spray with a sigh, luxuriating in the warm water on her skin. She scrubbed away the sweat, dirt and fear, washed the oil and despair out of her tangled hair. She spent far longer than she should have under the comforting spray but carefully cleaned the bathroom after, wiping down the shower and walls, then refolding the towel and restoring it to the closet. Unless someone were to inspect the room in the next hour, no one would be able to tell she had been there.

Ardeth picked up her abandoned clothes, and padded to the bedroom, not bothering to turn on the light. Clean now, she had no desire to don her stolen clothing again. Still, how much did she dare to take from her own closet? How much did she even want to? The clothes there were the skin of the old Ardeth, and she had shed that with the dirt that had covered her undead body. In the end she settled for clean underwear, a Black Sun T-shirt donated to the bottom of her drawer by Sara, and her battered black running shoes. She slithered back into her stolen jeans and kept Roias's leather jacket. The other dirty clothes she left by the door, to dump in a garbage can when she left the building.

She paused, wondering if there was anything else she could take. This would be her last time here, after all. Most of the things she had valued a week ago meant nothing to her now. But there were one or two items she could use in the creation of her new self. She hunted through the closet and drawers (she had almost stopped thinking of them as hers) and found a pair of wrap-around black sunglasses (a joke gift from a friend, she did not recall who) and a pair of earrings. The earrings had been a present from Sara, who had dared her to wear them. She never had. They had been too big, too unusual for the person she had been then. Now, the almost gothic look of the faces and spread wings and the blood-red stones dangling from the metal angels had an ironic appeal. She tucked them into the pocket of her leather jacket.

The last thing she took was the cache of money her former self had kept stored in one of her books. There were nearly three hundred dollars there, and Ardeth stuffed the bills into her back pocket. Even vampires needed money, she supposed, and she was not sure how she would get more. Could she work? The thought of being a vampiric night-shift worker made her smile, even as she rejected the idea. The old Ardeth would have dutifully gone out and got a job in an all-night cafe. Not the new one. The old Ardeth had been afraid of living. The new Ardeth, being dead, was going to make the most of the rebirth she had been offered.

She turned out the lights and slipped out the apartment door, locking it behind her. On the street, she started walking south, towards the bright glow of the downtown core. There, the city lived at night. And so would she.

At the edge of Chinatown, she found an abandoned house. Ardeth hovered on the sidewalk for a moment, studying the darkened houses surrounding it, then ducked between the overgrown hedges and approached the house. All the windows were boarded up and she could make out the dark tracings of cryptic graffiti on some. She moved down the narrow pathway between the house and its neighbour, stepping over broken roof tiles and scattered garbage. Maple trees hung over the overgrown yard and lilac bushes clustered protectively against the back of the house.

She pushed her way into the bushes and found the window screened and boarded like the rest. Did you think they'd conveniently leave it open for you? she asked herself sarcastically. She ran her fingers over the wood and found the cool metal head of a nail. The window frame must be wood, she thought, and found a narrow gap between the brick surrounding the window and the boards. She slid her fingers into the space and pulled, leaning backwards into the bushes until she felt the board yield beneath her fingers.

"Shit," Ardeth breathed, as one nail broke to the quick. She sucked the sore finger for a moment, then pulled off another board. Finally she had a hole big enough to wriggle through. She took the shattered boards with her and propped them against the window from the inside, some small concealment for the hole she had made.

After inspecting her camouflage, she straightened up and looked around. She had expected to find the house empty but there was a couch and chair in the room, dust-covered and forlorn. In the next room she found a table and four chairs, sitting in wait as if expecting the owners to return at any moment. One was on an angle, as if someone had just pushed it away from the table to rise. For a moment, Ardeth froze, afraid that someone shared her refuge. She listened intently; stretched out tentatively with the new senses she could barely feel. But there was nothing, only stillness and dust.

She shivered and moved into the next room. I could go upstairs, she thought. There might be beds, waiting like in some cautionary fairy tale. But the thought of sinking into stale, dusty sheets disgusted her and the upper storeys seemed somehow dangerous, exposed.

The basement, however, felt safe. It was unfinished and low-ceilinged, but the cold dampness didn't seem to penetrate her new skin and the weight of the house over her was oddly comforting. No one will come here, she told herself. Even if someone else, kids or squatters, breaks into the house, no one will come here.

She found a crawlspace behind the dead furnace and curled up in it, Roias's jacket pillowing her head. She wondered where Rozokov was, where he had found shelter. "You'll see," she whispered defiantly to the darkness and hugged herself, her arms tight across her chest, to hold in the sudden emptiness that filled her.

Chapter 17

The iron gates folded away before him, as if the name he spoke into the monitor was a secret password. Martin Rooke eased the Mercedes onto the road leading down into the valley of the Dale estate. His hands were steady; the shaking had stopped somewhere on the highway.

The car slid beneath the arches of the overhanging trees then out into the sunlight. These must have been lawns once, he thought, wincing as a bramble scraped against the side of the car. And gardens. He had a sudden vision of figures in white, playing croquet and sipping tea, overlaid like ghosts on the heavy growth of weeds and brush.

He swore softly. Ghosts . . . Christ! This was not the way to deal with this job. From the start, he'd looked at the whole mad scheme as just another business problem. It didn't matter whether or not he believed any of it—Althea Dale believed it. And the first thing he'd learned when he became head of Special Projects for Havendale was what Althea Dale believed, *was*.

Special Projects was the top, short of the President, or the Board of Directors. It was about as high in the corporate structure as you could go. When it came to status, nobody seemed to mind that no one knew precisely what Special Projects did.

No one in the mainstream company, that was.

For Havendale's shadowy underground corporate ladder, Special Projects was also the top. Whoever ran Special Projects got his orders from Althea Dale herself. Whoever ran Special Projects gave the orders that moved the drugs, the guns and the currency that were Havendale's *other* business. And for the last year, the man who ran Special Projects had been Martin Rooke.

Of course, after today, it might not be.

He stopped the car in the circular driveway at the base of the flagstone steps. From here, only the red tile roof of the Dale ancestral home was visible, lying like a bloody-scaled snake along the top of the low hill. Climbing the stairs, Rooke realized again how quiet it was here. The woods enveloping the estate swallowed all street noise, all voices, all sounds that would betray the fact that twentieth-century subdivisions surrounded the nineteenth-century mansion.

The grey fieldstone walls and the long, low length gave the house the look of an ancient stone fence, stretched across the ridge as if guarding something. But behind the house, Rooke knew, there was only an empty swimming pool and an old, unused tennis court. Or maybe what it was guarding was inside, he thought. The Dales had their share of secrets.

The elderly maid answered the door on the second clang of the heavy iron knocker. "Miss Dale is waiting in the office," she said slowly and turned to lead him down the dark hallway. He bit back the urge to say he knew the way; he knew she wouldn't pay any attention. He was never unescorted in the Dale house.

The interior of the house echoed the outside—the modern world had barely penetrated it. The lights in the hallway were electric, but their glow was filtered through dim, yellow shades and sucked away by the dark panelling and wallpaper. Portraits lined the walls. Five generations of Dale scions watched him pass, from old mutton-chopped Archer to soberly suited Arthur. Rooke suppressed a grin as he passed that last one. There was no hint in it that old Arthur was rumoured to have ended his days deep in Howard Hughes territory, a paranoid recluse with five-inch nails, poor personal hygiene and a reputation for business cunning that meant no one gave his eccentricities a second thought. There were other rumours too; whispers about women driven to the estate in dark limousines and well-paid not to talk about it, older stories of accidents that happened to people who stood in the way of what Arthur Dale wanted.

There was no portrait of Althea Dale yet. She'd better get one done soon, Rooke thought wryly, before she gets even crazier than daddy was. She might be crazy like a fox when it came to business—the bottom line in the four years since Arthur's death could attest to that—but this latest craziness could wipe it all away, Havendale, family name and all.

The thought sobered him, bringing back memories of the asylum and the edgy tension that always accompanied his meetings with Althea Dale. And that had been when things were going well . . .

The maid paused in front of the office door, knocking with timid knuckles at the dark wood. A muffled voice called out, then the maid opened the door and ushered him in. "Mr. Rooke," her voice whispered, then he heard the door close behind him.

Althea Dale was sitting at the massive old desk that looked like it must have first belonged to Archer. Rooke was once again struck by the contrast of the aging glory of the room, with its book-lined walls and ancient wooden filing cabinets, and the smooth blankness of that desk, marred only by the sleek grey metal of the computer terminal on one side and the compact black telephone on the other.

He knew his employer through those two things; through her voice on the telephone and her words glowing on the computer screen. He had only met her in person twice before. Once before his appointment to head Special Projects and once when she called him in to explain the true nature of her current obsession.

Like her father, Althea Dale never left the house.

"Rooke." Her voice was quiet, controlled.

"Miss Dale." He sat down in the chair opposite her and waited.

"How did it happen?"

"We're not sure. The lock to the cell wasn't broken so someone must have used a key. It might have been one of Roias's men, Peterson. We found his body in the cellar. The others, including the actors and the cameramen, were all killed near the studio. The films were all exposed or erased." He kept his voice calm, letting out no hint of what it had really been like to walk into the studio strewn with three-day-old corpses.

"How did he get away?"

"I'm not sure. The vehicles in the garage were all damaged. But the woods around there are pretty thick. It . . ." He caught himself suddenly, remembering her insistence on using the male pronoun, "he could still be there."

"He won't stay there. He'll come to the city eventually." She fell silent for a moment. Rooke watched her carefully. She'd grown thinner in the last year, face turning bony and gaunt, making her look much older than forty-two. The long, greying brown hair was caught back in the customary braid and she was wearing a white shirt and dark pants. He wondered if they were the same ones she'd been wearing the last two times he'd seen her.

She rose abruptly and paced across the room, hands over her elbows, holding her arms crossed against her body. Rooke felt the back of his neck prickle as she passed behind him, as if her brittle tension was communicable. He found himself unconsciously waiting for her to light a cigarette. As far as he knew, she did not smoke, but her angular edginess always seemed to suggest that she *should*, that her long, thin fingers were crooking to hold something besides empty air.

"What did you do with the bodies?" she asked at last.

"Called the cleaners in to bury them out in the woods, like Roias did with the women."

"Can they be trusted?"

"That's what we pay them for." He caught the swift, sideways glance of her sunken eyes. "We might have to eliminate them later."

"Why not now?"

"It's too soon after the others, those students."

"That can't be traced to us."

"Probably not. But if the police get too many unsolved murders they get nervous and suspicious. Give it a month or two." She frowned for a moment, then waved away the problem with a brief flicker of her hand. That meant kill them, Rooke decided. That was the one method of problem elimination that Althea seemed to consider foolproof.

"You will get him back." It wasn't a question.

"Of course. But he could have gone anywhere."

"No, he couldn't. He hasn't got a passport. He hasn't got any money. He doesn't know how to drive. He'll come back to the city, because it'll be the only place he'll find anything he recognizes."

"Toronto's a big place," he began carefully, watching her stalk towards the window to his left. She paused for a moment, staring out at something he could not see.

"He has to kill to survive. He will leave a trail, if you look for it in the right place." Rooke heard the impatience in her voice.

"I'll contact our people in the police department. If any unusual deaths or reports turn up, they'll let us know. And a reward promised to the right organizations should get their soldiers looking for him for us. I can take a print off that film of Roias's." She nodded, eyes still trained outward.

"Get the rest of the copies of those films back if you can find them."

"Buy them back?"

"Whatever." She shrugged the question away. "I want the laboratory moved here."

"Here?" Rooke couldn't help his astonished echo.

"Here." She looked over at him. "You made a mistake with Roias. I made a mistake letting you. When you get him back, I want him where I can see him. And maybe that will keep more of the scientists from hanging themselves." He should have known that was coming, Rooke acknowledged. If his mistakes were going to be itemized, Goodman's suicide was going to be right up there. Never mind that he'd used Havendale's resources and international crime connections to buy, bribe and blackmail five of the leading researchers in North America without causing any serious rumours in the scientific community . . . "There's a file on the disk in the computer. It has all my requirements for modifying the left wing for the laboratory. Get the workmen started tomorrow."

When it became apparent that she wasn't going to move, he rose and stepped around her desk to retrieve the disk. As he pocketed it, he glanced up and out the window past her still figure. Beyond the empty pool and the cracking asphalt of the tennis court, he could see the faint gleam of something against the trees.

"My father's grave," Althea said suddenly, as though she could feel his gaze through her back. "I had him buried there. Outside." The word came off her tongue as though it was wrapped in barbed wire.

It seemed like a dismissal. Rooke moved towards the door. Her voice caught him. "Get him back, Rooke. And for making me bring the laboratory here, in here," she paused in distaste, "*inside*, the modifications are coming out of your salary."

Rooke swore silently. Knowing her paranoia, the changes could cost more than two hundred grand. But he just nodded and shut the door between them.

The maid was waiting to walk him to the entrance.

He didn't look at the portraits this time. They didn't have the answers he wanted, not unless one of them had miraculously changed into a picture of Althea Dale's soul. He couldn't get a grasp on that, no matter how he tried. She should have been easy to read, with her neuroses and her tension and the secrets that lurked behind every closed door and lingered like the smell of sickness in the air. He should have been able to find the buttons to push, the weaknesses he could exploit to make her controllable. Every time he thought he found a way to twist her paranoia to his advantage, something would slip and he would catch a glimpse of an amoral, brutal madness that was so far beyond any motive he could understand that he would abandon his plans.

Arthur Dale wasn't the only one that there were rumours about.

It wasn't until the safety of his car that he let himself relax. Two hundred thousand dollars was a small price to pay . . . and there were always ways that amount could be reduced. He'd gotten off remarkably lightly, all things considered.

After all, the price for failure at Havendale wasn't a golden parachute. It was a long, long fall with no parachute at all.

Chapter 18

The sleep was heavy and dreamless. She woke in the same position in which she had gone to sleep, curled fetally behind the furnace.

Ardeth lay still for a moment, tasting her new awareness. She sensed the emptiness of the house and, beyond its walls, the heavy heartbeat of the city. She felt, deep within her, the faint stirrings of hunger. It is strongest in the beginning, Rozokov had said. She remembered the first taste of Peterson's blood, the dizzying sweetness, and sat up, shivering suddenly, torn between anticipation and a soul-deep revulsion. But *that* would have to wait, she thought with relief. There were other things to do first.

She glanced at the stolen Rolex and realized that she had slept for two days. The long night of her rebirth must have drained her more than she had thought. The hunger stirred again, more insistently, stretching in her guts like a waking cat.

She shrugged off the dust from her hair and jacket, left the house the same way she had entered, and began to walk south towards Queen Street. The back streets were quiet, but she could see the figures passing back and forth on the street ahead of her.

Queen Street. Sara's street, she thought suddenly and remembered her old, half-recognized envy of her sister's ease here, of her sister's presence here.

But now ... now Ardeth had a power her sister had never dreamed of. Now the street could be hers. Any of its

black-clad denizens, in all their power and style and preten-
sion, could be hers.

Be sensible, her reason told her, stay away from here—
where Sara could see you. But the remembered taste of
Peterson's blood in her mouth, the remembered feel of
Roias's mouth on her thigh, told her otherwise.

It was early evening and, even though it was Monday,
the warm weather kept the street crowded with people. In
the city's often careful divisions of neighbourhoods, this
was the home of the artistic and the left-wing, where appearance became a statement of purpose and the graffiti had
a decidedly political bent. It was home to some of the city's
coolest clubs and to a number of musicians, artists and de-
signers. Or those with aspirations—or pretensions—to any
of those callings.

Ardeth recalled Sara complaining that the second-hand
clothing stores were vanishing in favour of expensive de-
signers (albeit ones to whom black never went out of fashion), the used-book stores had gone, victim of rising rents,
and the restaurants were attracting as many slumming
yuppies as the genuine avant-garde. Ardeth had restrained
herself from asking how one told the genuinely avant-garde
from those who merely had the right clothes.

She smiled at the memory as she glanced down the
street. The difference between the pose and the person,
the artistic and the artificial, held little interest for her
now. What mattered was the ever-shifting population of
the street, by nature transient, and the loud darkness of the
clubs, where people pretended, with pale faces, black-lined
eyes and a carefully cultivated boredom, to the state in
which she now found herself. Hide, Rozokov had told her.
What better place to hide could there be than in a crowd of
vampire wanna-bes?

And . . . a secret voice whispered, they're the ones who
used to look right through you in your safe, dull little life.
Will they look right through you now, now that you're their
darkest dreams?

The wail of a distant siren brought her out of her reverie.
She wasn't ready for the street yet. There were still a few

important steps left in transformation, to ensure that no one would look at her and see long hours of study in libraries in her bones.

She spent some of her cache of money. It got her two black mini-skirts, a pair of flat black shoes, a black, narrow-strapped cocktail dress from one of the remaining vintage clothing stores. A trip to the drugstore added make-up and black stockings. Finally, she bought two black T-shirts from a sidewalk vendor. The shirts had fluttered behind him on ropes, the bright colours smeared against the sky. There were shirts with surrealistic representations of England's punk stars, fetishistic images of a 1950s bondage queen, and T-shirts with bats and salamanders printed on them. She was swayed by one bearing spiderwebs and bats, with the slogan "Sex Vampires" scrawled across the poisonous yellow background. But, though it made her smile at the irony of it, she turned away and settled instead for two in black, one with a gothic cross in pale grey emblazoned on the front and the other with wax-screened red lizards slithering up the chest.

She still had to do something about her hair. Something radical that would cause any eye seeking a fair-haired graduate student to slide right over her without a second glance. She could dye it herself, she supposed, using any brand available at the drugstore, but where would she do it? A public washroom seemed risky, too likely to draw attention to herself. Could she rent a room in a cheap hotel where cash would buy the blind eyes of the clerks and no names need ever be exchanged? Of course if she botched it, she might end up making herself more noticeable instead of less. She wanted to blend in on the street where flamboyance was the rule. A bad dye job might not be the best way to do that.

She still had money—why not do this right? Ardeth thought suddenly. The salons on Queen Street were open at night. Decided, she headed down the street and entered the first salon she passed. Luckily, there was someone free to do her hair right then. When the woman at the desk asked for her name, Ardeth paused for a moment, then smiled.

"Lucy," she said at last, "Lucy Westenra," and obligingly spelled the name of Dracula's first English victim.

"So, what are we having done tonight?" the hairdresser, who introduced himself as Doug, asked as she settled into the chair. Ardeth looked at herself in the mirror, grateful she still had a reflection.

"Something different. Something so that no one will recognize me." He raised one eyebrow in curiosity but when nothing further was forthcoming squinted at her reflection for a moment. At last he smiled. "I've got just the thing," he announced and, before she could speak, swept her up into the ritual of transformation.

Finally, he stepped back to let her look closely at herself for the first time. He had chopped her hair off at the jaw line, curved it delicately forward—an effect she knew she'd never be able to quite duplicate. Her part was gone, replaced by the sharp slash of bangs just above her brows. The colour was rich, glossy black. When she tilted her head, the light caught veins of blue in the sable. The dark colour did not look natural, but that didn't matter. The contrast turned her skin from ivory into alabaster and the cut altered the shape of her face, emphasizing the hollows under her cheekbones. "Well?" Doug asked.

"I look like that old movie star . . ."

"Louise Brooks. Very hot look right now."

"I like it," Ardeth decided and smiled at her reflection. "It's me."

In the salon change room she dug into her purse and pulled out the make-up she'd bought. She lined her eyes with Egyptian extravagance, and painted her mouth with a red that held the blackish hue of blood.

Ardeth stepped back and put on her sunglasses. Her features dissolved behind them until all that anyone looking at her would remember was their black line, balanced by the smaller red line of her mouth. She could walk by Sara on the street and her sister would never look twice. But others might.

Be careful, be anonymous, be safe, Rozokov had instructed, before he abandoned her in the night. The black-lipped demon in the mirror smiled grimly. What had safety done for her but given her this chance to be powerful, to be dangerous, to be reckless? Fear and caution seemed unsupportable by the new fire she felt pulse through her. Images flickered in her mind of late-night movie vampires, all sleek and stark in black and white, even when the films were in colour. *This* was what vampires were supposed to look like.

As she turned towards the door she realized, with a kind of relief, that she was still hungry. Everything was starting to fall into place.

She walked through the crowd with dizzy anticipation, her excitement showing in the faint smile that curved her lips, in the confident sway of her hips as she walked. She felt the eyes on her, felt them linger as she passed the sidewalk cafes and stores. The weight of those gazes was instinctively intoxicating, like a caress.

Still, even in the thrall of her new self, she knew that she could not completely abandon caution. And that she had not completely abandoned fear. Beyond the image she had created for herself, beyond the secret knowledge of her power lay the hard reality of her state, the price that would have to be paid over and over again. She had to feed. Blood must be taken, willingly or unwillingly, from the people who passed her on the street. They were not Peterson or Roias. Now there was no righteous hate to guide her—or to justify what she had to do.

She must be selective, Ardeth realized, as her black-lined eyes lingered on an attractive man sitting alone in one of the sidewalk cafes. It had to be someone who would not know what was happening to them—or would not tell. At least until she could master Rozokov's trick of hypnotism. That eliminated the man in the cafe, she decided, and moved on.

Johns, she thought suddenly. Surely a prostitute's customers would not be inclined to say anything if the woman engaged in an unusual practice. She paused at an intersection, watching the red light and considering the option.

It had its advantages: anonymity, a silent population of victims, and even payment for her actions. But there were dangers too—pimps, the increasingly vocal community groups in the "track," and, most importantly, the police. She dared not even imagine what would happen if she were imprisoned.

Besides, she thought, I never *wanted* to be a prostitute. I won't be anything I don't want to be, ever again.

She crossed the street before the light turned and was considering heading up one of the side streets when she saw him. He was no more than twenty, she guessed, with close-cropped dark hair and a gaunt, hungry face. He was panhandling, hand stuck out towards the crowd as he chanted his unending request for spare change.

Ardeth eased back from the passing crowd and watched him for a moment. Something in the monotonous voice and the lowered eyes suggested such weary resignation and despair that she almost kept walking.

But the sight had reminded her of her own hunger, which had turned into an insistent throb deep inside her. She shifted uneasily on the corner. He's been victimized enough surely, part of her mind suggested. Then once more won't matter, the cynical edge replied. Besides you don't intend to hurt him (but you might). You don't intend to kill him (but you might).

And if she did, Ardeth realized suddenly, no one would know—or care. The thought should have horrified her, but it seemed that her moral centre had gone too, burned out in the face of Roias's sadism and Rozokov's eternal imperative to survive.

That's all it is, she told herself desperately. My survival. I've paid too high a price for it to back out now.

She moved to stand beside the boy, who looked at her in dull surprise. "You got any spare change?" he asked.

"I might." She saw a spark of life in the dark eyes, then anger at her unclear answer, and his mouth opened to swear at her. Then he seemed to remember that she was a potential source of income and he snapped his mouth shut again. "Having much luck?" Ardeth asked.

"Some," he replied warily, eyeing her. "You looking to deal?" he asked suddenly.

"No, but I know someone who is. What do you want?"

"What's he got?"

"Come with me and find out," Ardeth suggested. The kid looked up and down the street nervously, as if expecting to gauge her trustworthiness by the signs of danger on the street. "Come on. It's not far. You'll be back here in twenty minutes." He nodded quickly, once. "Look, meet me down at the next corner down John Street in five minutes. Just in case, you know," she suggested and he nodded again. Ardeth smiled and dropped a quarter in his palm, then walked on.

Five minutes later she was standing in the alcove of a closed office building, waiting. The kid was on time, slouching with edgy bravado up to her. "Where to?"

"This way," she gestured with her head and led him down into the deserted blocks of warehouses and offices several streets to the south. In the shadow of an abandoned building, she drew him into a side alley.

"So where's the deal?" he asked uneasily, hands jammed hard into his jean pockets as he shifted his weight from one foot to the other.

"I'm the deal." Ardeth felt a tremor of pleasure as his eyes widened.

"Hey lady, what kind of game is this?"

"An easy one." She dug a ten-dollar bill out of her pocket and waved it gently. "I'll give you this . . . if you let me kiss you." :

"You want to *pay* to kiss me?" he repeated incredulously but his eyes were already hooked on the lure of the moving bill.

"Exactly. That's all. An easy ten bucks."

"Give it to me now," he said suddenly and put out his hand. Ardeth let him take the bill and then saw his eyes shift between her and the exit to the alley. They lingered on the empty street then returned to her. "OK."

She stepped up to him and put her hands on his shoulders. She realized with surprise that he was shaking. The thought set her own muscles trembling. The kid stared down at her, eyes moving uneasily from his own reflection in her sunglasses to her dark mouth. When she kissed him, she watched from behind her tinted lenses as his eyes closed.

To her surprise, he kissed her back. Her heart was pounding so loudly she thought her ribs would shatter and the hunger, tangled up now with a rush of desire, seemed to have expanded inside her, filling her body with heat. The kid put his arms around her and pulled her tight against him.

Ardeth thought she could feel his heart beating against her, feel every artery throbbing through their layers of leather and denim. The scent of his life, so close to her, was overwhelming. When he reached inside her jacket and put his hand on her breast, she made a soft involuntary sound of pleasure. "This'll cost you more," he whispered.

"It's all right," she murmured back against his mouth and his hands on her tightened.

If he had continued to kiss her, she might have let it go further, might have found the strength to wait. But she was too deep in it now, and too hungry. When his mouth released hers, she sought his throat with the blind instinct of a newborn creature seeking the teat.

She tasted his sweat, the bitter coat of grime on his skin, then she was in. The blood filled her, blotting out his cry, turning his sudden struggles into mere nuisances that she subdued with iron fingers. They sank to the ground and knelt there like praying lovers while she swallowed again and again. His head fell back in surrender and he groaned.

She felt the life go out of him, the heart stop with a suddenness that startled her. For a moment she crouched there, holding him, the blood curdling in her mouth. Then she stood up slowly, letting him fall.

There was a manhole cover at the foot of the alley and she pried it up, then dumped the body down into the sewer. She waited for the faint splash before replacing the cover.

Then she went back into the alley and vomited blood into a trashcan.

Chapter 19

"Hey Grey Man, you lookin' for some fun?"

"Grey Man, you got thirty bucks? You wanna blow job?"

"Girls, if Gris-Gris had thirty bucks, he'd have done drunk it by now."

The women lounged against the bus shelter on the street corner. He knew their names from time spent sitting on the park bench to their right, beneath the sheltering shadows of untrimmed hedges. Sheila was from somewhere far to the north, a ten-year veteran of the street at twenty-five. May was in late adolescence, he guessed, with baby-fat lingering in her round face, round limbs. Carlotta, who called him Gris-Gris, was from Haiti. She was the only one who was afraid of him, though she hid it with her merciless tongue.

Every night, they would stand by the bus shelter (their "office," they called it), clad in clothes so tight they outlined every curve, smoking cigarettes, chatting, and getting into the cars that slid in steady succession to a stop at the curb.

Rozokov didn't acknowledge their taunts as he shuffled by. He never did. He suspected that there was some rough affection in them, some acknowledgement of the kinship of the lost. Or perhaps it only gave them some pleasure to flaunt themselves in front of someone to whom they could feel superior.

"You'd do it to Grey Man for ten bucks? Girl, are you crazy?" Sheila said, loud enough for him to hear. "It'd take thirty just to ignore the smell. And who knows when the last time he washed that thing."

There was no denying the smell, he acknowledged with a smile he hid behind a bent head and a tangle of grey hair.

The derelict from whom he'd stolen the clothing had not believed cleanliness was next to godliness, or had not aspired to godliness at all. The shabby pants, dirty shirt and grubby grey overcoat all reeked of sweat, urine and liquor. Much as the man had.

It had been Rozokov's third night in the city. The first day he had spent in a sheltered drainage pipe in the ravine, the second in the dusty upper storey of a garage backing one of the mansions that rimmed it. When he woke in the early evenings, he had carefully tried to recover the resources he had secreted away against his awakening. They were all gone—or completely inaccessible to him as he was now.

His bank accounts had long ago been reclaimed by the banks, the trusts he had so carefully constructed for his "descendants" now required at least three pieces of documentation as proof of his parentage and he had none of the basic papers this age seemed to demand. He did not even know who to contact to obtain forgeries, such as had so often served him in the past.

And each time he stepped into a bank, he could feel the traces of footsteps before him, could sense traps set up to be triggered by his attempts to reclaim the last remnants of his old life.

On the third night, confused and angry, he gave up. He retreated to the shadows of one of the landmarks he recognized, a great church that was now dwarfed by the monolithic glass towers that loomed around it, just as it had once reached heavenward over the more modest buildings at its feet. He tried to think.

In the asylum Ardeth's stories had been, at first, a diversion, and then an affirmation that some life, some reason to endure, existed beyond the cruelty of Roias and the others. The world she described was both wondrous and recognizable. Despite the many strange and fantastic things she had told him, he had seen the seeds of war and technological development in his own day, had known that the pace of change had quickened over the span of his life. Such was the way of the world, he had thought. He would survive, just as he always did.

But when he was in it, in the heart of the vast city whose glow obliterated the stars, he found his certainty fading. The weight of the city's towers hung over him, blotting out the moon.

Sometimes, in the midst of all the alien glass and steel, he would find some remnant of the world he had known. A carved stone façade of a building, a restored "historical site" that had been new before he began his long sleep, street names that made a mockery of their own familiarity by being set in lighted boxes, or followed by the cryptic glyphs of Chinese or Hindi.

But more often he could find no echoes of the old city in the noise of the new.

More than the buildings had changed. The streets thronged with people of every race and colour. He heard Greek and Italian shouted on street corners, sat on a park bench beside two old women who gossiped in a tongue whose accents made him ache for the lost Russia of his childhood. And there were languages he did not know, Chinese, Portuguese, Urdu, and the thick sing-song patois of the Caribbean.

But when he looked at the newspapers, he realized that for all that he saw on the street, the world had not altered that much—the faces of those who ruled this vast, polyglot city were white and male. As they always had been.

Here, as everywhere and everywhen, money meant power. Those who pursued him had money beyond his comprehension. Trapped in this world whose inner working still eluded him, he had no way to fight that. He could not flee to some other land; Ardeth had made that clear. And the shelter of the gothic buttresses of his past was illusory. There was no sanctuary here. Somehow he had to find a way to elude the traps set for him and conceal his nature from the world until he truly understood the way this new world worked, until he could find the weapons this new age could offer him.

He stared out at the small park that lay before the

church, its salvation from the concrete that seemed to have been poured over every other blade of grass. Against the streetlights, the white eyes of the cars, he could see figures moving. Those on the sidewalk strode quickly, sure of their path through the night. The shadows in the park itself shuffled, seeking the shelter of tree-root beds or the bounty of wire garbage cans.

A dark shape lurched across his vision suddenly, exhaling alcohol and human stench as it stumbled into his alcove and leaned against the wall. "Fuck 'em, fucking assholes . . . that's what I say . . . fuck 'em," the man muttered, then seemed to see Rozokov for the first time. "Got a buck, mister," he demanded, leaning forward to peer into the shadows.

"No."

"Fuck you then. Got any booze?"

"No."

"Fuck you then," the man repeated, then slid down the wall to sit in a sprawl of dirty rags on the ground. "Need some booze," he announced at last. "Need some goddamn booze." The man's hair was long and unkempt, his features lost beneath a matted beard. His gaunt face and wild eyes reminded Rozokov of the religious hermits of his old land, drunk and demented by God. He twitched his nose in automatic distaste as the man shifted and the light breeze delivered the odour of urine, liquor and despair.

The mad eyes moved to him again. "Got a buck, mister?" the man asked. Rozokov shook his head.

"Nobody's got a fuckin' buck. Nobody's got a fuckin' drink. Fuckers don't even see . . ." the drunk muttered and his head slumped forward suddenly. He looked as if he were praying.

"Fuckers don't even see . . ." Rozokov whispered and the answer to his dilemma came to him. There were only two paths to anonymity—great wealth and great poverty. One was effectively blocked but the other lay before him, cloaked in the filth and miasma of alcoholism. "Friend," he said quickly and the man snorted, head jerking, then blinked blearily at him.

"Wha? What ya want?"

"Do you want a drink?"

"Ya got one? Where ya got one?"

"Here. Come closer." The drunk crawled deeper into the shadows, behind the rose bushes that sheltered them. Rozokov felt a stab of sorrow at his trusting desperation. The last two, the woman the first night, the man the second, had known nothing, remembered nothing when they woke in their ground-floor apartments. But this one—this one he could not spare, could not leave as a clue to his new identity.

"Where's the booze?" the man demanded plaintively. Rozokov moved forward, caught the filthy hair in his hand, and lifted the man's face up to his.

"Just look in my eyes. There is all the wine you want."

When he had drunk, he stripped off the man's filthy clothing and his own stolen attire. He could not help his shudders as he pulled the greasy, tattered cloth over his body, and eased his feet into the rotting shoes. He bundled up his old clothes—the drunk had no use for them. He crawled from the bushes without a glance at the huddled figure in the sodden underwear.

He had made sure the man did not suffer; that was the only comfort he took. Once he might have told himself that it was a kinder fate than the wretched existence of the street, a sweeter death than a long, drunken dying, but he was too old for that now. There were few, living or undead, who welcomed the end of whatever life they had. He killed, could not help killing, but he could not delude himself that it was mercy—or justice. It was only survival.

That had been a month ago. Since that night, his existence had been reduced to the essentials—to finding a place to sleep each day, to finding sustenance each night, to finding something to occupy the long hours in between. Ardeth's mention of abandoned houses had led him to a boarded-up warehouse and in its damp, earth-floored basement he found shelter from the sun. Sometimes, in the dark of midnight, he sat on the roof and counted the few stars that penetrated the clouds and the city's glow.

The growing warmth of the summer nights kept the city's homeless population on the streets and so solved his second dilemma. He was careful and wary, but his victims were often malnourished and ailing; there were deaths despite his caution, and rumours had begun to be muttered on the street corners and in the parks. They were easily dismissed, even by the street people themselves, but they made him even more wary, so that he lived with a constant edge of hunger rather than risk a mishap.

For the rest of the time, the hours between dusk and dawn, he hunted in garbage cans for newspapers and magazines, which he read word for word until the great gaps in his knowledge began to diminish. He stood outside electronics stores and pawn shops, watching the flickering images on the television sets in the windows. He visited the library in the early evening, poring through books on history and law and economics, seeking ways to penetrate the paper walls that kept him from his remaining resources. He researched the fire that had destroyed his resting place and discovered in the names the confirmation of his own suspicions about who was hunting him. He sat on park benches, invisible to the eyes of those who passed by, those who feared to look at him in case he asked for money and they'd have to decide between anger and guilt, and he watched.

He was watching tonight, in between careful perusal of *The Wall Street Journal* stock quotations. All business news had become part of his search for a way to deflect the pursuit set in motion by Ambrose Dale a hundred years earlier. He'd been fortunate to find a two-day-old edition in a garbage can on Richmond Street.

The street was quiet, except for the women's customers sliding up to the curb to pay court and then just pay. Rozokov finished the paper and watched the commerce for a moment, trying to decide whether to move on. He was restless tonight, and feeling some measure of his age as a weight on his heart. In a month, he had spoken to another being only rarely, and too often they had been words of hypnotism to lure already clouded minds deeper into darkness. For the thousandth time, he wished that he had not had to send Ardeth away.

Hunger nudged at his consciousness and he rose to begin

the shuffling search for sustenance. "Hey Grey Man," May called, "where ya going?"

"Grey Man's got business. Places to go, people to see," Sheila answered for him, as usual, and the trio dissolved into hoots of laughter.

Stirred by an overwhelming impulse, the sudden need to meet another's eyes, to use the voice that rusted in his throat, he stopped and looked at them. "Yes, I have business. Unless you fair ladies wish me to stay. Perhaps I could take you up on your so kind offers."

"Jesus," May breathed and he saw Carlotta's hand move, unconsciously sketching a half-remembered symbol in the air between them. Warding off evil, he realized and shuddered, then hunched away from them, muttering his borrowed incantation cursing the "fuckers."

They will not remember, he told himself. They will cloud their minds with drugs and drink and think they imagined it. And it will never happen again.

Resolutely, his disguise in place again, he shambled down the first laneway, seeking the various hunting grounds he now knew well. From an open doorway at the end of the alley, he heard the steady thump of the cacophony this age called music. It signalled the presence of one of the city's half-hidden nightclubs that seemed to bloom for a handful of nights on the back streets, then die as some other spot caught the attention of the fickle children who patronized such places.

He moved carefully then, staying in the shadows. The young moved in packs, and the boys could be dangerous in their alcoholic recklessness. Some nights they seemed to look for prey, and the old, shambling men who crouched in the alleys made suitable targets. He did not fear them but feared the risks he would have to take to defend himself.

There was a commotion at the other end of the alley and a group of laughing, shouting revellers appeared beneath the streetlight. He froze, invisible in immobility, and waited for them to move on. There was a dispute among them, some pointing down towards the door to the club, others clamouring for some other diversion. Finally, the schism deepened and half of them staggered off into the night. Rozokov waited impatiently for the three remaining to pass through the alley. They were two young oriental men, razored hair like black cockscombs over faces of almost feminine beauty. The third . . . his breath caught, and he wondered how he could have missed the glow of her presence. Once he recognized it, it blazed like the neon that coloured the city nights.

She looked completely different from the pale, haggard woman he had known in the asylum. Inky hair framed a pale face dominated by the red slash of lips. Her dress was short and black, revealing long legs in dark stockings, white arms that looked shockingly naked. Only her eyes, when she stopped and faced the darkness, were the same, incongruously soft among all her sharp angles and uncompromising colours.

She could not see him, her senses not mature enough to find him when he cloaked himself from her, but she stared uneasily down the alley until the young men tugged on her arm and pulled her into the dark mouth of the club.

Rozokov let out his breath slowly. Hide, he had told her. Change yourself so their eyes will not find you. And she had, with an efficiency that was almost fearsome. His heart ached for her suddenly, loneliness and sympathy combined. He knew the terrors of youth in this state, the desperate groping for some guide, when the only models were the one who had killed you and the accumulated misconceptions of the dark and fearful folklore. And you abandoned her to that struggle, his conscience reminded him.

He could force his way into the dark confines of the club, or linger amid the garbage bins to catch her as she left. But then the memory of Roias returned, along with the thought of what he could be forced to do if she were held hostage, and so he shuffled on, melting back into the skin of his disguise with more ease than he cared to consider.

Chapter 20

The street was in full swing by the time Mickey and Rick arrived to set up their gear. Memory of the day's ninety-degree temperatures hung like a scent in the sultry air. The heat brought out the crowds but stripped them of the leathers, boots and great coats with which they declared their allegiances all winter. Mickey had shed his customary leather jacket and rolled up the sleeves of his "Death from Above" T-shirt. Rick had even tied back his shoulder-length hair in concession to the heat. And, Mickey thought with a private grin, because with his hair tied back and his round sunglasses on, he looked just enough like U2's guitarist to get him a second look from the girls passing by.

There wasn't much room on the corner, but the recessed doorway to one of the used-clothing stores provided a space to duck when the flow of pedestrians got too heavy. The traffic crawled along, windows down and stereos blaring—competition they could do without on a night when they'd brought only the two acoustics.

"Holy Roller's here, right on schedule," Rick observed as he started to snap open his guitar case. Mickey finished slinging his Ovation over his shoulder and glanced down the street.

"He's closer tonight."

"I think the waiters at the Flamingo called the cops the other night. It made it hard for the people to eat on the patio with him ranting about AIDS and the wages of sin all night long. Wonder what the sermon is tonight?"

"I hope it's the evils of rock and roll. I like that one," Mickey joked, though he shot the preacher another careful

161

glance. The consensus on the street was that the Holy
Roller was harmless—just another lost soul driven crazy by
too much religion or too many drugs. He wasn't a street
person—he was too clean for that, a kind of hard-scrubbed
cleanliness that suggested that it ranked somewhere on par
with godliness. The face was craggy, edged in a shock of
muddy brown hair. It was very different from the bland vis-
ages and capped smiles of the television preachers. But if
his face kept him off the dollar-mill to glory on TV, his
voice put all the Falwells and Swaggarts of the world to
shame. Or it must have once, Mickey thought, with the musician's ability to hear the echoes of beauty in it. Now,
drink or illness or merely the endless duty of haranguing
their oblivious world had taken their toll and when the Holy
Roller preached, you heard crows, not angels. Mickey hated
to have to sing over that strident rant, though he and Rick
both took a wicked delight in playing songs that ran in
ironic counterpoint to the preacher's sermon.

The strum of Rick's guitar brought him back to the moment and they began to tune their guitars, pausing once in
a while to scan the street. When the two instruments
sounded almost like one, Rick settled his felt hat farther
over his eyes and grinned sideways at Mickey. "Well, pal.
Shall we try to make this week's rent tonight?"

"Why not?" Nothing else to do, Mickey thought with a
wry grin, realizing they were in for a long night's work.
"Start with 'I Knew the Bride'?" Rick nodded, counted in
with the bob of his head and they started out the night with
a quick pop beat.

An hour later, a small, shifting circle had gathered
around them. Some people stayed only for a bar or two,
some for a whole song if it caught their fancy, and some
hung around longer just to catch some free entertainment.
Or nearly free. Mickey's guitar case lay open on the
ground, a mute invitation for payment. As usual, they had
spiked the pot with a few bills of their own, just to plant
the idea of generosity in the audience's mind.

It seemed to have worked, Mickey thought, doing a

quick tally of their take. They might really make a dent in their rent, maybe even before midnight.

When he looked up again, the girl was standing in the front of the circle, watching him. Mickey stared for a moment, because he couldn't help himself. Her hair was startlingly black, a dye job, he realized. Beneath the line of ragged bangs, sunglasses covered her eyes. Trying too hard to be cool, he decided. Or covering up the bruises and lines of too hard a life. Her face was pale, except for her lips, which bloomed red-rose on her snow-white skin. There were faint lines around her lips, and a barely perceptible indent beside her mouth. Mickey wondered if she were chewing the inside of her mouth, keeping the tension inside.

She wore a battered khaki trenchcoat over a black miniskirt, dark stockings, and a loose black T-shirt. There was a faded design on the T-shirt but he couldn't make it out. He could only see the suggestion of a pattern and gothic lettering that shifted as she breathed.

The Holy Roller cried out, almost in anguish, and the girl turned her head suddenly. Blood swung in a glittering circle around her neck and Mickey started, staring, until he realized the red gleam was only a stone in her earring. She looked back and he saw the twin pewter winged faces suspended from her ears, red glass dangling from their throats like drops of blood.

She tilted her head a little and he felt the basilisk gaze of the sunglasses settle on him. Uneasily, Mickey dropped his glance, strummed aimlessly on his guitar. "For temptation is everywhere, my children, and we are lost in the wilderness. The wilderness is the devil's and the devil takes all forms here—many of them pleasing." The Holy Roller's rant echoed in his ears suddenly, the shattered voice rolling the last word around like a grape before spitting out the seed of meaning.

When Mickey looked up, the girl was still there, the black-lensed gaze turned to Rick. A sideways glance at his friend revealed the familiar slow grin of interest. Normally Rick's salivating over the women who gathered around them amused Mickey. Tonight, he wished the thin trickle of sweat down his back hadn't turned to ice.

"Come on, man," he said desperately and nudged Rick with his guitar. "Let's give the old Holy something to really rail about." The crowd had gotten restless and if they wanted any more cash that night they'd better start the show again.

"Huh? Oh, yeah," Rick answered, dazedly, barely looking away from the black-clad, black-eyed girl.

" 'Wild Thing'?" Mickey suggested.

"Yeah." The affirmative was stronger this time, and when his friend's gaze returned to the dark-haired girl, Mickey realized he'd picked the wrong song. But they were committed now, the first chords hit and the song begun.

To give Rick credit, he was trying to be subtle. He smiled at all the women in the crowd, and kept the lyrics and the chords straight. But he was singing it for *her*, his voice drawling and dipping over the chorus, stuttering and sighing over the verses. In the end, even Mickey was drawn into the intensity of the song, his guitar solo sliding achingly up and down the scale, echoing Rick's voice.

The girl stood there, smiling faintly, swaying just a little to the beat. The wind fanned her hair into a dark halo around her head and the streetlights fired the crimson gems hanging from her ears. For a moment, in the night heat and the thunder of the guitar rhythm, even Mickey wanted her.

Then the song was over, the last words a shout of "Wild Thing!" that the crowd joined. There was applause, and the clatter of money into the guitar case. All of which Mickey heard only distantly.

Because the girl had taken off her sunglasses and smiled at Rick.

You're not jealous. Staring into his coffee cup, Mickey repeated the words to himself. And knew that they were true. It wasn't jealousy that had made him angry when Rick started packing up his guitar, ignoring the crowd that thinned and drifted until only the girl stood there. It wasn't jealousy that made him insist that Rick meet him at the street-side diner in half an hour. It wasn't jealousy that kept him sitting here on the stool, staring out onto the street, while his coffee went cold and the blonde at the end of the bar went colder.

It was because the girl's eyes had flared as red as her earrings, just for a second, and her teeth had looked as sharp as ice beneath her crimson lips. It was because, just for a second, he had been afraid.

The girl's name was Ardeth. Rick said it over, once or twice, as Mickey stomped away up the street, carrying both guitars. "Ardeth. That's pretty." She smiled, lashes ghosting over her eyes for a moment.

"Thanks. You were very good."

"Thank you. It pays the rent, most of the time. Of course, we really want to get a band together and start playing the clubs. Then again, doesn't everybody?"

"Yes, doesn't everybody." Her voice was remote and a faint frown etched between her pale brows.

"You new around here? I've never seen you before."

"Maybe you just never noticed me before." Her smile was flirtatious but there was a bitter edge to her voice.

"Oh no, you I'd have noticed," Rick assured her and she smiled again. Her eyes were, incongruously, a soft hazel. She looked suddenly very fragile. "So, would you like to get a drink?"

"Yes. I would. Come on, I know just the place." She took his hand.

"Jesus, you're freezing."

"You know what they always say—cold hands, warm heart." She was tugging him along the street and he had to take a few quick steps to catch up to her.

"Do they?"

"Always." Her voice sounded weary but the smile she gave him was dazzling. "Just around here." She pulled him around the corner onto one of the side streets.

"Is there a bar down here? I never noticed it . . ." Rick began, then stopped as she turned into an alleyway. "Wait a minute, what's going on?"

She let go of his hand and turned to look at him. In the

faint light from the street, her face was all shadows and angles, alien. "Don't you want to?" she asked quietly. Rick
looked around at the four-storey walls bleeding moisture in
the heat, at the long shadow of the Dumpster touching the
edge of his boots. Someone had sprayed the slogan "Scary
World" on the container's metal side. In the silence, he
could hear the faint echo of the Holy Roller's voice coming
down the far end of the alley.

"Don't I want to what?"

She took a step backward, shrugged. The trenchcoat fell
to the ground. The black T-shirt was emblazoned with a
faded sun symbol. Then it was gone too and he had a quick
glimpse of her gleaming bare breasts before she disappeared behind the Dumpster. "Don't you want to?" her
whisper came to him, half-haunting, half-promising.

Games. All right, if she wanted to play games, Rick
thought with sudden anger, and followed her, seizing the
cool, bare arms and pulling her against him.

It was easier than he had thought it would be. For all his
boasts to Mickey, he didn't get that many girls, and had
never simply fucked a girl in a dark alley after exchanging
five sentences. Even now, part of him was afraid, afraid of
the diseases you could get, afraid of the possibility of failure, afraid even of the dark. It didn't help that he could
hear the Holy Roller and the echoes of a long-forgotten religious past. "I am the resurrection and the life," he heard
the Holy Roller cry as the girl fumbled with the zipper on
his jeans. "Whosoever believeth in me, shall not die, but
shall rise again!" He wondered distantly why the girl was
laughing, but then he was inside her, and she was wrapping
her legs around him as he pushed her back against the wall,
and he didn't care at all.

The triumph, the pleasure was so intense that he barely
even noticed when she started to kiss his throat. By the
time he felt her teeth, he couldn't have stopped even if
he had wanted to.

The first thing he saw when he came to was a rat the
size of a small cat. It stared at him from across the alley,
red eyes gleaming. When he moaned and started to sit up,

it vanished with a whip of its snakelike tail. Holy fucking Christ, what happened? His head felt as heavy as a lead weight on his shoulders, and when he tried to lift his hand, it moved as slowly as if through water. Dizzily, he tried to remember.

The girl . . . Ardeth . . . he recalled meeting her, remembered fucking her in the darkness, even vaguely remembered the orgasm that buckled his knees and tumbled them both to the littered ground. After that . . . ? After that, there was only darkness.

He opened his mouth to call out to her, to anyone, but only a rasping croak came out. How long had he been here? Mickey must have left . . . Jesus, Mickey'd be furious. He had to get up and find Mickey, tell him what had happened.

Rick pushed himself to his hands and knees and swayed there, breathing deeply. His knees hurt, and his back, and his throat. At the thought of the pain in his throat, a vague memory stirred inside him, but it only confused him and he pushed it away. Clinging to the side of the Dumpster, he hauled himself to his feet and started down the alley.

Twice, he had to stop while the world spun around him, but at last he made it to the street and staggered onto the sidewalk. The streetlights flared and unfocused suddenly and he took a step towards the street, struggling to maintain his balance. When his vision cleared and he looked up, he saw a slender figure in a khaki trenchcoat standing on the other side of the street, farther up towards Queen. Red glittered in her black hair.

"Ardeth," he croaked, stumbling forward. "Ardeth." The curb came too suddenly and pitched him out onto the street. She turned her head just as the cab's brakes squealed. Rick saw her eyes widen, spark red beneath the headlights, and then the impact threw him headlong into the gutter.

Chapter 21

The people crowding the Yorkville sidewalks were as sleek and well kept as the Mercedes and Jaguars lining the streets. Ardeth slid like a shadow among them, black leather jacket over short black dress, hair tucked up under a battered fedora. She kept her sunglasses on, to hide the hunger in her eyes. Her back teeth worried unconsciously at the flesh inside her lower lip. She was now able to feed only every third night. It had been four since her last meal.

It had gotten . . . simpler . . . since that first night two months ago. Then, she had learned how easy it was to drown in the pleasure of the blood. It had taken two more deaths to teach her not to kill. Her mental powers had increased and now she could blot the memory of her sharp kiss from her victim's mind, though only if they were distracted by alcohol, drugs, sleep or sexual pleasure.

The street kid's body had just been found by a sanitation worker, but by this time the rats hadn't left much. The other two hadn't been discovered. She scanned the newspaper carefully each day, just to be sure. The only slip had been that musician two weeks ago . . . but surely it wasn't her fault he'd stepped in front of that cab? And that one had never made the news at all.

The articles about a missing twenty-eight-year-old graduate student had gradually stopped as well, resurfacing only when another woman disappeared. Then her name would join the recitation of mysterious disappearances: Susan B., who drove home after a party, made a cup of coffee and vanished; Lila S., who disappeared between the shopping mall exit and her car; Ardeth A., who walked down the street, around the corner and onto the lists of the lost.

She spent most of her nights prowling Queen Street; or Yonge, with its steady stream of cars and people cruising up and down the street on an endless treadmill; or the parks off Carlton and Jarvis, where the bums and the gays searched for their own satisfactions. She had been to Yorkville only once or twice before.

Like Queen Street, this place had once intimidated her, with its rows of expensive shops, the lines of BMWs and Ferraris that prowled beside the sidewalk, the throngs of exquisitely dressed, exquisitely coiffed and exquisitely funded inhabitants. "Flaming shitheels" a friend had once called them, contempt and envy mingled. Now she felt like a shark in a school of neon-coloured fish who flitted and flared in the shifting light, blissfully ignorant of the dark shadow gliding among them.

The street vendors were out on this hot summer night as well, hawking everything from silk scarves to knock-off Rolex watches. There had been an influx of fortune-tellers since the last time she'd prowled these streets—plump, middle-aged European-looking women who wore print dresses and called themselves Madame Marisa, Madame Elana.

One didn't fit the stereotype, Ardeth noticed. She could be no more than seventeen or eighteen, still slender, still beautiful. She had the long oval face of a Renaissance madonna, framed with wings of black hair. Wearing a sleeveless white T-shirt dress, she sat behind a table labelled with a crudely handmade sign promising "excellent, true fortunes." Ardeth doubted she was really the "Madame Adela" the sign mentioned. She was probably a daughter, granddaughter or niece, apprentice in the trade of fleecing the gullible, temporarily abandoned by her tutor.

She didn't, however, lack for customers. Her darkly innocent beauty attracted a group of young men, who were watching as she turned the cards up on their friend's future. Intrigued, Ardeth skirted around them to edge up onto the steps of the building behind and to the left of the girl's ta-

ble. She settled onto the top step and watched through her
dark glasses.

The fortune the cards foretold seemed standard—wealth,
love, happiness, health. But the patrons in this part of town
expected only entertainment value and it would take a
braver or more foolish novice than the madonna to try any
more elaborate con here. After a few moments of fruitless
flirting the men wandered off, well satisfied that their own
expectations of high-paying jobs, beautiful women and long
lives had been confirmed.

Ardeth remained where she was, elbow propped on
knee, chin resting on the heel of her hand, watching the
crowd. A young man wandering up the street caught her attention. He had the slightly unsteady air of someone who
had spent too long celebrating, or too long drowning his
sorrows, in the warm haze of the street's bars. He was handsome, in a bright, blond way that was so different from the
pale, dark-haired intensity of the crowd she usually moved
in. His hair was the colour of butterscotch, or honey turning
crystalline. He was younger than she was, Ardeth realized
suddenly, despite the expensive suit, the champagne stagger.

He almost walked past the girl's stall, then seemed to see
it for the first time. He wavered a moment, then Ardeth saw
his "why the hell not?" shrug and he approached the table.
He squinted at the name on the placard, then at the smooth
face in front of him. "You're not Madame Adela," he announced.

"No. I am her granddaughter, Marisa. But I know the old
ways. I can tell your fortune," the girl said softly, her voice
full of demure promise. The man laughed and hunted
around in his pocket until he drew out a battered five-dollar
bill. He tossed it onto the table.

"OK. Go for it."

Ardeth saw Marisa's eyes flicker up and down for a moment. Checking the suit, the left ring finger, the eyes, she
thought. Looking for the clues to say whether the drunken-
ness was celebratory or despairing. The girl shuffled the
cards and then placed them in front of him. "Touch them
once," she instructed and he did. She cut them once, twice,

then began to lay them out along the table. When there were six cards lying there, patterned backs upward, she crossed her hands in her lap and closed her eyes for a moment, lips moving. Praying she does it right, Ardeth thought with a smile. From her vantage point, with her heightened vision, she'd be able to see the cards before the girl revealed them to her customer.

"This is your past," Marisa began, turning up the first card. "The coins mean wealth. You come from a rich family." How'd you tell? Ardeth asked the girl silently. Must have been the way he wears that suit. No *nouveau riche* yuppie here. More cards turned over, to lie like patterned jewels on the white cloth. "You have recently been rewarded, a job promotion." The man nodded almost absently, eyes fixed on the cards. "This has brought you joy, but also concern. Do not be concerned. The cards indicate great success, great power." He grinned self-consciously, as if to indicate that he did not believe her but that her prediction would undoubtedly come true. "This is the card that shows your health. It means you must guard against illness of the heart. There have been some in your family, so you must be careful." Not so hard to have guessed that, Ardeth thought. Rich family, probably classic type-A personalities. Bound to be some history of heart attacks there. But the man was nodding again, the doubt in his eyes beginning to waver.

"Next is your heart card," Marisa said, her voice taking on the sing-song intonation of a chant. "The Queen of Swords. She is a card of the future, for there is no one with you now. This card represents a woman of great beauty and power."

"How far in the future?" the man asked suddenly, finishing the question with a self-mocking chuckle.

"This last card will say." She lifted it up and froze, the card still turned to her. Ardeth squinted through her sunglasses at the card in the girl's hand. Oh dear, she thought with sudden sympathy. You weren't supposed to show him that, were you? You weren't even supposed to have that card in your deck.

"Well?" the man demanded, and Marisa turned the card over slowly, revealing the scythe-bearing skeleton.

"This card means that your love will last until death. And that your future is very close to you." He stared at the card, blinking, as uneasiness warred with the warm glow of alcohol. "The cards have shown you a good fortune, sir."

"Right, yeah, thanks." He backed away from the table, uneasiness winning. Ardeth stood up and stepped down onto the street. When he turned her way, she took off her sunglasses.

It turned out that he was celebrating. His name was Philip. Son of an industry scion and newly appointed Vice-President of Public Relations for one of his daddy's companies. Ardeth let him buy her a glass of wine at one of the outdoor cafes, let him tell her his life story with the unselfconscious confidence of someone who believed his life story would matter to the world.

She told him her name was Carmilla and, when he finally asked, that she was a writer. It was not her favourite story, but she had to vary them. "Really? What do you write?"

"Gothic romances. Under another name, of course. You probably haven't read any."

"Probably not. That's funny, I always thought that romance writers were middle-aged and sort of . . ." he groped for the word, then announced it triumphantly, "fluffy."

"Some are."

"You're not fluffy at all." He grinned. "Is Carmilla your real name?" Ardeth laughed.

"Unfortunately, yes. My mother was a big Le Fanu fan." He didn't understand the reference but shrugged it off, either not caring to reveal his ignorance or not caring at all.

"So what were you doing here, all alone?"

"Research," she replied, and let herself savour the irony of it for a moment. "A little people-watching."

"Seen any interesting ones?"

"A few." She smiled and allowed her gaze to linger on his for a moment, before glancing at the street. "I saw several men trying to impress the world by talking on cellular phones while walking down the street. I saw far too many women wearing clothes far too tight. I saw two kids trying to figure out if they could hot-wire a Porsche parked behind that building without getting caught." Philip laughed.

"Did they do it?"

"No."

"You've got to give them credit for taste, anyway."

"I suppose so. Did you steal cars as a boy?"

"No. But when I was fourteen, some friends and I broke into almost all the houses on our street."

"Why? For money?"

"No, our mommies and daddies had lots of that. For kicks, mostly. To prove we could do it. To see what would happen if we got caught."

"Did you?"

"Of course. One of the guys told his parents."

"What happened to you?"

"I got sent to boarding school in Europe," he said with a triumphant grin.

"Must have been terrible for you." Ardeth swirled her drink in her glass, while an idea drifted into her mind. A way to get him alone, without risking his place, or a hotel, or the alleys that were far less numerous and far more brightly lit up here in the "platinum mile." She took a sudden gulp of her wine, hoping the motion had the right edge of recklessness. "I've always wanted to do something like that."

"What? Break into houses?"

"Yeah. Something daring . . ." Ardeth's voice trailed off and she leaned forward, her eyes holding his. "Come with me."

"You mean break into a house? Now?"

"A deserted one. Why not? It's nearly midnight. No one would see us. No one would care. We could just go in for a minute."

He glanced around, guilty in advance. "We're not exactly dressed for breaking into buildings."

"It'll be easy. I walk by one all the time and I know there's a window loose."

"Yeah but . . . aren't there often squatters, you know, skinhead kids and drunks, in those places?"

"In Yorkville? Come on—what's the worst that can happen?" He couldn't think of an answer to that one. Ardeth didn't offer him one.

Ten minutes later, she led him behind the darkened shop on the corner to clamber through a gap in the wooden fence. He came through behind her, brushing worriedly at his jacket. "Carmilla, I don't think this is such a good idea." She held her fingers to his lips, then gestured to the house.

"You can see the window, up on the second floor. We just have to climb up on the porch roof and we're in," she whispered. He squinted up at the boarded window.

"I don't see a way in."

"Trust me." She led the way through the overgrown bushes to the back of the house. When he caught up to her, she pulled him into the shadow of the porch, against her body. "This is where the girl died. The one that was stabbed in the cult killing last year."

"Jesus." He looked up at the house looming over them, then back at her shadowed face. "You want to go in there?"

"Why not? There's nobody there now." She had made sure of that when she was considering the house as a resting place during the day. He shivered, his gaze returning to the blind, boarded windows. Time to up the stakes, my girl, time to give him the little jolt he needs to go over the edge. She shifted, let her body lean on his just enough so that he could feel her breathing, feel the tremor in her body. She knew from the fearful fascination in his eyes that some measure of her hunger had leaked through, had escaped to glow like a flaming corona around the reassuringly ordinary colour of her eyes. But that was all right—one hunger, one tremor could easily be mistaken for another. She brushed a kiss against the corner of his mouth.

"I don't think we should . . ." he whispered uneasily, as she took hold of the drainpipe, put one foot on the window sill and swung herself lithely up to the roof of the porch. She knelt at the edge, looking down at him.

"Of course we shouldn't. That's why we're going to. You want to do it, don't you?" It was not really a question. He wanted to. They all wanted to. The long-dead girl she had been had wanted to. Wanted the forbidden and feared it. *Wanted*—despite society, morality and judgement. Wanted to do whatever they desired, right here, right now, and most of all, wanted something stronger, something darker than themselves to come along and *make* them do it.

He looked up at her for a moment, then with a whispered curse, or prayer, scrambled clumsily up beside her. "What if somebody sees us?"

"No one will see us."

"What if they hear us?" She took his chin in her hand, leaned over to kiss him again.

"Shut up and they won't." Her smile softened the words, but kept him quiet. The boards loosened under her strong fingers then came away. She slithered through the narrow space into one of the second-floor bedrooms. He followed with controlled nervousness, torn between his fear of discovery and his fear of tearing his expensive suit on the ragged sill.

"Christ, it's dark in here. How are we going to see?"

"Wait." She could see perfectly, of course, but let him fidget in the darkness for a moment before she lit the candle from her purse. She held the flame up between them and smiled. "Come on."

The house had been empty for more than five years, occupied only by dust, mice and a steady succession of transients. Then the previous summer, the mutilated body of a missing girl had been discovered by a safety inspector. Rumours of satanic sacrifices screamed across the tabloid headlines for weeks, to be supplanted by the next scandal when no arrests were made. Ardeth didn't know if anyone had ever been arrested—it didn't matter. All that mattered was that this house was one place this carefully groomed, carefully protected yuppie would never confess to being in, no matter what post-coital suspicions he might have about the true nature of his seduction—or his seducer.

Philip followed her up the stairs, at her heels, as if he feared to get too far from the flickering circle of light she held. She paused on the first landing, leaned over the railing to look down two storeys, holding up the candle. Red dots flared briefly below, then vanished in the patter of feet. "Rats," she said and he shuddered, drawing closer.

"Carmilla . . . you were joking, weren't you? About this being the house where they found that girl?"

"No." She took his hand and started up the last flight of stairs. "The girl was here on a school trip . . . from some high school up north. A Catholic school, I think," Ardeth said, not looking back at him. "They were staying at the university residence. She went out to get a newspaper or something. The police think she was kept in the basement for a couple of days—there were some chains down there. There are no windows in the basement and the walls are pretty thick, so no one would have heard her scream. Of course, they might have gagged her." Behind her, Philip stumbled on the stairs and she paused while he got his balance, then she continued, embroidering the few known facts of the case with imaginary details. Fear could be an aphrodisiac for them, as long as in the end they thought they conquered it in the possession of her body.

"On the night of August first, that's Lammas Night, they brought her up here. They didn't drug her, so maybe she fought them all the way up these long stairs. Then again, maybe she didn't." For a moment, the world slipped sideways in the flickering light and she saw a narrow staircase, damp, bleeding walls. "You don't always, you know. You can be so scared you can't move. And you think that if you just obey them, if you just 'be good,' that it'll be OK. That they'll let you go. They don't . . . didn't . . . though."

They reached the top floor at last. There was only one door on the landing. It was open. Ardeth felt Philip's hand tighten in hers, but she did not look at him. "They took her in there." She lifted the candle, sent the flickering light to stroke the edges of that interior darkness. She stepped forward, his hand dragging on her, holding her back, until she exerted her inhuman strength and pulled him with her into the darkness. "They cut pentagrams into her body. She bled a lot—but she lived a long time. You can, you know. You can lose a lot of blood and still survive, if you lose it a little at a time. That was important to them. That she stay alive to the very end. When they cut her heart out."

She lifted the candle again. There was no altar, but the outlines of pentagrams rippled like black snakes along the walls. Ardeth closed her eyes, saw a lightbulb swinging in a slow arc in the darkness, saw the shadow of bars along the floor. "That's very important to them. That you don't die until they're done with you. That you don't die until they kill you. Because then you've spoiled the fun. Because then you might come back." She didn't realize she'd spoken her thoughts out loud until she heard her voice echoing in the empty room.

"Carmilla . . ." His hand was gone. She turned around, tried to force some semblance of the practised seductive smile back onto her lips and knew from his stumbling backwards step that she had failed. In the candle's unsteady glow, she saw the realization burn away the champagne haze and knew he saw her more clearly than she had ever intended. As he backed through the door, the candle went out.

He was on the landing, reaching for the railing. His fear was like an aura of pale light. "Philip," she said, intending to calm him, to win her way back into his trust or hold him still and wait long enough to let her hypnotic powers lull him into acquiescence. At the sound of her voice, he jumped and groped for the stairway, stumbling on a rotting board.

His hands closed on the railing even as the wood at its base splintered and arched him out into the darkness of the stairwell. She heard his indrawn gasp, but he hit the floor before he could cry out.

She waited at the top of the stairs for a moment, listening to the rush of blood in her ears, drowning out the distant echoes of screaming. Then she stepped to the edge of the landing and looked down. The body was crumpled on the dusty floor.

Ardeth swore silently. It was not supposed to have ended this way. Finally, she started down the stairs. His blood wouldn't be cold for a while yet.

Chapter 22

The girl was tall, with long, tawny hair hanging loose over her shoulders. She stepped out onto the street as the light turned yellow, then stopped with an awkward jerk. Sara, walking behind her, felt her heart contract in sudden pain. Ardeth did things like that, like getting caught between the urge to race the light and retreat to the safety of the curb. Even the woman's hair looked like Ardeth's.

For one dizzying moment, Sara thought, "Maybe it *is* . . ." and then her heart expanded so suddenly her chest hurt. But no, the girl was too tall, the walk was wrong, the clothes were wrong.

She let her breath out slowly and fought the rush of tears. Sometimes she wondered why it hurt so much. She and Ardeth had never really liked each other all that much. But her older sister's absence was a great, cold vacuum in her heart.

She had accepted a thousand other uncertainties without question. Where she would sleep, where she could get her next meal, whether the guitarist she'd rehearsed with would show up in time for the gig or whether she'd have to find someone else, all those things she'd taken in stride. She'd shrugged off the might-have-beens as easily as unremembered dreams. But Ardeth, Ardeth had always been unchanging. Always in school, always rational, always careful. It disturbed Sara more than she could admit that her sister's disappearance had shattered every preconception she had held.

Maybe she just ran away—to Paris, or Tahiti, or Tibet. To someplace as frivolous as she was sensible. Any day now, Sara told herself for the hundredth time in the last two months, I'll get a postcard or a telephone call. And then

Ardeth would be laughing and saying, "I finally did it, Sara. I finally learned to have fun. No more dependable, average, scholarly Ardeth."

The furious honking of a car horn brought Sara out of her reverie and she realized that she had walked an entire block without knowing it. She was now sauntering casually through an intersection as the light turned yellow. She paused to gesture obscenely to the driver, who gestured back, then she jogged across to the curb.

Enough, she thought, pushing her sunglasses back from their perch at the end of her nose. Thinking about her doesn't bring her home. You've done everything you can. The police, the papers, your friends, they all say the same thing. She's gone missing. They said other things too, but Sara steadfastly refused to consider them.

She heard shouting from behind her, a man's voice yelling "Hey, you!" She paid no attention until someone grabbed her shoulder and spun her around.

"What do you think you're doing?" she demanded, when she realized that the rough, attractive face didn't belong to anyone she knew. The man stared at her intently for a moment, his hand still on her shoulder.

"I remember you. You didn't count on that, did you?" he said harshly.

"What are you talking about?" she countered, reaching up to try to pry his hand off her. His fingers refused to loosen.

"What happened to Rick?" The dark eyes beneath the thatch of spiky brown hair grew bright with outrage and Sara felt the first touch of fear trace ice up her spine. It's broad daylight, she told herself. Surely he can't hurt me on a busy street in broad daylight.

"Rick who?" Her voice was sharp with her own anger and fear. The man seized her other shoulder suddenly.

"Didn't even ask his name, did you?" he sneered. "What did you do to him?"

"I don't know what you're talking about!"

"Yes, you do. Two weeks ago, Friday, the corner of John and Queen. Rick. The street musician you picked up. The one who ended up in a gutter when a car hit him. Now, what did you give him?" He was shouting at her, fingers bruising her shoulders as he shook her.

"I don't know what you're talking about. And get your fucking hands off me before I start screaming for a cop."

"Not until you tell me what you gave him!"

"All right, all right," Sara lied quickly. "Let go of me and I'll tell you." She prayed he would loosen his grip enough for her to break away and run. Out of the corner of her eye she could see the passersby hastening around them, eyes lowered. Some help they'd be, she thought in disgust. Her only hope was to get into a shop, maybe even to The Gold Rush.

The man stared at her face for a moment, then shifted one hand down to hold hers. She winced in pain at the grip of his short, strong fingers. "All right. I'm waiting."

"Please believe me. Whoever you think I am, you're wrong. I'm sorry about your friend, but I didn't have anything to do with it."

"You're not *that* forgettable. Even if you did get your hair cut and dye it red instead of black. I remember you." There was no doubt in his voice, but his eyes had lost their bright, fanatical gleam.

"I'll prove it to you," Sara said desperately. "Come with me."

"Where?" His hand tightened again and she bit her lip to keep from crying out. His fingers unclenched suddenly, as if he had just realized that he was hurting her. But he didn't let her go.

"The Gold Rush." He glanced towards the neon sign half a block up the street.

"OK. Let's go."

Danny was at the bar when they entered, leaning idly over the counter watching the game of pool in process farther down the room. He glanced up and grinned. "You're here early, Sara."

"I need your help." The bartender glanced curiously at the man by Sara's side and shrugged.

"Name it."

"Where was I two weeks ago, Friday night?"

"Here, of course."

"For how long?"

"Jesus, I don't know. You got here around 9:00, I guess."

"When did this happen?" Sara asked the man, who was watching Danny suspiciously.

"Eleven-thirty or so," he replied and she felt his grip on her hand loosen a little.

"Where was I at 11:30?" she asked Danny.

"On stage, where you usually are Friday nights. What the hell is this? Do I get a prize or something?"

"Just one more question. What colour was my hair two weeks ago?"

"Red. Just like it is now," Danny replied in bewilderment.

"There." She turned to the man next to her with a triumphant smile. "Now do you believe me?" He looked at her for a moment, then closed his eyes wearily.

"I am such a fucking asshole sometimes," he muttered, releasing her hand. He opened his eyes. "I am really sorry."

"Yeah, well." Sara felt her anger fading. "It's OK. Must have been tough. Your friend dying, I mean."

"I was just so sure. You look just like her, except for the hair. You even dress the same."

"Hey, on this street, some days *everybody* dresses like this," she said, gesturing to her black mini-skirt and loosely draped top.

"Yeah, but not everybody has earrings like that." He gestured towards her then started to turn away, apologizing again. Sara reached up instinctively, suddenly unable to remember what earrings she was wearing that day. The metallic winged heads were cool beneath her fingers and she felt the pinprick of pressure from the loose catch on one of the red stones.

Well, at least her double had good taste, she thought absently, then her eyes widened. She had bought these earrings from her friend Mira. They were one-of-a-kind. Or almost. Mira had made two pairs and Sara had bought them both. She had given one pair to Ardeth for her birthday.

"My God," she whispered and looked up to see the door closing as the man left the bar.

She caught up to him halfway down the street. "Wait a minute," she gasped, seizing his arm.

"I said I'm sorry. At least let me escape from the scene of my crime," he began and she waved him to silence.

"Are you sure, are you positive the girl you saw was wearing earrings like these?"

"Yeah. It's not something I'll ever forget."

"Then tell me everything that happened that night," Sara demanded.

"What's this all about? Do you know that girl?"

"There are only two pairs of earrings like this in the city. I have one pair. My sister has the other."

"Then you *do* know her. Where is she?" His voice had gone cold and angry again.

"I don't know. That's the point. She's *missing*. She's been missing for two months. Now, if you've seen her, it means she's all right. She's not . . ." Sara felt her voice trail off, unable to say the word even to deny it.

"Oh Jesus," the man said softly.

"I waited for two hours for Rick. Eventually I just went home. The next day, the hospital called. Rick had died from internal injuries," Mickey finished, staring down into his coffee. They were sitting in a diner, uneasy introductions over.

"What makes you think Ardeth had anything to do with the accident?" Sara asked in confusion, still trying to reconcile his description of the dark-haired, black-clad woman with the memory of her sister.

"The cab driver said Rick just fell into the street, like he was drunk, or on something. When he was playing with me, half an hour earlier, he was straight."

"Did they find any evidence of drugs or alcohol in his blood?"

"I don't know. They wouldn't say. There was something weird about that too. The police just wrote it off, didn't charge the driver. I guess it really wasn't his fault. But when I went to the hospital, one of the doctors asked me if Rick had given blood lately, because he'd lost more than the accident could account for. Rick never gave blood. He hated needles too much."

"All right, I'll admit it's pretty weird. But I still don't see what you think Ardeth had to do with it. Did anyone see her at the scene of the accident?"

"No. Look, I know it sounds crazy. But you didn't see her that night." He paused uneasily, glancing around the room as if he wanted to look at anything but her. "She was spooky."

"What's that supposed to mean?"

"I don't know. There was just something about her . . . that's why I thought maybe she was on something. Something she gave Rick that made him walk in front of that cab."

"Ardeth never took a drug in her life. She hardly even drank," Sara said vehemently.

"Yeah, and she didn't have black hair and disappear either, right?"

"Forget it then. Thanks for the information," she snapped, starting to rise. He was right, that was what hurt. Ardeth had obviously changed more than she had ever guessed.

"I'm sorry. Sara, sit down, please." She sank back onto the vinyl bench and ran her hands through her short hair.

"You're right. It's just so hard to believe. She was so straight it was unbelievable. Maybe somebody just stole the earrings. Maybe it was someone else that you saw."

"Someone who just happens to look like you?" he countered and she sighed, abandoning the comfort of the idea of theft as quickly as she had clutched at it. "When did she disappear?" Mickey asked.

"I'm not sure. The last time anyone saw her was at a class back in March. I'd called her a couple of times but there was never any answer. Then I got a call from her friend Carla, wanting to know where Ardeth was. Nobody had seen her, or heard from her, in almost a week. Carla and I reported her missing the next day."

"What did the police say?"

"What could they say? She's a grown woman, she could do what she wanted. They checked her apartment, her bank account. Nothing was missing. They put out a report and asked a lot of questions, searched a lot of ravines. I told them Ardeth would never just disappear like that. She was too responsible, too predictable. You know what the sergeant told me when I said that people like Ardeth don't just disappear? He said, 'Ms. Alexander, people like your sister are exactly the type of people who just disappear.' But after a while, they stopped looking very hard. They think she'll turn up as Jane Doe in the morgue someday."

"Well, at least you know she's still alive. And she's here somewhere."

"And she's in trouble. I know she is."

"Why not go back to the police? I'll tell them who I saw."

"And let them think she had something to do with your friend's death?" Sara challenged him. "Why should I do that? If she's in trouble, I'm not going to make it worse by dragging in the cops. I'm going to find her myself."

"You don't know what kind of trouble she's in. Maybe you should just let it be," Mickey suggested carefully.

"She's my sister. She's all the family I've got left. I want to find out what happened to her."

"Sara . . . maybe she doesn't want to be found. She's been here all along and she's never called you."

"Then she can tell me that herself. I've got a right to that much from her."

"How are you going to find her?"

"I don't know yet. But I'll think of something. If you saw her, someone else must have. Someone else will."

"Oh, shit," Mickey swore suddenly, glancing at his watch. "I'm late for a job, I've got to go." He started pulling on his jacket and fumbling in his pocket for change for their coffees. The money clattered on the Formica tabletop as he stood up. "Sara . . . good luck. I hope you find her."

"Thank you."

"And," he paused, "if you're ever in the market for a guitarist . . . oh hell, that's an opportunistic thing to say." Anger flared up inside her for a moment, then died. She smiled sadly.

"Nature of the business. Give me your number." He scrawled it on the napkin she extended, then dashed out of the diner. A moment later, his face appeared in the half-open window beside the booth. "Sara, listen, I've got it—a way we can find your sister. I'll come by The Gold Rush tonight and tell you, OK?" Before she could do more than nod, he was gone.

Sara stared at the number on the napkin for a moment, then looked around at the diner's clientele, eyes searching each feminine face, seeing Ardeth's eyes in one, the line of her jaw in another. From Mickey's description of the woman with the earrings, Ardeth had changed so completely it would take recognition that subtle to find her. For two months, she had searched the street for the sister she remembered and might have walked by Ardeth without a second look.

Black hair, white skin, wild, spooky eyes. It was not the sister she knew. Not straight, dependable, dull Ardeth.

And face it, that's what you thought of her. Hell, that's what she thought of herself. Was it the image she'd rebelled against? Sara asked herself. You always told her to. Told her to loosen up. To risk something once in a while.

I did, I know I did, she thought in sudden despair, but oh Ardy, I didn't mean for you to risk *everything*.

Chapter 23

She was near.

He had wandered up from his usual haunts farther south, pretending that he might make it to the central reference library before it closed at nine o'clock, but knowing in his heart that it was her scent on the breeze that drew him.

Stay away from her, Rozokov told himself. There was someone asking questions of the old men at the Salvation Army shelter yesterday. Ambrose Dale's great-great-granddaughter has not stopped looking for you—and you have not found a way to stop her. Until then, you have to stay away.

He walked up Yonge Street, feeling her presence somewhere to his west. Pre-occupied by his awareness, he was standing at the great glass doors of the library building before he realized that it was dark and empty. He paused for a moment, hand on the door handle, staring at his reflection in the glass. You are being a fool, he told the ghostly figure there, and if you persist in it, it will not be Jean-Pierre who goes down in flames this time. It will be you. Or it will be Ardeth.

"Sorry, you just missed us." The voice from his right made him jerk around, hand tightening so hard around the door handle that he heard the glass rattle in reaction. A young woman stood there and he realized that she must have been sitting in the shadow of one of the scraggly trees the city planted in granite pots in fragile, futile defiance of the concrete that seemed to cover everything else. "I was just trying to sort all this out so I could cart it home." She gestured to the collection of magazine-filled shopping bags piled at the edge of the planter. "Sorry if I startled you."

Rozokov let go of the door handle and felt a smile beginning on his lips. It was well past nine and full night was on the city, touching even this brightly lit thoroughfare. And this young creature was apologizing for startling *him*. Even as it amused him, it reminded him achingly of Ardeth and her odd courtesies to him in the strange hell of the dungeon. "That is quite all right. I was overly optimistic." He looked at her more carefully, sensing something familiar in her voice and the way she pushed the tortoiseshell glasses back up her nose. "You work here, do you not?"

"Yeah. I stayed tonight to finish some work . . . and collect these." She gestured to the magazines again. "They let me take them home after the microfilm versions come in." She shifted forward a little, studying him curiously. "I've seen you here a few times. You're the one who actually reads things."

"The literate bum. Not just one looking for a place to sleep." The faint light did not completely conceal her blush.

"Well, you know, a lot of you ... of them ... just sit around and ..."

"I know," he rescued her, suddenly glad he was wearing relatively clean clothing tonight and he had forgotten his shambling, swearing ritual in his concentration on Ardeth. He glanced at the collection of bags. "Do you have to carry all those?"

"Well, I thought I could. I don't live very far away. Just over in Rosedale." She gestured with her head. How young was she? Rozokov wondered suddenly, still uncertain about the signs of passage in this new world. Younger than Ardeth surely.

"I am passing that way myself," he lied. "It would be my honour to escort you."

She laughed uneasily. "Are you really going that way?" she asked and beneath the slight tone he recognized the threads of caution, uneasiness and fascination that he had so long ago learned to exploit.

"I am a gentleman of leisure, as you can see. I have no previous engagements and Rosedale is as pleasant a destination as any. But you are quite right to be concerned about being escorted by a stranger. So permit me to introduce myself. I am Dimitri Rozokov." It felt good to say his name again. Even the foppish bow he finished with felt good, a moment of the humorous frivolity that he had so long denied himself.

Her giggle signalled her surrender, her inability to fear for long anyone who spoke with such elaborate and foolish gallantry. "I'm Eleonora Holmes. But since the great-aunt they named me for is safely dead, I usually go by Ellie."

They collected up the bags, two each, and she led him up Yonge towards the city's most expensive neighbourhood. It had been that in his day as well and he remembered watching the mansions there glow like jewels against the trees and the darkness, recalled the long lines of carriages drawing up to release their impeccably dressed cargo at the doorsteps of the city's elite.

Beneath the streetlights he could see that she was younger than he had thought, no more than twenty. Her auburn hair was long and loose, framing an oval face with a wide, full mouth and narrow, brown eyes. Her features were almost anonymously pleasant but the animation in her face as she talked fascinated him. She punctuated her comments with grimaces and grins, her weighted hands coming up as if she was used to gesturing with them and even the heavy bags could not stop her. She wore black pants and a loose, sleeveless tunic caught at her throat with an orange, glittering brooch.

She was nervous, careful to keep distance between them, and talked to hide it. In quick succession, he discovered that her father was a lawyer, her mother a hospital administrator and her older brother a stockbroker. She herself was going into her second year at university and her future appeared to be of central concern to the rest of the Holmes family. "Of course, Dad would love it if I were a lawyer, Mom would prefer a doctor and Paul just doesn't want me to embarrass him too much at his old alma mater."

"And what do you want to do?"

"I don't know yet. I like working at the library, even if the pay makes my parents cringe. I'm majoring in biology at university and I like that. That's my problem. I find *everything* interesting. Sometimes I wish I was one of the people who knew from the time they were five they were going to be a neurosurgeon."

"Curiosity is a rare trait. You should value it," he commented and he caught the edge of her careful glance.

"What about you? What did you want to be when you were young?"

"Not what my father wanted me to be." She grinned and turned a corner, leading him off Yonge and onto a side street without seeming to notice it.

"And what was that?"

"A good son. One who stayed home and had sons to carry on the name."

"What did you do?"

"I left. I travelled and studied and . . ." He caught himself abruptly, remembering suddenly that this was not Ardeth, and they were not in the asylum, where all lies were meaningless. He was walking into the wealthy heart of the city, dressed as a vagrant, with a child whose blood drew him as much as her charm. It was madness. This was no half-conscious wino, no drugged prostitute. If he bungled this, he might as well raise one of the strange bright neon signs above his head and wait for Havendale to get him. And he had told her his real name.

For a moment he almost dropped the bags and fled. But the hunger for blood was a sharp ache in his gut, the hunger for her careless, casual youth even stronger. The wildness, the intoxication of his dark power, was much older than the caution to which he had schooled himself a hundred years ago. You might chastise Ardeth for it, he thought ruefully, but cannot even kill it in yourself.

"Mr. Rozokov?" Her voice was hesitant, hovering between sympathy and fear.

"And that was another country, in another time," he finished at last and managed a smile.

"What happened to you?"

"That I should end up like this? It is a long story and not a very interesting one, I am afraid. Why not amuse an old man by telling him what else about the world you find fascinating?"

Her lip curled for a moment, halfway between pout and scowl, then her mobile features cleared. "I don't think you're nearly as old as you let on. And you're the most interesting thing around at the moment. If you don't tell me about yourself, I'll just make it up."

"Go ahead."

"All right." She squinted at him theatrically for a moment, not even noticing that a man walking his dog across the street had given them a long, lingering look. "I'd say you're from Europe somewhere. Your family was probably wealthy, or noble, if you were supposed to carry on the family name. When you left home your father disowned you." She managed that much correctly, Rozokov had to admit, but then the tale spun out into tragic, secret loves and scheming brothers out to ensure that he remained disinherited. "So here you are, stuck in Toronto, reading the newspapers to try to find some clue to the whereabouts of your long-lost love. How did I do?"

"Perhaps you should be a writer instead of a biologist," he suggested with a laugh.

"Dad would love that. Writers make even less than librarians." She paused suddenly, standing at the head of a short driveway. "We're here." Her voice sounded bewildered and uncertain.

Rozokov surveyed the house for a moment, looking for windows fringed with light, or the shadow of a face watching them. There was nothing but a lamp set over the front doorway. Behind the veil of cedar hedges that framed the front lawn, he could hear faint noises from the house on the right, but the one on the left was still and silent. "My parents aren't home yet. But they should be in a little while." The words came out in a rush, as if speed could disguise the lie.

"I'll leave you here then," he said but did not put down the bags.

"Are you hungry? Thirsty? I could . . ."

"I am not hungry." His own lie came out so much more smoothly.

"I'd invite you in but . . ."

"I understand. I could be anything. It might be dangerous." She teetered there for a moment longer, torn between her fear and her curiosity, between a thousand warnings and her belief in her own invulnerability.

"If you're a thief, it doesn't matter. Everything's insured. And . . . I don't think you want to hurt me. Do you?" She looked at him, dark eyes intent, features for once still and open.

"No, Eleonora Holmes, I don't want to hurt you." That, at least, was the truth.

So she opened the door and let him in.

The house was cooler than the air outside, chilled by modern machinery and the stark white of the walls. Everywhere the light touched, metal and leather gleamed. Black furniture and chrome shelving stood in glacial elegance against the walls, set off with large paintings in icy blue. Ellie looked around the open living room and sniffed. "Maybe not," she decided. She switched off the light and led him down to the kitchen. "You're sure you don't want something?"

When he declined, she unlocked the back door and ushered him out onto a screened porch. "How's this?"

"An admirable compromise," he observed and her brows lifted curiously. "I am not exactly 'in' the house. In case your parents have any injunctions about strange men."

"I'm an adult," she said, stiff and dignified. "They don't make rules like that." She settled onto a wicker divan and watched as he sat down beside her. The trees and hedges grew tall and shadowing back here, he noticed, and behind them was a high wooden fence. Their voices might carry as a murmur to anyone outside in the yards surrounding them but surely would not penetrate houses with windows all closed to keep in their artificial air. She had not turned on the porch light. There was a long silence, not entirely companionable. "What are you doing here? Why did you come with me?" Ellie asked at last.

"I thought that I would enjoy your company. I was right. And," he paused, momentarily reluctant to use the truth as part of his seduction. "And you reminded me of someone."

"Your long-lost love?" There was a grin in her voice but he could almost hear it fade, just as he saw it slip from her face. "Is she dead?"

"After a fashion. She was young and loved learning, as you do. I spend my time in the company of old or lost men . . . or in no company at all. There are times when I need youth and life."

"I knew you weren't as old as you pretend to be."

"I am much older than I pretend to be. That is why I need what you have so much."

"Do you want to fuck me?" The obscenity came out sharp and jagged, as if she used it as a defence against him.

"I am long past that, I am afraid. But I would like very much to kiss you." She sat still for a moment then shifted to face him.

"All right." He felt the breath of the words as much as heard them. He put one hand against her hair and leaned over to touch her mouth. For a moment, her lips were tense against his, then they softened and she returned the kiss. "Do I kiss like her?" she asked when he lifted his mouth.

"No. You kiss like you."

"My parents are up north. They're not coming back tonight."

"I know." This time her mouth was waiting for him.

She was not much like Ardeth after all. Her body was rounder, her breasts fuller, her passion more vocal. When he slid his teeth into her throat, he put his hand over her mouth to hold in her cry and she bit the edge of his palm. Her blood was unutterably sweet, fresh with her youth and spiced with forbidden fruit.

Sated, he drowsed against her longer than he had intended. At last, he eased his arm from beneath her head and sat up. She stirred, eyes opening slowly. "Ssh." He put his hand against her lips. "You are very tired. It was a long walk home with all those bags." His thumb shifted to smooth the frown forming between her brows. "You were so tired that when you got home, you came out here and fell asleep. You had a dream."

"But . . ."

"Just a dream, that's all. Just a dream that you will forget in the morning."

"Don't want to forget," she managed mutinously, fighting the lull of his voice and the drowsiness in her limp body.

"Very well. Remember the dream then. Only the dream."

She sighed and surrendered, sinking back against cushions. Rozokov almost left her there but then remembered that, even in this neighbourhood, there might be predators abroad without his courtesy and so he carried her into the house and left her on the black leather sofa to sleep.

On his careful way back to his own territory, he tried to regret her . . . but could not. He had been too long with only hypnotized whores and unconscious winos to whom he was not even a dream. He had gone so long without hearing his own name on another's lips that he had almost forgotten it. He had confused caution with inertia, fear with prudence. It was time to change. It was time to act.

Some night soon.

Everything
That Rises

She says one day soon
you and I will merge
Everything that rises must converge

From the Diary of Ambrose Delaney Dale

25 September 1898

It succeeded—this plan that I have spent all summer orchestrating has finally succeeded! The prey has eluded me, it's true, but now I know his name and his face. There is nowhere he can run now.

They all came, all those I had reason to suspect. The ruse of a social dinner, in aid of broadening the membership of our city's business association, seemed to have deceived them all.

It was maddening at first. They all passed every test I had devised. All entered without being invited—but perhaps written invitations suffice. All appeared in the mirrors I carefully placed about the foyer and dining salon. Some arrived with wives, overdressed and as respectable and ordinary as any merchant wives. All ate the fowl, despite the heavy dose of garlic in the sauce. None cowered before the crucifix I set on the mantel, or the crosses woven into the pattern of the tablecloth. They seemed an average selection of foreign businessmen, some pompous and loud, some quiet and careful, some charming and astute.

As the evening wore on, I had almost given up in despair and was prepared to send away Collins, who stood guard in the hallway in the guise of a servant, and the men he had hired. I left the parlour and proceeded to my study, confident that Collins would follow me to receive his instructions.

The door was open when I arrived and I knew at once

that I was not alone. I had not made this room off limits, of course, and so a fire burned low in the fireplace, casting a faint, flickering light that let me see the man standing in the shadows by the far wall. He was staring at the shelves of books there. I had time to realize that those shelves housed my collection of occult volumes—and that the fire could hardly have shed enough light for any normal man to read the titles there—when he turned around.

As his eyes flared red, I knew that he was the one I sought. Once recognized, it came as clear as day and I wondered how I could have looked at that narrow face, those pale eyes and not have seen it immediately.

But as I knew him—he knew me!

I could see by the sudden light in his eyes that he realized that I knew the truth. For a moment, we stared at each other, then he moved, lunging at me more quickly than I would have believed possible.

There was a thunderous sound in my ears and the smell of cordite in the air. The creature's forward motion reversed, and he staggered backwards, clutching at his chest. I could see the white front of his shirt start to darken.

I heard Collins swear behind me and feared for a moment we had both been wrong . . . that an innocent man was dying in front of us.

Then the vampire spun around and dove for the window, crashing through the glass and out into the gardens beyond. "Go after him!" I shouted at Collins and, to his credit, the man did not flinch, but hurled himself across the room and out the same window. Outside, I heard him shouting for his men.

Almost instantly, there was a babble of voices behind me. Henry, Elizabeth, the guests . . . clamouring to know what was happening. I managed to placate them with stories of a prowler and that set them off into tales of crime in the city and much head-shaking and tongue-clucking about the sad state of the modern world. Fortunately, Elizabeth persuaded them to return to the dining salon to do it.

* * *

It is now almost dawn. Collins has not returned. I have begun to think perhaps he will never return. That is inconvenient . . . but not an insurmountable setback. There are plenty of men like him in the city, who for a fee will believe any lies I choose to tell them. If Collins does not return, I will hire someone else today to begin the search of the vampire's property.

I have not slept. I cannot sleep.

It is very hot here in the study, despite the broken window. My head pounds incessantly and that strange, tight feeling in my chest has come back. To think that in a while none of these things will trouble me!

I hear Carstairs at the door, no doubt with breakfast. Maybe this pain will go away after I eat.

Chapter 24

The death of Philip Campbell Jr. was a tabloid publisher's dream. "Millionaire's son dies in Horror House," screamed the headlines. Young and handsome, Philip's image stared out from every front page. The cult-killing case was regurgitated in nauseating detail in inner spreads. The building's absentee owner, who had found the body during an inspection, reluctantly submitted to interviews yet again.

The next day Martin Rooke read the details the papers didn't print. The police didn't know much. Philip had died of internal injuries and a broken neck suffered in his fall from the third-floor landing of the infamous "Horror House." His blood alcohol count was too low to qualify as legally drunk, but he had definitely been drinking. No one knew why he had gone there. He'd been with friends until 10:30 on Saturday night, but that was the last time they'd seen him. Police were questioning restaurateurs and shop-keepers along Yorkville Avenue in an attempt to trace his movements.

And the coroner had asked them to examine the death scene again. To find the blood that was missing from Philip's body.

The next transmission brought more news. Campbell had been seen at 11:00 in a cafe, in the company of a young woman. An hour and a half later he was dead. The young woman was described as dressed in a black dress and wearing a hat and glasses with snap-down sunshades.

There was a note beneath the official report. "Street musician killed in car accident on June 10th—friend claims he spent last hour with 'weird' woman in black. Autopsy reports slightly lowered blood level, but nothing conclusive. Checking it out." Rooke snorted. He wasn't sure whether he was pleased by the report or not. He didn't care whether Philip Campbell Jr. had been killed by a woman in black or a transvestite in pink chiffon. It was the grey-haired monster he needed. But the blood loss was important.

Had it started recruiting its victims through others, using women as the lures? It was a way to hunt without exposing itself to the city's eyes. There was nothing in any of Roias's reports to indicate that it could do that—but Roias had badly underestimated it from the beginning.

It couldn't still be in the "Horror House"; the police had searched that thoroughly. But maybe it hadn't gone far. Rooke sketched a brief note to himself. There were strings that could be pulled to allow a search of abandoned buildings to find fire code violations. One of Havendale's construction subsidiaries could handle the credentials; Thompson's men could handle the searches. And the city councillor with a half a million in Havendale kickbacks in a Swiss bank account could handle the formalities. *Would* handle the formalities.

Rooke glanced out at the last reflection of the setting sun, a band of flame across the gold-plated windows of the Royal Bank building. It was almost time for his report to Althea. At least this time he had something to say.

He used the computer and made the leads sound as positive as possible, outlining the action he was taking and daring to estimate a capture within two weeks. It was his longest report in a month. It got the same reply he always did, two words shimmering on the screen in silent accusation:

FIND HIM

There was no argument for that, no discussion. He was dismissed. Rooke sighed and erased the text.

At least the lab transfer had gone off without any major screw-ups. And he'd managed to keep the expenses down, what with switching the halon system in the lab to sprinklers and keeping the modifications to the upper storey at the bare minimum of Althea's requirements. It still meant more than one hundred and fifty grand out of his pocket, but it could have been worse.

He needed a drink. That, and noise, and live bodies to take his mind off the mechanics of recapturing the dead. He glanced at his watch. There was time to head out for a beer and still be back here before the computers spit out the next batch of stolen data cross-referencing Campbell's death.

Out of the shadows of the towers, the heat clung to the concrete of the city, even as the last edges of sunlight disappeared behind the horizon of buildings to the west. He lit a cigarette, inhaled smoke and car exhaust, and walked towards Queen Street. As they always did now, his eyes flickered over everyone who passed, ignoring the uniforms of suits or leather, and looking for the signs of a memorized skull beneath the placid faces.

At the corner of Queen and John, he waited for the light to change, wondering if he wanted a beer at the Rotterdam or a margarita at Santa Fe. His gaze drifted over the streetlight pole beside him. It was covered with paper posters, layer upon layer plastered over each other. Did people really pay to see bands called Barbie Goes to Hell? Did they enjoy it? And that one—was it a band ad or a real notice? The poster showed a sketch of a woman's face, angularly lovely and oddly unreal, surrounded by blunt, dark hair. The caption below said, "Have you seen this woman?" He skimmed the handwritten text. Missing since April . . . seen in July at Queen and John . . . anyone having seen her, call. . . . Ardeth, please call home. That's an odd name, he thought, wondering why it sounded familiar. He glanced back up into the handwriting, found the full name. Ardeth Alexander. Then the light changed.

He was halfway across the street when it hit him. There was something else that Roias must have lied to him about. But now he knew who the weird woman in black was. He knew who had lured Campbell into the death house. And he knew how to find the vampire. One of them, anyway. And either one would do.

Chapter 25

"Sorry, Sara. Nothing at all."

"Thanks anyway, Danny. Let me know if anyone calls."

"You know it."

She hung up the phone, turned off the bedroom light and stepped back out into the living room. Pete, Derek and Steve were sprawled on the floor amid a litter of pizza boxes and beer cans. Mickey sat with his back against the couch, a little apart from them. They were getting along, as far as she could tell, though she knew that the band members were curious about Mickey's motives. Getting into her was one thing—and her business. Getting into the band was another.

She had some misgivings about his motives herself. He'd arrived at The Gold Rush that night a week ago with the poster scheme, promising that an artist friend of his could do the sketch, they could get them printed up cheaply, and he'd distribute them when he did his regular midnight post-

ering runs for one of the clubs. After that one clumsy over-
ture in the diner, he never mentioned joining the band
again. He never played for her, not even when she left her
own guitar lying around the living room of Ardeth's apartment. She never invited him to, for fear her artistic judgement would end up ruining the tentative friendship she
could feel developing between them.

"There's only one inning left," Tom was saying, watching the television. "The Jays are gonna make it."

"In your dreams," Derek retorted cynically. "They're
gonna choke. They always choke. It's the unwritten rule of
Canadian sports—to join the union, you have to choke."

Baseball, Sara thought in disgust, wending her way
through the outstretched legs and beer cans to retrieve her
empty glass and head for the kitchen. She was pouring herself another glass of wine when there was a sudden ragged
cheer from the living room. She looked up as Mickey came
in. "The Jays scored?"

"Yeah." He leaned against the wall, watching her.

"You're not into baseball, are you?"

"Not much," he confessed.

"Neither am I. But . . ."

"But the band is."

"The guys are. And it's noise. I need noise here."

"So that's why they're always here." Sara laughed and
sat down at the kitchen table.

"It's not the only reason. But, well, I spent a few bad
nights here when I first moved in, just after Ardeth disappeared. I don't know, maybe I think if I keep a bunch of
drunk, pizza-eating Jays fans around the place long enough,
she'll get so outraged she'll come back and throw us all
out."

"Nothing from the posters yet?"

"No."

"It's only been two days. Give it time."

"I hope so. I hope she calls. I hope she's not angry I'm
staying here." She contemplated the bottom of her wineglass for a moment, as he settled into the chair across from

her. "I haven't unpacked. I just put all my stuff in a heap on her floor, just like I always did."

"So you can pack up and go when she comes back?" Mickey asked. "You think she'd throw you out?"

"She never did before. She wanted to sometimes, but she never did. Of course, she never gave me a key either. I had to get the one I have now from Carla. But now . . ."

"She's changed." She nodded.

"Ardeth and I . . . we weren't exactly friends."

"Ever?"

"I don't think so. But we had a good time together sometimes and usually we could be civil the rest of the time."

"I have an older brother. He's an engineer. At family gatherings he punches my shoulder and asks me when I'm going to get a real job. We probably say about twenty-five words to each other all day and five of them are 'How was the trip down?' " Mickey told her and she laughed.

"We usually managed more than that. Not much more, mind you. She," she paused, "I always thought I was supposed to live up to her somehow. The typical kid stuff, you know. 'Mother always liked you better.' "

"Did she?"

"I don't think so, not really. Ardeth said once that she thought Mom liked *me* better, so who can tell. It got worse when our parents died. Ardeth started to act as if she were my mother. Sometimes it was like we spoke different languages—so that even if we meant the same things, it all came out sounding like a reason to fight." She tilted her chair back, looked up at the ceiling, then back down at the glass twisting in her fingers. "One time, when we were just kids, I was in a school play. It was some Greek myth or something. We had these white sheets we had to wear as Greek gowns. Ardeth loved that shit, mythology, history, anything old and dead—she loved it. So she found a book that had designs of Greek jewellery and she made me this necklace. She made it from papier mâché and painted it up in gold and blue and red. I suppose it was probably pretty sad—Ardeth's strong point is her mind, not her hands. But I felt like the Queen of Olympus in that thing. Because it was the first thing she ever really gave *me*—the me that was just learning to sing, that was just starting to really be *me*. I wore it every time we did that play. I kept it for years. Because it meant that, at least once . . ." Her voice broke and she stared harder at her hands, blurry behind her tears, "she must have liked me."

"Sara . . ."

"Jesus, I'm sorry." She tossed her head back, blinked up into the light as if the electrical heat could dry her tears. "I thought I was over this. I sound like a fuckin' Disney film."

"I don't think you're allowed to say 'fuck' in a Disney film," Mickey pointed out and Sara laughed, harder than the joke warranted, and let the laughter explain her tears and flushed cheeks when the band put their heads into the kitchen to announce that, due solely to their moral support, the Jays had staved off the dreaded Canadian choke syndrome for another game.

"Well, now that we've once again consumed your food and watched your TV, we'd better be going. See you at the Rush tomorrow night," Tom said. "We're heading downtown, Mickey. You want a ride?"

In the sudden silence, Sara felt Mickey's eyes on her, waiting for a sign of what she wanted. What do I want? If she asked, they'd all stay, let her sleep with them in a heap of covers and pillows on the living-room floor, like they'd crashed on so many floors before. If she asked, Mickey alone might stay, might drive Ardeth's ever-present memory out of the cold bed in the next room.

She said nothing.

"Sure," Mickey answered after a moment. The chair scraped on the floor as he stood up. In the empty kitchen, she wiped her eyes and listened to the rustle of leather jackets being pulled on, the ritual banter of the band as they prepared to leave. She waited until she heard them open the apartment door, until it was too late to call them back with any dignity, before she got up and went out to the small entrance hallway.

They were already on the way down the hall, pausing to wave and mouth goodbye in an exaggerated concern for silence, mocking her insistence on not ruining Ardeth's reputation with her neighbours. It was almost funny—she who had hosted lease-breaking parties that summoned squad cars insisting on silence.

Mickey hung somewhere between the apartment door and the exit and when she appeared, he drifted back to her doorway. "You'll be OK alone?"

She looked at the closing door at the end of the hallway. "I'll be fine. Thanks."

"If you change your mind, I can bike back up here."

"To sleep on my couch?" The question came out sharp and jagged, studded with memories of Tyler, and false comfort promised by other arms.

"Wherever. Whatever." He met her gaze squarely, while she considered the angles, considered what it was he really offered. And what he wanted in return.

"If I need someone," she said at last, "I'll call." He smiled then leaned over to kiss the corner of her mouth lightly.

"To keep the ghosts away. See you tomorrow." He was gone before she could speak, vanishing down the hall in pursuit of his ride home.

Sara stood for a moment in the hallway, then turned back to the empty apartment. Without the television, without the laughter, the silence had a chill that made her shiver. To keep the ghosts away ... but who's haunting who, Ardy? she thought in sudden pain. She closed the door, pressed her forehead against the cold metal surface. Are you the ghost haunting this place—or am I?

Sara dreamed. She dreamed of a soft voice whispering in her ear, asking her to open the door. In the dream, it was perfectly reasonable that it was the balcony door she rose to open, to admit a sliver of night that drifted into one shadowed corner of the bedroom.

She woke with a start, breath caught in her throat, heart racing. She lay in the darkness, wondering what had wakened her, suddenly sensitive to the faintest sound. Her breathing seemed to echo in the darkness. She had almost

drifted back to sleep again before she realized that it was
not an echo.

Terror raised a sudden heat beneath her skin, propelled
by the triple-time pounding of her heart. The ancient dilemma of childhood returned—was it better to face the
thing looming over your bed, or hide beneath the sheets and
hope your own blindness would conceal you?

At last she sat up and said, with as much bravado as she
could muster, "Who the fuck are you?"

The dark shadow in the rattan chair in the corner stirred
slightly. "It is better that you do not know. But I mean you
no harm." The voice was low but clear, with the tantalizing
rhythms of a foreign accent.

"What do you want?" Her vision was improving. The
shadow had resolved itself into a recognizably human form,
though the face was still no more than the suggestion of
features.

"I have news of your sister."

"Ardeth? You've seen her? Where is she?"

"She is dead."

"I don't believe you," Sara said fiercely.

"Your sister is dead," the man repeated.

"How do you know that?"

"I know."

"When did she . . . ?" She let the question end, the hopes
she'd held beginning to unravel within her and dissolve into
the darkness in the corner.

"A while ago." His voice was steady but she doubted
him suddenly. Mickey had seen Ardeth only three weeks
ago. She was still alive.

"She's not dead. Someone saw her." There was a moment of silence.

"That may be. But she is still dead to you. She *must* be
dead to you. And you must stop seeking her."

"Why?"

"You endanger her."

"How?"

"The world must believe her dead. She is in great danger

otherwise. Your questions, your posters, may have already alerted her enemies."

"I don't understand."

"Let her go, Sara."

"No. She wants to be dead, that's fine. But she can tell me that herself."

"You may be watched."

"They can't watch all the time, whoever 'they' are. I want to see her. I won't believe you, I won't believe anyone until I see her." There was another long silence and she heard the rustle of cloth as he shifted position.

"I will do what I can," the man said, after a moment.

"These enemies of hers—are they after you too?"

"With any luck, it is still *only* I they seek."

"Who *are* you?" she dared at last.

He rose from the chair and stepped forward. In the faint gleam of light slanting through the blinds, Sara could see that his clothes were shabby and ill-fitting. But there was something aristocratic in the narrow lines of the face beneath the dishevelled smoky hair and something compelling in the pale eyes. She was suddenly aware that she was still sitting among the tumbled sheets, wearing only her briefs and her tattered, threadbare Sex Pistols T-shirt.

"It is still safer that you do not know," he said softly.

"What have you got to do with my sister?"

"She is my blood," he replied cryptically and for a crazy moment she wondered if he were some long-lost relative, some forgotten second cousin twice-removed. "I will see what can be done. I will contact you. Tell no one of this." He reached out and slid back the balcony door. "Goodnight, Miss Alexander. Sleep well."

"After this? I'll probably have nightmares now," she said caustically. He turned back to her for a moment and she saw the faint gleam of his smile.

"I do not think so . . . Sara. Not tonight." There was an edge of wry amusement in his voice, then he bowed slightly and the blinds swung shut behind him.

By the time she had scrambled to the door to lock it again, the balcony was empty.

Chapter 26

The fragrance of night woke her—dark-blooming flowers, car exhausts, the distant scent of the lake. She shifted on the narrow cot then opened her eyes to the darkness. There was no light here in the basement of the church tower, but when she emerged through the trap door to the main floor, moonlight strained through dusty stained glass patterned her naked body.

Ardeth stretched and climbed the stone stairway that wound up the interior of the tower, pausing when she reached the narrow platform by the window. Earlier, she had brushed away the dirt from a section of clear glass and she looked through the tiny spyhole to the street below. She heard mothers calling late-lingering children home from the park, the blare of ghetto-blasters from the teenagers waiting for the night's rituals to begin, the quiet chatter of the elderly Chinese men who sat on the benches outside the tower. In another hour the park would be quiet, except for the occasional drug deal, hurried sexual encounter or snoring drunk.

Her gaze shifted to the ivy covering the tower's outer walls. The breeze caught it, made it ripple like the skin of a great beast shifting its muscles. She wished she could open the window, breathe in the scent more deeply. She imagined someone seeing her pale face up in the open window, like a maiden in a fairy tale. Like Rapunzel, she thought, and smiled at the thought of what would happen to the prince who tried to scale her tower. No one ever seemed to consider that Rapunzel might have been immured in that tower for a reason . . .

The tower of the Church of St. Sebastien stood alone, the original church long since burned down and replaced by an anonymous modern building separated from the tower by hedges and walls. Someone had lived here once, had left the cot she had moved down to the basement, but in the month she had made this her resting place no one had come near it. The tower was quiet and dark, and it appealed to her sense of irony, but sometimes time passed very slowly within its narrow walls. Waiting for the full night she needed to leave it undetected, Ardeth found herself longing for warmth and light, and perhaps a book to occupy her. But that longing seemed to belong to the living and a world she had lost, so she sat on the landing, letting the moonlight paint the haloed head of the martyred saint across her skin.

When the voices from the street faded, when the insistent thump of rap from the ghetto-blasters followed its owners down to the street, she went back down to the basement and dressed. She dared not wear the fedora since the death of Philip, so she left her dark hair free. She put on a loose black jacket over her Black Sun T-shirt and short skirt, put on her round glasses with the snap-down sunshades. As she dressed, she felt the first stirrings of hunger.

It had been two nights since she'd fed. She was restless and edgy with the mingled anticipation and uneasiness the hunt always stirred. The feeding, the satiation of the gnawing hunger, was still sweet, especially since she had learned some control over the urges that could push her over the line between seduction and murder. But afterwards . . . there was a lingering guilt and dissatisfaction that undercut her reckless pleasure, a childish fear that punishment would follow indulgence. The uneasiness lay like a weight inside her, making her draw out the ritual preparations for the night.

Stop it, she told her reflection in the mirror propped on one wall. No one will reward you for depriving yourself. What did doing without ever get you? A memory flared suddenly, bright and shiny under the moonlight. A child waiting in a supermarket line, while her mother says no, no candy, forgetting promises made to a little girl trying hard to be big. Sara leaning on the other counter, hanging from the edge by grubby fingers. Sara turning around, grinning her wide sneaky grin, her mouth full of red, red gumball. Opening her own mouth to tell—but too late. The gumball vanishing into her sister's smile.

A rush of anger and hunger washed away the dread. The taste of something hot and sweet, better than any candy, filled her mouth. She snapped down her glasses and went out into the night.

She paused for a moment at the edge of the park, torn between entering its darkness or heading down towards the lights of Queen Street. There was something in the air, not quite a scent, not quite a sound, that drew her off the sidewalk and onto the manicured lawn of the park. She walked slowly towards the manor house that marked the park's northern boundary. Nothing stirred under the trees, no bums stumbled from the bushes, no one offered to take her pain away with chemical or physical oblivion. On the path now, she kept walking, waiting.

There was a man sitting on the steps of the manor, a shabby figure of worn cloth and grey hair. Her gaze touched him, slid away into the shadows, then returned. The night shivered, faded away as the truth suddenly blazed before her, for a brief moment as blinding as the half-forgotten sun. Her heart caught, froze his name in her throat, and she closed her eyes. When she opened them, the trees and path had resettled themselves around her—but he was still there.

She made herself walk slowly, slowly, counting each step until she arrived at the foot of the stairs. "Ardeth." The tenderness in that single word broke her control, sent her up the stairs into the arms he opened for her. His kiss was like it had been in the asylum: light in the darkness, warmth in the cold, solid sanity in the shifting madness. All the embraces of her victims, the blind gropings in alleys and empty houses that she had thought were pleasure she realized now were just pale substitutes for this first passion, this first hunger. She forgot her anger at him, all her stubborn resolutions to freeze him out as he had frozen her. She forgot everything but the knowledge that she was not alone.

"You are a mess," she said at last.

"Be thankful these are my good clothes, else I would smell as well," he replied with a laugh as she shifted up behind him on the steps and began to brush out his hair with the comb from her pocket. They sat in silence for a few moments, then she took his hair in her hand and pulled his head back.

"You left me." The accusation hung in the air for a moment.

"Ardeth . . ."

"You left me. Don't. Not again."

"It is not that simple." She let his head go, and dropped her hand back into her lap.

"It's as simple as we make it. And don't tell me we're solitary creatures. You missed me." She said it fiercely, clinging to the memory of her name on his lips, his arms opening to her.

"More than you know. More than I thought I would. But . . ." Rozokov stared out at the park for a moment. "We are dangerous to each other."

She heard the ghosts of old sorrow in his voice again. "It's not just Armitage, is it? It's something older than that . . . whatever made you leave Europe." She saw his shoulders tense and he kept his gaze fixed on the dark heart of the park. After a moment, he began to speak.

"It was Paris, in 1865. Oh, if you could have seen it. The city was bright and terrible, with pleasures that went on all night, and pain that never slept. I met Jean-Pierre there. He was the only other vampire I had met since my transformation. We first saw each other at the opera, when both of us were hunting. At the intermission, we circled each other like wolves, determining threat, trying to establish dominance. In the end, he sent a bottle of wine, very old wine, to my box.

"We started with that truce, then as our paths crossed more often in the salons and clubs and mansions, we became acquaintances, then friends. Perhaps we were both lonelier than either of us had known. He was younger than I, and much wilder than I had been, even at my maddest. There was a fierce recklessness about him that was contagious. I loved him like a brother, like the mad, self-indulgent, fascinating younger brother I had not had. And had not been.

"We both had considerable wealth, though he spent his faster. I moved into his ancestral home where he had lived alone since his transformation twenty years earlier. In its gloom we would sleep away the day and rise at twilight to sample the rich tastes of the city.

"We were welcome in the best houses in Paris; the most beautiful women in that most beautiful city in the world sent us scented letters inviting us to their bedrooms. We went, sometimes together, and left them with dreams of ravishment and no memory of what we really took from them.

"We had lived like that for a year of nights when I met Roxanne after she tried to pass me false coin one night. She was seventeen, two years out of the countryside, which she'd fled to escape the attentions of a stepfather she despised and a future of babies and harvests and early old age. On the streets of Paris she had found only poverty, pimps and the choice between living on the city's dark side or not living at all.

"I would have killed her without a second thought. But she looked in my eyes and did not flinch and that stayed me long enough for her to start talking. She swore to serve me, to keep my house so none would suspect my nature, to be my sustenance if it would not harm her, inventing outrageous reasons why my existence would not be complete without her services.

"So in the end I took her back with me, after I had laid on her all the hypnotic control I could to prevent her from betraying us during the daylight hours. She was right, in many ways. Our existence was somewhat easier with her in attendance. She was quick-witted, possessed of a sly sense of humour, and, once washed, quite lovely. Very soon, we could not imagine our household without her.

"At first, neither of us touched her. Our morals fluctuated greatly, you see—we could be wicked beyond belief, guilty of almost every evil ascribed to our kind—but we would not stoop to abusing our servant. Then one night, after she had been with us for several months, we both returned from our separate ventures restless and unsatisfied. To our surprise, when we confessed our failures, Roxanne berated us angrily, saying that what we needed was right there, unless her blood was not aristocratic enough for us. We were startled, and then Jean-Pierre rose to leave. I suppose that he felt my claim on her was stronger. But she bade us both to stay, unless we thought it would harm her. So we knelt beside her chair and drank from her wrists for the first time.

"From that moment on, she was not just our servant, but our sister, our friend, our lover. And, in some strange way, our mother. She would call us her beasts, just as a mother calls her sons 'little animals.' She gave us what neither of us had ever expected to have again . . . a home and a family, however strange it might have been.

"The end came suddenly. I still do not know which of our many mad, reckless acts alerted them, or which one of our companions, friends, or victims suspected us. But one did. I had been roaming the city, too restless to go home, and when the golden sky finally drove me towards the house, it was already in flames. Jean-Pierre was doomed from the start. I saw Roxanne through one of the upper windows, her hair in flames, then she was gone.

"The next night, I set about gathering all my money and bought passage on the first ship leaving for the Americas. I came here and lived carefully, fed only from the poor and helpless who would not know me, killed no one, knew no one, loved no one, felt nothing to excess. And tried to forget."

She touched his hair. "It wasn't your fault."

"I was older, I was supposed to be wiser. I should have been more careful."

"That's why you say we are solitary creatures." He nodded and she let her hand slip down to caress his cheek, turn his head to face her. "But you were happy then. Were you happy here, all those years ago? Were you happy these last months?" He shook his head silently. "No. You were just trying to be safe. There's no happiness in safety. I learned that lesson in the asylum."

"There is no guarantee of happiness in risk, either. Jean-Pierre learned *that* lesson in Paris," Rozokov countered harshly.

"Then there's no guarantee of happiness in anything. So don't leave me again." She met his gaze, would not look away despite the sadness there.

"I make you no promises, understand that. We have an eternity in which to break them and the odds are far too great that we shall," he said at last and Ardeth felt a surge of triumph. What he said was true, of course, but eternity was still far in the future. "Now, I have lingered too long in the past. I found you to talk to you about our present dangers."

"Oh, are you ready to talk to me about that now?" At his startled glance, she grinned. "I've always suspected that you knew more about what was happening than you let on."

He told her about his encounter with Ambrose Dale almost one hundred years earlier. "After I fled from his house, I hid myself in my warehouse and set my body to the deep rest that can hold us for years. I did not know that the next day he suffered a stroke and the hunt for me ended. Until this year," he concluded. "And now we have not only Havendale to contend with . . . but your sister as well."

"Sara? What has she got to do with this?"

"She knows you are not dead. Did you not see her posters seeking you?" Ardeth shook her head. "Then perhaps I managed to find and destroy them all. But she will not stop looking for you, and sooner or later her attempts will alert Havendale."

"How do you know she won't stop?"

"I asked her to and she refused."

"You asked her to," Ardeth repeated incredulously.

"I went to her at your old apartment and told her to stop

searching, that you are in danger unless all believe you to be dead. She insisted that she would accept that only from you. She is very determined. You will have to speak to her, convince her that you are safe only as long as she abandons her search for you."

Anger surged through her suddenly, at her past dragged back into her present, at Sara for trying to bind her with ties best broken, at any connection between her wild, unpredictable younger sister and Rozokov. "I don't want to see her. I don't know why you did. Why is she looking for me anyway?" she demanded, to the night as much as to him.

"I suspect that it is because you are her sister," Rozokov suggested carefully.

"So? That never mattered to her before, except when she needed someplace to sleep. Why won't she just let me go? I won't see her."

"Ardeth, we are not invisible here, no matter how we try. I saw traces of you in the death of that young man in the old house. Someone else may have as well. And your sister, in all her misguided love for you, may provide them with the final clues. The price of her silence is proof from you. It may be the price of our survival. Surely it is not so great a thing to ask of yourself."

"If I do it, what then? Even if she stops, we can't go on trying to be invisible forever." In the heady heat of the last months that truth had been easy to ignore. In the reasoned chill of the first honest conversation she had had in those months it could not be. And now that it had been acknowledged, she had to *do* something about it. Rozokov's obsession with safety had always seemed a denial of the wild power she felt singing in her veins. It was Havendale that should be afraid of them, not the other way around.

"I know. But we need the time, the freedom, to deal with this threat on our terms, not theirs."

"All right. I'll see her. But then we take Havendale down."

"Then we take Havendale down," he agreed. "So now, if

you can bear to be seen with such a shabby creature as I, we should go and watch your sister sing."

Chapter 27

The Gold Rush was packed, the front room full of drinkers and pool players, all the tables at the back occupied by people waiting for Black Sun's second set. Ardeth and Rozokov worked their way through the crowd lingering by the front doors and moved through the smoky air towards the back room. As they found standing space in an unoccupied corner, Ardeth remembered the few times she had come here to watch the band. Then, she had hated the noise and the smoke and the long hours spent sitting at a table waiting for the show to finally start. Most of all she had hated the feeling that she was either invisible to the people around her—or awkwardly and noticeably out of place.

She could feel some of that emotion seeping hatefully back, making her feel suddenly exposed in the short black skirt, gawky and unsteady on her black heels. She clenched her fists in her pockets and willed herself to remember what she was.

Despite Rozokov's concerns, they elicited no second looks. With his hair combed back, he no longer looked like a half-crazed street person and in the darkness, the shabbiness of his clothes was unnoticeable. On the way to the club they had stopped at the row of street vendors and he had bought her, with surprising courtliness, a long, gold-shot white scarf to conceal her black hair. He insisted that she take off her sunglasses as well, to look less like the description Sara had publicized in her posters.

"Does she know we're here?" she asked at last, unwilling to say her sister's name, here in Sara's domain. Rozokov shook his head. "Wouldn't we be better to wait for her outside, at the back?"

"And look like vagrants or thieves? No, we are safer in here. She has not seen my face in the light and the drawings of you were . . ." he paused and looked at her with a curious air of realization, "harder, stylized."

"What am I going to tell her?" she asked after a moment, leaning close to keep her words to him only, over the roar of the music.

"Whatever you have to. Whatever words she will believe."

"Even the truth?"

"If necessary, even that." Ardeth closed her eyes and put her head against his shoulder. His coat smelled faintly of mothballs. *Whatever words she will believe . . . what words are those? What words would I believe?* When a voice announced the band, she still had no answer.

It was harder than she had thought it would be. Only Rozokov's arm around her shoulder kept her there through it, through Sara's voice calling her back to her past, through the familiar sight of her sister's black-clad, auburn-haired form moving on the stage. Though the crowd bouncing appreciatively on the dance floor would sometimes blot out the vision, nothing could block out the sound, twisting things in her heart she thought well-dead and deep-buried.

They played for an hour, from kinetic dance tunes to ballads full of eerie, ragged harmonies. Seen from the corner, from the distance she fought to maintain, Ardeth realized for the first time what gifts her sister really had, from the sly, sad, off-centre view of the world to the melodic sense that could find beauty in contrast and power in voices never quite in perfect tune.

Called back for the encore, the band began a slow, haunting tune, a delicate dirge. Sara stood still at the microphone, head bent to conceal her face as she began to sing.

> There's a girl walking down the street
> She walks just like you

And I call out your name again
Though I never mean to
She turns around and there's a stranger
Looking out of her eyes
And I look away when I realize
That the thing I was looking for
Has gone missing

Ardeth felt her heart contract. That's me, that's me she's singing about. The pain in Sara's voice was a clear, hard counterpoint to the lilting music, stilling the crowd to silence. Ardeth's hand went to her shoulder, closed hard over Rozokov's, clinging to his older, darker strength against a pain that was not nearly old enough to fight alone.

I used to laugh at you
'Cause you were always on time
You used to yell at me
'Cause I was always changing my mind
And I can't help but believe
That it really should have been me
Yeah everybody thought I'd be the one
To go missing
While I was out dancing on the ledge
You just fell right over the edge
And disappeared into the night
With all the missing

And no one will say it
but I see it in their eyes
You'll be just another Jane Doe
The dental chart identifies
As the better part of someone's heart
That went missing.

As the music died, Sara looked up for the first time and said with the weary resignation of repetition, "Ardy, come home." She left the stage as the applause began.

"Damn her," Ardeth whispered, closing her eyes against

the sudden lights, the noise of the crowd, wishing she could shut out the tangle of emotion twisting inside her.

"I did not know about the song," Rozokov said quietly. "I am sorry."

"I can't talk to her, not after that. Don't ask me to. Don't ever ask me to again." She pulled away from him and started to struggle through the crowd. He caught her arm and pulled her back.

"What is wrong?"

"It's none of your business," she flared, the black rage that had waited inside her since the asylum surging eagerly towards her heart.

"It is. You know it. Now tell me." His grip grew gentler. "My poor dark daughter, tell me."

"I ... It was mine, what happened to me was *mine*. It was the one terrible thing that made me different. And she has to try and take that too. She has to turn me into just another song, *her* song. I hate her for that." The words spilled out of her, incoherent and anguished, whispered fiercely against the music and the crowd. "But I never thought ... all this time I've never once thought that anyone would miss me. I never thought that it would hurt her."

"You never thought that she might love you at all," he finished for her. She nodded slowly, feeling the black fog in her mind receding with the echoes of Sara's lament, her anger fading to a dull sadness.

"And now it doesn't make any difference."

"To what we must do tonight, no."

"I'll talk to her. The truth is, I didn't miss her yesterday, and I probably won't miss her tomorrow. Let's just make our peace tonight and then it really will be over. But," her voice faltered, "not yet." He nodded and let her lean against him in the dark corner, and did not protest when she put her sunglasses back on.

A half an hour later, they were in the back alley behind the club, concealed in the shadows of the Dumpster. "She might have left," Ardeth said, half-hoping it was true.

"She does not usually leave so early."

"How do you know that?"

"I have watched once or twice, to be sure." The back door of the club creaked suddenly, then swung open. A dark figure emerged and dashed down the alley. It hovered on the sidewalk for a moment, peering up and down the street, then the man turned and walked slowly back towards the door. He had almost reached it when he froze.

"Who's there?" Ardeth held her breath unconsciously. "I know there's someone there." He took an uneasy step towards the Dumpster. "Ardeth? Are you there?" asked the unfamiliar voice. She looked at Rozokov in surprise, found no other conclusion in his eyes than the one she had already reached. She stepped out of the shadows, Rozokov behind her.

"You're Ardeth?"

"Yes. How did you know?"

"Sara's been looking for you. You're just in time," he said, voice hard and bitter. "Someone just kidnapped her—and you're the ransom."

He introduced himself and explained what had happened. Sara had left the stage as usual, gone alone to her dressing room. Mickey had been playing pool in the front part of the club, waiting for her, when the bartender had received a call concerning Sara's missing sister. He had passed it over to Mickey, and over the din of the bar, a cold voice had told him that they had taken Sara.

" 'You tell Ardeth Alexander—and the monster too—that we want both of them. Remind Alexander that we have uses for her sister. For a while,' " Mickey recited. "I tried to tell the bastard I had no idea where you were but he didn't seem to believe me. When I went backstage Sara was gone and I found this," he held up a shiny object, "right where they said I would in her dressing room." Ardeth recognized the band of silver as one of the many rings Sara habitually wore on every finger. She almost put out her hand to take it but Mickey's fingers had clenched possessively over the ring before she could move. Their eyes met. I know him, Ardeth realized suddenly, though she could not remember where or when they had met. But even that knowledge did not explain the cold anger she saw in his eyes.

"How are you—or we—to contact them?" Rozokov asked. Mickey held out a bar napkin with a phone number scrawled on it.

"Call any time, day or night, the man said." His voice was razor-edged under the flippancy. "If she's Ardeth, does that make you the monster?"

"It is not the first time I have been called that," Rozokov replied with a faint smile. "I would prefer you judge that for yourself."

"Can we call from the club without anyone seeing us?" Ardeth asked, the first thing she had said since Mickey's story began. His voice, quoting the kidnappers, echoed in her mind. Tell Alexander that we have uses for her sister . . . They must mean the pornographic movies, she thought. Not the other ones. Those died with Roias. They *must* have died with Roias.

"Ardeth." Rozokov's voice caught her attention, dragged her from the terrifying memory of Suzy and her naked, blood-smeared body on the altar of her death. "It is I they want, I they have always wanted, from the time I began my sleep to the time they woke me up. I will go."

"They know about me," she pointed out. "They want both of us. Do you think they'd let one of us escape after what happened at the asylum?" She turned to face him, caught the fraying lapels of his coat in her hands. "And they're right. No matter what they did, no matter how deep they buried you, I'd find you. And I'd kill them all this time."

"Shall I let you be like Jean-Pierre after all? Let you burn for my mistakes?"

"We won't burn," she said with all the certainty her black rage, coiling like waiting serpents in her heart, could give her. "And if we do, they'll burn with us."

"This battle of the martyrs is very touching, but neither of you has given me any reason not to call that damn number myself and turn you both in," Mickey interrupted. "If you've got one, you'd better give it quickly." Angrily,

Ardeth turned back to him and she saw his face pale for one moment as he faced the fury flaring like flames behind her eyes.

Rozokov's chuckle caught her and drew her gaze back to him. "That is a very sensible question. Martyrdom has never been one of my ambitions. I appreciate the reminder of that. As for your answer, when they have what they want, they will undoubtedly kill Sara anyway," he concluded reasonably. "Her best hope is also ours. Let Ardeth call and discover their terms. Then we can decide how best to proceed." Mickey looked at them for a moment, then nodded.

"There's a phone at the back of the kitchen. With any luck nobody will see us and start asking questions."

The phone rang twice, then a man's voice answered.

"This is Ardeth Alexander." She said nothing else, afraid of making a mistake that would doom Sara, determined not to let her voice betray any of that fear, or her anger.

"So soon?" the voice asked mockingly. "And is the . . . Rozokov . . . with you?"

"No. I don't know where he is," she lied, to see if she would be believed.

"In that case, we have nothing to talk about."

"I really don't know where he is. Whatever you wanted from him, I can give you."

"And I can end up like Roias, right? No. The price includes both of you. You find him and be where I tell you, or I'll let Roias's successor have your sister. Do you understand?"

Ardeth closed her eyes in resignation. "Yes. I'll try to find him. Tell me where you want us to be."

He gave her a location and time. She repeated them to the dead air, then hung up the telephone and turned to face Rozokov and Mickey. "He wants us both at the railway lands at 5:00. There'll be a van to pick us up."

"What about Sara?" Mickey demanded.

"He says they'll let her go there."

"Do you believe him?" Ardeth looked at him squarely,

facing the mysterious dislike in his eyes. In the aftermath of the call, she felt terribly weary.

"No. Whoever these men are, they've already killed at least two innocent people on the faint chance that they could know something. They won't let Sara go."

"Then what the fuck are we going to do?" The words came out in a tight whisper.

"We are going to leave here, go someplace private to think. You will say nothing to anyone, not the police, not Sara's friends. Go home to her apartment, if you can, and wait," Rozokov ordered him. Ardeth heard the threads of hypnotic persuasion in his voice and for a moment Mickey started to nod in agreement. Then he shuddered slightly and stepped away from them.

"No. How do I know you won't just leave town and let them kill her? And if they do let Sara go, then somebody has to be there to get her. Look, I don't give a fuck what these people want with you. I don't care who or what you really are. I just want Sara back."

"If you insist then," Rozokov said and Ardeth stared at him in surprise. This was the last thing they needed, she thought in disgust, to be saddled with this angry, bitter young man who seemed to have hated her on first sight. "But you will ask no questions and when we are decided on a course of action, you will make no protests." The grey gaze caught the younger man's, held it still under the bright overhead lights. "I can make you leave. I can make you forget all you have seen and done tonight. I leave you your freedom and your will on sufferance. Do not forget that."

"So you say," Mickey retorted with a bravado that hung like a lie in the air between them. Rozokov smiled suddenly, with humour as genuine as his threats had been.

"So I do. Now, you must . . ."

"Wait," Ardeth broke in. "Sara's stuff, her purse . . . are they in her dressing room?"

"Yeah, I think so," Mickey answered.

"You have to get them then . . . or else Pete and the others will get suspicious."

"Right, right," he agreed, then looked at her sharply. "So

you can disappear into the night? Nice try, but I'm not fall-ing for it."

"Ardeth is not deceiving you," Rozokov said.

"Yeah? Then one of you come with me."

"And how will you explain me?"

"I don't know. You're my second-cousin twice removed, just in from Timiskaming or something. Good enough?" They stared at each other for a moment, then Rozokov shrugged and glanced at Ardeth.

"We will be in the alley in a few moments," he promised and let Mickey lead him away into the labyrinthine corri-dors of the club. Ardeth watched them go, then hurried back to the alley, to wait fidgeting in the shadow of the Dumpster as each moment they were gone dragged by with agonizing slowness.

At last, the back door opened and they emerged, Mickey carrying Sara's black duffel bag over his shoulder. "Did anyone see you?"

"Yeah, Steve was looking for her. I said she wasn't feel-ing well and had gone out to get a cab home."

"Did he believe you?" She saw his lips tighten around a sharp retort, then Rozokov intervened.

"Yes, he did. Now take us someplace where we can dis-cuss this problem with some privacy."

Mickey led them out of the club by the alley entrance and down the quiet backstreets. As they walked, Ardeth was aware of the weight of his occasional glances. Finally, waiting on a street corner, he said suddenly, "So, what did you do to Rick anyway?"

"Rick?" she repeated in confusion. The name was famil-iar, as Mickey's face had been, but the memory could not surface through her worry about Sara.

"You know, the street musician you picked up a few weeks ago. The one who stepped in front of a cab and died. What did you give him?"

"I didn't give him anything," she protested, then remem-bered. "You were the other guitarist, weren't you?"

"Yeah, the one you didn't pick. Not like lucky Rick. Only he wasn't so lucky, was he? So," Mickey continued,

turning to watch her as they crossed the street, Rozokov a
silent presence behind her, "what did you do to him?"

"I fucked him in the alley," she flared back. "Are you
suggesting that *I* killed him? I'm sorry about his death—but
I wasn't responsible." She said the words vehemently, remembering the sight of the body flung across the street, the
terrible thud as it hit the curb. It had not been her fault. She
had killed the boy in the alley, and the others, but not Rick.
Not Rick.

"Yeah, right. Just like you're not responsible for Sara either. She was better off thinking you were dead." His cynical voice cut her, twisted at her heart, and suddenly
revealed the weapon she could wield back at him.

"And how did she know I wasn't? The only way she
could have known was if someone who'd seen me told her.
Do you suppose that's what happened?" she asked casually.
"That must have started her looking for me. And if she
hadn't started looking for me, none of this would have happened. So it would seem to me that whoever told her is the
one who is really responsible for what's happened to her."

He rounded on her suddenly, and might have struck her
except for the hand that caught his arm. Rozokov moved
between them. "Stop it, children," he said sharply, still
holding Mickey's arm. "Let it be. You will not save her by
blaming each other for her danger."

Mickey jerked his arm, trying to free it, and his eyes
widened when he found he could not move. Rozokov let
him go and he stood, rubbing his arm and wincing. "All
right," he muttered at last and turned to lead them down the
street. Ardeth stood still, watching him go, then looked at
Rozokov.

"I didn't kill his friend," she said slowly.

"That is between you and your conscience, Ardeth. Not
between us."

"I thought we didn't have consciences."

"Things would be much simpler that way, I admit. But
all that died in the asylum was your body. Anything else
that seems missing now, you yourself have buried." His
voice was gentle but the words seemed to set fire to the

guilt and remorse she had struggled to reduce to ashes in her heart. "But this is not the time, nor the place, for this. Whatever has given you the strength to survive these last months, hold on to it now. We will have need of it."

In the silence, a voice called to them and Ardeth turned away gratefully. It was easier to face the heat of Mickey's hatred than the cold, implacable intimations of morality in Rozokov's words.

Chapter 28

The freight elevator clanged and clattered, echoing in the post-midnight silence of the old warehouse. Mickey watched the ancient pointer creep in its slow semicircle towards the Roman numeral that signalled his floor. Anything was better than looking at the two silent figures who shared the dimly lit elevator with him.

All this time, he had wondered what he would say if Ardeth really did reappear. He knew the questions had to be asked, even if he never mentioned them again to Sara. But somehow he had always imagined that the confrontation would come after the sisters had made peace, as Ardeth was conveniently exiting the scene again, so that whatever truth he discovered would leave with her and not hang around to mess up his relationship with Sara.

Your relationship with Sara, his mind mocked him. What relationship? One kiss, one moment when you thought she might have wanted you to stay. Probably the only reason she let you hang around at all was the lure of her missing sister that you dangled in front of her. But he didn't believe that, not in his heart.

And now she was gone. Dragged into God knows what

horror and all because of her sister. He dared one flickering glance at Ardeth. She was watching the floor pointer as well, face uptilted so that the faint light illuminated her features. The strangeness he had sensed on the street was still there, though more elusive, as if she had gotten better at hiding it. But he remembered seeing her eyes spark red in the alley and something in his gut tightened. He couldn't reconcile that memory with Sara's story of the sister who had scheduled her whole life, who had lived in that neat, booklined apartment, who had made a clumsy papier mâché necklace. The images remained separate, refusing to overlap into a coherent picture. He tried to imagine what might have happened in the last few months to shatter the personality Sara had thought was carved in stone and create this new, utterly alien woman.

Remind Alexander that we have uses for her sister, the cold voice had said. Mickey took a sharp breath and tried not to think about what that could have meant. Or what might happen to Sara's soul under the pressure of those mysterious threats. The elevator shuddered to a halt, and, grateful for the chance to move again, he pulled open the metal mesh door.

The lights in his apartment were too bright, banks of overheads that suited the office this had once been. In the harsh light, the large single room and its contents looked stark and shabby. Mickey had a moment of dislocation, seeing the room through a stranger's eyes: tangle of tape recorders and guitars, faded sheets on the unmade futon, neon graffiti scrawl of a former tenant covering one wall and the ancient, noisy refrigerator. He tried not to look at the far corner, where Rick's paraphernalia had once been.

"Well, this is it. Home Sweet Home," he said, hoping the sharp edge of sarcasm in his voice hid his sudden disorientation. "Have a seat, have a beer, make yourselves at home." He sat down on the unmade bed and instantly wished he hadn't, as it forced him to look up at them.

After a moment, Ardeth sat down on the armchair in the corner. Rozokov settled onto the stool Mickey normally sat on to record. There was a long silence. "All right, what are we going to do?" he asked, when he could stand it no longer.

"Ardeth will go to the meeting and you and I will follow her," the grey-haired man said.

"They said they wanted both of you," Mickey reminded him. "What if they kill Sara because only one of you shows up?"

"Sara is the weapon they will hold over Ardeth to ensure her co-operation. Ardeth is the weapon they will seek to use against me. They cannot afford to jeopardize either of them."

"Even if they believe me," Ardeth interrupted, "they'll be waiting for you to try something. They'll have guards, maybe more of those machines."

"Of course. But they will not be expecting Mr. Edmunds here. They are counting on the fact that they are taking you near dawn and that I will be helpless to move about during the day. With you," he bowed slightly in Mickey's direction, "as my navigator, my eyes and ears, there is no reason we cannot follow them during the daylight. I will not be able to attack until night, it is true, but we will have had time to observe them and formulate a viable plan by then. We must assume they will not be expecting us to enlist any aid."

"So I just let them take me." Her voice was so strained that Mickey looked at her sharply, surprised out of the questions swirling in his mind by the pain and fear he could hear for the first time. Maybe her strangeness, the sleek confidence suggested by the dark clothes, was an illusion after all. Maybe the sunglasses were to hide more than the red fire in her eyes.

"You must. And, unless your survival depends on it, you must not let them know our true strength. They are still guessing about that, they still have only the old myths to guide them." That brought the questions back. There was some subtext here he couldn't grasp, something that their conversations hinted at that slipped with eel-like ease from his fingers every time he thought he understood. Ardeth was nodding slowly, but her hands held her elbows against her body, and her knuckles were white.

"This is all sounding very good so far, but I have a bit of bad news. I don't have a car so I'm not sure how you expect to follow these guys. I don't think they'll be taking public transit," Mickey pointed out, relieved to find some realistic objection to lend some solidity to this strange, slippery conversation. Rozokov looked at him again, the odd, pale eyes meeting his. In the bright light, he realized how shabby the older man's clothes were, worn castoffs not even acceptable to the Salvation Army any more. The contrast between the clothes and the man's quiet confidence, the angular aristocratic lines of his face, was suddenly clear and bewildering. "The monster," the kidnapper had called him. Mickey remembered the hard, unbreakable grip on his arm and the lulling persuasive voice. "I don't care who or what you are," he had declared. *What* you are. . . . He shivered but would not let his gaze drop.

"Have you no friends who could be persuaded to lend theirs? Can we rent one at this hour?" Mickey checked his watch. It was 3:30. Mitchell was probably home, might be convinced to part with his old van if they made it worth his while.

"You have any money?"

"Some. How much will it take?"

"Give me fifty bucks and I'll be back in a few minutes." Rozokov hunted in the interior pockets of his battered coat for a few moments, then handed Mickey three twenties.

Mitchell was just awake enough to be angry when he finally staggered to the door of his apartment two floors below. Mollified somewhat by the sixty dollars and the promise of no more disturbances, he gave Mickey the keys and said, "Have it back by tomorrow night."

"Sure, no problem," Mickey promised, knowing it might be a lie. He'd have to get another fifty off Rozokov to placate Mitchell later. Later, he thought in sudden giddy humour. After you've rescued Sara, disposed of the mysterious bad guys and figured out who and what the hell

Ardeth and the old man are. If you manage to do all of that without ending up dead or in jail. Yeah, later.

They were still back in his apartment, waiting, when he returned. "All right, I've got a van. But before I drive it anywhere, you'd better tell me what is really going on."

"Did I not say no questions?" Rozokov said and the quiet voice did not conceal the ominous undertone there.

"That's right, you did. But I didn't agree to it. And now you need me."

"What difference does it make to you?" Ardeth demanded, rising from the chair. "You say you just want Sara back. If that's true, then what difference does it make if we tell you or not?"

"*You* say you want her back too—after three months of letting her mourn for you. Maybe I'd be more inclined to believe you if I knew what happened to you, what's happening right now."

"I will tell you what you need to know. After we have gone to meet the kidnappers." Mickey opened his mouth to argue then met the cold gaze and decided against it.

"Good enough. What do we need besides the car?" The list seemed strange, but he found it all—two blankets, an old fedora he no longer wore and a pair of his sunglasses. "Shouldn't we have some guns or something?" Mickey asked, watching Rozokov tuck the sunglasses and fedora into the capacious inner pockets of his coat.

"Can you obtain some for us?" Rozokov inquired curiously and Mickey was forced to shake his head.

"No. Not at this hour in the morning." What I really wanted to hear was that we wouldn't need them, he thought with regret. "Well, come on. If we want to get there before they do, we'd better go."

The instructions had been explicit. Ardeth and Rozokov were to be waiting outside an abandoned one-storey building that sat alone in the middle of the railway lands. The lands themselves lay in a strip of rusting steel and stubby grass between the raised highways and office towers of the city core, awaiting redevelopment. In the daylight they'd be visible to a thousand passersby, but in the pre-dawn darkness only a trucker or two might notice movement in the empty yards.

The nearest place to hide the van was half a mile away, in the shadow of an overpass. Mickey had to drive without lights through an empty field to reach its sheltering darkness. He surprised himself by praying under his breath the whole way. Whichever god he was praying to didn't seem to mind the blasphemies he threw in for good measure; they made it to the overpass without losing a tire.

"We're here," he said, turning to look at the two figures crouched in the back of the van. "It's almost 5:00."

"I'd better go," Ardeth said, voice tight. Rozokov reached out to touch her hair and Mickey turned away, trying not to listen to their voices or watch them in the rearview mirror.

"Remember the asylum," the man whispered, grey head bending close to hers. "We survived. We will survive this." Mickey heard her draw a slow, ragged breath.

"They'll burn. And we'll be free."

"Yes, my beloved, my salvation, we'll be free." In the mirror he saw them kiss, a slow, lingering caress that made something in his heart catch as he dropped his eyes. Then the panel door slid open and she was gone, walking across the rusting tracks towards the building.

"She'll be OK. They'll both be OK," Mickey said awkwardly into the silence. There was a rustle of movement as Rozokov moved into the front seat beside him. He sat still for a moment, watching the dark figure moving away from them.

"You wanted to know what is happening," he said at last and Mickey nodded, then said "yes" when the man did not take his eyes from the retreating figure. "I know only part of the explanation and much of that I have only guessed. But here is what you need to know. She and I are . . . afflicted . . . with a condition that makes it difficult for us to move about in daylight. This same condition can also mean a longer lifespan. It appears that someone has discovered our existence and sees some profit in exploiting it. They have been pursuing me for a long time now."

Mickey sat still for a moment, absorbing the words. The man sounded sincere but . . . he remembered the persuasive power of that voice. "Wait a minute. Ardeth didn't always have this . . . this condition or whatever you call it. Sara would have mentioned it."

"That is true. She was afflicted because of me."

"Are you saying it's communicable?"

"Only under *very* specific circumstances. You certainly cannot be infected by sitting here with me." Rozokov's voice held a hint of humour. Mickey looked hard at him for a moment, at the grey hair and the faint lines around his eyes and mouth.

"If this condition means you live longer, you could make a fortune on it yourself. Lots of people would consider staying out of the sun a small price to pay."

"It has other prices." Rozokov stiffened suddenly and gestured towards the dark bulk of the rendezvous point. Mickey heard the faint grumble of an engine and saw a dark van jolting its way towards the building. The white banner of her scarf was all that was visible at this distance. The van rolled to a stop, between their vantage point and the waiting woman. It paused for a moment, then they heard the engine being gunned and it turned and moved, more quickly this time, back the way it had come. Ardeth was gone.

Mickey reached for the keys to start the van but Rozokov stopped him. "No. Not yet."

"We'll lose them."

"No. We do not need to see them to follow and we will be too conspicuous on the streets at this hour."

"Don't need to see them? Then how will we find them?"

"An advantage of my condition. I can find her wherever she goes." Mickey saw the sideways gleam of the man's smile. "Blood calls to blood, as they say."

"Has this 'condition' of yours got a name?"

"Back in the old days, they called those who suffered from it vampires," Rozokov replied, taking out the fedora and settling it over his pale hair. "You may start the van now."

"And what do they call them now?" Mickey asked, as he began backing out from under the overpass.

"The same thing, I would imagine."

Mickey glanced over, expecting to see the man smiling at his own joke. But Rozokov's mouth was still and straight, and if there was any amusement in his eyes, it was safely hidden behind the blind, black stare of the sunglasses.

Chapter 29

"They're bringing the woman in now," Elder reported. Lisa Takara nodded and took another sip of her coffee. They were all drinking it, even Parkinson, who normally disdained anything but decaffeinated. They had been dragged out of their beds at her summons; she'd been dragged out of hers by Rooke's voice on the telephone . . . "Get up and get ready. We're bringing them in in one hour."

They didn't need an hour's notice, of course. The laboratory had been functioning for close to two months. Two months in which they had had nothing to do but test and re-test equipment, read old books full of superstition, and try not to learn too much about each other. Even the move from the first anonymous location to this equally anonymous one was only a minor diversion. They had no more freedom here, in this place that was obviously a house, than they had had in the converted warehouse.

Conversations during the long, dull days were restricted to who had studied what with whom and the latest theories in their related fields. No one mentioned families or life outside the confines of the laboratory they were not allowed to leave. No one discussed the "terms" of their contracts and what combination of money, blackmail and coercion had brought them there.

Lisa had her own theories. Martinez, the neurologist, was probably in it for the money, though she was astounded that he believed he would live to collect it. Elder, the aging bacteriologist, was fighting a severe alcohol dependency; it was either blackmail or lack of better opportunities in his case. Parkinson's pinched face and tired eyes convinced Lisa that it must be threats that had drawn her into the web. She had once seen the other woman hiding a photograph of a young boy in her room. Hanick, the hematologist, watched the sports station in their common room almost constantly and Lisa suspected he must have had gambling debts that had finally been called in.

In the case of Goodman, the team leader, the holds had not been strong enough. After three weeks, he'd escaped at the end of a rope wrapped around his neck. Lisa didn't like speculating about *that*. Working with a leading immunologist like Goodman had been one of the few things that could have made this "project" endurable. And his death had left her, the secondary expert, in reluctant charge.

And then there was her own motive. Was it any more or less believable than the tales she spun for the others? She tried not to think about it, but during the long hours of idleness, her mind would return and worry at it, as if it were a formula that would not make sense or a secret cell that repeated viewing would reveal. But there was no mystery to it—only a terrible logic.

If Hanick had debts, then so did she. They were her father's debts, true enough, incurred forty years ago in another land, but they were just as entangling. She had not known any of it until three months ago, when her father summoned her to her brother's house where he now lived. She had gone expecting only to hear another of his pleas for her to get married, or the increasingly rambling complaints of an old man against the perfidy of ungrateful sons and upstart wives.

Instead, her father was sitting in his upstairs room, dressed in a suit and tie, clinging to the frail dignity she had forgotten he possessed. Seated beside him was a middle-aged man with smooth, impassive features and cold eyes.

"This is Mr. Moro," said her father.. After pleasantries, she served the tea he had set out, and she waited, wondering what her father intended. Not an arranged marriage, surely not that. The cold black eyes that watched her were covetous but not, she decided, of her body. Finally, after rituals of tea and conversation were observed, her father spoke.

"In Japan, after the war, I was greatly assisted by Mr. Moro's esteemed organization. Now I have an opportunity to repay that debt."

"How?" Her father deferred to Mr. Moro.

"An organization with which we have done business has inquired after the services of a qualified and experienced immunologist for a confidential research project. Such are rare. If you were to consent to provide such services, we would be most obliged."

"What sort of research?" He shrugged and spread his hands. His shirt sleeve slipped downward to reveal the tattoo around his wrist. As she was sure he had intended it to. "What if I am unable to participate?" she asked carefully.

"A debt unpaid is a great burden. It would no doubt weigh heavily on your father's heart were he to die with such a favour still owing. It would bring great dishonour to his family. And perhaps great misfortune as well."

She thought briefly of rebellion, of police, of flight. But only briefly.

"I could not allow that," she said at last. There were more ritual pleasantries, then polite mentionings of the time, and Mr. Moro's graceful offer to escort her to her car. She was careful not to look at her father, so that he could not see the anger in her eyes, or she the sorrow in his.

Mr. Moro's car waited by the curb. She saw the shadowy shape of a driver behind the smoked glass. "Here is the number of the man you must contact. He will expect your call tonight." He spoke in English, handing her a card that she put away without looking.

"You are yakuza," she said and he did not reply, as if insulted by her stating of the obvious.

"The other number on the card is for one of our men. You will inform him of the progress of your work. If our associates have something of value, we want it." There was no politeness in his voice now. "You do not work for them, Dr. Takara, you work for us. Your father's debt is to us." She stood at the end of the driveway, watching the dark sedan pull away from the curb and vanish down the street. When she looked back at the house, she thought she saw her father's face in the window, watching her, but when she blinked, it was gone.

So here she was, bound by her father's forty-year-old debt to the yakuza, forced to take an "emergency leave" from her research position at the university and trapped for two months in the sterile, windowless lab. She had not been able to call the second number. She did not know what she would say even if she could. If she told them the truth, they would most likely not believe her. And if they did, that might be even worse. The yakuza would have the same uses for the vampires—and the scientists—that Rooke did.

She heard a door slam, somewhere down one of the long white hallways. "It's them," Martinez said unnecessarily. Lisa put down her coffee cup and joined the others, gazes fixed on the doorway.

Now we see. Now we see if these old bogeymen we've been brought here to study are real—or just a figment of some mad imagination. I hope they're real, even if it breaks every rule of science and logic and reason. I don't want to be the one to discover they aren't. I don't want to die for someone else's fantasy.

The door opened.

The cold-eyed lab guards came in first, then the dark-haired, dark-clad woman, and then Rooke. She's so young, Lisa thought involuntarily. Her face was pale beneath the dark hair and the odd, sharp angle of her shoulders was explained by the elbow-to-wrist metal and leather restraints. There was an odd clatter as she moved and Lisa realized they had fastened steel fetters around her ankles. They looked shockingly shiny against the black stockings and shoes.

Rooke pushed her forward, holding the ultrasound at her back. "Dr. Takara, she's all yours." His voice was mocking, implying an authority she did not have. He was watching her, waiting to see how she reacted, if she recalled the instructions they had been given. She looked at the other scientists, but they were all watching the still figure flanked by the guards.

"All right, get the subject into the chair. We have thirty minutes till dawn and I want full samples done by then." There was a moment of silence, then Martinez and Hanick moved forward to take the woman's arms. Rooke handed the ultrasound to one of the guards. Lisa met his gaze for a moment. I remembered it all, Mr. Rooke. Do not call the subject by name, do not speak to her, observe full security precautions. And always remember that you're watching me. Always. She turned towards the examination chair, making every line of her back a cold dismissal.

She watched as Martinez and Hanick undid the arm restraints and, still holding on to her arms, eased the woman into the chair. It had been an ordinary dental chair until it had been fitted with metal wrist and ankle restraints. It had looked like some ludicrous torture device the first time she had seen it, and her mind and her heart rebelled at putting anyone in it. Not even the films Rooke had forced them to watch had changed that.

He had done that the day he finally revealed what the nature of their research was. Or rather, he had used the film to reveal that nature, taking her alone into the video control room and fast-forwarding through the entire first hour of the film before he let the final moments run at regular speed. Then he had shown the tape of the film studio a week later, watching her face as the camera lingered over the dead bodies sprawled about the cavernous space. He had hoped to shock her, to frighten, and he had. The films, if they were genuine, were testaments to the physical existence and violent power of the creatures she was to study. But the image that lingered with her was not that of the sharp-toothed monster or the broken bodies but of the man in the expensive business suit fast-forwarding through the sadistic prelude to the murder. The monster he had revealed, she thought later, was perhaps not the one he had meant her to see.

The young woman did not resist as they strapped her into the chair. Lisa pulled on the rubber gloves as Elder pushed up the sleeve of the woman's jacket and wrapped the tourniquet above her elbow. Dark hazel eyes focused for a moment on the needle in Lisa's hand then flickered away. Lisa felt the flinch the woman hid. She's afraid of needles, she thought suddenly. Not the fear of a Frankenstein monster for fire or of tuxedoed celluloid vampires for crucifixes, but the common, human fear of needles.

As she rubbed alcohol onto the delicate, trapped inner arm, Lisa almost said, "It's all right, it'll be over in a minute." Remembering Rooke, she kept quiet as she slid the needle into the blue vein and snapped vial after vial into the cylinder. The blood looked human. Lisa stepped back to let Parkinson start to collect the skin samples.

They were moving smoothly, grateful for the chance to act, to sublimate their fears into the skills they knew so well. Hanick took the blood samples from her and began labelling them, separating them for the tests he wanted to run. Martinez was bringing around the specially designed EEG machines, beginning to attach the spidery wires and pads to the still figure in the chair. Elder went through the rituals of measuring pulse rate, blood pressure, the contraction of the pupils, the twitch of reflexes in the black-sheathed legs.

Sometime during the initial examination, Rooke vanished, leaving the silent guards beside the door as a reminder of his presence. The team ignored them and Lisa felt the white-hot ache between her shoulder blades ease, freed from the weight of Rooke's gaze.

They had completed the first set of samples by the time sunrise (according to the chart posted on the wall; they had no visual clues to follow) arrived. The EEG whirred on, needles scratching out the mysterious rhythm of the subject's thoughts. The woman's half-closed eyes slid shut, the

scratching slowed and settled until Martinez reached out
and switched off the machine. "She's out," he confirmed.
"Should we keep going?"

"Let's stick to the plan. We've enough baseline indica-
tors to keep us busy today." Lisa turned to the guards. "You
can take her now." They did, one hoisting her over his
shoulder, the other holding the ultrasound as they carried
her into the narrow steel-walled observation cell that made
up one side of the laboratory.

As they moved, a streak of white slid from her pocket to
coil limply on the floor. Lisa leaned over to pick up the
scarf, the sheer silk running through her fingers in a fragile
white stream.

She put it in her pocket, then turned back to the lab tables where the anonymous woman's blood and skin and
brain patterns waited to be sampled, sliced and spread naked beneath the remorseless eye of science.

Chapter 30

Ardeth swam up from the warm, comfortable darkness of
sleep and surfaced into painful, fluorescent-lit reality. She
lay still, eyes closed against the almost palpable weight of
the light, testing the world around her. Far off, at the edges
of her awareness, she could feel Rozokov's presence, drifting like a persistent memory along the edges of her mind.

Falling back into her body, she became aware that she
lay under a blanket. Her shoes had been taken off. She
could feel the faint pressure of the bandage they had put
over her vein. At the memory of the needle sliding into her
skin, the silent indignities of examination, she felt the black
anger begin to swell up inside her. She clamped down on

it, but let it linger, knowing that it masked the paralyzing fear she had known in the asylum.

She stirred beneath the sheets, shifting one arm to cover her face as she slitted her eyes open and looked around. This cell was as white as the previous one had been dark; as modern as the other had been old. But the taste of the place was the same, she thought—stale sweat, urine and the copper bite of fear.

There was someone in the narrow room with her. A dark figure lay stretched along the other bed, one knee crooked up against the other raised leg, foot twitching rhythmically while the hands tapped a silent accompaniment on the sheets.

Ardeth closed her eyes for a moment. You knew this would come, she thought, angry at the sudden fear that suffused her relief. Be grateful she's safe, worry about what you'll tell her later.

She forced her eyes open, then sat up. On the other bed, Sara echoed the movement, coming up off the mattress in a spurt of pent-up energy. She stopped just as suddenly, halfway between their two cots, as if she had run into an invisible wall. "Well. You're awake. I thought whatever they gave you would never wear off."

"Whatever they gave me . . ." Ardeth echoed in momentary bewilderment.

"The drug that made you sleep like that. I saw the bandage over the needle mark. Are you all right?"

"I'm fine. How about you? Did they hurt you?" Ardeth asked awkwardly, noticing suddenly the bruise on her sister's left cheekbone and the ripped shoulder of her T-shirt. Though of course, she thought distantly, the rip might have been intentional.

"Not as much as I hurt them, I hope," Sara replied with a brief smile. She seemed to notice that she was still standing and sat back down on the edge of her bed. "They sent a message that you were waiting for me in the alley. When I went out, they jumped me."

"I was at the club. I must have just missed you."

"How did you . . ." She stopped, ran her hand through her coppery hair, then started again, "What happened?"

"They called the club and talked to your friend Mickey. He told me what they wanted."

"You." Ardeth nodded slowly, aware that with each awkward word they were edging closer and closer to the questions she dreaded.

"I'm sorry, Sara. This never should have involved you."

"I was right though. You weren't dead."

Ardeth took a breath and glanced around the room, to keep her eyes from Sara's. She saw the camera mounted over the door, angled to encompass both of them in its dark lens, and noticed the long mirror on the wall over Sara's bed, a window masquerading as a reflection. *What will you tell her?* they seemed to ask. *What will you tell me?*

"I *am* dead."

"Don't give me that symbolic bullshit," Sara said, the formal courtesy between them shattering with the abrupt obscenity.

"I died of loss of blood on April 8th. At least, I think it was the 8th. I lost track of the days. I was buried in the woods somewhere northeast of the city. There were four or five other women buried there too." The words came out easily, as if they had been waiting to be said. *I've wanted someone to know,* she realized. *All along, I've wanted to tell someone, just once.*

"Ardeth." There was mingled anger and pleading in her voice.

"I'd better tell it from the beginning, or you'll never understand. It all started the night of Peter's party, the night you were waiting for me to come home." It was easy at first, a clear, concise storyline that led from Tony to Conrad to her own descent into the asylum dungeon. There, the story started to flounder on the rocks of words that belonged to the alien world of fiction and fantasy. "They had taken me there rather than kill me immediately because they needed me. There was another captive, someone they had to keep alive. The easiest way to do that was with my blood."

"Your blood? You mean they took your blood and gave this person a transfusion?"

"No. I mean they made me put my arm into his cell and he drank it." Ardeth was grateful for the sudden, shocked silence. It gave her time to think. She couldn't tell the whole truth, not with the silent witness crouched over the doorway, but she *needed* Sara to know it. To know the essence of what had happened to her.

Sara opened her mouth, closed it again, and waited. Ardeth told her about the snuff film and the rape attempt by Peterson. She told her about her own fears, her fruitless plans of escape, the final realization of her inevitable death. She did not say Rozokov's name or the word "vampire." "I went too close to his cell. I may have done it on purpose, I don't really know. He'd known all along that there was only one way to escape. I couldn't stop him. I didn't even want to. I let him make me drink his blood and then he drained away mine." The lie was hard, remembering the true nature of the night, and the way her life had slid from her on a path made warm and slippery by pleasure.

"They buried me in the woods where they buried the other women. But the next night I woke up and went back to the asylum. We killed them all. We stole a car and came to the city. Then he left me." *That* was the truth and for a moment the loneliness flared up in her heart, as sharp and desolate as it had been that night.

"Ardeth . . . I . . . What did you do then? Why didn't you come home?"

"Come home? To what? I went to my apartment but it was no more than a hotel room to me. And I had to hide from Havendale. As long as they thought I was buried, I was safe."

"You could have come to me."

"And said what? 'Hi, sis, I've come home. By the way, have any B positive blood in the fridge?' I'm a vampire, Sara."

"You really believe this, don't you?" There was weary wonder in Sara's voice. Anger sparked along Ardeth's taut nerves, flamed into life.

"You're right. I can't be a vampire. I must be crazy. Poor, pathetic Ardeth runs off and thinks she's a vampire. It's the quiet types, you know, they always crack," Ardeth said with sarcastic flamboyance. "Or maybe it was pre-thesis trauma. Maybe that made me give up everything, run off to live in abandoned buildings, and prowl around downtown looking for dinner."

"Why did you, then?" Sara flung back. "Why come downtown, why make yourself look like that? If you really had to hide, why make yourself look like a B-movie vampire?"

"Because I needed to look different. Because I *wanted* to look different."

"Looks to me like you wanted to look like me."

Ardeth was on her feet before she knew it, the black rage goading her muscles into action while her mind was frozen beneath the cold core of truth in Sara's words. She stopped herself somehow, found the invisible wall that had stalled her sister and kept herself behind it. Suddenly, she felt alien and awkward in her self-created image, a child caught playing make-believe in her mother's clothes. Her armour of blackness was shredding, fading, and she felt the Ardeth-that-was forcing her way back into life, threading blonde back into her inky hair, turning her limbs soft and ungainly.

Then she looked at her sister's white face and horrified eyes and knew that Sara didn't see any cracks in the armour, didn't see anything frightened and human beneath the vampire mask. For a moment, triumph flooded through her, washing away the old life trying to gain a foothold in her heart. Now you see, now you see what I really am! Not at all what you thought, am I, little sister? You're not angry that I look like you—you're angry that I look better than you. And that's the one thing you never thought you'd see. But the exultation only lasted a moment, then Sara's stricken expression wiped it away. She's not the enemy, Ardeth told herself. What you wanted, what she was, doesn't matter now. What's left to compete over? You don't even exist in the same world any more.

"You see now, don't you?" she said quietly, still standing. Sara nodded slowly.

"Ardeth, what . . ." She groped for the words, then laughed unsteadily, "Jesus, what do I say? I'm sorry you're a vampire? I'm glad you're still alive, sort of?"

"Don't be sorry. I'm not." Ardeth settled back onto her bed, suddenly weary. The burst of anger had set her adrenaline pumping; coming off it, she realized it had awoken the hunger. She was aware of it as a constant, nagging ache, like a headache waiting to happen. Hurry up, Rozokov, she thought to the distant smoke on the horizon of her awareness. God knows what they plan to feed me. *If* they plan to feed me. She glanced at her reflection in the false mirror and had the uneasy suspicion that putting Sara and her together had been more than a way to make her tell her story.

"The vampire," Sara began suddenly. "The one who made you. What did he look like?"

"Grey hair, grey eyes," Ardeth replied warily. "Terrible and beautiful at the same time. Why?"

"One night, at your apartment, there . . ." She stopped suddenly, eyes flickering sideways towards the camera for a brief moment. For a briefer moment, Ardeth saw suspicion in her sister's eyes. She may believe the vampirism, but she hasn't bought it all, Ardeth realized. "I had a strange dream, that's all." She shrugged the subject aside as abruptly as she had raised it. "Can I ask you something?"

"Sure."

"What happened to Mickey's friend Rick? He was a street musician. Mickey thinks you killed him."

"I didn't kill him. He was hit by a car. I took his blood, but not enough to kill him." Ardeth leaned forward a little to catch Sara's uneasy gaze, compelled suddenly to tell the truth, to put an end to the sudden relaxation, the complicity between them. Her death had cut the ties between them forever; this belated truce was just a ghost of whatever friendship they had once had. "But I *can* kill, Sara. Don't think that I'm still the sister you knew, who was too squeamish to kill spiders. Don't think that I'm anything like her at all."

"Then what are you doing here? If you're not Ardeth, if

you're not my sister, why didn't you just walk away?" Sara asked, voice ragged with pain and defiant refusal to *believe*, just as she had refused to believe Ardeth was dead. Ardeth's heart caught for a moment, overcome by sudden, blind desire to refute everything she had just said, to pretend that somehow the hard facts of her second birth did not irrevocably sever her from the bonds of her first. She had come to make Havendale pay, to end the threat to Rozokov and her, that was true. But first of all, most of all, she had come to save Sara. And if Sara saw that truth in her eyes, she would clamp down on it with her bulldog persistence and not let her deny it again. And then they would go on haunting each other forever, just as Sara had haunted her through the creation of her new self, and she had haunted her sister through the nightly outpouring of loss and longing strung on electric guitars.

"Because," she began slowly, looking past her sister's dark gaze to the darker ones waiting behind the mirror. I'm not telling them anything they don't already suspect, she thought, to excuse the half of the truth she was about to reveal, to hide the deeper one. "I got tired of hiding from them, running from them. Of always being so damned careful because of them. I wasn't careful that night in the asylum—and you know what, Sara? You were right—not being careful was fun. It was the best fun I'd ever had."

She leaned back against the wall behind her cot with a slow, lazy stretch, and put her sunglasses on. The camera could see only the predatory smile frozen on her lips. It could not see the disbelieving horror in Sara's eyes. It could not tell that, behind the shelter of the black lenses, Ardeth's own eyes were shut tight, so she would not have to see it either.

Chapter 31

Mickey yawned and stretched surreptitiously, wincing as the leaves around him stirred at his movement. Come on, you weird old bastard, hurry up, he thought to the cooling night air. Rozokov had woken up about an hour earlier and vanished back into the woods surrounding the house. Mickey supposed it was too much to hope that he was going for doughnuts and coffee.

They had been stuck here for more than sixteen hours now. After tracking the van to the entrance to the estate and noticing the two guards posted at the gate, they had parked in a mall parking lot on the far side and gone over the ten-foot stone wall. Mickey grimaced and sucked at the cuts on his fingers for a moment. The height and the barbed wire at the top hadn't seemed to slow Rozokov down—he wished he could say the same for himself.

Circling around towards the house, they'd had to crouch in the brush while someone stamped through the woods off to their left. Some sort of perimeter alarm, Mickey had decided and spent the next too-long moments preparing his excuses before the man wallowed back the way he had come, apparently writing off the warning to either raccoons or kids, both of which probably snuck onto the estate with annoying regularity.

I suppose we should be grateful old Althea hasn't bothered to keep the gardener on, Mickey thought idly, glancing up at the lights from the house through the screen of lilac bushes. It was only fifty feet from his vantage point to the nearest door, but the shadows of the overhanging oaks and the dense branches of the bushes seemed to have kept him invisible all day.

Watch them, Rozokov had told him, before retreating farther into the woods to sleep. Mickey had tried to argue, suggesting that shifts might be more practical, but the old man had rejected that sensible idea. "I have no power until dusk," he had said and there didn't seem to be any argument for that. Mickey had ended up sleeping anyway, catnapping when the heat and heavy, green-scented air lulled him into drowsiness. But he seemed to jerk awake every time someone closed a door, so he didn't think he'd missed anything.

Not that there was much to miss. Once in a while, the door at the end of the house would open and a man would walk down the long driveway towards the gate or make a circuit of the house. There didn't seem to be any pattern to their movements and he never saw more than one man at a time. For all he knew, there could be two men inside the house . . . or twenty. The only thing he knew for sure was that they were armed; he'd seen enough movies to know a sub-machine gun when he saw one. It was not a reassuring sight. It made him suspect that Rozokov really didn't know much more than the few details about Althea Dale and Havendale he had been persuaded to part with before he went to sleep.

Something moved behind him and he twisted around as a dark shape settled into the bushes at his side. "Nice to see you," Mickey said sarcastically.

"I had some business to attend to." In the darkness he couldn't see the man's smile, but he was sure it was mockingly amused.

"I don't suppose it involved getting reinforcements."

"No, regrettably not. I was just finding some nourishment."

"Jesus, you ate and didn't bring me anything?" He managed to keep the accusation to a furious whisper.

"I did not think you would care for squirrel."

"Squirrel? You ate a squirrel?"

"Not 'ate' precisely but . . ."

"Never mind," Mickey interrupted, suddenly certain he did not want to hear any more. "Now that you're back, what are we going to do about Sara and Ardeth?"

"What happened today?" Impatiently, Mickey outlined what he'd seen during the day. "No one came from outside?" Rozokov asked curiously.

"No. No one left either, not since the van this morning." The silence lingered on for a moment and Mickey squinted at the pale shadow beside him, making out Rozokov's profile as he studied the house. "So how are we going to get in?"

"The man who called you . . . he should be coming back tonight. We will get in with him."

"And if he doesn't come?"

"I cannot believe he will stay away. But if he is not here by midnight, we will try something else." He sounded so certain that "something else" would occur to them that Mickey was almost convinced. Almost.

It was nearly eleven o'clock when they saw the headlights flickering through the trees lining the driveway. Rozokov was gone without a sound, slithering up through the weeds to crouch in the shadow of a tree at the edge of the driveway. Mickey started after him, froze as the headlights swept the patch of ground where he lay, then forced himself on. The car pulled to a halt just beyond Rozokov's hiding place, at the base of the stone steps that led up the hill to the house. The brake lights winked as Rozokov's shadow moved across them; then Mickey stood up and ran.

He reached the far side of the sleek convertible sports car just as the driver saw the dark shape standing at his door. "Good-evening," Rozokov said pleasantly with a smile that had too many teeth.

Mickey saw the man lean sideways, his hand snaking towards the glove compartment. He lunged forward without thinking, catching the man's wrist. There was a muffled grunt from his left and he glanced over to see the man held against the door, Rozokov's long fingers over his mouth.

When the glove compartment snapped open, he found what the man had been so desperate to reach. He hoisted it up at Rozokov with a grin, then pointed the gun at the man in what he hoped was a professional manner.

Rozokov's hand left the man's mouth and he kept it shut, eyes trained on Mickey. The free hand vanished like a pale spider into the man's coat and came out with a wallet that it tossed onto the seat.

"Martin Rooke," Mickey announced, checking the driver's license. He studied the photograph of the lean, dark-haired man and then looked back at the real thing; for once the photograph didn't lie. Rooke's suit might look like a genuine Armani but his face looked like a genuine killer, all angles and bones and blue arctic eyes. He checked the business card. Vice-President, Special Projects, Havendale International.

Rozokov's hand on Rooke's collar tightened and hauled the man up and over the closed door of the Jaguar. When his feet hit asphalt, Rooke pulled himself up and leaned as far away as Rozokov's grip would allow. "A pleasure to meet you, Mr. Rooke."

"You're Rozokov, I assume." The voice was cold and steady, recognizable even without the backdrop of bar chatter.

"Of course. Now you will escort my associate and me inside to Ardeth and Sara. If you try to warn anyone, or to mislead us, my associate will shoot you. Is that clear?"

Rooke nodded. Have to give the old bastard credit, Mickey thought with distant humour. He puts on a good show. And he's avoided mentioning my name, which is considerate of him, I suppose. Though I hope to hell he doesn't really expect me to shoot Rooke. The gun felt suddenly awkward and heavy in his hand, like a prop he had no idea how to use.

They walked up the stairs in silence, Rozokov at Rooke's right shoulder, hand on his arm, Mickey at his left, gun against the man's ribs. We won't fool anyone, he thought, as they approached the far door and he saw the camera above it. But when they reached it, Rooke pressed the buzzer on the door lintel and nodded up into the lens.

Mickey noticed that Rozokov hung at the edge of the light, face tilted away from the camera's curious gaze.

Something clicked deep within the door. Rozokov was at Rooke's shoulder again, reaching past him to open the door. There were guards on the other side, rising inside their glassed cubicle with curious expressions. Mickey saw their eyes flicker over Rooke's face, slide past his own, and widen when they saw Rozokov. Mouths began to open, arms jerk back to grope for guns. The gun, he thought, they have to see the gun. He raised his own weapon, jamming it hard into the side of Rooke's throat.

Rozokov was in the cubicle before the guards' guns were clear. He caught the first man's jacket and held him still for the fist that caught him in the throat. The body was sliding bonelessly to the floor when the second blow sent the other man slamming into the wall so hard Mickey was sure he heard the skull crack.

Mickey felt Rooke's muscles tense under his hand and he tightened his grip, pressing the gun behind Rooke's ear until it forced his head to tilt awkwardly to the side. Rozokov came back out of the cubicle. "Very impressive." Rooke managed to croak.

"Did you . . ." Mickey started, then felt his voice trail away as the words got stuck in his throat.

"Of course he killed them," Rooke answered contemptuously. "That's what he does. You don't have any idea what he is, do you?"

"I don't give a shit. I know what *you* are," Mickey answered and shoved Rooke down the hallway after Rozokov. They were halfway down the corridor when Rozokov suddenly cried out, his body jerking as if struck. Rooke started to run, pushing his way past the stumbling figure. The gun came up before Mickey had time to think about it but his attention wavered between Rooke's back and the figure crouched on the floor between them and then the moment to act was gone, swallowed up as Rooke vanished through the steel door at the end of the corridor.

"The machine," Rozokov gasped out, eyes wild in a face gone grey with pain. "Shoot the machine."

"What machine? Where?" But the only reply was a cry, smothered as the man bent over in pain. Machine, what the fuck was he talking about? The only machine was the camera ahead of them. Mickey ran forward, skidded to a halt beneath the black box. It wasn't a camera after all, he realized, as he raised the gun and fired. The machinery exploded into a hail of metal and sparks.

When he turned, Rozokov was hauling himself back to his feet, leaning hard on the wall. "What happened? What was that?"

"Where's Rooke?" The words came out hoarse and ragged.

"Through there." Mickey jerked his head towards the door. "What do we do now?"

But Rozokov didn't answer that question, just slumped against the wall drawing in slow, shuddering breaths. After a moment, Mickey put his back against the wall beside him and looked down at the door shining with implacable serenity at the end of the hallway.

Oh Christ, Sara, he thought, what am I going to do now?

Chapter 32

Glancing from the window to the video monitor's image of the two dark figures in the tiny room, Lisa Takara muttered a steady stream of imprecations under her breath. The guard behind her, seated at his own set of monitors, shifted uneasily but, not understanding her, did nothing else.

Videotapes keep giving you away, Rooke, she thought bitterly. If the last one hadn't shown me what a monster you are, this one would have. Whether that woman in there is crazy or a vampire, it was your kind that made her that way. It was clever of you to kidnap her sister to get her, to put them together to make her talk. But you should not have made me study her while she did. Because now she has a name and a life that your company ripped from her and gave her this madness or this curse in its place.

And now you are making me sit here and watch in the hopes that the hunger you put in her will drive her to the unspeakable.

Behind her, beyond the guard, the other scientists were still working, poring over the microscopes and computer reports. There was nothing conclusive yet, nothing more than a few anomalies in the blood tests and Parkinson's suspicion of a shift in the tissue structure of the skin samples. She knew that they all glanced her way occasionally in guilty, reluctant fascination. On their way across the lab they would pause and stare for a moment into the narrow cell. There was one proof that could not be denied—and they were all waiting for it to happen.

Ardeth knew they were there and Lisa suspected that at least some of Ardeth's words and gestures had been aimed at the watchers, not her sister. But there were things she guessed the other woman would have hidden if she could: her restless shifting on the cot, the fingers curling and uncurling in the sheets, the almost imperceptible twist of her mouth as she gnawed at her inner lip.

"Subject A increasingly agitated, restless. Subject B has tried several times to engage her in conversation but failed." She jotted the notes in her own cryptic shorthand, English and Japanese characters combined. Then, without thinking about it, she wrote in Japanese only: "Subject A is waiting for something to happen."

The guard behind her swore suddenly. Lisa turned instinctively and caught a glimpse of the monitors over his shoulder. There were three men moving down the hallway towards the lab. She recognized the middle one as Rooke. The one in the lead had smoke-grey hair and a narrow face. Beautiful, terrible . . . the words echoed through her mind.

The guard hit one of the mysterious switches littering the console. The lead figure jerked spasmodically and then

Rooke was moving, vanishing out of the camera's sightline for a second. A second switch triggered the grinding unlocking of the lab's door, then Rooke was inside.

"Lock the door," he said, breathing hard, face pale beneath the gleam of fear-sweat. Lisa barely got out of her chair before he reached her to push her aside. She eased herself towards the back of the lab, where the knot of her fellow captives stood frozen.

"What happened?" the guard asked.

"The monster's here. He took out Buwoski and Noble. Call down to the guardhouse and get them up here." He leaned over the monitor, obscuring Lisa's view, while the guard picked up the phone. "Shit. That little punk shot out the ultrasound."

"Carnegie and Singh are on their way. Give 'em five minutes. Should I call Ms. Dale?"

"No! We'll handle this," Rooke snarled, staring at the screen. "They can't get in here." It sounded almost like a prayer.

"We can't get out," the guard observed cautiously. Lisa caught the edge of the withering glance that remark received.

She heard rustling behind her, the creak of a stool as someone settled onto it. In the sudden silence, each sound seemed to reverberate and the hum of the computers was unbearably loud. She glanced into the cell and saw that Ardeth was sitting up straight, sunglasses gone, staring at the mirror-window as if she could see the confusion beyond it. Can she? Lisa wondered suddenly. Or does she see it with senses other than her eyes?

Rooke straightened up suddenly, shoulders tightening as he glanced around the room. Lisa felt ice track down her spine as the pale blue eyes slid over her. He was scared, she realized suddenly. And we all saw it. That is something he cannot bear, that the monster frightened even him in the end—and that we know it.

The cold gaze settled on the mirror for a moment, then she saw a smile crack across the thin mouth. "Bring me the ultrasound and open the cell." The guard froze for a moment. "Now, Banks." Banks unslung his rifle, fumbled with the machinery, and moved to the door.

When it opened, Sara stood up. Ardeth did not. Rooke leaned against the lintel, ultrasound wand dangling almost negligently from his hand, Banks at his shoulder with the rifle ready. "Come out."

"And greet your guests?" Ardeth asked casually and the device in Rooke's hand swung up.

"Come out and keep your mouth shut until I tell you to open it." She shrugged and leaned down to pull on her shoes, then rose and walked towards Rooke. He backed away with equal nonchalance, ultrasound always between them. "Bring the other one." Banks pointed the gun at Sara in response and she went to the door, stiffening when he gripped her arm and pushed her out into the laboratory.

Beside her, Lisa heard Martinez swear softly. Someone sucked in their breath and let it out in a rattling sigh. Rooke glanced their way briefly. "Dr. Takara, turn on the intercom." She moved to the console, surprised to find she was pleased to be able to see the monitors again, to observe the two men hovering outside the door. It gave her the illusion of control. She found the intercom button among the others and pressed it.

"Hello, Rozokov," Rooke said. "Can you hear me?" Lisa saw the men start in surprise, then the pale grey head nodded. She glanced at Rooke and saw the flicker of his eyes towards the monitor. "Good. Now tell your friend to get rid of the gun and the both of you lie down on the ground." The man's shrug was expressive. "Why? Because if you don't I'll try out the ultrasound on your girlfriend here. Or I'll shoot her sister."

Lisa saw the distress on the young man's face. His hands moved in controlled panic, gesturing with the gun at the door. Rooke's grin told her he had seen it too. Rozokov did not move. "I forgot. I can see you but you can't see me. So you'll just have to listen."

Lisa heard nothing but Ardeth's sudden scream. The black-clad form arched and crumpled. Sara's cry came a moment afterward, and she lunged forward, wrenching her-

self from Banks's grip. Then the gun butt cracked across
her shoulders and she fell to her knees. Ardeth was huddled
on the floor, fingers clawing at the white tiles in time to her
hoarse, shuddering moans.

On the monitor, Lisa saw the young man surge towards
the door, his mouth opening and closing in soundless
shouts. The old man's eyes closed in pain. She felt a sudden throb in her fingers and glanced down in surprise to
discover that her hands were digging at the metal console.
Her thumb touched something; the switch that controlled
the door.

I wonder what would happen if I pushed it, she thought
distantly. I wonder which monster scares me more.

No, I don't wonder that at all.

From somewhere far away, she saw her thumb flatten
and press, heard her voice shout "The door's open" before
she flung herself backwards off the chair. The sudden clatter of Banks's rifle came on the heels of Rooke's cry.
Someone screamed and glass shattered behind her.

Reality caught her as she hit the floor and rolled beneath
the console. The metal door was grinding open with agonizing slowness. Rooke swung towards it, the ultrasound
moving with him. On the floor in front of her, she saw
Ardeth gather herself up, limbs moving with slow spider
grace. Beneath the veil of black hair, her mouth opened like
a wound.

Then she was on him, breaking his grip on the ultrasound with the snap of his wrist, dragging him around into
her savage embrace. She held him for a moment, spun him
around in a strange, violent dance. For one endless moment, Lisa saw only their white faces pressed together, his
pale with fear, hers bloodless with exultation. Then she let
him go, hands flashing up to catch his shoulders as she
turned him and slammed his head into the computer screen
that was still flashing the secrets of her blood.

Lisa put her face into her arms, shielding herself from
the sudden crack and the flash of light as the vacuum inside
the screen exploded. Something struck her and pattered

away with a sound somewhere between liquid and glass. The smell of blood and burning circuitry filled the air.

Shaking, she forced herself to look up, past her blood-spattered arms, past the mess of the red and grey on the floor. Into the ancient eyes of the beautiful, terrible creature standing over her.

Chapter 33

When he came through the door, Rooke was beyond his rage, locked in Ardeth's death dance, so Rozokov took what vengeance he could, tearing the gun from the guard's hands and swinging it against the blank, terrified face.

For a moment he could only stand there, waiting for the red madness to drain away, for the echoes of Ardeth's anguish to be replaced by the sounds of Rooke's dying, Mickey's murmurs to Sara, the strange, distant moans and queries from the far side of the laboratory. When he found himself again, he turned slowly to look around.

Mickey was crouched beside Ardeth's sister, helping her to sit up. A man lay in a puddle of blood against the far wall. A weeping woman shook the shoulder of another, older man as he sprawled beside her, face down. A dark-haired man was moaning as he tried unsuccessfully to sit up, clutching his shoulder, blood seeping from beneath his hand. Stretched beside the bulk of a console was another woman, her arms around her head.

Rooke's body was still, dangling from the shattered computer like a limp, useless cable. The scent of scorched hair and smouldering flesh lay under the sweet, heavy smell of blood. And beside him, Ardeth huddled, her face hidden by the fall of her hair.

He moved towards her, pausing briefly as the prone woman lifted her head to gaze up at him, and he looked down into dark, almond eyes. Then he crossed the slippery floor to crouch at Ardeth's side. When he said her name, there was no response. He reached out to touch her hair, tilt her face up to him. For a moment he thought it was only Rooke's blood on her face, then he saw the jagged piece of glass embedded in her cheek. When he touched it, she winced a little, but the blankness did not leave her eyes.

She was in shock, he realized, shattered by the ultra-sound and the aftermath of her savage violence. He plucked away the first shard of glass, then saw the second glittering in her hair.

Behind him, he heard the insistent buzz of the doorbell, then voices over the intercom. He turned to see the oriental woman pulling herself to her feet. "They called the other guards," she said slowly and Rozokov recognized the voice that had screamed to them over the sound of Ardeth's pain.

"Can you keep them out?" She blinked distractedly for a moment, then shifted with painful slowness to stand in front of the console. As he turned back to Ardeth, he heard her talking, telling them that Rooke was busy and to return to their posts. If they believed her at all, it would not be for long.

His oldest, strongest instincts screamed at him to take Ardeth and run, praying that the death of Rooke would be enough to end their pursuit. But he knew that it would not. Everything in this laboratory could betray them and beyond it, somewhere in the rest of the house, was the woman whose will had revived the nightmare left unfinished when he fled this house one hundred years ago.

He glanced over at Sara Alexander and saw that she was on her feet. "Sara, take her out of here. Take out all the glass you can find."

"Glass . . .?" she echoed in bewilderment, but she was moving already, stooping beside him to touch Ardeth's arm. Her face paled when she saw the blood and glitter on her sister's hair and skin.

"You will do her no harm. Go on." He helped to raise

Ardeth to her feet, then surrendered her into Sara's hands, refusing to look as they limped from the room. "We have to destroy the laboratory. Mickey, do whatever has to be done to the computers." He waved his hand at the machines he had never used. Mickey stood still, staring at him. "Go on ... unless you want Sara to be a hostage to this forever." Under the lash of that threat, the young man moved.

Rozokov stepped past the dying men and shaking woman without looking at them. He found the blood samples in the test tubes in the refrigerator and poured them down the drain, then followed them with the skin samples. A sudden burst of gunfire shocked him around. Mickey stood in front of the row of computers, the guard's gun clamped against his side, emptying the magazine into the machinery. Rooke's body jerked each time the bullets swept across it.

As the echoes of the shots died, Mickey looked around with a strange, sardonic smile. The oriental woman eased herself back up from her crouch behind the console. "Is that everything?" Rozokov asked her.

"They recorded the examination and the conversation in the cell. The tape is in the machine here." She gestured behind her, a vague, distracted movement. "There are other tapes as well, but Rooke has those."

"Takara!" the dark-haired man said in sudden reproof.

"What tapes?" He stepped closer.

"The movies they made. The asylum afterwards." She looked up at him, dark eyes unreadable.

"Why?" She shrugged.

"There are monsters, after all. But you are not the worst of them."

"I should not let you live," he found himself compelled to point out.

"No. You probably should not."

The hallway did not seem safe enough, so Sara took the first door that opened. Inside the darkened room, she settled her sister's unresisting body down on the couch. "Ardeth?" She wished that her voice didn't sound so small and frightened, that the bloody face and blank eyes staring up at her

weren't so disconcertingly disconnected from any semblance of the sister she remembered. When she took a limp
hand in hers, something sharp stabbed her thumb. She
forced herself to close her eyes and pull out the thin sliver
of glass.

She found more in Ardeth's hair and hands and down the
length of her torso. Ardeth shivered as each shard was removed but she said nothing. She didn't even close her eyes.

To Sara's relief, the wounds only wept thin blood for a
moment and then seemed to close. She found a cloth by the
room's small sink, dampened it with water, and wiped away
the blood that was painted across Ardeth's face. As she
smoothed the last of it away, her sister stirred, blinking
slowly. "Sara." Her hand lifted a little and Sara caught it,
leaning closer.

"It's OK. Mickey and . . ." She paused, groping for a
word to define what that grey-haired man must be to
Ardeth. She could not find one but remembered a name
coming from Rooke's mouth. "Rozokov came. Rooke's
dead. You're safe now."

Ardeth shook her head with sudden strength. "No. We're
not safe . . . not until Havendale burns. Where is he?"

"Back in the lab. I think he and Mickey are destroying
it." She caught Ardeth's shoulders as her sister struggled to
sit up. "You're in shock. Just rest for a moment."

"I can't rest. He'll go on without me."

"No one will leave you. Just lie still. You're not strong
enough to move yet." She tried to soothe her, brushing back
the blood-matted hair, her fingers holding tight to the cold
hand.

"She'll be waiting for us. He'll die if he goes alone."
The hoarse whisper was frantic, the eyes, no longer blank,
were wide and frightened. "I have to go with him. I have
to be strong enough to go with him."

"You'll be all right."

"I could be," Ardeth said, as if she hadn't heard. "I could
be strong enough if I had something to," her voice trailed
off. Sara felt her heart constrict suddenly. She remembered

the flippant voice from the prison room: "Got any B positive blood?"

She'll be all right. She'll be fine without it. She's just scared and in shock. She's not thinking clearly. For a moment she clung to the reassuring chorus of refusal, then felt the certainty shred and fade away.

"How much?" she asked carefully at last.

"Not very much. Not enough to hurt anyone." Sara glanced guiltily at the door, waiting for Mickey or Rozokov to interrupt them. Wishing that they would. But the door stayed closed and she looked back at her sister's pale, desperate face. There was no sign in her of the cool, savage woman gloating about the night in the asylum. "Sara, if anything were to happen to him, I'd be alone. Forever. These last three months have been like a terrible dream, a dream that terrifies you and thrills you until you can't tell if you want to wake up or keep dreaming. And it'll go on and on . . . for years, for centuries, forever. If I lose him again . . ." She shuddered, her grip on Sara's hand tightening cruelly, "it would have been better for them to have killed me."

For a moment, Sara wanted to pull away, to retreat from Ardeth's terror, from the implications of her words. I should have let you stay lost. The thought stabbed through her then dissolved into pain. But I didn't. I asked you to come home. And even if you can't, I still owe you whatever I can give. "All right. What do I have to do?"

"Just this." Ardeth drew her hand up, turned it to bare the wrist. "Don't worry, it won't hurt." Sara felt the warm mouth touch her skin and managed to hold down her sudden revulsion. There was a brief, sharp pain then nothing but the sensation of pressure and the heat of Ardeth's mouth. See, no worse than giving blood, she told herself resolutely, no different at all. Of course, there's nobody to give you cookies and orange juice afterwards but that's all right, 'cause it really doesn't hurt at all . . .

And then the door opened.

* * *

I wish to Christ somebody would tell me what's going on around here, Mickey thought wearily, watching Rozokov and Takara. The air stank of gunpowder, smouldering wires . . . and something worse. His stomach turned over ominously but he decided it didn't matter—he didn't have anything in it to throw up anyway. And now on top of everything else, Rozokov was talking about killing more people, including the one who had helped them. Rooke's voice echoed in his mind: "Of course he killed them. You don't have any idea what he is, do you?"

She knows though, he thought with mutinous envy, watching Takara's face as she looked up at Rozokov. But on the heels of that thought came another, darker one: if Takara and the others had to die, what did that mean for Sara and him?

He shifted the gun in his arms uneasily. He had felt a guilty pleasure at his wild destruction of the computers, and even the way it had spooked Rozokov, but what would he feel if the old man said the scientists had to die? And if he didn't agree, what was he prepared to do about it?

At last, Rozokov smiled sadly and lifted his shoulders in a resigned shrug. "But who would believe you anyway, if you chose to tell the truth?"

Mickey saw Takara's rigid spine slump in relief. She bowed her head and then stepped past Rozokov to kneel beside the man clutching his injured shoulder. Mickey felt his own shoulders ease down, his death grip on the gun relax.

Rozokov retrieved the videotape, turned it curiously in his hand for a moment before the long fingers broke it into two with chilling ease. He tossed it to the floor by Rooke's body and looked at Mickey. "Is there more ammunition for your weapon?"

Mickey looked down at the sub-machine gun still clutched in his hands and fought the urge to laugh. He'd emptied the clip into the computers, his finger frozen to the trigger by his terror of losing control of the deadly thing jerking in his hands. Good thing you didn't have to make any big moral decisions . . . not with only an empty gun to enforce them. He dropped the weapon and retrieved Rooke's gun from his belt.

He looked back at Rozokov. "There's just this."

"Come, then. Let's find Ardeth and Sara."

As he left the room, Rozokov behind him, Mickey heard voices rising in argument, Takara urging flight, a man suggesting they just lock the door again and wait for the police. I'm with you, lady, Mickey thought with an inward grin. But nobody ever listens to me either.

Ardeth and Sara weren't in the hallway, so he tried doors until one opened beneath his hand and he stepped inside. He saw Sara first, face turning towards him as the light from the hallway spread across them. Ardeth was stretched on her side on the couch, holding Sara's hand against her face. As she lifted her languid gaze, Mickey saw her eyes spark red.

Like a lion looking up from a kill. The thought seared through him, burned away the half-hearted rational explanations struggling to form in his mind. Images flashed by with quick-cut intensity: Ardeth's eyes in the alley, Rozokov sleeping beneath the trees, his strange, sharp-edged smile. On the sound track was Rozokov's voice . . . and Rooke's . . . and Takara's. They called them vampires—they still do. . . . Of course he killed them, that's what he does. . . . There are monsters, after all.

Ardeth released Sara's wrist and wiped her mouth.

"Sara . . ." He managed her name then heard a sound behind him. He spun to face the dark figure outlined against the door.

"Now you know."

"You," Mickey began, then caught his breath, fumbling for the words and for some way to make his mouth say them. "You're vampires."

"Yes. I told you that, as best I could. As best I dared." His voice was too damned reasonable so Mickey made himself look at Ardeth, sitting up slowly beside Sara. The hot, angry loathing that he had felt for her after Rick's death returned.

"You were drinking her blood." Deny it, he thought desperately. Please just deny it.

"That is what we do to survive. But she has done her no harm," replied Rozokov in his quiet, seductively sane voice.

"She drank her fuckin' blood!" The gun came up before he knew it, pointed futilely at the centre of Rozokov's chest. This won't work, this won't stop him, Mickey thought dizzily, but he couldn't move his hands, they were frozen holding the deadly, ridiculous toy like a talisman between them.

"She's my sister," Sara snapped. As if she were angry at *him*—as if *he* were being unreasonable. "I said she could."

"You said she could?" he found himself echoing in disbelief. "And that makes it just fine that they're . . ."

"Monsters?" Rozokov's voice was dark with sadness, edged in old pain. "Rooke's word. Perhaps he is right. But ask yourself, have I harmed you in any way? Have I lied to you?"

"Because you needed me," Mickey flung back at him, aware that the muscles in his arm had started to tremble, that the gun barrel was wavering between them.

"And if I were a monster, would I need your help? Would I have asked for it? Mickey, if you shoot me in the chest, you will do me no particular damage. If you mean to destroy me, between my eyes would probably do it."

The gun shifted upwards, almost by itself. Distantly, Mickey heard Ardeth's angry protest and Sara saying his name. He fought the shaking in his hands and let the gun's aim settle somewhere in the centre of the narrow face. Kill him, kill *it*, some primal part of his brain whispered. Kill it before it kills you. Then he remembered the silence in the van, watching Ardeth walk away through the darkness, remembered the moments of the quiet humour, the brief, sidelong smiles, the sad shrug as he gave Takara back her life.

"We do not have much time. Kill me if you are going to."

He felt his finger spasm, cramp against the trigger. His adrenaline-soaked nerves, the ancient, terrible fear in the pit of his stomach urged him to kill the thing, to drive out the darkness in the flash of gunpowder. But . . .

But he had no proof that Rozokov really *was* a monster. He had no proof of anything at all. Except that if he surrendered to the violent, terrified thing in his mind that demanded the death of anything different, anything whose face did not reflect back the known, familiar lines of prejudice and certainty, then Mickey would have more proof than he had ever wanted that *he* was no more than a torch-wielding peasant, a pinstripe reactionary bigot hiding under a leather jacket.

He let the gun drop and closed his eyes.

"Come," Rozokov said softly.

Ardeth stepped onto the narrow beam, moving her eyes from Sara's teetering figure to watch her own feet settle easily onto the four-inch board of wood. For a moment, she waited for dizziness to unbalance her ... but felt nothing. She could do this easily now. Her body, this new thing of blood-driven sinew and will could do it, could do anything.

She started to walk, the close, dark heat of the attic seeming to clear her head, to thaw the chilly core of dislocation that had held her frozen since Rooke's death. She had followed Rozokov and the others blindly, accepting his decision to try the upper storey when it became apparent they could not reach the other half of the house from the ground floor. When the upper hallway had ended in another reinforced steel door, Mickey had found the trap door to the unfinished attic.

Her feet paced out the path of the board between the seas of ancient, decaying insulation. It didn't matter to her that the dirty, fly-specked windows kept out most of the moonlight, but she could see Sara easing her way carefully along the plank, nearly blind, arms outstretched with the unconscious grace of a tightrope walker.

How long had it been since Rooke had arrived at the door of the cell? Ten minutes? Twenty? She wasn't sure how long she had been in shock—or if she were truly out of it. She could still feel the echoes of the explosions that had stunned her; one when Rooke's head had breached the vacuum of the computer screen and the first, the stronger, when she held him in her arms and the wild hunger had blazed through her like a star going supernova. It had left a black craving in its wake, pulsing far away in the darkness inside her.

Ardeth thrust that image aside and forced herself to concentrate on moving forward. There were still things that had to be done ... and thanks to Sara she had the strength to do them. That was all that mattered. She couldn't afford to drift into either indifference or madness.

Ahead of her, Rozokov and Mickey were crouched on a small patch of solid floor, peering downward. Sara joined them in two long strides, Ardeth bent beside them a moment later.

"Hear anything?" Mickey asked and Rozokov shook his head. He reached down and lifted the board covering the trap door to the attic slightly. Ardeth saw a faint light edge the wood but there was still no sound. He lifted it higher, drawing it slowly up to rest on the floor beside him. He lay still for a moment, head bent, then slithered forward, and his torso disappeared into the trap. After a moment, the grey head resurfaced.

"All clear." He sat up, swung his legs into the hole, then vanished. Ardeth heard a faint thump as he reached the floor. Sara went next, dangling with her fingers gripping the edge of the trap until Rozokov caught her legs and brought her down. Ardeth followed Mickey, tugging the board back into position as Rozokov held her up to reach the nine-foot ceiling.

Feet back on the floor, she glanced up and down the corridor. At one end, dark wood gleamed in the soft light, the banisters that lined the stairs down to the ground floor. Two sets of closed doors faced each other across the hallway, the shadows in their frames unbroken by light. Ancient wallpaper garlanded by faded roses covered the walls but the wine-red carpet beneath her feet was lush and barely worn.

At the far end of the hallway was one last door. No light seeped through its dark defences but Ardeth knew. She looked at Rozokov and he nodded.

The carpet swallowed their footsteps and brought them to

the door without a whisper. Rozokov's hand closed over the polished brass knob. Ardeth caught her breath, panic and eagerness closing her throat.

The door surrendered with a sigh and let them in.

Chapter 34

The room was dark, illuminated only by a circle of light from the spidery black lamp on the desk and the faint grey gleam of the monitor screens banked behind it. Ardeth's eyes flickered around the room, seeking threat and shelter in the same moment.

Heavy wooden bookcases lined the wall beside her, leatherbound texts mingling with garish paperbacks. The right wall was swathed in heavy velvet curtains, keeping the waning moonlight at bay. In the left wall there was another door, neatly closed.

Behind the desk, a shadowed figure looked up. Ardeth saw a flash of movement and darted forward instinctively. Her hand closed on a wrist so thin her fingers wrapped it easily, stalling it on its path to the phone. "No," she said softly and looked down into the white, upturned face.

It was almost a skull, sharp cheekbones and hook nose slicing through skin as dry as chalk. Her eyes were sunken, the skin around them bruised. Her hair, caught in a thick braid of mahogany, was threaded with grey. But she was younger than the deathshead face suggested, Ardeth decided, no more than forty. She was wearing a man's dressing gown, faded from scarlet velvet into patchy rose.

Then Rozokov was beside them, his hand on the woman's shoulder as he pulled the chair away from whatever other weapons she might have concealed in the desk. "You are Althea Dale, I assume."

"Yes."

"You know who I am."

"Yes. I thought you might try to come here."

"And you let me?" Rozokov's voice sounded skeptical and amused.

"The guards are watching the doors downstairs. I thought that would be enough. How did you get in?"

"Through the attic." Althea's eyes closed briefly.

"I never should have trusted Rooke with that," she said after a moment.

"But it is better that we talk, you and I. Without Rooke, without outsiders." Her gaze moved across them, dismissing Sara and Mickey where they stood against the closed door, lingering for a moment on Ardeth before returning to Rozokov, apparently satisfied.

He settled back against the desk and Ardeth moved to lean against the bank of monitors. She spared a glance at them as she did so; two showed the empty hallway corridor outside the laboratory and the other two revealed only static and snow.

"How did you find out about me?" Rozokov asked at last.

"Great-great-grandfather's diaries. They were in the attic with all his other books. He gave me everything but your name." The answer was prompt, edged with confidence and triumph. She *wants* to tell us, Ardeth realized. She's proud of it . . . she wants us to know what she has done.

And I *do* know. I know she killed Tony and Conrad and me. I know she would kill anyone who stood between her and whatever she wanted. The rage ripped up through her again, jagged daggers turning in her heart, and she jerked away from the proud head balanced so precariously on the long, fragile neck. She had to move away, stay where she could control the murderous urge that swept her, so she walked to stand behind the old love-seat on the other side of the room, and looked at the bookcases.

Her eyes slid over the assembled library, catching titles

in faded gold on brittle leather—*Malleus Maleficarum, The Vampire in Myth and History, Dracula*—and garish paperbacks in red and black. All of them were on vampires or the occult. She pulled one out at random and flicked it open; Latin words crawled across the page.

"And Havendale?" she heard Rozokov prompt gently, inquisitively, giving her a chance to fill his silence with a celebration of her own cleverness.

"When Daddy died," she said, her voice bitterly amused, as though she were laughing at some secret joke, "it became mine. I do a better job of running it than he ever did."

A set of narrow booklets on the bottom shelf caught Ardeth's eye and she bent to look more closely. They were exercise books, she realized, the pale buff ones given to every public-school student. Curious, she took the first one out carefully and flipped it open.

The childish scrawl covered the pages, intense and dark, pressed deep into the page in places, legible to her nightsight even in the dim light. She paused to read occasionally, caught by a word or a date.

September 5, 1962
Mother took me to tea in the big store today. It was supposed to be a special treat for my eighth birthday but Daddy was mad when he found out and made me take two extra baths.

October 15, 1963
Mother caught me in the attic playing with great-great-grandfather Dale's trunks. She scolded me (as usual) and told me to get downstairs. I suppose I'll have to stay out of them for now but I don't know why they care. It will all belong to me someday anyway. And lots of the books are in a funny language—so all I can do is look at the pictures. I like the one of the man with the horns and the sharp teeth best, though it scares me a bit, when it's dark.

April 14, 1964
I can hardly write, my hands shake so much. But I have

to. Mother died today. She got hit by a car when she was shopping. Everyone is crying (me too, you can see the tears on the page if you look). Even Daddy. But then he got angry and yelled about how she shouldn't have gone out and that's what happens when you go out there. Then Nurse came and made me come up here. . . .

April 17, 1964
They buried Mother today. Daddy's right. I don't want to go out there any more.

"So you made Havendale search for me?"
"Of course." Her voice held a trace of contempt.
"How did you know I was still in the city?"
"I didn't. But everything I knew about you dated from 1898, so that's where I had them start."
"And when you found me, you had Rooke kill the men who did it and the researchers who had done the work for you."
"I told Rooke to eliminate the loose ends. That was his job. What you are was too important to risk." There was calm certainty in the cool voice and Ardeth clenched her teeth, forced herself to crouch by the bookcase and endure the casual dismissal of her life, her self, as a "loose end." To distract herself, she snatched out another exercise book, staring resolutely at the pages. The writing was adult now, a smooth, practised script.

Dec. 24/83
Daddy spent tonight in his room. I was very angry at him and yelled at him for missing Christmas Eve. He just laughed and said he wasn't feeling well. He thinks I don't see. He thinks I don't know about the cars that come at midnight and the women in them. He thinks I don't know what dirty things he does with them, the filthy games he plays. There are times I'd like to kill him.

May 15/84
Daddy has finally agreed to stop bringing the women to

the house. We've fought about it for weeks but then, when he got sick last week, he finally realized that they're bad for him, that they bring in all kinds of germs and filth and danger.

Things are going to be good again.

For the first time, Ardeth felt a ghost of sympathy for the woman, trapped in the strange household her diary described.

June 3/84
Daddy in a foul mood. He's drinking, yelling for Carl to get him some girls. Carl won't, because I've told him I'll tell Daddy about his advances to me if he does. Must go calm Daddy down. . . .

There was a brief break in pages as Ardeth flipped through the blank sheets to find the next entry.

"And what was I?" she heard Rozokov say behind her.

"Immortality," Althea said quietly. There was a long silence.

"Mickey, Sara, go out and keep watch in the hallway." His voice was quietly implacable and Ardeth glanced over to see her sister and Mickey protest. "There are still two guards out there, as well as whatever servants this household has. Go out and keep watch."

She heard the door open and shut, then her attention was dragged back to the words in front of her.

I just read my last words. Calm Daddy down. And I did. He was angry, banging with his cane on the wall as he rampaged about the library. I told Carl and the others to go back to their quarters.

The writing grew fainter, as if its author was afraid to press too hard and make her story visible, make it real.

I didn't have any choice. He might have gone out! He might have ruined everything. He said he would do it since I had taken his women away and given him nothing in return. So I had to do it. It was just as disgusting as I thought it would be but it seemed to calm him down.

Maybe he will forget all about it. Maybe I will. I pray I do.

June 5/84

Daddy called me into the library tonight. He said that I'm a poor substitute for his whores but if I don't want him to go out I'll have to do.

I can't let him go out. He'll die like Mother did. The whores have already made him sick. As long as he stays inside, I can make sure that everything is under control. I can make sure everything is right. I can make sure he does what he's supposed to do.

He said he'd have to teach me what to do, starting tonight.

I still hurt and there are bruises I'll have to hide from the servants. But I won't let him go out. I won't let him get away. I won't.

Ardeth closed her eyes, fought the unexpected invasion of tears. This woman killed you, killed your friends, would have killed Sara. She left Rozokov to be tortured by Roias, she let—she ordered—Rooke and Roias to hurt people in the name of profit. What is on these pages doesn't make any difference to that.

"Do you want to live forever?" The question was quiet, doubting.

"Of course. Everyone does. And they'd pay for it. They'd give their souls for it." Althea Dale's voice was fierce and defiant.

"But it is not the world's soul you want to ransom, though I can see you'd take every coin the world had to offer and it would not be enough. It is your own, is it not? You are dying."

Ardeth turned and saw Althea Dale's burning eyes widen in pain, saw her pull back helplessly, trying to get away as the truth in his words broke through her composure. "I won't! I won't die. Your blood can cure me. With your blood, I won't die." The words came out in a harsh rush, a snarled mantra of irrational belief.

With your blood . . . the words echoed in Ardeth's mind and then she knew what Althea Dale was dying of, what had killed Arthur Dale. His daughter had been more right than she ever knew, when she blamed the prostitutes her father had brought into the house in the middle years of the 1980s. Against the odds, the unknown virus had passed into him. Against the odds, he had given it like a legacy to his daughter/lover.

With that realization came an understanding of what the laboratory had been set up to do. If there was something in their blood that could cure her disease, she could make the world pay twice—billions for the answers to the AIDS crisis, billions more for the secret of immortality. Though no doubt, she'd reserve the second secret only for the highest bidders. For something like that, killing a few whores and graduate students would seem like a small price to pay. At least to men like Roias and Rooke.

"So I should save you then. Let you drink my blood?"

"Yes, if that's the way it works. Don't you see, I can give you everything you need. A safe place to stay, all the blood you need, whenever you want it. Whatever price you have, whatever you want, I'll pay it, I'll do it." She had regained control of herself, finding strength in the mechanics of bargaining and the certainty that everything could be bought.

"You would, I do believe. If you cannot have me by force, you would do it by money. If I asked you for a dungeon full of victims, if I asked you for skulls to drink my pleasure from, you would give it to me, yes?"

Before she could answer, the door opened and Mickey leaned in. "I hate to interrupt but I think the other end of the house is burning," he said, his voice surprisingly calm. "Probably the computers in the lab."

"It can't be the laboratory," Althea replied. "The halon gas system would kill any fire." Along with any scientists still trapped there, Ardeth thought. Althea turned her head to look at the static-smeared screen and suddenly laughed bitterly. "Rooke. The stupid bastard put in sprinklers."

"You and Sara leave if you think it necessary. We will not be long." Mickey shrugged and vanished. This time, he left the door open. Ardeth put her hands on the back of the love-seat and felt them tighten on the wood as she tried not to imagine how fast the fire could be spreading. Rozokov moved to crouch beside Althea's chair, looking up into her face.

"You have not answered my question."

"I'll give whatever you want, whatever you ask," Althea agreed, her body hunching forward, eager, hungry. She had forgotten about the fire already, Ardeth suspected. She saw Rozokov's hand go out and touch one chalky cheek.

"Poor mad one, you truly believe that might buy me."

"But . . ."

"Should I let you live forever, so that you can gain more wealth, more power and grind more lives under the wheels of your progress? Should I sacrifice another Ardeth to your fear of dying?"

"What are you talking about? You're a vampire. You prey on people, you feed off them. You preyed on *her*." The dark head gestured savagely, the fevered eyes met Ardeth's with hot envy. "You made her like you. Why not *me*? I can give you everything."

"That is what you do not understand. I do not want everything. I want only peace from your pursuit. Can you give me that?"

"If you made me like you, yes, yes, I would leave you alone."

"Would you? With the secret that we held, could you risk it? With the ransom of the world to be ripped from our blood, without a drop of yours being spilled, would you let us go? Have you done a single thing in the last months to make me believe that?" After a long moment, Althea shook her head. "You do not need my help to be a monster, Althea Dale. You have been that all along. And now you know what I must do."

"But . . ."

"Ssh. You knew the stakes in this game when you started it. But do not fear, I will be quick. This is more than you gave the women who died for Roias's films, more than you gave Ardeth when you made her a tool to be used and destroyed. But I will give it to you nonetheless." His voice was still gentle and reasonable but the will behind it was inflexible. He rose and walked around behind her.

Ardeth opened her mouth to tell him what she had discovered about Althea's past and the things that had reduced her reality to herself and her own desire, turning the rest of humanity into unreal objects that either did her will or were destroyed without a single thought. Then she saw his eyes, and the pain burning through them like fire through parchment, and she closed her mouth.

No matter what she said, he had to kill Althea Dale. There was no point in making it harder for him.

I wanted this, she thought. I imagined this in gleeful detail a hundred times. I almost broke her neck myself five minutes ago. I should be ecstatic, triumphant. But all I feel is empty.

Rozokov's hands settled on Althea's hair, shifted gently around her skull. The woman's eyes were wide and frightened but she did not move. "Do not fear," Ardeth saw his body go suddenly still, his shoulders tense, "it will be over . . ." His arms moved, snapped hard to the left, "in a moment."

When he let go, her head dropped forward. His own drooped in echo, shoulders slumping.

When Ardeth put her hand on his arm, he turned and pulled her close, face against her throat. For the first time, she felt the truth that he had tried to tell her all along, that every death they caused, no matter how necessary, was murder and whatever curse or mutation made them different from the rest of humanity did not absolve them of it, any more than Althea Dale's tragic life absolved her of guilt.

She thought of Rick and the boy in the sewer and Philip and wanted to weep, to scream, to flee back into the glorious, insulating madness that had sustained her. Her old anger at Rozokov rose, anger that he had left her to commit those crimes, even irrational fury at his seduction of her in the asylum.

She pulled from his arms, trembling, and said, "We'd better go." Her voice sounded harsh and hateful but he only nodded.

Mickey and Sara were waiting at the top of the stairs, pacing edgily. For the first time, Ardeth could smell smoke and in the distance she thought she could hear the faint wail of sirens.

There were no guards at the door and they left unnoticed. When they reached the woods, the laboratory side of the house was being eaten by flames. Rozokov stared up at them for a moment, face drawn and empty, then Ardeth caught his arm and pulled him away into the dark shelter of the forest.

He guided them to the edge of the estate, near the place where he and Mickey had climbed over the wall eighteen hours earlier. Ardeth followed him silently, grateful that the mechanics of winding her way through the darkness, Sara and Mickey strung behind her with hands linked like blind children, required her full attention. She did not want to think about the rage and guilt twisting inside her, waiting impatiently to explode.

But when they reached the fence, she caught Rozokov's arm. He studied her face for a moment, then glanced at Mickey. "Wait for us at the van." Ardeth didn't watch as they went over the wall.

"Ardeth . . ."

"We're free. No more Havendale. We can start again." There was a plea in her voice she couldn't hide, couldn't articulate. "This is the new world. No Havendale, no ending like in Paris. No rules." She wanted him to agree, to repudiate the weary pain she'd seen in his eyes, to give her back the sweetness of the night and the hunt.

"There are always rules, child. Althea Dale lived by the ones that her father taught her. Jean-Pierre lived by the rules of his day, that said all things were allowed to the powerful and the wealthy and the beautiful. And you, my dark daughter, what rules did *you* follow in re-creating yourself?" The criticism in his voice stung, despite his gentle tone, and she stepped away from him.

"You left me. How was I supposed to know what to do? How was I supposed to know how to be a vampire? I did the best I could."

"I know. And you are everything a vampire is supposed to be—you are beautiful, seductive, deadly. Were I mortal, I would fall at your feet and let you drink me dry."

"Don't laugh at me!" Her heart was torn by the thought that he found her laughable, that he mocked her for trying to pretend she could be any of the things he had said. She was at the wall when he caught her.

"I do not laugh at you, oh love, believe me. You are right in all your accusations. I drained your life from you and left you alone to survive the most dangerous months of our kind's existence. You have done so magnificently. But I wonder, when you look in the mirror, what do you see?"

"I see what I am." She couldn't look at him, remembering her moments of pain in the church tower a night ago, Sara's horrified expression, her own fear of losing her armour of her new self.

"You see a vampire. Only a vampire. Ardeth, do you love me?" The suddenness of the question took her breath away, shocked her eyes back up to his.

"Yes."

"Do you love my teeth, my dead flesh, my red eyes, my hunger for blood?"

"No . . . yes . . . I don't know what you mean. Those things are part of you."

"Part of me, yes. Not all of me. I have struggled for five centuries to keep that true." He took her face in his hands. "In Paris I was a vampire. I drowned in it, in all it meant to me. Jean-Pierre, for all his charm, had never been anything but a vampire, even when he was alive. In Toronto, a century ago, I was just a vampire, too fearful to let myself hope to be anything else. In the asylum I was a vampire.

They forced me to be that . . . and only that. Until you. And now . . . now I am going to try very hard to be Dimitri Rozokov again. Who loves Bach and hates Liszt, who wonders what made the stars, who misses the sun and vodka, who needs blood only the way other men need food. That is what I want you to learn to love. That is what I want you to *be*."

"It's not easy."

"No. It is the hardest thing we can do. But if we do not try, what has immortality made us but undying beasts in an eternal jungle? What then is the difference between Althea Dale and us?"

"What I've done . . ." she began, her voice shaking, thinking again of the dead she had left in gutters and sewers and broken on decaying floors.

"Is done. Just as the women I killed in the asylum. Our guilt will not bring them back, nor will our grief. All we can do is go on and try to find some way to survive that does not drive us mad."

She sighed and rested her forehead against his, his hands in her hair. Ardeth drew a long breath. "Maybe . . . it was hard to be . . . so vampiric . . . all the time. But I thought I had to. I thought I wanted to." She was surprised to find herself chuckling softly. She put her hands in his hair, and tilted her head to look at him. "You won't leave me."

"No promises. But I won't leave you now." Then he kissed her and something inside her cracked open, just as it had the last night in the asylum. At last, he pulled away. "We had better go."

Ardeth smiled and followed him over the wall.

When they came around the side of the van, they found Sara and Mickey sitting between the open doors, untangling themselves from an embrace. Ardeth met her sister's eyes and smiled, wanting to laugh at the guilty look on Sara's face. Go on, little sister, you deserve him—you deserve a man who would brave vampires and killers and nightmares for your sake.

"All done?" Mickey asked.

"Yes," Rozokov replied, and for the moment, Ardeth was content to believe him.

Epilogue

The fire engines began to leave the Dale estate at dawn, followed by the black-and-white police cars that had arrived in their wake six hours earlier. Last in the procession were the ambulances, lights as still and dead as their charred cargo.

The house was a ruin, roof gone, stone walls standing but scorched and black with soot, the interior gutted. Once the fire had escaped the sterile confines of the laboratory, it had devoured the aging wood that had sheltered five generations of Dales.

From the back of the police car, Lisa Takara watched the remaining investigators begin to wrap the smouldering shell in yellow ribbons.

They had been kind to her so far, accepting her clumsy answers and blank passivity as evidence of shock. So far she had told them only the truth—that she had fled the laboratory alone when it became apparent that Martinez and Parkinson would not leave. That she had hidden in the woods in fear of the confused guards, who had now vanished. That she had no idea what had happened in the rest of the house.

But they would want more than that sooner or later and she needed the safety their solicitude brought her to give herself time to think. Telling the rest of the truth led to only two possible fates, each of them unbearable. A discreet stay in a psychiatric ward "for her own good" and the end of her future in the scientific world if she were disbelieved.

And if she were believed, a repeat of Havendale, with only the names of the masters changed. She would lose more than her reputation . . . she would lose her freedom. And so would they: the woman whose terrible story she had over-heard, the man who had stood with her life in his hands and let her live.

At last, the house vanished behind the trees. She turned around in the seat, tugging the smoky blanket closer about her shoulders. In the rear-view mirror, she saw the young police officer's eyes flicker towards her. "You all right back there, Dr. Takara?"

"Yes. Thank you. I might just close my eyes for a moment though."

"Go ahead. I'll wake you up when we get to the station," he said solicitously. Lisa nodded and closed her eyes.

Behind the safety of her mask, her mind formulated and tested the composition of possible lies, while her fingers absently folded and refolded a scrap of paper in her pocket, a tattered card bearing a phone number she had never called.